The Witness

ALSO BY SADIE RYAN

The Proposal
The Secretary
The Housekeeper
The Witness

THE WITNESS

SADIE RYAN

Choc Lit
A JOFFE BOOKS COMPANY

Choc Lit, London
A Joffe Books company
www.choc-lit.com

First published in Great Britain in 2025

© Sadie Ryan

Cover art by Nick Castle

ISBN: 978-1781898369

To Harry, Charlotte and Stephen.

And to Ian Cooper, my recipe-swapping buddy.

PROLOGUE

Taking a wrong turn, she felt vulnerable being on foot when she found herself in unfamiliar territory, a little run-down street in London, and she desperately needed the loo.

To her left was a scruffy pub with a typical Victorian green-tiled facade. She could nip in, use the loo and be out in a flash. Flyers adorned the door, and litter carpeted the red scuffed steps. Ordinarily, she would avoid a place like this.

The heavy, brass-adorned door insulated her from the acrid smell of stale beer that assailed her nostrils the moment she pushed it open. Recoiling, she hesitated before stepping inside, but it wasn't the smell that had her heart racing: something chilling swept over her almost like a foreboding. But Jane didn't believe in superstitions, except for a moment there where she thought she might. She contemplated finding somewhere else, but then her need was greater than her apprehension.

It was difficult to see if the dirty brown carpet was brown by design or just filthy. She crinkled her nose as she hesitantly entered, the low lighting taking some getting used to. An unnatural quiet hung in the air, tingling all the fine hairs on the back of her neck. She should have turned around and walked out, but she didn't. Her thoughts skimmed over all that might be wrong with this decision, touching like ghostly tendrils on so many possibilities, all of which dissolved like mist on a windscreen before she had time to dwell on them.

She rounded the bar and stopped suddenly as if she'd crashed into an invisible wall. A full-body crash. Good. God. She couldn't believe her eyes.

A man in a vest with blooded fists, a beard, scruffy hair and a tattoo on his shoulder knelt over the broken body of a bloodied young man. He lifted his gaze up to her. Deep blue, beady eyes she'd never forget smiled at her in surprise. It took him a moment before recognition lit up his face.

Blood roared through her ears. Her mind raced desperately trying to find a way to get her out of there.

Something rotten jammed in her throat; the vomit she wanted to throw up. As her mind filled up with flashbacks of her past catching up with her body and insides turned to cement. She knew this man. What were the chances of walking in on *him*! Seeing him again after all these years. This was not good. Maybe if she left, turned and walked out as if she'd not even been here. There was no sense in talking to him. It was bad enough that he had recognised her. Talking to him would only make things worse. For her. A man she'd hoped never to see again. *My God.* She felt a sharp bite of fear tear at her, at how this could destroy her beautiful life. No need to prolong her stay. She had to get out of here. She'd block it from her mind like she'd done with her past. She could do that. She had to do that. As she got feeling back in her limbs, turned to leave, a hand on her shoulder stopped her and a hard voice she'd hoped never to hear again, said, 'Janey.'

She lurched backwards, away from him.

My God, she thought, *this was real.* She felt real fear creeping through her and she began to tremble as pent-up memories charged at her, unrelenting.

She had long since stopped remembering her past, and *him*. She had seen him do this.

He wouldn't forget it was her. Again, just like the last time — she was the witness.

CHAPTER 1

Ten years later

Jane was totally engrossed working on her illustrations in her top-floor home office. Jasper kept her feet warm under the desk.

The Jack Russell jerked up, ears pricked, startling her. Jane's own ears now tuned into the sound of a car pulling up on the drive. He barked then raced downstairs, yapping.

Patrick was home. She glanced at the time; Christ, he was home early, and she'd lost track of time.

As she stood up, she stretched, relieved at having an excuse to stop working on the latest illustrations for a children's book. Her eyes settled on the many snow globes collected on their travels and smiled. She kept them in order of visits on the shelf above in front of her desk, beneath a row of books she'd illustrated over the years.

Patrick's footsteps crunched the gravel on the drive. She rushed to the bathroom, put on some lippy and took down her practical ponytail, combing her hair then groaned when it simply wouldn't do what it was supposed to but insisted on sticking out in all the wrong places. She looked a bit of a sight and did the best she could with it, grabbed a T-shirt from the freshly washed pile of clothes on her bed and slipped it on.

She liked to dress comfortably when Patrick was away; no bra, lounging in comfy joggers, or shorts — as she was in the moment due to the current heatwave. She hated him seeing her looking a mess. Being a drummer on tour as a session musician he was often away for chunks of time: this one had been six weeks. She poured out mouthwash into a glass and rinsed her mouth then smiled into the mirror.

Knowing Patrick, how she looked wasn't going to be the first thing on his mind. A little flutter of anticipation in her tummy made her giggle. Their attraction to each other was still as strong as when they met.

She heard him playing with Jasper in the hallway before calling out to her. She leaned over the banister, saw him tickling Jasper's tummy before Jasper ran to get his ball. As far as he was concerned his playmate was back and everything was good in the world once again.

At the top of the stairs, she watched her husband. He'd never changed from that young man she'd met twenty years ago at a party when she was twenty-two and he was twenty-eight. She'd met Patrick while out with Suzanna, her publisher, on some literary do. He'd been her plus-one. Patrick and Suzanna had been friends for years. They'd met at university. They made a gorgeous couple standing together. Thankfully, Suzanna wasn't into men, but you'd never have known it from the body language they gave off. He was muscular and tall with a European look about him, maybe Italian. He was British through and through, he'd told her. 'There's nothing continental running through my veins, sadly,' he'd said to her when she'd pointed it out. Their daughter, so like her father in looks, had inherited all his gene pool. There was little of herself that she could see in Lizzie who was nineteen, dark-haired, and olive-skinned like her father. Light grey eyes, a blend of her father's grey eyes and her pale blue ones. Tall with legs a mile long and hair that always shone in stunning waves down her back. What she did have of hers was her flamboyant way of talking and using her hands to get her point across.

The desire she'd felt for Patrick that first day was so hot she'd felt as if her thighs were on fire. His smile was still a winner. Broad and welcoming. Now, he rushed up the stairs two at a time, wrapped his arms around her and hugged her tightly to him. 'Hey, my darling girl, I've missed you,' he said softly. His lips closed to hers. He gave her a warm kiss, gentle and loving. He tasted of stale coffee and smelled of a long day. He kissed her neck and hair.

'You need a shower,' she said pushing him gently away.

'I do. Fancy joining me?'

* * *

Later they waited for Deliveroo. Patrick hummed in the shower in the steamed-up en-suite and she reposed on the bed after their lovemaking. Stepping into the bedroom, drying himself off, he asked, 'How are the illustrations going? Last time I asked you said you were nearly done.'

'Nearly, yes and I'm ahead of schedule. I'm so pleased with them. I think Suzanna will love the pieces — and the author, of course. It's been so immersive. I'm so incredibly lucky to have a job I love doing.' And it was true, she did. 'We both are, I suppose.' She watched him as he walked around the room with the towel wrapped around his hips, marvelling how he was still able to make her feel the flutter of gossamer wings in her stomach. She smiled at him, knowing how much he adored his music too. They really were lucky with their work. She heard so many people talk about hating their jobs. She couldn't imagine doing anything else.

'That's great and you've time for the last few tweaks you like to put in.'

'Yep.' She got up and dressed, slipping back on her shorts and T-shirt. He really was wonderful the way he invested time to understand and care what she did for a job. They were both that way, two peas in a pod so to speak.

'What's this story about?'

She watched him dry his hair with a towel, feeling a cosy warmness in her belly.

'An angry but loveable bear. He's angry because he has a thorn in his paw which is infected, and the little girl who's befriended him in the woods by giving him honey brings her mother's tweezers one day and removes it. All the outlines are done, I'm just filling in with colour.'

'It'll be great as always.' He smiled broadly. 'And then when you're finished, perhaps we should take a break somewhere. Where d'you fancy going?'

The thought of having him all to herself with no interruptions from his agent or hers, not even from their beloved daughter, was something they needed. Besides, Lizzie was grown up now and didn't need them around all the time. While at home at the moment for the summer break from university, she had plenty of plans of her own.

'Somewhere warm and relaxing, with no children, blue waters and white sands.' He was right. They'd not been away in ages. They could do with a holiday.

'We ought to go somewhere tropical like St Barts, it has perfect weather all year round,' he said. 'Yes! Let's go for it. I'll sort it, it'll be a surprise.' He grabbed her by the shoulders, pinging her bra strap. 'Think of all that uninterrupted time we'll have.' He nibbled her neck. God, it felt good having him home.

She wrapped her arms around his neck and pushed herself close to him. 'I can't wait. No work. No responsibilities for a whole week.'

'A week? Let's make it two. It's too far to go for one.'

She wrinkled her nose. 'Ten days. You know I hate leaving Jasper. And with Lizzie home, I want to spend some time with her, don't you?'

'You know I do but you also know she's got plans for festivals and the like.' He sighed dramatically. 'OK, ten days.'

He stroked her cheek, the longing in his eyes nearly making her weep with desire. God, how had she got so lucky finding this man. She knew she was lucky. She never took him for granted. Never would. He grinned. 'Let's go one better. Let's push the boat out. I've been paid really well for this last tour. Let's go first class.'

'Really?' She pulled back, surprised by his extravagance. 'Can we afford that? Maybe business might be better.' He wanted to spoil her, she knew that. He always did. She was the sensible one, the one who put the brakes on. Business was good enough for them. Butterflies of excitement fluttered in her tummy and made her smile when he ran his finger along the pulse in her neck.

'We can do first, you know.'

'I know, but it's so extravagant, business will be just as nice.' Patrick's frivolousness scared her sometimes. He often laughed that she was too cautious and had to live life. She couldn't help it though, being cautious was ingrained in her. She never took all they had for granted. She was too afraid of losing it all. She was always aware how easily life could change. She was happy, very happy; she didn't see the point in throwing money away just because they could.

He smiled, shaking his head. 'If you say so.' He tilted her head up with his finger to look into her eyes. 'Jane Carmichael, I fucking love you.'

* * *

The next morning, they sat in the kitchen having breakfast. Jasper started barking all over again.

'What's got into him?' asked Patrick, buttering some toast. 'Here, look at these hotels, what d'you think? Any take your fancy?'

She shrugged. 'You choose. Surprise me. We have a family of squirrels that are driving him crazy, which is what's with the barking. Though I think the postman just arrived.' She'd heard the slam of a car door and now the snap of the letter-box. 'I hate him chasing the squirrels. They can be vicious sometimes.'

'Right, well not a lot we can do about them. We'll just have to keep an eye on him until they decide to go. What time did Lizzie get back? I didn't hear her come in?'

She sighed. 'Lucky you, I did. It was around two. She woke Jasper but he settled quickly. You were out for the count and snoring like a hog.'

'Really? Sorry. I was whacked. It's not easy touring with lads twenty years younger, you know. They never want to sleep.' He bit into his toast. 'Always wanting to party. While I can't wait to get home. In my own bed next to you is the pot at the end of the rainbow.'

'That's cheesy,' she said giggling as she buttered her own piece of toast. 'Didn't you party at all?' She knew he wouldn't have.

'No. Not at all. I forget how much energy you have at their age. Honestly, Jane, it makes me feel bloody old. I don't have the same energy that I used to.'

Jasper ran in with the post.

'Postman's early, isn't he? He doesn't normally come till after ten,' Patrick observed. 'Jasper come here, drop it. I thought he'd stopped nicking the post.' Jasper ignored him and ran back to the hall with the post.

'Sometimes he does,' she said wondering where he'd put it this time. Sometimes he'd drop it back by the door, other times in the lounge. She was sure he did it on purpose in play.

'Listen,' she said forgetting about it. She wanted to show him her island and what she'd done with it while he'd been away. 'Fancy going out to the island? I've made it lovely these last six weeks. The weather's been brilliant, and I've really got stuck in. I think I got carried away a bit though. But it's lovely now. And it's such a beautiful day.' It was twenty-five degrees centigrade, and only 9 a.m. The forecast was tropical for the next few weeks at least. She rested the cool orange juice carton against her face. August was usually a washout as she remembered from Lizzie's school holidays. They'd all been excited by the heat initially but as the days went on with no reprieve from the suffocating temperatures it was becoming more of an ordeal than a pleasure. Particularly when the heat inside the house was smothering, especially at night.

She had spent a considerable amount of time since they moved here two years ago cutting back thick bushes on the island, which was just beyond the house on a lake that skirted their property. She wanted to make it her restful retreat among nature. Somewhere she could go and draw in peace. They lived on the edge of Balcombe Lake, north of Ardingly Reservoir in Sussex, in a crescent of three houses. She had claimed the island as her own when they moved in although the other houses had access just that they didn't choose to and had been happy for her to chop, chop, chop and do with it what she may. Politely, she had offered that they could, of course, come and spend time there. Thankfully, it wasn't up their street so to speak and she certainly hadn't pushed it.

She grabbed the keys off the hook by the utility. 'I'll get the boat ready. You fill the flask with coffee and join me. Jasper loves it there. Come on, Jasper, let's go, sweetie.'

Outside, her eyes caught the fleeting movement of a heron on the edge of the island before their noise scared him away and he took off gracefully into the denim blue sky. Jasper, once he realised where they were going, bolted ahead, leaping into the boat where he waited for her to catch up. She untied the cleats from the post at the edge of the lake and pushed the ten-foot *Clinker* into the water, just as Patrick arrived with the flask.

When he was onboard, she pulled the cord on the engine, and they made their way smoothly across the still lake. Jasper perched along the side next to Patrick, his eagerness keen in his wagging tail. The boat made ripples across the water, and she wondered if the heron was watching them, waiting for when they left to come back. Their house and where it was,

was all she'd ever wanted. She looked back at the distance growing between them. Finding it had been a little miracle. She lifted her head upwards, squinting in the brightness of the day. She was blessed to have found this life, she really was, and she told the universe quite often that she was. She'd read somewhere that you ought to say thank you for what you had, which in turn gave you more of the same.

She sat at the rear, her hand on the tiller. There was something magical about being out on the water like this. She loved it. To the right of the island was the strip of land that led towards the small town, country roads, farms, schools and shops. All of them shielded from the lake by the giant overhanging trees. Behind them, tucked at the end of the strip of land, was their crescent. It had once belonged to a rich merchant who in the nineteenth century built an imposing mansion near the lake which had since fallen into disrepair and had been demolished. The land was sold off and bought by local developers who shared it out between the three houses in the crescent. Theirs had the best outlook onto the lake. They'd built a sound studio for Patrick alongside the house when they moved in, it was the first thing they did. And it was where Patrick spent most of his time.

Pauline and Tony lived in the first house as you drove in, theirs was at the bottom and Penny and Gordon with their two little girls lived to the right. Since they'd bought a static caravan in Mumbles, South Wales, close to her family, they spent nearly all their holidays over there.

As they got close, she eased up on the throttle, coming to a gentle stop.

'Here we go. Mind you don't trip on some of the loose stones at the edge,' she said turning off the engine. Jasper leapt out, running straight into the bushes, barking happily at the wildlife hiding from him.

Following Jasper they arrived at the space she had turned into a cosy spot with wooden steamer chairs and cushions she kept in a watertight garden box that was also filled with plastic glasses and mugs, bottled water, a torch, tea, coffee, powdered milk, batteries, rope for emergencies and a little camping stove to heat a tiny kettle to make a hot drink should she ever forgot to bring a flask.

'Jane this is fantastic,' Patrick said looking around surprised by the change. 'You didn't do all this by yourself, surely?'

'I could take all the credit. But I won't. Ralph helped. He's been marvellous.' Ralph lived in one of the other three houses in the crescent and he and Lizzie became great friends quickly after they moved in. They were now at the same university in York. He spent a lot of time at theirs.

Patrick settled himself on one of the chairs after Jane had pulled out the cushions.

She poured out two mugs of coffee and handed him one.

'Isn't this lovely? Can you see why I love to come here and draw? It's so peaceful.' It was the quiet she loved the most. The all-consuming quiet that filled her up with calm and happiness. It was quite something when they weren't that far from a main road. Here, she was able to let her imagination roam and create her characters for her books.

'I can, but the idea of you coming here when you're on your own worries me. What if you fell in the lake?'

She laughed. 'Don't be so daft. I'd swim, obviously. Now don't start with the drama, Patrick. This is my place, and I don't what to think of what ifs, please. Besides, Ralph is always around.'

'He's a nice lad, and it's great for Lizzie him being so close and going to the same uni. I like that he looks out for her. I hate thinking of her partying up there where we have no idea what she's up to.'

'Yeah, but she's sensible, Patrick. She's not one of those ravers that you hear about. It is great for Lizzie to have a close male friend, I agree.'

'It's great to have her home, though,' he said smiling.

'Of course. Anyway, stop fretting about her. I love this place. Best of all I love having no mobile. Nobody to bother me and—'

He held up his hand, a look of horror crossing his face. 'OK, OK, I won't say another word about what ifs. But not bringing your mobile is crazy. No, Jane, please, just be sensible. I know you hate the things, but what if I need to get hold of you or better still, Lizzie. Or the boat won't start. Think about it.'

She had thought about it. A lot. And she didn't know what she'd do in all truthfulness. It didn't bother her though. What were the chances of such an emergency? *Tiny*, she thought weighing up the cost to her of having it with her. Just knowing it was on her person was enough to bother her and make her switch it on. To take a look. A just in case moment. She hated that about them. 'OK, well to put your mind at rest I have a basic Nokia in the box. No internet. It's switched off and only for emergencies. Happy now?'

'Much,' he said smiling to himself.

She understood his worry though — she'd be the same. And if he was away, it would be a preoccupation he could do without.

Contented that she was going to be safe now, he reclined back and closed his eyes. 'Shall I put on some gentle jazz?' He opened the iTunes app on his phone and soon the tranquillity was complete.

They stayed that way, the two of them, quiet, listening to the music and the gentle lapping of the water, the occasional barks from Jasper deep in the bushes, the rustle of his scampering. The heron came back, landing quietly on the edge of the water, elegant, regal, looking out into the distance. She liked that he came while they were still there. Or maybe he didn't know they were because they were so quiet. Apart from the music. Maybe he liked jazz. You never knew. She'd read it once, somewhere or heard it on the radio, that animals liked music. Anyway, it didn't matter, did it? He was there. With them. Did he feel as contented there as she did? Had this been his island before she came along, or did he come now because she had made it so appealing? She'd never know. He dipped his head into the water and when he popped it back out, he'd caught a fish. How lovely. She thought that was lovely.

Jasper shot out of the bushes like a greyhound out of a trap and in a streak of movement was next to the heron. He was no fool and heard him before Jane did and took off serenely into the sky with his fish, leaving Jasper yapping after him, annoyed he'd lost out. Silly boy.

It was time to go back. They packed everything away and then climbed back into the boat. Jane started the engine and they quietly sat as the engine powered them back to the house, safely. Patrick sat next to her, his arm around her shoulders, there being no need for words. It was as if they knew it would break the magic of the serenity they had captured on the island.

Once she was back in her kitchen, life went back to normal. Patrick went upstairs to change into fresh clothes because he said he was all sweaty and she collected the post from whence Jasper had deposited it, this time on the sofa in the lounge. Tiny tooth pricks marked the brown envelope addressed to her.

She ran a finger under the flap and opened it. As her eyes ran over the words a couple of times, her blood pooled in her ankles. She focused on the words that stood out to her. *Curtis Murk.*

Curtis, bloody, Murk.

She couldn't believe it.

Curtis bloody Murk.

This couldn't be happening, not now. No, it must be wrong; they must have made a mistake. They told her, she was sure. She was definitely sure they told her this wasn't possible. What now? What if it was true? What was she going to do? This was her life. Her beautiful life. Her beautiful husband and daughter. What did that mean for them? For all of them? And now there was *bloody Curtis Murk.* She couldn't quite believe it and leaned against the sofa at her side to steady herself. It was a shock. A bloody big shock, that's what it was.

She read the letter again. It had to be a mistake. She'd call them. Tell them it wasn't on, that making a mistake like this was nasty, unprofessional; she could have died from shock. They ought to get their facts right before sending their letters out. Unprofessional, that's what it was. Bloody unprofessional.

She reread the letter, her hand shaking so badly she had to hold it with two hands. It had happened two weeks ago. *Why am I only receiving this now?*

Victims Care Scheme

Dear Mrs Carmichael

As requested by yourself, we are informing you of the early release on parole of Curtis Murk. He was released on 20 July.

It has been considered by the parole board that he is no longer a danger to the public and has served his time with good behaviour and rehabilitation.

If you have any questions, please contact us on the number above . . .

She should never have put in the request for this. *What was I thinking?* She'd wanted to know at the time. Of course she did, anyone would have. Or maybe they wouldn't have. Ignorance was bliss, wasn't it? Or dangerous? She didn't know.

Considered by the parole board? *Considered*? The words were like acid on her tongue. What was the parole board made up of, muppets? How could they say "he is no longer a danger to the public"?

Her mind froze as if he had reached out from the letter and grabbed her by the throat. Flashbacks came at her, one after another in quick succession, quick, quick like being fast-forwarded on the TV. Blood on her hands. Tears spilling from her eyes. A dead body. White walls. Lots of white walls around her. She was trapped in the white all around her. She squeezed her eyes shut. No. No. NO! *I can't go there. I CAN'T!* She trembled. Her flesh crawled with goosebumps as she tried to stop the memories surfacing. Clenching her head wanting to rid them out. She stepped backwards, lost her footing and dropped to the ground on her arse. Light-headed she read the letter again.

Then she heard Patrick coming down the stairs, quick steps, calling her name. She screwed up the letter and jammed it into the pocket of her shorts. She couldn't let him see her like this. She swiped at her eyes with her hand. Took a deep breath. *He can't ever know. Not ever.*

CHAPTER 2

'Jane? Where are you?' Patrick called out. She took stock of herself, breathed in and called out. Horrified he was going to find her this way, she tried to get up. 'In the lounge.'

He walked in, reached down to her, taking her hand. 'What you doing on the floor? What's up? You look like you've seen a ghost.'

'What? I . . . err, no, no, not at all. I just had a funny turn that's all.' She fanned herself with her hand. 'This heat, I've probably not drunk enough water, that's all.'

'Let me get you some,' he said.

She relaxed her grip on his hand, letting him go. She should tell him. *For heaven's sake, Jane, tell him. You don't have secrets.* But that was a lie. She did have a secret. One she could never tell anyone. Especially Patrick. *I should have told him from the beginning.* It was too late now. She'd thought she'd never have to. Murk was in prison, and they told her he'd never get out. But she'd never told Patrick about Curtis Murk, because that was inconceivable. Patrick would never understand. He just wouldn't. How could anyone understand? Curtis Murk was a monster. This wasn't a secret; it was a nightmare. She thought of the letter, again. He was out on parole. She had asked to be kept informed and now they had. She wished they hadn't. She wished she knew nothing about him. She wished he was dead. Dead. Dead. Oh, God. How had this happened? They told her he'd never get out. She screamed inside her head with all the pain from her past rushing up to meet her. Now he was free. What did that mean for her?

After drinking the water she sat up straight, feeling slightly better. 'I'm OK now. Look, why don't I make us some lunch? I could do with a bite to eat. Maybe that was part of the reason for feeling a bit off.' She needed to keep busy. Have something to do. Her mind was busy worrying, so she needed to have her body doing something. 'I'll go fetch Lizzie. She's having one of those lie-ins she likes so much.' Her world was shifting beneath her feet. He was out on parole. He wasn't a danger to society anymore. Of course he wasn't.

* * *

Inside the house she felt safe. She exhaled, letting out the pent-up air trapped in her lungs. Her eyes swept the garden and lake. She didn't know what she was looking for, only that she was in an agitated state and couldn't relax.

'Dad!' exclaimed Lizzie rushing over to him. 'I didn't know you were back. I wouldn't have had such a long lie-in.'

'Hi, sweetheart. Great to see you.' He gave her a bear hug and they hugged for a good long while before Patrick extricated himself. 'Enough, you're cutting off my circulation.' He laughed. Jane saw how his eyes crinkled at the corners when he smiled and felt a small sharp jab in her chest.

Lizzie laughed too. 'I forgot Mum said you were coming back last night. Oops, sorry, Dad. I didn't get in till late.'

'So I hear. Your mum heard you, but I was zonked.'

'Come and tell me how it was? Did you enjoy playing with *young* musicians that are my sort of age?' She giggled. Patrick always said that he felt like everyone in the music business was getting younger and younger all the time and it made him feel his age.

'Yes, loved it. Getting to play to a live audience is always amazing no matter what. Their style of music isn't my taste, you know I love rock, but it's still an amazing experience.'

'Did you get autographs for me?' She kissed him on the cheek.

'Lizzie, how old are you?' he joked, loving her enthusiasm. 'Yes, I did, sweetie. I have them upstairs.'

'Brilliant.'

He'd toured as a stand-in drummer for one of the big boy bands Lizzie really liked. She was into music like her dad — not that she was musical; the most she'd ever played was the recorder at school and she'd not been much good at that. Lizzie liked having music on wherever she was. It wasn't Jane's taste, and she was pleased when she bought noise-cancelling headphones. Lizzie was into music festivals too. It worried Jane, letting her daughter go. It all seemed such a hippy way to spend a weekend, living in tents and going to Portaloos that were no doubt disgusting; she didn't want to think about that. You had to let your kids do these things. It was what they enjoyed. It wasn't about what she liked.

'How long you back for?' Lizzie asked, beaming at him. Lizzie had always found it difficult having him spend long tranches of time away from them when she was little.

'Well, a little while. I haven't any gigs planned at the moment. Listen, while we're all here, your mum and I are thinking of taking a holiday.' He saw the look of excitement in her eyes. 'Just the two of us. We haven't been away in so long. You OK with that?' Jane struggled with the look on Lizzie's face at the mention of it being just the two of them. Lizzie enjoyed going away with them on their trips, despite being a teenager. She wasn't a sulky teenager who thought she was too grown-up to do such a weird thing like so many of her peers. To her it was a paid holiday, and she wasn't going to turn that down, why would she? They'd always been close. She had to admit since going to uni though, she'd become more independent. It's what was supposed to happen, and she was pleased it was. It didn't stop her resenting her little girl growing up. But she couldn't keep her that way forever. It was life. You nurtured them, prepared them for the future to be grounded adults then you let them fly. That was what you were supposed to do. For the most part they did. Patrick was much better at it than she was. The tight pull of a mother was tough to break.

'I guess so.' She pretended to sulk, then perked up. 'Anyway, I have some festivals lined up, so they'd probably clash.'

'Well then, we're all sorted,' Patrick said looking relieved. 'Is Ralph going with you to the festivals?'

'He is. Well, to some of them. We'll look after Jasper when you go and if we're at a festival, his mum wouldn't mind, I'm sure.' Pauline was a retired vet and Jasper liked her a lot. 'So, where you thinking of going? Any ideas? Oh yeah before I forget, he asked me to ask you, if he can shadow you in your studio over the summer to get some experience and maybe play with you a bit? He's been trying to get some experience in some of the studios around us but there's only a handful and they all said no. The big ones in London haven't been interested. Plus, it's not easy for him to do things in term-time being based in York. Would you? Please, Dad?'

'Of course. Remind me again what he plays?'

Jane watched them chatting away while going over in her mind, for the millionth time, what the letter had said. *Parole. He got fifteen years, and they've let him out after ten. How is it right that people can say one thing then do another? It wouldn't work in my career. Imagine saying I'll illustrate like the author suggests in her story and then do what I want. How would that work? Nothing would ever get done. There'd be chaos.* But it seemed that in the hands of people with power it was OK to say and do something totally different.

'You know he plays the guitar, but he can play anything.'

'Oh, yes, I forgot. Very talented young man.'

'He's brilliant on the guitar, you said so yourself. Did Mum mention he'd changed uni this last term?'

'She did.' He smiled at her.

'He went originally to Manchester but hated it there, so he changed and came to York. Isn't that great! I'm so pleased. We get on so well. It's like having a big brother. So, can he? Please? It would mean so much to him.'

'OK, slow down. You're talking so fast I can't keep up. That was a hard sell and it didn't need to be. Did you think I'd say no? Of course, tell him I'll be delighted.'

Lizzie gave him another kiss on the cheek. 'You're the best, Dad.'

Patrick didn't take his eyes off Jane, who was looking out the window.

'So, Jane,' he called out to her. 'Looks like Ralph will be even more of a regular visitor than he is already.' Jane stared into the middle distance. 'Jane!' he said again. 'Jane!' he called out louder the second time.

'What?' *Oh hell, what had she missed?* 'Sorry, I was off with the fairies . . . thinking of that holiday.' She beamed, pleased she'd come up with a reasonable excuse.

'Ralph? Lizzie was asking if he could get some experience in the studio over the summer.'

'Yes, great, sounds great. He's a nice lad.' She felt uncomfortable that she'd missed what they'd been talking about. 'I told you he helped me. Yes, he's a very nice boy. Can't fault him.' *Her imagination* . . . was like a frightened wild horse galloping at top speed heading into God knows where.

Lizzie stood up. 'Right, well I'll leave you both to catch up. I'm going for a shower and meeting some friends in town.'

* * *

They made lunch together, with the distant hum of the radio in the background. She prepared the salad, grabbing some of what she needed from the walk-in pantry at the back of the kitchen, and Patrick grilled some prawns on the stove, cut slices of French bread and arranged a couple of pieces on each plate then plated the prawns on one side ready for her salad. From the kitchen, Jane heard the front door slam then the start of Lizzie's little Fiat Uno that they'd surprised her with on her eighteenth. She tossed the salad in the flowery ceramic bowl they'd brought back from one of their many holidays abroad. The sight of it took her back to that holiday, sunshine in Greece, long wine lunches, people-watching when life looked like it would never change.

'Here you go, Jasper, my little boy,' Patrick said as Jasper, at his feet in anticipation of some falling morsel, looked up and snatched the crustacean from his fingers.

She heard Patrick's voice so full of love for the little rescue dog they'd adopted five years ago. He showed the same love to his whole family.

'Right, all ready?' She grabbed the wine from the fridge together with the salad bowl and walked outside, Jasper at her side.

All she could think of was that she had to tell Patrick about the letter, about Murk. She should have told him at the time. But the shock of witnessing it had been too shocking. She had just wanted to block it out.

They sat in the shade, she poured the wine, he dished up the salad. She was hungry but she wasn't, that was a bit of an oxymoron. Her appetite disappeared as the image of the letter popped into her mind. She just couldn't stop thinking about it.

'There's a couple more gigs coming up that my agent's asked if I'd be interested in.'

'Oh, good. When?' She tried to take an interest in what he was saying; she always took an interest in his career. 'Will we still be OK to take that holiday?'

'Bloody will. I emailed my agent from my phone after we discussed it, you know, to make sure he knew what we were thinking and when we're thinking of going. I know the dates aren't set in stone, but I think we should work around them. These gigs aren't for a little while.'

She glanced up at the still handsome man. He kept himself fit, running and going to the gym. More than she did; he always made her feel guilty. The thought of it all made her queasy.

They drank a couple of glasses of wine then relaxed back in the comfy chairs. But she couldn't relax.

'Is something up, Jane? You seem distracted?' He'd turned to look at her.

'Distracted? Well, maybe a bit, yes. I've got a bit of work to finish. The illustrations aren't going to finish on their own.' She drained her glass and felt a little light-headed. Better not have any more.

'You know I'm glad Ralph's at uni with Lizzie. I'm pleased she's got someone to look out for her.'

'Yes . . .' She played with the stem of her glass. He was right, she was distracted. She wanted another one but that would be silly. She had a deadline, and she already felt she could do with a snooze.

'Come on, love, tell me. Has something happened today? You've been uncharacteristically quiet since we got back from the island.'

Uncharacteristically quiet, is that how he sees me? Because inside she was a mess. Her thoughts, her guts, her heart were all out of sync and tying themselves up in knots. Knots she didn't know how to undo. Honesty would help. She smiled at him, and he smiled back. A welcoming smile, inviting her to talk to him. To tell him what was bothering her.

'Patrick. I . . .' She was scared out of her wits about how to say it. But they didn't have secrets . . . *other than this* — and this was killing her. 'Well, the thing is, today . . .'

His phone rang. 'Sorry, Jane I must take this. Can it wait?' He was poised to press the green button.

'Yes, it was nothing anyway. Take your call.' And just like that her courage disappeared.

She stood up, smiling encouragement for him to continue his call, and collected the dirty dishes.

He hung up a few moments later. 'Jane, sorry, darling. Come on, tell me now what you were going to say.'

'Oh, no, never mind. I've got to get on. It's not important. Deadline, remember?'

He made her a cup of herbal tea. 'Take this and go lock
yourself away until you're done. I'll be in my studio if you
need me.'

She took the tea and looked into his face. They said they
wouldn't keep secrets. She just couldn't tell him about Murk.
She couldn't do it. He kissed the top of her head.

Her mobile rang, startling her. She looked at the screen,
No Caller ID. caller ID. *Unknown number.*

'You going to answer that?' he asked, waiting for her to
make a decision.

'What? Oh, no. No.' She stopped it ringing then put it
back in her pocket as a feeling of dread slowly climbed out of
her stomach and crawled over her. 'I never answer unknown
numbers. You know that.'

CHAPTER 3

Two days later, she was on her way to London. She hated going to London. It brought back so many bad memories. But it was the only way to meet up with her publisher.

The roads were thick with standing traffic, honking and pedestrians shouting and talking on mobiles as they weaved between traffic to get to the other side. It was *so* loud. The vista up ahead was of multi-storey car parks, office buildings with the skyline intermittently giving way to skyscrapers in the distance.

She pulled her phone from her handbag and put in the address of the restaurant where she was meeting Suzanna. It was a short walk, a gorgeous day and she didn't fancy getting a taxi.

A message from Suzanna popped up on her screen, reminding her to post photos of her trip to London on Instagram. Damn. She hated all that stuff and had managed to avoid getting sucked into social media until recently. 'There's no such thing as staying under the radar, Jane. You have to be seen,' Suzanna had said. Jane had looked at other accounts and wondered how they did it and how they sounded happy about doing it, which baffled her the most.

She strolled down the pavement, thinking about the illustrations that she'd sent in and hoping they were OK. She'd had no confirmation from Suzanna either way. Jane always thought the worst, and that she could have done better. Being a perfectionist added to her stressful nature. It drove her mad how she always felt so negative about her work when she had to hand it in. She got such a buzz working on the briefs but waiting for Suzanna and the author to approve them was torture. In the meantime, in her mind, she almost made herself believe she'd made a complete hash of them. Not that there was any reason to be that way. She'd never had a problem in all her career. She was a busy children's book illustrator and much in demand. Clearly, she was doing something right.

Patrick would tell her to feel positive. She would do just that. They were great, she was sure of it. They always were. She had nothing to worry about. She was worrying about nothing. This was the same routine she went through every time she handed work in.

She straightened her back and walked with confidence, matching the stride of the busy Londoners. She started laughing to herself for being so silly and imagining Patrick getting cross with her for allowing herself to put herself down. She giggled aloud, garnering odd looks from passers-by.

Looking down at the map on her phone, she didn't see the man in the hoodie carrying a coffee and fast approaching. He body slammed into her, throwing her to the side, and she nearly dropped her phone. He apologised, throwing her an innocent grin as he carried on past. She rubbed her shoulder as he disappeared into the masses. She tightened her hold on her handbag. She mentally told herself it was just an accident. As she walked down the road, she was actually aware how vulnerable she was.

She walked down Melton Street, crossed the road in-between a line of taxis and standing traffic, past Euston Square Gardens and stopped at the lights on the crowded pavement.

The girl next to her was talking loudly on her phone about her date the night before and about sex and how many times she'd done it. Jane's eyebrows rose. *Christ, she must be exhausted.*

The lights changed. She checked which direction to take on the map and stepped out — a car blew its horn, forcing her to jump back onto the pavement. *Jee-ZUS!*

She glanced at the car moving past. She was sure that a face she recognised turned around to look at her. She had to stop winding herself up like this.

The girl next to her raised a middle finger in the direction of the car then looked at her, smiled in solidarity, and rolled her eyes. Jane smiled back. She looked nice in her flowery summer dress and Doc Martens.

The smart bijou restaurant was just around the corner from her publisher's office. Jane climbed the steps. At the top, she felt the urge to look behind her.

Suzanna Broome had been with Rebel Yell Publishers for six years, before that she'd been with HarperCollins and before that . . . Jane couldn't remember. Being freelance meant Jane herself wasn't tied to any one publisher. Most of her work came from Suzanna. She was amazing at her job.

The waiter brought their drinks. 'I pre-ordered your favourite,' Suzanna said, smiling. Jane took a big grateful gulp of Merlot, feeling the instant effects of the ruby liquid as it slid down her parched throat and asked them to leave the bottle. Suzanna didn't touch her soda water.

'So, Jane, how are you?' Suzanna asked. 'It's about eight months since we saw each other.' Her blue eyes smiled. She always looked like a glossy magazine cover. And Jane always felt all of her five foot four inches in her tan ankle-grazer trousers and white shirt. She ran quick fingers through her chestnut hair, aware how immaculate Suzanna looked.

'I'm well, thanks. Gorgeous weather, isn't it? I've forgotten how busy it is in London. So many people everywhere. I'm not used to all the people and the noise anymore. It's so quiet where we live now.'

'I couldn't leave London. You were so brave to leave. You're right about this weather and thank God for air conditioning.'

'We never lived in the actual city though, not like you.'

Suzanna tucked her blonde bob behind her ears. Strands of platinum hair escaped and fell into her eyes. She took out her lipstick and touched up her lips using the silver single flower vase on the table as a mirror. Then capped the lipstick and dropped it into her handbag.

The waiter arrived and they ordered. Jane, realising how hungry she was, ordered the fish and chips with mushy peas. Suzanna, the Caesar salad with chicken.

'OK, so we all loved the work you sent in. And I was wondering if you were free to take on something else as the author is a huge fan but it's a book that's running late so timings are tight.'

'Sure. Sounds great. You know I like to keep busy.' *Especially now.* She sipped her Merlot, feeling the relief that her work was well received relax her a little.

'I know you do, that's why I thought of you, but Patrick's back and I'm wondering if it's going to be too much. You haven't seen each other for ages.'

She was right. He wouldn't be too happy about her locking herself away working. But she wanted to do it. He'd understand. She needed to keep her mind busy right now anyway so this would be a godsend. They'd work it out, they always did.

'You're right, but I've nothing else on, so it's fine. He'll be fine about it. We're going to go for a little holiday but that's not yet. I'll give you the dates I'll be away when I know them. He's booking us a special getaway.'

'That sounds amazing. I could do with a getaway. Anyway, it's the deadline I'm worried about. The thing is, you're great with those children's books.' She paused. 'And the author's seen your work and asked for you. She loves what you do. It's her début, she's nervous, you know how it is — I think she's desperate. Like I said, the deadline is super close.'

'Oh, cheers for that.'

'Oh, I didn't mean it that way. She's just been really picky, and I happened to mention that you might be free, and well, she practically begged me to ask you.'

'OK, so when's the deadline?'

'Three weeks. Four at a push?' said Suzanna. Jane's face said it all. 'Too short, I thought so.'

'No, no, I'll do it. Send everything over and I'll get onto it first thing tomorrow.'

Suzanna made a face of sufferance. 'Really? I don't want to be the cause of marital problems with Patrick.' Suzanna talked her through the new job. It really would be great to be busy. Nothing better than having a busy mind to keep her thoughts linear.

'Right, that's out of the way,' said Suzanna, tucking into her salad. 'Have you photos of your island?'

'God, I don't want to bore you,' she said, pulling up the pictures on her phone. 'But it is wonderful. Look at this one in full sunshine. Isn't it fab? You know the photo doesn't do it justice. You ought to come over and stay. Patrick would love it. You haven't visited since we renovated and cleared the island.'

'I know, I know, I'm just so busy, and yes I know it's a cliché. But when I do have free time, I like to travel and get some proper sunshine, you know what I mean? God, it makes me feel alive, all that vitamin D.'

They both laughed. Jane topped up her own Merlot rather than wait for the waiter. Sometimes she thought Suzanna's life was amazing and wondered what it would be like to be so busy all the time. It wasn't for her, though, she would hate it after a while. It just sounded so fascinating. She made her feel exhausted just listening to all that she did. She never seemed to sit down and just simply chill.

The London sun coming in through the windows behind her felt warm on her shoulders. The rumble of a lorry going past made her turn and look out the big picture window. For one moment she thought she saw the face of the man who'd knocked into her.

Suzanna laughed, still holding the phone and flicking though the photos. 'Oh, look at him, still handsome. How is he doing? Is he still enjoying touring?'

As Jane was about to turn away, she did a double take and gasped.

'Are you OK, Jane?' asked Suzanna looking up, suddenly worried.

'What? Oh, yes, sorry, I err, I just thought I saw somebody I recognised. But I was wrong. Sorry, what did you say?'

'I asked if he was still enjoying touring?'

'I'll say, he loves it.'

Suzanna handed the phone back. 'Does it bother you? Him being away for chunks of time like that?'

'Sometimes, I guess, but I'm usually busy. I have a devil of a publisher who's constantly giving me work.' She smiled mischievously. 'Joke.'

'Do you remember that first night you met him? I knew the two of you were right for each other.' Suzanna finished her salad and daintily wiped the corners of her mouth with her napkin.

'You mean when I tripped right in front of him, catching my heel in the carpet, and nearly falling into his arms and a clumsy attempt to appear not interested?' said Jane, reminiscing how her attraction to him had turned her legs to jelly.

Suzanna laughed quietly. 'How could I forget?' She changed the subject. 'And the house? Still loving it?' Suzanna took the cheque from the waiter and handed him her card.

'The house is wonderful. We're so pleased we made the move.'

'Darling, I'm so pleased for you both. How long is it now? Two years?' Jane nodded. It felt like time had flown by. 'Tell Patrick I'll call him. We really need a catch-up. Listen, I'm just going to pop to the loo.' Suzanna grabbed her handbag and headed to the back of the restaurant.

Jane was happy to sit and watch the world go by through the window. She knew her imagination had run away with itself earlier, gasping out loud like that, Suzanne must have wondered what on earth was wrong with her. She drank more Merlot and turned to casually watch the diners chatting and laughing, the sound of cutlery against china and the low hum of conversation adding to the relaxed atmosphere. She was feeling a little light-headed and put her glass down. Perhaps she'd had enough.

The restaurant was filling up fast and getting tight with bodies; nearly all the tables were occupied.

When Suzanna was back at the table they gathered their things. 'OK then, I have to get back to the office,' she said. 'I'll wait for you to send me the rough concepts.'

'That shouldn't be a problem,' said Jane wondering if she was being a bit too optimistic with the time frame.

A different waiter appeared at their table with a tray of cocktails. They looked surprised. 'These are for you, ladies, compliments from the gentleman by the bar.'

They glanced over. A tall, large man with his back to them stood up and left. Jane blinked and he was gone out the door and down the street. *Oh God. He'd been here all the time! In plain sight.*

She must have paled because Suzanna asked, concerned, 'Do you know him?' She let out a nervous laugh watching Jane's reaction to the cocktails. 'God, who is it, Jane?'

Jane turned to the window, her gaze searching the street full of bodies walking past but he was gone. Vanished into the crowd. She was certain it had been him. She saw the back of him standing proud in a sea of heads. She called the waiter back over. 'The man who sent the cocktails, was that him?' She pointed nervously to the back of a man's head moving down the street.

'How would I know?'

'You saw him,' she insisted, her mouth paper dry, her hands clammy.

'Yeah, but he was with those two guys — if you want to ask them?' He pointed to the bar area.

She glanced at the backs of two men drinking at the bar, joking with each other. She went over, nervously. She could ignore it, drink the cocktails and think nothing of it. Or just walk out, leaving them on the table. Or she could find out for sure. If she didn't find out for sure it would play on her mind. 'Excuse me,' she said standing behind them. They turned to face her. 'That man that was with you, who was he?' Her tone was spiky.

They laughed at some private joke that made her nervous. Were these his new friends? The ones who were helping him find her? Because now he was out of prison, she was in no doubt he'd be looking for her. She took a step back.

'Didn't you like your cocktails then?' one of them asked, smiling as he drank his beer, looking her over lasciviously.

'Why did he send them? We don't know him. Why would he do that?' She sounded like an idiot. Men did that sort of thing all the time.

Both wore well-cut clothes, so not some backstreet yobs he might have hired. Clean-shaven and both bald.

'Chill out, he was being nice. He liked the look of your friend that's all.' The man talking nodded in Suzanna's direction. 'Why don't you pull up a chair with your friend and join us for a drink?'

What a ridiculous idea. 'What's his name?' Jane asked wanting answers.

'Martin Thompson. He does a bit of boxing. You might have seen him on the telly.' She hadn't seen him on the TV because he wasn't on there. It was a lie. 'You think if we gave her his number, she'd call him?' She laughed at his stupidity like they would do that. 'He's a nice guy. Had you pegged right, though. Said you'd be a bit spiky.' She was tempted to pour their drinks over them.

She was certain it had been him. And that would make her spotting him earlier a real possibility.

'Cat got your tongue, *Jane*?'

Christ, they know my name. She stepped back.

A frisson of fear trickled down her spine. How did they know her name if it wasn't him?

The other man roared with laughter. 'Don't look so scared. We're not scary people.' The laughter brought them to the attention of the other diners who looked in their direction. 'You are called Jane, aren't you?'

'That's none of your business.' She sounded like a fool getting irate with them.

The first man who spoke grinned at her. 'Here's Martin's number.' He handed it to her written on a cocktail napkin. 'In case you wanted to call him,' he said.

She didn't take it, just stared at the napkin then him, like he was holding out something distasteful.

CHAPTER 4

After yesterday's trip to London, and Suzanna's email first thing, she needed the time away from everyone to get the rough concepts finished. She was already stressing she'd made a mistake agreeing to this tight time frame. What had she been thinking? She needed to be better at saying no.

She hadn't intended on coming to her island this morning but what she needed was time away from everyone to get them finished. No distractions.

She couldn't escape the feeling something wasn't right in her office. She couldn't quite put her finger on what it was, but she felt like things had been disturbed. One of the snow globes had been moved. It wasn't in its shelf space but on the end of her desk next to the purple jar where she kept her pencils. She didn't remember putting it there. She'd returned it to its rightful place and arranged them all, once again, equidistant from each other. It was her least favourite. She kept it at the back for good reason. It was the second time it had happened. She was certain she hadn't touched it. Maybe it was Lizzie showing Ralph. She'd overheard her telling him about them.

As it happened, she'd overslept today, and it was now nearly midday, and she really hadn't got through as much as she'd wanted, even on her own here on the island. Patrick wanted to go out for lunch, and she felt rotten having to turn him down.

It was another scorcher of a day, muggy with little wind if any and the air felt heavy. The lapping of the water was restful. She looked over at her home and a tight knot built up in her chest, knowing she still hadn't told Patrick.

The Merlot was giving her a headache. She shouldn't have brought it with her. It was too hot to drink, and it was making her sleepy. She'd thought it might relax her, help her concentrate, calm her nerves and take her mind off seeing *him* yesterday. Had she though? She really couldn't be certain.

After a couple more hours concentrating on her sketches, she decided to put down tools and let her mind roam. Her head was pounding. Luckily, she had a packet of painkillers in her supply box with all her necessary bits and bobs. She really had thought of everything.

The island was just a quarter of a mile from the house, with her binoculars she could see Patrick and Lizzie in the kitchen talking and laughing. She wanted to be there with them but knew that would be fatal to her getting any work done. Jasper too was feeling the heat, lying on the edge with the water gently lapping over his paws. He must be dreaming as little squeals and grunts escaped him and occasionally his legs moved as if he was dreaming that he was running.

The silence here was what she loved most of all. And the birds with their birdsong. They had jack snipes that dived and drove Jasper potty, chasing them into the water looking for them. The moorhens were friendly. They came when Jasper was foraging. When she came here alone, she found them inquisitive. She never fed them, not wanting to encourage them in case Jasper might one day catch one. It was insanely quiet considering they weren't at all far from town. Patrick said it was all the trees that kept them insulated. He must be right because even though the island was only half a mile long and less than a third of a mile wide with most of it uninhabitable, you couldn't hear anything but the water lapping. The chunk she'd carved out for herself was much less than half a tennis court if that, and some of that was still overgrown. They'd pulled out a lot of dead bushes and Ralph and Lizzie had been great in helping with the heavy work.

She wiped the sweat from her brow with the back of her hand and that's when she saw something out on the water in the distance. Jane picked up the binoculars and focused on it. It was a small boat, bobbing in the distance where their inlet opened to the mouth of the river.

She rarely saw anyone else with a boat along here. She had seen teenagers a few times messing on the water in boats, but it wasn't very often, and they were usually further down, well away from the crescent and the island. In fact, she didn't know anyone else who had a boat close by. But then she didn't know many people further down the lake. She magnified and gasped. Her body went rigid. They were looking at *her* through binoculars. She dropped hers. Then squinted. Unable to make out the form, she picked them up again. It was a man. The salt from her sweating brow dripped into her eyes; she wiped it away with the end of her T-shirt and looked again.

The boat was bobbing away further into the distance.

But whose boat was it?

Ha, she tried to rationalise. It had to have been her imagination that they were looking at her. Nobody knew what she had done here. In fact, they had purposely left so much of the foliage in place to keep her hidden. They couldn't have been looking at her. She probably wasn't allowed on here and didn't fancy having to deal with council bureaucrats. Maybe someone did know what she'd done and was out there checking up on her. Their two neighbours were the only ones who knew, and they weren't bothered. They wouldn't have said anything to anyone. She dismissed it. She certainly wasn't going to start worrying about that. Like she didn't have enough on her plate already.

A snap of a twig made her bolt out of her chair and spin around. *Je-ZUS*. Jasper shot up, barking furiously having been woken suddenly. 'It's OK, Jasper, calm down.' She was a little scared to send him off to investigate and grabbed him. *Oh, God, was it a water rat?* Yuk. She didn't want him going after that. Too late, he was off like a rocket, yanking himself free from her grasp. It could of course be more squirrels. Could they swim? She thought they might. There was a medium-sized lump of vegetation stuck in the lake between them and the island towards the end of their boundary. Maybe they swam to that, rested then swam to the island. Could be, she supposed. She had seen an owl once that wouldn't crunch a twig though. A couple of months ago she'd seen a duck and a drake and found a nest with some eggs; she'd had to keep Jasper away for two months until they'd hatched and gone. She'd seen an occasional otter since they'd moved in but not too often. There were always noises here, scuffling, rustling and fluttering in the bushes. But today, that snap of a twig was different. It sounded different.

The more she thought about what she'd seen in London, the more she was convinced she *might* have imagined it. It wasn't improbable. After all, he was all she could think of since that letter had landed on the doormat. And now every sound and odd thing that happened, she thought of him.

She turned back to see if the boat was still on the water, but it had gone. She sighed with relief. It was probably someone from further down the river that they didn't know and nothing to do with the council or checking on her. Although it was unusual for them to come up this far. OK, she had to stop second-guessing every little thing. This wasn't doing her any favours. All she was doing was winding herself up. For what? For something that might not happen. It was easy to make every little thing seem as if it was connected.

Jasper started barking, trying to get her attention from deep in the undergrowth. She moved towards the thick foliage and called out, 'Come here, Jasper, come on.' But he just carried on barking. Damn him, she wasn't going in after him, it was too dense for her. She had treats and got one out, trying to coax him. He wasn't having any of it. Stubborn little bugger. It really annoyed her when he ignored her this way.

God this heat is awful. She pulled her T-shirt out to let in some air and wiped her brow. Her mobile rang: Patrick.

'Hi,' he said. 'We can see you. Are you OK?'

'Yes, it's Jasper. I think he's found something in the bushes and won't come out. I can't come back until he does.'

'D'you want to come and get me, and I'll have a go? He can spend ages chasing stuff.'

She thought about it but then she'd have to go back, and she was stressed about the work she had to do. 'No, I'll get on with my work and hopefully by the time I finish then he'll have got tired enough to come back. If I can get a chunk of the illustrations done, I'll be much happier.'

She settled back down with her pad and pencil and by the time she looked up again the light was beginning to fade. Hell, how had she done that? A ghostly mist was forming over the water. She'd heard this sometimes happened out here on the lake in hot weather. The warm air encountered the cool surface of the lake causing tiny droplets of warm water in the air to rapidly cool, causing it to change from invisible gas to tiny visible droplets that made the mist. Her stomach growled in protest. She hadn't eaten since lunch and not very much then. She was starving and snatched a biscuit from the stash she kept. Looking back at the house she saw the lights of Patrick's studio on, neither had he, she'd bet. You could still see the extension to the right of the house set back a little, but the mist was coming in quickly.

Patrick must have lost track of time too. It wouldn't be too long before the mist was too thick to see the house. She noticed a text from Lizzie that she'd also missed, saying she was going out for pizza with Ralph several hours ago.

'Jasper, come on, we have to go.' *Hell, I might have to get Patrick after all.* She hated the idea of leaving him here alone, especially with that mist coming in while she fetched him. *Where are you?* He'd been quiet for a long time, she now realised, and began to panic. Just as she was about to call him again, he let out a squeal as if he was in pain. 'Jasper, quickly, come here. Come on!' She threw herself at the bushes trying to break through to get to him. Dammit, it was no use and a loose branch slashed her cheek. 'Ouch.' She was about to call again, more angrily this time as he'd ignored her, but he flew out, startling her and ran towards the boat, whining. Annoyed, she scolded him. 'I told you to leave whatever was in there alone.' She immediately felt bad for shouting — he looked so frightened. Now she'd have to take him to the vet if something had bitten him. He was so naughty going after anything that moved.

But when she looked him over, she found no wounds, but his ribs seemed tender. Curious, she touched him again only to hear him yelp and pull away. A rustle from behind startled her. Jasper growled deep in his throat. She imagined the rat coming out after him and quickly tried to think what she could grab to defend themselves with. But Jasper growled again, baring his teeth this time, and that was enough for her to decide to go back to the house. *We're off matey, let's go home.* She gave him fresh water from her water bottle and grabbed her stuff. 'I can't believe you stayed in there for so long you naughty boy?' she said, soothingly to try to calm him a little, even though she wasn't. He was still on edge, not taking his eyes off the bushes. Whatever had hurt him still spooked him. And now she too was spooked. She berated herself for forgetting about him while she worked, worrying that he might have been trapped and she'd not heard him. How could she have done that?

She grabbed him, put him in the boat, and pushed off. The boat journey only took ten minutes but tonight it felt a lot longer as they rode into the mist. She rubbed the back of her neck to ease the odd feeling someone was watching them and looked around for the little boat. Jasper moved to the back of the boat, looking back at the island, staring intently, a low growl emanating from him with the occasional bark.

Whatever it was that had frightened him he wasn't happy about it. She looked back, just as a shadow seemed to move out of the bushes. She pushed the boat on, faster, and shivered. It was just the disappearing light and the mist sending her thoughts dangerously spiralling. *Calm down, Jane you're going to spook yourself if you're not careful and then you won't want to come back!* She really had to stop thinking this way.

'Come here, Jasper, give me a cuddle.' He always liked to sit with her on the way home. But tonight, he stayed watching the island.

When they landed, Jasper leapt out and raced back to the edge of the water, growling again into the mist that was now thick and edging closer to them.

She fastened the cleats securing the boat and followed him, glancing behind her into the mist as they walked towards the house. The air was cooling and she rubbed her arms to stifle the uneasy feeling that wouldn't leave her. Apart from an eeriness surrounding them she saw nothing — except for one second as she turned to go inside and glanced once more behind her. She caught a glimpse of something before it was swallowed up by the mist. A second later and she'd have missed it. The tail end of a small boat, perhaps? Had she really seen that?

She glanced at Patrick's studio just visible from where she was standing to the right of the kitchen and already shrouded in thick white mist. She bet he didn't even know the mist had fallen. He'd be as surprised as she was at the speed with which it had wrapped around their house.

Jasper was by her side now, staying close to her. She walked to the studio and peeked in through the window. Seeing him with his headphones on and drumming, she decided not to disturb him; there was no need.

Inside with the doors closed she felt better, although it was really too warm to close them. She loaded the dishwasher, binned the rubbish. The kitchen was a mess, and she was a bit annoyed that Lizzie had gone out and left it this way. She wiped over the surfaces with anti-bacterial spray. Then she gave Jasper a treat. He ran off back to the patio doors as if guarding them. She had to admit, his behaviour unsettled her no matter what she told herself.

She sat in the comfy armchair in the lounging part of the kitchen with a glass of Merlot and tried to unwind a bit. It was just the one. That's when she saw the untidy pile of newspapers on the mat by the front door. She picked it up. It was unusual to see a real newspaper in the house; they only used them for the log burner; they both read the news online these days. Pauline and Tony liked real newspapers and collected a few at a time then dropped them off when they were done. Similarly with Gordon and Penny, but some of theirs usually had kids' drawings on or bits of paint from the children's crafts that made the log burner whoosh. She quickly flicked through them before putting them on the pile for the log burner. Just as she was coming to the end of the last one, she dropped onto the chair as if someone had kicked her legs from under her and scanned the article in horror.

MAN RELEASED FROM PRISON AFTER ONLY SERVING TEN YEARS OUT OF FIFTEEN FOR THE MANSLAUGHTER OF—

She couldn't read anymore. She didn't have to. She knew what it said and more. About how Murk ran gangs in London before going to prison. And the witness whose evidence helped put him away. Her hands felt clammy. She put the Merlot down before she dropped the glass. *Who'd put it through the letterbox?* Pauline and Tony or Gordon and Penny? *Or someone else? No, no, I know that's not possible. This is a freak coincidence her seeing this. It's just by chance I chose to look through them. Nobody could have predicted I would. I hardly ever do.*

It wasn't the main heading but a sub, big enough for her not to miss, but she might have if she hadn't had the time to flick through. He couldn't have anything to do with this. It was a coincidence. That's all. *Yes, yes, I mean, it has to be, right? I mean what are the chances I would have read it? I'm starting to panic, and I need to stay calm. I need to stay focused. This means nothing. Right? Right.*

Her jaw set rigid and she shuddered.

She didn't want Patrick to see her anxious like this. A chill swept the room as if she was being watched. She rubbed the back of her neck. He'd be unhappy about her going to the island if she told him she'd heard weird noises and felt someone watching her. So, she thought the best thing to do was to bin the paper in the recycling bin outside, she didn't want it in the house, sitting there until they needed a fire, staring at her, goading her. She'd bin it together with the empty bottle she'd brought back with her and decided, for now, it was best not to say anything. The pressure in her head was building again. She shouldn't drink any more that wasn't helping. But she needed something to calm her nerves. She grabbed a couple of painkillers and swallowed them with her wine. What was she going to do about *him*? She was naturally risk averse and that hadn't helped her in the past. This wasn't something she could avoid, though. And yet, she was trying to do just that. She felt she was navigating a dark tunnel with him at the end, waiting, coxing her towards him. Murk had few if any boundaries he wouldn't cross. She knew that.

She sent Patrick a quick text telling him she was back in the house.

She sat and drank her wine knowing she shouldn't really be drinking it but enjoying it all the same and the feeling of her body beginning to relax. Soon her eyes grew heavy. She felt unusually tired. She shouldn't have wound herself up with the mist and Jasper's behaviour and the damned newspaper. Concentrating like she'd been with her work always wore her out. Murk was a low life. She had dismissed him once before and she'd do it again. He would have to be mad to come for her. She closed her eyes; a power nap was what she needed. Her eyes grew heavy. Before she knew it she was out like a light.

She woke to the front door banging closed and checked the time.

My God, where was the time going to, today? She wiped the dribble off her chin. *Yuk*. She got up and set to making a late dinner.

Lizzie and Ralph came in as she was putting some potatoes on the boil.

'Mum! Have you seen the mist outside? It's so spooky, don't you think?'

'I know, we got caught in it on the way back from the island. I think it really bothered Jasper.' She wasn't going to mention how distressed he had become.

'Oh God, scary,' Lizzie said, poking her nose out the window. 'It's like a Stephen King film.'

'Mrs C, do you mind if I go and speak with Patrick?' He flushed vermilion as if he was embarrassed to ask.

'Not at all. You take him, Lizzie. It's a good opportunity for Ralph to ask about when he can start shadowing him for production experience. Tell your dad dinner will be about twenty minutes. Oh, and Ralph, you don't need to keep asking permission. Just knock on the studio door in future.'

Ralph was a good-looking boy with thick blond hair and intense blue eyes. He was clean-shaven unlike a lot of youngsters these days. She liked how he called her Mrs C instead of Mrs Carmichael, or Jane. Ralph slipped through the internal door off the kitchen into the studio behind Lizzie.

When Lizzie came back to the kitchen by herself a few minutes later, Jane said, 'You know, he's so polite.'

'He is, but why are you surprised? All my friends are polite. You make them sound like they're all down-and-outs.' Jane shrugged. 'Oh, Pauline said she had some tomatoes from her garden and would drop them off at some point. I hope it clears up — we want to go out later.'

'Oh excellent, the last batch she gave me was gorgeous. Have you been over there this afternoon?' Pauline was lovely. Her husband, Tony, a retired teacher, was in awe of Patrick being a musician, himself being a wannabe musician but totally tone-deaf.

'Yeah, after we came back from lunch we stopped there first. You know they've got air conditioning and, God, it's so nice and cool.' She pulled a drained expression. It was stifling in the kitchen even with the windows open. She didn't want to open the patio doors.

Jane sidestepped the new persistent nagging about AC. 'Pretty handy for you this hot summer then.'

'Why don't you have it put in? You'll love it when you do.'

'I bet. I just can't justify it when we only get a couple of weeks a year of hot weather.' She glanced out of the window. The mist combined with the heat trapped in the house was eerie and unsettling like they were cocooned in some strange land.

'That's so old-fashioned, Mum.'

'No, it's not. I take umbrage at that, you cheeky madam. It's called being sensible.'

Lizzie laughed. 'You're so weird sometimes. It's not like we can't afford it. Dad's booking a luxury holiday for you,' she said, texting at the same time.

'That's different.' She didn't want to get into it.

She took the potatoes off the heat and drained them. 'Will you make the salad, please?'

Lizzie came off her phone. 'Shall I lay the table too? We can't eat out there with that mist.'

'Great, please. I think the dishwasher's finished. You might as well empty it and use that instead of getting more out.' She was right about that and glanced once again out the window; it wasn't budging. She remembered Pauline had told her the mists didn't generally last long. But how long was long?

'Have you and Dad sorted where you're going to go, yet?' Lizzie asked.

'I think he's still researching it. You know what he's like. It takes him an age. I'll have to give him a nudge at some point otherwise we'll still be here at Christmas. Oh, look, damn, are you two really hungry? I've not made enough potatoes. They've kind of mashed up in the pan.' She'd overcooked them, she realised, spooning them out of the colander back into the saucepan.

Lizzie wasn't one of those high-maintenance girls, in fact she was a bit of a tomboy. She wore ripped jeans and cropped tops with trainers and her long, dark wavy hair was always swept back in a ponytail. She was incredibly smart and doing an Electronic Engineering course at uni. Jane was so proud of her.

'Famished.'

Oh, to have that metabolism again. 'Even after your pizza?'

'Yeah, Mum, that was hours ago. What dressing do you want me to put out for the salad?'

'I don't know, whatever you fancy. I think we all like what's in the cupboard. Choose one.'

Jasper was by Jane's feet chewing his bone and in doggie heaven oblivious to anything but his little treat. He seemed to have calmed down but refused to leave her side.

'Knock, knock, it's only me!' Pauline sing-songed from the patio doors, as she stepped in carrying a small bowlful of plum tomatoes. 'As promised. I hope Lizzie told you I was coming over with goodies. Lordy, Lord how bad is that mist? I got halfway and thought I'd made a mistake but thought I'd keep going. I followed your fence. We haven't had one this bad in years.' Although she was well-spoken, Jane detected a hint of the East End slip in and out with the odd word. She didn't talk about where she was from much. Jane got the impression she was insecure about her background. She had mentioned occasionally that she'd grown up in Barking but was quick to change the subject.

'Hi there,' said Jane smiling and side-stepping Jasper to not trip over him and took the tomatoes from her. 'Just in time for Lizzie to chop them in the salad. But really, you shouldn't have come over in this. You could have tripped and broken something.'

Jane handed them to Lizzie. 'Now, stop fretting, you forget I'm used to them. At least it's starting to cool down a little.'

She wiped her brow. 'But your house is far too hot for me. I won't stay long if you don't mind.'

'I was just telling Mum about your amazing air conditioning, but she won't budge.'

'Shut up, Lizzie, and chop the tomatoes,' Jane said pretending to be annoyed. 'Thanks, Pauline but you really didn't need to come over with them right away.' She felt bad and worried about her getting back home safely.

'It's fine. I wanted to check if Ralph was eating with you or us anyway? He's not answering my texts.'

'Oh, he's in with Patrick so probably in music heaven. I was cooking for him, I just assumed. Lizzie—'

'Here, we're going to see a film afterwards. Is that OK with you, Pauline?'

Pauline laughed. 'Of course. I might bring all his stuff over too seeing as he practically lives here. Mind you, I can't see this lifting that quickly.'

'It's not on till late and besides, Ralph said sometimes it only hangs around near the lake and the rest of town is fine.'

'True, true,' said Pauline. 'Best walk up to the main road to check though, first.'

'Sorry, Pauline,' said Jane. 'Were you cooking something for him?'

'What are you sorry about? I was joking. It's great these two are such good friends.' She laughed her big baritone laugh. 'Especially after his upheaval with changing universities. God, it's hot in your house.' She fanned herself with her hand frantically. 'I'm going back, if you don't mind. I don't mean to be rude.'

'I'll call Ralph to walk you back,' said Lizzie.

'You'll do nothing of the sort. I'll be OK.'

Jane reached for her glass of Merlot and watched her leave as she wondered what else was quick to cook and would fill Lizzie and Ralph.

* * *

45

She checked the clock on the wall. She'd overrun but was pleased the boys hadn't come searching for food yet. The fries in the air fryer had another ten minutes.

'Shall I go fetch the boys? How long's left?' asked Lizzie.

Jane looked at the air fryer. 'Ten minutes.'

Alone, she leaned back on the cupboards looking at the wall clock ticking away, enjoying the peace it brought her.

Their home was in a very peaceful, safe area. The sound of traffic was hardly ever heard. They didn't have many visitors, not having lived here all that long. Sometimes when she was alone on her island, she imagined she was alone in the world, and you could quite easily believe it. She focused on the ticking of the clock, thinking about earlier on the island and if that feeling of safety would still be there the next time she went over.

Jasper growled and raced back to the patio doors.

'Jasper, be quiet. Don't start that again, please. It's probably Pauline coming back to ask Ralph to help guide her back home after all,' she said slightly nervous by his sudden actions and more to convince herself than him. Pauline didn't appear. And he hadn't barked at her earlier anyway. She looked out the window into the thick inky blackness, amazed Pauline had gone out in this. Jane couldn't stop her mind from returning to the boat she'd seen earlier. It was really bothering her.

Jasper was getting quite frantic now at the patio doors. Leaping up and scratching at the glass. Lizzie's comment about Stephen King hadn't been helpful that was for sure. She put on the outside lights. The mist bounced the light back. Jasper didn't let up barking and scratching.

'Just a moment, let me see if there's something out there,' she told him, not wanting him to race out, again and get hurt a second time.

She opened the kitchen window above the sink, leaned out, not wanting to open the patio doors in case Jasper shot out, and heard a heavy thud that startled her. She stepped back, looking at Jasper who'd wound himself up even further by the patio doors. That wasn't a fox or a squirrel. He cocked his head, making a deep throaty growl and baring his teeth like the last time. Had she imagined the noise? No, Jasper had heard it too. Maybe it was a branch snapping off a tree and hitting the floor. *But there was no wind.* There was nothing for it. She had little choice but to open the patio doors now, slowly, and stepped out followed by Jasper who bolted down the garden and disappeared into the mist like one of the hounds from hell. The night was still.

She stared into the mist. It was impossible to see through it. The thick white candyfloss hanging all around felt creepy. She shivered then tuned in towards a sound she caught in-between Jasper's barks. A scraping sound. Heavy and solid. Like a boat being dragged off the land into the water. The heavy splash of a heavy object hitting the water.

The mist hid the garden and beyond.

'Jasper, come back. Jasper!' She really didn't like him out there on his own. He was locked on whatever he had found. In the mist. Out of sight. She shouldn't have let him out.

Then she heard it. A cough. There was someone out there. A neighbour perhaps? It would be unusual to hear them but it *could* be one of the neighbours. Maybe they dropped something, and the sound carried over.

She held her breath, straining to hear. Afraid to make a sound. And like in all good horror movies the mist was dense, the air thick and heavy with not a sound to be heard but the lapping water at the edge of the garden. Very Stephen King. And Jasper had disappeared into it. And as in those films, the protagonist slowly walked into the whiteness while viewers screamed, *no, don't go in there!* And you know nothing good is going to come out of this situation. So why was she stepping into the unknown? To help her dog. You always had to help the dog. Didn't you?

The barking stopped. Creepily sudden. Her heart rate sped up. She waited to hear him bark again but there was nothing. Then laughter, young people's laughter. Teenagers out on a boat for a spooky trip? *That would make sense, right?* She felt jittery from the sudden spike in adrenaline but let out a breath of relief that that was probably all it was. But then the quiet was back again with just the lapping of the water making her pulse race. *Was Jasper hurt? Was that why he'd stopped barking?* Against her better judgement she stepped carefully into the whiteness. Patrick and the kids were only in the house if she needed help. What could happen? *Stop it, stop it, I'm being over dramatic that's all.* 'Jasper? Where are you? Jasper? Jasper, baby come here. Come on, come back?'

Walking trepidatiously down the garden her attention was drawn to a rustling and splashing sound ahead of her. What were those kids doing so close to her garden? Or was that Jasper? She followed the sound, using it to guide her. Maybe they didn't know where they were. Maybe they were lost. Was that Jasper in the water? Was he in distress? There was a lot of splashing. Were they hurting or teasing him?

'Jasper? Come on, boy. Come here,' she called out, hesitantly. But her words hit the wall of mist and bounced back. She felt something touch her arm and jumped away. It was only a branch. Pressing on, her foot twisted on the uneven lawn. She yelped. 'Fuck.' She had no idea where in the garden she was. She'd been following the sound of Jasper in the water but now there was nothing.

She couldn't hear any water splashing. That was not a good sign.

She didn't know why but cold sweat broke out over her body as if she had a premonition something bad was about to happen. Oh, God. And then she heard him again. Relief flooded her. *Thank God.* She moved a little quicker towards him. Her head felt woolly for some reason, her earlier headache still there in the background. The painkillers hadn't worked.

She saw him at last, growling and snapping at the water's edge, and sped up. She felt relieved he was fine after everything she was thinking. He was half in and half out of the water, snapping at something in the lake that she couldn't see from where she was. Trying to grab it. But clearly not comfortable going in after it. 'Jasper, leave it alone. Come back. Come on. Leave it.' She stepped a little closer. 'Bloody dog, what's got into you? You're really scaring me. Come here.' It was probably a piece of driftwood from one of the trees. Or something the kids had thrown in to antagonise him. She was convinced it had to have been them teasing him. Maybe that had been the thud she'd heard? Whatever was in the water still had him agitated. The hairs on the back of her neck tingled. There was no one around but Jasper and she heard no more laughter.

She stretched forward when she got to him, intending to pull him out. Her feet slipped on the muddy floor around the edge of the water, unbalancing her a little. She reached out further to grab the floating mass in front of her, seeing as she couldn't grab him. Jasper leapt on top, excited she was helping. A body burst through the surface, sending her toppling backwards. She screamed. Her blood ran cold and she went under, into the cold water. Then burst out gasping for air. Jasper barked louder, thinking it was a game. Patrick wouldn't hear a thing inside his studio and neither would the kids, she suddenly realised. Nobody would hear her scream. *Oh God.* She splashed and spluttered trying to right herself. Her feet slipping on the floor as she scrambled to get purchase. She was afraid she'd be dragged under if she didn't pull herself out. Fear sank its fangs deep within her and she began to scrabble on all fours to the edge like a drowning woman.

Kneeling on the water's edge, gasping, her fingers touched something that felt like hair in the water, but it couldn't be. They curled around the mass. She didn't want to think about it. She yanked it out of the water expecting it to be heavy, to be attached to a body, but it ripped through the water easily. Startling her. 'Jesus!' She flung it onto the grass, wiping her hands on her jeans in disgust, horrified the hair had come away in one piece. Jasper ran around barking and growling at it. Pulling it along the grass and fighting with it. It was a wig of long brown hair.

She stood up too quickly then pitched back into the water when something hard bumped into her side, knocking her off balance. Sending her back under. She swallowed water, choked and broke free through the surface, gasping, splashing around, disorientated. Terrified. Seeing Jasper, she made her way to him, stumbling. A body floated face down next to her. She was on her feet instantly, slipping and sliding to get back on the bank. Away from it.

She had only ever seen two dead bodies. Her father and that poor boy at the pub. The memories hurled themselves at her, taking her by surprise. She didn't want to remember. She'd promised herself never to think of them. She had taught herself well to block it all out. But this wasn't a body. It was a mannequin.

Standing up, she pulled it out from the water, dragging it to the bank. Jasper growled, staring at it, waiting for it to move. It wasn't lost on her that the wig resembled her own hair. She flipped the mannequin over with the toe of her shoe. *Janey* was written in thick, black letters across the forehead. She drew her foot back as if it had scorched her. Ice chips replaced her blood.

CHAPTER 5

Jane grabbed Jasper and rushed back to the house as fast as she could through the mist, tripping and twisting her ankle a second time. At one point she walked into the weeping willow they had in the garden. Finally, she made it. Gasping for breath and exhausted, she burst into the kitchen. There was nobody there. She walked to the studio trying to calm down a little. Jasper ran off upstairs.

Patrick had his back to her, sat in jeans and T-shirt at his electronic drum kit. A faint trickle of music escaped his headphones. Lizzie and Ralph were listening to something through headphones too and were watching him with smiles on their faces. All oblivious to her startled entrance.

Jane grabbed his arm. Startled, he flinched. When he saw her distress, and wet clothes, he yanked off his headphones in a panic.

'What's wrong? What's happened?' His eyes bore through her as he tried to fathom what was wrong. What had frightened her. Both Lizzie and Ralph turned around. They took off their headphones and looked at her stunned, waiting for her to say something.

'Mum! Sorry, we got sidetracked. Is the food ruined?' Lizzie thought that was why she was distressed. *God, if only.* 'What's happened? You're soaked.'

She felt a hand grab hers. It was Patrick. His worried features stared back at her. His thick dark hair, speckled with grey was now flat on top where the noise-cancelling head-phones had sat. His grey eyes, which she'd always been able to melt into and feel safe in, swallowed her right up. He had a unique aura that made her feel he would protect her from the world she realised. That he would fight off any demons to save her. She never used to put that thought into words, but suddenly finding out that a violent criminal she knew was out of prison and looking for her did that to a person.

'You all right, Jane?' he said and sat her down in a nearby chair. 'Why are you soaked? What's happened?'

She sat down and replied to Lizzie first, unsure how to go about explaining what had just happened. 'No. It's not the food.' She sounded a little dazed.

'Then what's happened?' Lizzie asked. 'You look like you've seen a ghost.' *She wasn't wrong.*

'Jasper was barking by the lake . . . I tried to stop him . . . It was floating in the water . . . I thought it was a body . . . Jasper wouldn't shut up . . . I . . . I was scared it would hurt him . . . I tried to help him . . . It's horrible,' she babbled, dropping her head into her hands, angry with herself that she couldn't get her words out straight. *But that name. God, it was true then.* It couldn't be a coincidence. He *was* looking for her. And he'd found her. That bloody name.

'Jane. Slow down. Did you fall in the lake? I can't make out what you're saying. What's horrible? Where's Jasper? Is he OK?' asked Patrick, kneeling in front of her and taking both her hands in his. 'What's happened? Talk to me.'

She nodded. 'He ran off when we got back inside. The mannequin. It wasn't a body. It's a mannequin. In the lake. It has — it has a name on it. A girl's name. Jasper was trying to pull it out. I fell in trying to stop him.'

'What mannequin?' He looked bewildered, throwing a glance at Lizzie who shrugged as confused as he was. 'What has a name on it? Look, take a breath. Slow down, Jane. Jasper's all right, is he?'

She closed her eyes for a second and nodded. 'He's fine.' *God, that bloody name.*

'He didn't get hurt?'

She shook her head. 'No, he's fine.' She couldn't slow her breathing down. She was becoming dizzy. She reached out to him for support.

'Slow down. Breathe, Jane. Breathe slowly in through your nose, out through your mouth. Do you know what she's talking about, Lizzie?'

'No, I came in to tell you dinner was ready then got sidetracked by what you were working on. I didn't know she'd gone outside.'

Jane was calmer after the breathing exercise. Her heart rate slowed. But her headache was still there, and her head was still woolly. She rubbed her temples as if trying to get rid of both.

'Tell me again, Jane. You said there's a mannequin in the garden? I don't understand?'

Thinking of telling them what had happened in her head sounded nuts. She didn't know for how long she sat there going over it with herself. It was like suddenly someone had unlocked her memories. She didn't want to remember her past, but it was all coming back like a tidal wave of horror and fear. Patrick was watching her, patiently, waiting for her to speak. Worry etched all over his face. *I must look and sound totally bonkers to them.* She glanced at them suspiciously. They all watched her, waiting for her to explain. Confusion and worry on their faces.

She cleared her throat about to speak, but Patrick spoke for her. It was clear that he sensed she was having trouble getting what had happened out in words. 'Shall we go outside?' he offered. 'Will it be easier if you show us?' he said gently, then grabbed a discarded hoodie from a chair in the corner of the room and draped it over her shoulders.

She took a breath. Yes, that would be easier. Better. The malevolence that was out there on the lawn wasn't something she wanted to see again. And yet, what choice did she have if she was to get him to understand? But understand what? That a mannequin had washed up on the lake? And scared her half to death? Now that did sound crazy. Without the backstory what were they to make of her near hysteria?

Where to start though? With the sightings in London? Of which she hadn't told him because of exactly this same situation. She just didn't feel safe which was hard for her to explain to him because she'd need to mention the letter and that damned newspaper pushed through the door.

If she told him about the letter then she'd have to tell him what she'd witnessed, and about Murk, and then that would lead to how she knew him and then she'd have to tell him about that and her father's dead body and she wasn't ready to do *that*. . . not yet. No. Not yet.

'Who would put a mannequin in the lake?' asked Lizzie questioningly.

'It must have come down the river. Perhaps from the town,' said Ralph. 'Mum said she'd seen a bunch of teenagers out in a boat a couple of times. Maybe it was them messing about, larking about in the mist, that sort of thing.'

'That's probably what it is, darling . . .'

'Yeah, but Dad, you haven't seen the mist out there. It's really spooky. It's so thick you can't see anything in front of you,' Lizzie said.

'Really?' Patrick glanced at the window then went to look out. 'Wow, I see what you mean. I suppose finding something like that in the water in this weather would freak you out. I can't believe how quickly this came down.'

'It does happen,' said Ralph, 'something to do with the temperature of the water and the air. I don't really know enough to explain it.'

'Right, right,' said Patrick coming back to Jane. 'Silly, you probably wound yourself up if you couldn't see anything and then Jasper making a fuss compounded it. Do you want to show us? Or do you want to wait till morning? It's up to you, sweetie. But if we all go and see it, it might make it less spooky for you.' She could tell he was really worried about her.

'Yeah, he's right, Mum. I told her it was like a Stephen King movie when we came back from Ralph's.'

'There you go. Lizzie saying that clearly made an impression. You had that thought in your mind when you went out there.' He laughed. 'Come on, let's go there and check it out and put your mind at ease.'

She stayed mute, worrying what to say and said nothing.

Lizzie crossed the floor of the studio and put her arms around her, hugging her tightly. There was a memory of her doing that to her daughter so many times to try and comfort her as a child. Her daughter was growing up fast; she had the same sensitivity of her father picking up on silent emotions.

Jane wiped her face with her sleeve, feeling ridiculous. She hadn't realised she'd been crying.

'You OK now?' Patrick asked, picking up on her silence.

'I'm fine now,' she lied. 'You're right. The Stephen King reference probably did it.'

He squeezed her arm supportively. Then laid a gentle kiss on top of her head. It sent a warm feeling spreading throughout her.

'Tea everyone,' Ralph announced, pushing open the door carrying a tray of steaming mugs. Jane hadn't seen him leave. 'I thought a sweet cup of tea would help Mrs C and it looks like the mist is beginning to thin out a bit. It might be easier if we wait a little longer before going down to the lake.'

'That's kind of you, Ralph,' said Patrick.

'Yes, thank you, Ralph.' Jane took the tea. 'The salmon in the air fryer and the fries are probably dried out by now.' She wanted to laugh that that was what was worrying her right now.

'I'm sure it will be fine, Jane. You feeling a bit better?' Patrick asked after she drank some of her tea.

'Yeah,' she nodded.

A chill had run through her when she'd spotted the name on the mannequin, the brown-haired wig strewn at the side, the dark eyes of the doll staring back at her blankly. Her eyes involuntarily wandered to her family, to what they might be thinking about her story. She forced herself to look away.

She had kept her past successfully hidden for years, locked away inside her head like a safety deposit box only she'd thrown away the key. This wasn't the first time she'd wanted to tell Patrick everything about her past. She'd been plagued with insecurity her whole life and with the need to lessen her guilt for keeping such a big secret from him because it was against the ethos of their relationship. The need to finally open up and shed the guilt and shame she carried and tell him the truth about her past was sometimes overwhelming. But never so much that she gave in. When they married, she wanted to do so with a clean slate. But she never found the courage and it had always bothered her if that was why she felt slightly removed from him. She didn't want to be, of course. But keeping it hidden all this time now made it so terrible. It showed a lack of trust in him that she didn't believe was there. Only, she was so afraid that she might be wrong and that their relationship might not stand the admission.

She held Patrick's gaze feeling conflicted about what to do. *I'm not sure he's strong enough to hear it.* Finding Patrick and falling in love with him was the best thing to ever happen to her. She'd dreamt of such a wonderful relationship but never dared to believe she deserved it. And that was why she desperately wanted to protect it. Even if that meant keeping secrets she knew might destroy it.

CHAPTER 6

After she finished the cup of tea Ralph had brought her and was feeling a little better for it, they still all needed to eat. So she insisted they all sit down at the kitchen table Lizzie had laid up earlier while she served up the overcooked food, feeling slightly embarrassed by it and by what had passed. They couldn't go out right now anyway, it was best to wait for the mist to lift.

Patrick had a calming way about him, never showing worry or tension; it was one of the things she'd first noticed about him when they met at Suzanna's party. It was comforting and always seemed like a safe place for her to cling to. If Patrick was calm, she was generally calm too. He would always listen to what she had to say and make her feel cherished, looking logically at everything that she worried about and finding a solution. It was him who told her once, there are no problems, Jane, only solutions. It was the mantra she liked to live by. She wasn't sure how that applied to this problem, though.

She wanted to call the police to come out and see the mannequin, but Patrick convinced her they would look ridiculous to call them out for this. He was right of course; it was a dumb idea. Did she really want to involve the police? Probably best not to. Not yet anyway. No. She had to handle this by herself.

'The shop around the corner from the old bank building just changed hands,' Ralph added, helpfully chewing on a piece of rubbery salmon. 'It used to be a women's clothes shop. Maybe she named all her mannequins, and the kids took it from the skip.' He could be right; the woods did butt up along the side of the lake further up. 'But naming the mannequins? That would be a weird thing to do, though.' He wrinkled his nose and looked at Lizzie. Both giggled conspiratorially.

'The kids probably did it,' echoed Patrick with logic. 'It's probably someone at school they know or a sister or some stupid challenge.'

'Yeah, Mum, I've seen the skips at the back of the shop,' said Lizzie. 'It's going to be a craft shop, I think. Can't see that working in the town, can you? I mean, who does crafty stuff these days? You can probably get it cheaper on Amazon and they deliver.'

She sighed. 'I know you're all right, there's always a simple explanation,' she said trying to sound convinced while looking at Patrick, his strong face and comforting eyes filling her with his much-needed calm. A bubble of panic rose inside her chest, catching her off guard as a memory intercepted her thoughts. Her past was coming back to haunt her.

'I think . . .' she blurted. She cleared her throat. 'I think that . . .' She marshalled her thoughts. She did truly want to tell him and to relieve herself of all the stale emotions from her past. It was all bubbling up inside her that she needed to get it out. *I'm not being fair to him.* She knew the longer she held on the more damage and destruction to her beautiful life they would impact. The more she thought he wouldn't be able to handle it the more she believed that he would. Because he loved her. And yet . . . when push came to shove, she couldn't do it. She clammed up again.

Patrick finished his dried-up salmon and fries. 'What d'you think, darling?' He looked at her, waiting for her to say what she was struggling with.

'I need to talk to you, Patrick. I need to say something.' She tried again. 'To tell you something. I need to tell you something . . .' She put down her cutlery with more of a clatter than she expected. It brought them all up to attention. The three of them watched, waiting for her to elaborate. She looked around. No. This wasn't the right place. Not in front of the kids. What the hell was she thinking? Was she truly insane?

I'm standing there looking at the body of my dead father on the floor. A dark red mass spreading from his head along the floor. So much blood. His eyes staring at me, blankly.

The flashback came at her so unexpectedly, so fast and violently that she was struck dumb. She had to take a ragged breath. Her eyes were drawn to Lizzie then Patrick knowing how much telling them would hurt them.

She felt the pull of fear and horror in her bones that she had actually considered telling them about her past. About Murk.

Patrick stood up from the table saving her. 'I tell you what. Let's all go and see what's at the edge of the lake, I know it's still bothering you. With the mist lifting a lot since we've eaten, it won't look quite so scary, you'll see.'

They just wanted to put her mind at rest that it was silly teenagers messing about and she'd overreacted in the mist and darkness and had got herself worked up.

'OK, yes . . .' She supressed a raging urge to tell them that she knew it wasn't teenagers. That only one person would know how the name *Janey* would affect her. It felt unsettling to say that name even in her head.

Patrick took her hand. 'Lizzie, grab the torch from under the sink. The mist is lifting just as you said, Ralph. We'll need it now.'

She placed her hand in his large, solid one feeling the comfort of his warmth run though her. He smiled down at her comfortingly.

'You OK to do this? We can wait till the morning if you prefer.'

'No, I'll be fine.' She hadn't expected to feel quite so nervous about going back out there, but she had to see it for herself, if for no other reason than to prove to herself that *Janey* was written on the mannequin.

They walked down to the edge of the lake solemnly. At the edge the four of them stood looking around. They'd left Jasper locked in the house. She saw a look pass between Patrick and the others as he looked over his shoulder.

There was no mannequin.

* * *

A little while later, Jane was in her bedroom, staring out the window, still feeling confused where the mannequin had gone. She'd thought there might have been a possibility that she'd imagined it, but not much of one. She'd been so certain it had really been there. The only explanation could be that the water had dragged it back in and taken it further down the river. That's what Patrick had said, and he was right, of course; it was the logical explanation. But it didn't sit right with her. She couldn't help thinking there was more to it.

She decided to go to bed early, leaving Patrick to sort the kitchen, but sleep wouldn't come to her. Ralph and Lizzie had gone to the cinema. The mist had practically all gone. And her small nightmare seemed watered down. While feeling slightly ridiculous that there'd been nothing there to prove why she'd been so scared. She decided not to express her concern that somebody had moved it, and it hadn't drifted down the lake. It didn't stop her thinking it though.

She grabbed her phone, sat up in bed, and scrolled through Facebook then stopped. *Oh God.* Someone she didn't know but whom she followed had posted an old newspaper article. The photo was grainy, but she was in no doubt it was her as a child in the picture. The article copy was cut, leaving just the picture of a sad young girl, with fear in her eyes being taken from a house by the police. She stared into the young girl's eyes, large and vacant, and the past came rushing at her like a train crashing into her, leaving her breathless with a pain inside that made her whimper so profoundly that Jasper leapt up to comfort her. She gripped the phone until the knuckles of her hand turned white.

She clicked on the person who'd posted. She didn't know her, if indeed it was *a her*. It could be a false account. If could be *him* masquerading as this woman. She followed lots of people because of her work, most of them if not ninety-five per cent she didn't know anyway. There was nothing about this woman that made her stand out. A mother, photos of kids, holidays, pubs, girls, family and friend's nights out. Why would she post this? Further down, she saw this was not unusual. She posted all sorts of random press cuttings about terrible family tragedies. She looked more carefully at the other articles. Each one was posted on the same day and month as the original had been published in the newspaper. She scrolled back up. She clutched her throat as if she was drowning. Of all the articles out there how had she come upon this one? *He* must have sent it to her. It was too much of a coincidence.

Without thought she typed in his name. He popped up. His smiling face not dissimilar to the last time she'd seen him. There was a candid shot of him in the pub holding up a pint as if in salutations for his parole no doubt. Her lip curled with numb disbelief. She stared at him, taken aback by his happiness and by his lack of awareness of what he'd done and why he'd been in prison. She clicked his profile; it said his location was London. Not on her doorstep but not exactly bloody Scotland either. The internet was her friend, now she could see him, sort of keep an eye on him if she wanted. It was also her nightmare showing her how easily he could access her if he wanted. There was no friend request thank God, though she wouldn't put it past him to send one, arrogant sod. She took a moment, a breather. Well, all that was well and good, but the fact of the matter was he hadn't any idea where she lived. Seeing the absurdity of her earlier worry, she thought how utterly ridiculous it was to waste so much energy on whether he was happy or his bloody lack of awareness. She knew he hadn't any.

She found it hard to convince herself she was safe even though she knew she was. It was an annoying niggle in the back of her mind, like a nasty itch. He didn't know where she lived. But there it was, the reality; she was safe, here in their lovely home with her lovely family and he was far away. She must remember that. Of course, the mannequin had been just kids, of course that's what it was. She was the one making it more than it was. Silly really, she was scaring herself half to death with her own runaway imagination. Just to be doubly sure, she set her privacy settings to private.

* * *

The following morning, the temperature was still in the high twenties and the three of them had breakfast on the patio under the umbrella. Jane buttered a slice of toast, struggling to swallow each bite. She'd had a dreadful night's sleep, thoughts of Murk loose in her subconscious which upon waking had annoyed her after her pre-bedtime speech to herself. It wasn't as if she wanted to worry. It was her mind worrying for her. Being a natural worrier and stress head that went hand in hand with her perfectionist trait was like a ball and chain. The blinds were drawn to keep out the sun and keep the kitchen cool. It was muggy inside the house and much better outside.

'I thought you'd have a longer lie-in. You were very restless last night,' Patrick said taking time out from reading the newspaper on his phone.

'It's too hot upstairs. Are you going to see Ralph today?' she asked Lizzie, not wanting to think about her bad night's sleep and definitely not wanting to talk about it.

'Maybe later. I'm going shopping with some girlfriends this morning. I think he's coming over to work with Dad. Is that right, Dad?'

'Oh, yeah sometime later this morning, I think.' He didn't look up, scrolling on his phone.

'Sophie is picking me up in half an hour. I need some more shorts. It's too hot to wear anything else. What you up to?'

'Me? Working, I have that deadline to deal with.' She pressed her cold glass of orange juice to her face. Lizzie was right about the heat. The weather forecast kept saying it was going to cool, clearly not around here. She felt hypercritical wishing for it to cool after always moaning how little sunshine they got.

'How'd you feel after last night? You OK now, Mum?' Lizzie asked, drinking juice and watching her over the rim of her glass. There was worry there and Jane didn't want her daughter to worry about her, that wasn't fair.

'Oh, I'm fine this morning, sweetheart,' she said cheerfully trying to convey it was all in the past. 'You know, the mist the darkness and your silly reference to Stephen King just got the better of my imagination.'

Jane saw Lizzie's relief at her words.

'You did a lot of tossing and turning,' Patrick said putting his phone down and picking up his coffee mug.

'Oh, really? It felt like I did this morning though. It must have been the heat bothering me.' She didn't want to go into it anymore.

It made her happy that Lizzie was going out with friends and not feeling she had to stay in with her. Thinking back, she had sounded a bit of a basket case last night; it must have sounded so bizarre to the three of them. Worrying over a mannequin of all things. The thought made her cringe. What would Ralph have said to Pauline when he got back? Heaven only knew. One thing was for certain, she didn't want Pauline feeling she had to keep popping over to check she was OK. She was that sort of neighbour. Good-hearted and all that but that type of thing could quickly become quite bothersome. Lizzie stood up and wrapped her up in a massive hug. It felt good. What she had to do was put it all behind her and move on.

* * *

After clearing up the breakfast plates and spending some time with Jasper in the garden throwing a ball, Jane finally sat down and opened her laptop to check her emails.

She took a couple of ibuprofens to relieve the tension in her shoulders then leaned back in the garden recliner under the willow tree. She longed for cool air to fan her hot skin and put a stop to the hemmed-in feeling that was only accentuated by the muggy air.

She was a little surprised there was no email reply from Suzanna after sending her the first few rough concepts. So she checked her junk file only to see it empty then looked in her sent file — the same. Curious where all her deleted and sent files had vanished to — she'd prepared the draft email the day before then sent it yesterday morning. She never liked sending emails late in the day as they always ended up down the list at the other end, much preferring to send it first thing. That way it was less likely to get missed. And she most definitely had sent it. So why wasn't it showing in her sent folder? She thought it better to call and check she'd received it.

'Hello, there, so glad you phoned. I was beginning to worry about you,' said Suzanna.

'No need for that, it's all going fine. But I sent you some rough concepts yesterday morning. And, well not hearing from you, I was getting concerned.'

'I emailed you back. God, it must have got lost in your spam. There was nothing attached to your email.'

'Oh!' She hadn't thought about *her* spam file. Could it have gone there? And why would the attachment go missing? 'OK, sorry about that. I'll have a check.' She hadn't double-checked it before she hit send, knowing she had put in the attachments. But then, maybe she hadn't. She supposed it was

64

easily done. She quickly re-typed the email and sent it again with the attachments. 'OK, I've re-sent it now.'

'Great, it's just arrived. Brilliant, thank you so much, Jane. I'll get back to you ASAP if the author approves them.'

'So, while you're on the phone, will you check your diary and see if you have a free weekend to come over for lunch? I know you said how busy you are but it would be lovely to see you socially and I know Patrick would like to see you.'

'Gotcha, I'll look at some dates and get back to you. Speak soon. Got to go — my next appointment just arrived. Hugs to Patrick, too.'

* * *

A little while later, Patrick came out with a cold lemonade; she heard the clinking of the ice before she heard him.

'Thought you might like this to cool you down. Bloody scorcher today. I've just looked at the weather and it could well be here for the next few weeks. Shouldn't complain, but Christ, it's impossible to concentrate. It's the mugginess that gets me.' He was in long shorts and T-shirt, a tan nicely developing on his face and limbs. It didn't take long for him to catch a tan.

She smiled at his very British complaint.

He sat next to her on the other recliner.

'You can't moan, you have air conditioning in your studio.'

'I know, but the minute I come out it's like walking into an oven,' he said.

Against her better judgement she broached the subject of the mannequin, only because she really wanted to know what he was thinking. She was pathologically immune at letting things drop, which was why the letter was having such an effect on her. Despite her best efforts to put it to the back of her mind. Her own neurosis was driving her to believe that Murk was definitely coming for her even though she told herself that she might be imagining it all. So, she had to be sure.

'Patrick, I know we said last night the mannequin must have washed down the river if it had been there at all.' He looked surprised that she thought there was another explanation. 'But, well, I want to go check a little further down, and, well, the thing is, I don't want to do it on my own. Will you come with me?' He might look shocked, but this was her husband, and she knew he loved her and would not say no if he thought it would help her.

'God, Jane, really? Are you sure you want to do that?'

Uneasily, she wondered what he meant by that remark and why he was questioning her. She honestly thought he'd just agree to go with her without calling her out on it.

He must have had a shower to freshen up before coming out to the garden, she could smell the lemon shower gel on him. There were a few droplets of water on the tips of his hair too.

She wished she wasn't being so obsessive about all this and feeling fixated about the damned thing.

She turned, arching an eyebrow, unable to help it. It annoyed her a bit that he was questioning her like this. She didn't want to start an argument. That would make it worse. She just needed to do this and explaining that to him without sounding weird wasn't easy.

He seemed to dither a little, drinking his lemonade and clearly thinking the best way to approach what she'd asked without sounding insensitive. 'OK, if you want to, that's fine, darling. Best to get clarity on it. I agree.'

Together they walked down to the bottom of the garden, along the edge of the water and beyond their house. Here the path became narrow and if there had been a mannequin, she was sure it would have snagged along the water reeds.

They looked as far as they could down the lake, which was far enough to see anything that might be tangled in the bank.

He did that thing with his face when he wanted to say what he really thought but wondered if perhaps he shouldn't.

She was so damned sure she'd seen it. This wasn't good. It could only be that someone had moved it. Maybe the teenagers who might have put it there came back for it? Maybe. Or maybe not. If only she could be sure she had seen it! Jasper could have been barking at there being someone on the water, the teenagers for a start. She had been wound up, stressed and worried for him. It had been creepy. Then hearing the cough. But it could all be attributed to the teenagers. She closed her eyes remembering a time when remembering had been difficult and recalling events unclear. Her doctor had told her stress could make the mind create and erase events that it thought might be too upsetting. He'd said it was the subconscious protecting her. She was certainly stressed. Was that happening to her now? Was she seeing what she wanted to see to make what she was worrying about real?

'It was kind of eerie last night,' he said. 'Lizzie didn't help with her slant on things. You OK?' He gave her a thin-lipped smile. 'Lizzie mentioned she'd seen one of those mannequins dressed up by the side of the road the other day. Had to be teenagers messing about. Maybe it was the same crowd on the lake, and they came back for it.'

She flashed a quick familiar smile back, there was nothing more she could say. She hadn't expected to feel how she had all those years ago, but everything happening was leading right back to Murk, she was sure of it. He was the cause of her anxiety now just like the death of her father had been then.

CHAPTER 7

'We need to spend more time like this,' Patrick said a couple of days later, standing behind her in the kitchen as she stirred a tomato sauce on the hob. She dropped a piece of chicken on the floor for Jasper, wagging his tail like a propeller at her feet. Patrick wrapped his arms around her middle and held her close as the rich aroma of garlic and tomato filled the kitchen. They were having a Saturday evening dinner party with their neighbours. The date had been in the diary for weeks. They were due at seven and she wasn't even changed or showered. She'd chosen spaghetti with a salad and crusty bread as an easy choice for tonight.

'Did you manage to get any work done today? You've been locked in your office most of it,' he asked taking the salad vegetables out of the fridge and starting on chopping and slicing. 'Are you pushing yourself too hard with this extra work? You haven't had a break since the last pieces you sent in. You always need a break. You always say you need to clear your mind so that you can function going from one to the next.'

'I've only one more concept to send.' He was right, totally right, but she had to finish it and there wasn't a choice on that. She shouldn't have accepted so readily. She knew that. But other things had been at play at the time. So, it was what it was. She poured out a glass of Merlot for herself, knowing he preferred white wine, and fetched the bottle for him. 'I shouldn't have said yes to Suzanna, it's my fault. But I can't *not* do it now, I'm committed. Besides, I wanted to take it on before we went away.'

She put down the wooden spoon she was stirring the sauce with and stared out of the window, directly down the garden to the lake; it was so peaceful. She never tired of looking at it. The sun was beginning to go down but there was still heat in it. Her petite frame was suddenly wrapped in Patrick's arms, making her feel cocooned and safe.

'Jane, why not call Suzanna and explain to her it's too much after the last job? You need a break, darling. You're so tense I can feel it.' He massaged her shoulders. 'This stress that's come over you, isn't you. I'm beginning to worry you're pushing yourself too hard to please everyone.'

'No, Patrick, love, really. I know I shouldn't have accepted it, but I did and now I must see it through. I'm nearly there. Then we can go away and get some rest.' She leaned back into him.

'Which reminds me, did you check out those hotels I emailed you?'

'Oh! What hotels? I didn't get an email from you.'

'Oh, right. I'm sure I sent it you. I'll re-send it. Then we can narrow it down to two or three.'

'It's probably my email. I've been having some issues with it recently. I'll check the spam as it might have gone in there.'

'Anyway, you're sure there's nothing else wrong that you're not telling me about?'

'Why would you say that?' She stiffened a little.

He shrugged. 'I don't know. I get the feeling there's something else bothering you.'

'No, love, there's nothing else worrying me.' Her worries, reflected in her pale blue eyes, scanned the garden from the window, grateful he couldn't see them. Her thoughts kept coming back to the mannequin and how it had disappeared so quickly without even Jasper hearing anything. It really had felt real. She'd touched it. Felt it in her hands. Her mind wasn't playing games with her, she was sure of it. It wasn't like the last time. It felt different, somehow. But someone was. She pulled his arms tighter around her and rested her head back against his chest, closing her eyes and willing the thoughts away. She couldn't bring it up again, there was no evidence, only her word. Everything seemed to be happening too quickly, and she felt her heart race and her guts tumble, one of the signs of her anxiety spiking.

'OK, but if there was something . . . you'd tell me, wouldn't you?' It was her turn to feel the tension inside him. 'I mean you wouldn't keep something terrible from me.'

'Like what?' she asked, a little panicked, going stiff in his arms.

'If you were sick, I mean. Because you know I'm here for you, don't you? And things are always better when they're shared.'

Tears pushed to get out, hearing the pain in his words that she'd do such a thing if she were sick. She clung to him. Her heart aching to console him. 'It's OK. I'm OK, there's nothing wrong with me, I promise.'

'But I can tell something is bothering you.'

She sniffed back the threatening tears, trying not to let him see and changed the subject. 'Any news on those extra dates you mentioned?'

'As a matter of fact, yes. I got an email earlier. It's just a few dates. They want me in London again, but nothing's been confirmed yet, but as soon as they are we can push on and make the holiday booking.'

'OK, great. I'll let Suzanna know when we book the dates and, in the meantime, I'll look over the hotels you sent me.'

* * *

Sometime later, Jane came back downstairs after showering and changing. She checked the time on the clock on the kitchen wall: two minutes to seven. She wore cream linen trousers and a striped shirt in candy pink that she wore loose. She'd applied only a little make-up, enough to give her a glow. Her chestnut hair was in a messy bun, the loose strands already sticking to her neck. Too hot to eat inside, she laid the table on the patio and put out a couple of hurricane lamps with citronella candles to keep the mosquitoes away. She staked half a dozen around the perimeter of the table to give them enough light to eat.

Pauline and Tony were never late, and didn't have any excuse to be living across the road. She checked the sauce and put on a pot of water to boil for the pasta. They'd been ever so kind since they moved in. Pauline especially had been there for them with any questions they'd had, and they'd been over to theirs for dinner a few times. Tony loved listening to the stories Patrick had to tell of his friendships with famous rock stars. No doubt he'd be bending his ear again tonight. He was like a child in a sweet shop. Overcome with the fact that he had met some of his musical heroes, Gene Simmons from KISS being his all-time favourite.

Ralph walked in through the patio doors with Pauline and Tony in tow. A tall blond boy with hair to his shoulders and tied in a ponytail, he looked very rock and roll. Smouldering chatoyant eyes always alert, with sinewy strength hidden beneath his skinny body. For such a tall boy he was phantom-silent with fluid movements, which always surprised her when he suddenly appeared in the room without her hearing him. He resembled Pauline in lots of ways, colour of hair, alert blue eyes, but she struggled to see Tony in him. His height was a mystery — perhaps one of his grandparents was particularly tall.

'Hey Mrs C, you look amazing,' he said giving her his best smile. 'Is Lizzie ready? We're supposed be going out tonight.'

'Probably not, you know what she's like. Never has anything to wear and is probably stressing about being late. Go and see if you can calm her, will you, sweetheart?'

'Aah, she's all bark.' He gave her a knowing look she knew all too well. Rather him than her going into the lion's den. He pilfered an olive from the dish on the counter, smiled and shot out of the kitchen to find her.

'I didn't know what to bring so I brought champagne. You can't go wrong with champagne, can you?' Pauline said kissing her on both cheeks and putting the wine in the fridge. 'It's been in the fridge all day, so no need to worry about chilling it.'

A hint she wanted champagne. Pauline always did that.

'Fancy a glass then?' Jane asked cheekily.

Pauline laughed good-heartedly. 'Go on then, if you insist.'

'Hey, did you know Ralph and Lizzie are off to a party? Do you know where?' said Patrick, coming into the room looking and smelling drop dead gorgeous. He was wearing her favourite aftershave, musky and seductive in long shorts and black polo. He welcomed Tony with a pat on the shoulder.

'It's at the White Lion in town. It's not a party as such. I think it's one of her friends' birthdays. Will you check if they'll be drinking and if so, they're to leave the car and get a taxi back.'

'Already done, don't fret,' Patrick said kissing Pauline welcome.

Jane popped the champagne cork and handed Pauline a glass. 'There you go, take one to Tony would you?' Pauline sipped hers and sighed as if it were pure nectar. Jane laughed. It was good to laugh and she felt the tension slowly leaving her body. She was going to enjoy tonight by thinking of nothing but small talk.

Sinatra came on the speaker. *In the wee small hours.* 'I've put a playlist together for tonight.' Patrick stretched out his hand to her. 'My lady, may I have this dance?' He twirled her around the kitchen to the oohs and aahs of their guests.

With everyone sat at the table, Jane served up the food, making sure everyone was topped up with alcohol. 'Such a shame Penny and Gordon are away at their caravan,' she said. It was great having excellent neighbours. But she missed Penny when they went to the caravan to stay with her family in the school holidays. She missed her when she was away. She didn't miss the scrutiny Patrick gave her. He'd made a passing comment the other day that he thought she was drinking too much. Which was ridiculous. She might be having a little more, but then she had a lot more on her mind. It had caused a little argument and now made her conscious every time she did have a drink. She tried not to let it bother her. She poured herself a glass of ice-cold champagne and sat down to enjoy her meal.

'This is delightful, Jane, as always,' Pauline said. 'D'you have any idea when Penny's back?'

Jane found she really didn't have much of an appetite though. She hadn't had one since the arrival of that damned letter. 'She didn't say. I think they're playing it by ear. You know what her family's like, they'd have her moving back if they could. I think she stays as long as she can bear it.'

'God, Patrick,' Pauline turned to face him. 'I don't know how you can bear to tear yourself away from this woman. Don't you miss her wonderful cooking when you're away?'

'Pauline, stop,' Jane said feeling embarrassed and twirling spaghetti onto her fork, secretly chuffed at the compliment.

'It's true. Oh, look at little Jasper asleep on the cushion under the willow.' Pauline made little cooing sounds. Jasper opened one eye to see who was talking to him then closed it again.

Tony reached over for the crusty bread. 'Pauline told me there was a weird bloke around the house this morning. Did you find out who he was? We don't get many strangers around here what with it being a private road and all.' It was an off-the-cuff remark but it made Jane falter.

She stopped eating, a lump of spaghetti stuck in her throat. 'What man? Delivery man?' she asked, taking a sip of champagne to wash it down. Tony bit into the bread and shrugged.

'Well, I don't know, Jane,' interjected Pauline. 'He was snooping around your front door like he was in two minds whether to ring the bell or not.'

A thought struck her that it might be a parent of the teenagers who had been messing with the mannequin. Maybe he came over to apologise on their behalf for trespassing. If he'd seen the dummy in the boat he'd have questioned them and when he found out what they'd been up to felt obliged to come and apologise.

Lizzie and Ralph walked in, chattering loudly and breaking the spell. At a loss, Jane put down her fork and reached for her drink, emptying the glass and refilling it instantly. Suddenly wired from what Tony had said, a violent nausea gusted through her, wiping away the little appetite she'd had.

'Right, Mum we're off,' Lizzie said oblivious to what Pauline had dropped on them. She looked giddy with excitement, looking forward to a night out with her friends. 'We'll get a taxi or an Uber back. Don't look at me like that.' Lizzie mistook her uncomfortable look for her own situation. 'Dad's already laid down the law. We're leaving Ralph's car in the pub car park. We might go on to somewhere else. Don't wait up.' She wouldn't get much sleep tonight anyway, not after what Tony just dropped on them.

Pauline turned around to face Ralph who stood behind her. 'Ralph, you saw that odd man this morning, didn't you? The one I pointed out to you, looking around Jane and Patrick's house. We were just talking about him.'

'Oh, yeah, he was a big guy, tall and wide. Had a baseball cap on and a heavy sweatshirt. I thought it was odd he was wearing that in this weather.'

Very odd indeed, you're not kidding, Jane thought wiping her top lip with her serviette.

Patrick was looking worried. 'What was he doing? Did you speak to him?'

'Oh, no, no, no,' said Pauline. 'That would be nosy. We just watched to see if we could be of help but then he just upped and left like he changed his mind or something.' Jane's stomach tightened. 'He wasn't a delivery driver that much I'm certain of. I mean there was no van, he was on foot. I see all the delivery vans from the kitchen window. Well not all of them, obviously, I'm not sat there watching, you understand.' She chuckled.

'How can you be so sure?' asked Patrick. 'I mean that it wasn't a delivery?'

'Well, he didn't have a van as I said. Or a sack. He was just on foot like he came to see you then changed his mind. I wouldn't worry, he was probably lost.'

Lost? Here? You can't actually walk from town. Nobody would do that.

'Maybe,' said Patrick, 'he was lost and left his car at the top of the lane. The pot holes could have put him off. The satnav has been known to drop people off at wrong locations. It could simply be that? It's unnerving, nonetheless.' That could be another explanation, she supposed.

'I'll keep an eye out, don't go worrying yourself. This is a safe close. You shouldn't have mentioned it, Tony, now they're in a bit of a flap.'

'I didn't mean to start anything. By the way, Jane, this is delicious, it really is.' He mopped the sauce up with a chunk of bread.

Her problem now was that Ralph's description of the man unnerved her. It was too much of a coincidence, wasn't it? A large man at their front door? In a baseball cap kept low — to what? Hide his face? He would have seen their camera, not that it worked, but still, he didn't know that. Murk was pretty distinctive looking. She wouldn't need to see his bloody face to know it was him. But from what Ralph said, it was enough to shake her up and start her mind rambling, again.

Why not approach the other two houses? Ask them for directions, if he was actually lost. Or ask them if they were in if he wanted to apologise. They were in, the cars were on the drive. There were too many things that didn't add up.

'But we were at home,' said Jane, her succinct response more about how she was feeling internally than what was being discussed.

'I don't know, dear,' said Pauline in such a casual manner that Jane tried not to let on how flustered she was.

Nevertheless, she put her fork down with a loud clank. The words spoken about this man being at their house, looking at their house even, wrapped around her, tightly. This was too much. First the newspaper then the mannequin that was there one minute then gone the next and now this stranger hanging around their house? She felt unnaturally hot. Ralph said he was a large man. Murk was a large man. But there was a rational explanation for all of them. And there wasn't if she let herself believe that.

She screwed up her eyes, trying to stop the thoughts flooding her. 'Excuse me.' She left the table and went inside quickly. It was all getting to her too quickly to process. She poured herself a glass of water to cool herself down and fanned herself with a paper napkin which was proving next to useless. No good was going to come from thinking the way she was. Fear was insidious. Once it started it was hard to stop. She knew that. But this, this revelation was so sinister it made her toes curl.

She wasn't sure how long she stood there, holding the glass of water in one hand and fanning herself with the other. It could have been seconds, but it felt like hours. The problem was that she knew how terrible this could get. He did bad things. He was dangerous and he was coming for her. And all these things could be him letting her know he was here, watching her. Or not, because there was a rational explanation for all of them. But if he'd been at the house. What was he planning on next?

She wasn't eating properly or sleeping. Her night terrors, the visions, the memories of screaming and blood and chaos tormented her every night. Not that she could share any of it with her husband. Her lovely, wonderful husband who might not understand. And then the other thoughts and memories, her dad on the floor with blood pouring from his head. The look in his eyes. The doctors, the police. The voices, so many voices talking, talking to her. But it was the blood that she saw mostly. Blood everywhere.

She managed to control the visions for a while, fall asleep but then she'd jolt awake, sweating, terrified she might have spoken in her sleep. Said something Patrick would question. The fear she had running through her veins was quickly turning chronic. Making her drink more than usual and Patrick was noticing. It was just a matter of time before he said something else about it. She had to take control of herself, or she was going to spin out. She was forgetting things or so she thought but she didn't believe she was. My God. She sounded nuts. She couldn't tell anyone any of this. It sounded unhinged. She wasn't going to go back to that place of loss of control, where nothing felt real and yet it was. Is that what he wanted? To send her mind into that state of flux, again ? Hadn't he done it once before?

For the hundredth time she saw the dead body of her father in front of her. Her shock, fear and the pain inside at how it had happened scratched at her, fighting to be let out. She snapped those thoughts closed as quick as a mousetrap.

She fought back hot tears that sprang into the corners of her eyes. She was bloody terrified, she wasn't going to deny it. She had to tell Patrick. She just didn't know how!

Warm arms encircled her. She brushed the budding tears away with her fingers. Patrick's lips on her neck instantly relaxed her as they always did. And increased her guilt for keeping Murk a secret from him. She wanted to push back and get inside him, to hide, to feel safe once more. *Oh, God, I so want to tell Patrick everything.* It physically hurt not to. He turned her around to face him. She was sure he saw all kinds of reactions on her face that he couldn't understand. From fear, to sadness, to need. After their last conversation when she assured him she was hiding nothing, what was he to think now?

'Jane,' he said wiping a stray tear away with his thumb, his voice a low, gentle hum against her face. 'What's wrong? You left the table in such a rush, everyone's worried about you.' She looked up and saw the bewildered expression in his face at how horror-struck she must look. She forced a smile. 'Was it what Pauline said about that stranger? You know what a nosy parker she is and how she likes to gossip. She's more than likely over-egged it. It worried me, too, until I realised it was probably nothing quite as dramatic as she made out.' However much she wanted to tell him the truth, she felt inside that this wasn't the right time. They were so close to one another she could see the tiny specks of green in his iris that gave him that unusual grey colouring. Was there ever going to be a right time? He gave an anxious smile. Probably wondering if what it was she was keeping from him that made her this sad and fearful was something as awful as a cancer diagnosis.

She shook her head in response to his question. She had nothing to offer him. Then she remembered he'd mentioned something about some dates in London for some session work. 'It's you going away again so soon.' She gave a small laugh. 'I've only just got you back. And got used to not being alone here. Silly, really, I know. I don't want you to feel pressured or anything like that. I just thought we'd have more time together and the holiday before you had to go away again. Don't mind me, I'm being selfish and daft as well.'

His face slackened and she saw the worry begin to slip away, silent acknowledgement that his worst fears weren't real. 'You had me really worried there, sweetheart.' He stroked her hair. 'You don't normally react this way when I go away. You always say you like your space. You're sure that's all it is?'

She smothered a sigh. He was right. She didn't normally react this way. No wonder he was concerned about her. She gently kissed him, smiled, reassured him all was OK; that she was simply being greedy wanting him for herself.

Back on the patio, they sat down again at the table. 'Have the kids gone then?' she asked, wanting to move things on.

'Oh, my dear, yes. They left, afraid they'd be late. Are you OK, Jane? You paled so much I thought you were going to be sick.'

She forced a smile. 'I was feeling that way. I think it's this heat and maybe I drank a little too much wine.' She let Pauline prattle on. Listening to her now, she realised that Patrick was probably right, and she had elaborated quite a lot. It didn't take much for her imagination to pick up the baton and run with it. But in the back of her mind the seed of doubt that she might be right was beginning to germinate and that really frightened her. Despite saying the wine had made her feel unwell, she needed it right now to help her unwind.

Patrick cleared away the plates and brought out the fruit bowl with clean plates and cutlery. 'We thought it was too hot to spend more time in the kitchen than was necessary. Besides, I think fruit after a bowl of pasta is exactly what's needed. Grapes, Jane?' he prompted after serving their guests.

She sat quietly contemplating what Pauline was saying now about the delivery drivers, the bin men, the odd cold caller and it became clear to her that she did indeed over-egg everything. Was it because she was bored being at home so much of the time? Tony golfed but Pauline, as far as she knew, didn't do much of anything. Oh, she did yoga twice a week.

* * *

Later the two of them cleared up. Loading the dishwasher, Patrick asked, 'How are you feeling now? A little better?'

She detected something in his tone, in the way only someone who knew a person well could tell that something was . . . off. She didn't need to read his mind to figure out what. She had drunk too much. She'd seen him watching.

'Yes, I think you're right. It was Pauline making more of it than it was.'

He sighed. 'That's good. I won't deny that I'm concerned for you right now, Jane. Something is going on. You drank an awful lot tonight. And I can't think it was because of what Pauline said.'

'You're not seriously thinking I drank all the wine, are you?'

'I didn't say that, but you drank a lot. A hell of a lot of it.' His tone was hard.

'I was trying to relax, Patrick, that's all. What's wrong with that?' She hated how defensive she sounded. Or guilty more like.

'I'm sorry, I shouldn't have come out and said it that way. It came out wrong. But what am I to think? You *are* drinking a lot and acting weird, and I know there's something wrong and you won't talk to me. How do you think that makes me feel?'

'I didn't drink that much!' she snapped. *Christ, I don't want to get into this again.*

'What just happened here?' he asked, evidently perplexed by her mood change. 'Why are you so defensive?'

'What happened here is that you don't believe me when I tell you that I didn't drink a lot. What? Were you watching me? Counting the glasses I drank?' Why the hell was he being so picky with her? 'You know what, actually I feel hurt that you said that. It's kind of insulting to be truthful.'

CHAPTER 8

Jane stomped upstairs to bed not wanting to argue anymore. Not being *able* to face arguing any longer was more the truth. And she hated the way she had lashed out at him. He was right, she was drinking more than usual but not that much, she didn't think. She jumped in the shower, letting the warm water wash away her anxiety over tonight's dinner party and their bitter words to one another. She shouldn't have bolted like she had. She couldn't help going over and over what Pauline had said about the stranger at the door. She shouldn't have lost her temper like that with Patrick, either. *I don't actually know why I did.* He'd only been asking about her drinking. She couldn't shift the feeling it had been Murk nosing around their house. *I know it. Deep in my fucking bones, I know it was him.* She scrubbed at her skin with the loofah until it was red.

When her husband finally came to bed a little while later, the tension between them filled the bedroom with a heavy gloom. He went straight into the shower without saying a word. She waited in bed, wanting to repair the damage she'd caused before they went to sleep. It wasn't good to fall asleep on an argument.

He walked into the bedroom from the en-suite, water dripping from his hair and watching the football highlights from earlier on his phone.

'Do you want me to stay home? I can cancel the sessions I'm booked for,' he asked, climbing into bed. She could still tell he was cross with her; his body language was taut.

'I thought you said they were important and paid well?' Her voice was welcoming and more agreeable now that she'd had time to calm down. And no, she didn't want him to do that. That was ridiculous and selfish; she wouldn't ask that of him.

'I did and they do, but if you'd rather I stayed at home because you're feeling out of sorts, I can do others in a few weeks or when we get back from our holiday. By then you'll have sent in your work to Suzanna and hopefully the stress will be gone. And you'll be back to normal. Right?' She wasn't going to ask him to do that. He switched off the match and plugged in his phone to charge. 'Look, Jane, if you want me to stay, just say so, please. I really don't mind.' There was a small pause as if he was gathering his thoughts before he spoke again. 'I'm sorry about what I said downstairs. It was an observation that's all. Maybe I went over the top a bit. And don't get yourself worked up about what Pauline said earlier. You know she's a gossip and exaggerates everything. I think she's bored to be honest. Which reminds me, so you don't panic, I've ordered a Ring doorbell off Amazon so there will be a delivery man coming.'

She nodded, hating that she felt he was treating her like a child. That was a great idea though, why hadn't they thought about it before? Why hadn't she?. 'I guess she is, you're right. I overreacted.' It was probably best to leave it now. 'I'm sorry too. I shouldn't have snapped the way I did.'

They lived in a place where bad things could happen without any witnesses. Private and secluded with neighbours in big houses who wouldn't necessarily hear or see anything.

'I don't want to keep on about this, but remember that Sainsbury's order that arrived two days ago and you said you didn't order?' How could she forget? She was sure she hadn't ordered it. She'd dismissed it at the time, saying she must have simply forgotten about it. She'd certainly been out of sorts with all the weird stuff going on. But it had bothered her since, and she'd been avoiding discussing it as she didn't have answers. 'How was it ordered on your card if you said you didn't order it, that's what I don't get?' He stretched out in the bed with the single sheet only covering his bottom half and turned to face her.

'I don't know.' She put her phone down. That was why she hadn't wanted to talk about it. She'd seen it on her card statement. But she was sure she hadn't ordered it. She slid down the bed, put her phone on charge and turned to face him. She didn't have an answer. She didn't want to talk about it. Why wouldn't he just let it go?

'But it was on your card, Jane. You must have done it.'

'I know. OK, then I must have. I told you that. I just don't remember. Can we leave it at that? I mean no one's pinched my cards so it must have been me. I thought I was on the island that day but I must be mistaken.'

'So maybe you came back and ordered it.'

'Maybe, or it's a glitch on their system. Why are you so bothered now?' She really didn't want to discuss it further. He was making her feel so uncomfortable.

Patrick frowned. 'Because you said you don't remember doing it and that's odd, Jane. It worries me. It tells me that you're under a lot of stress if you're ordering stuff and not remembering.'

'Patrick it was just the one time. It's not like stuff is being delivered every day. Look, maybe I was putting in an order for tonight's party, meaning to save it on the system. I was thinking of doing that anyway. I do that sometimes and accidentally hit pay automatically.'

'But you only ordered Merlot. Not any food. That's odd, right, don't you think? I mean that the order was for Merlot, and you drink Merlot.'

'I've no idea. Why is it odd? We drank Merlot tonight. All I know is that I didn't remember ordering it but maybe I did order it and simply forgot.'

'Lizzie thought you might have been looking at it online or put it in your basket for tonight's party too. Maybe you did click "pay" out of habit without realising it.'

'There you go, she thinks the same. Can we leave it now, please?' She was getting frustrated with him.

'Well, I suppose there's nothing to it. You have a lot on your mind with work and you don't handle stress all that well either.' *I know that, Patrick, thanks for reminding me.*

'Patrick, just let it go, please.' *I really don't want to be reminded that I'm forgetting stuff.*

'I was just trying to prove that you hadn't had your cards cloned or something. There's no hidden agenda, Jane. You can't be too careful these days.'

She turned away, not able to look him in the eye. She didn't believe that was what he thought at all. *He thinks I might have a brain tumour or something, I bet he does. So, I should tell him the truth to stop him worrying, shouldn't I? Only I can't.*

And let's face it, she really didn't believe she'd fucked up with the order either, but she wasn't going to say as much. That way madness lay.

***

The next day, she woke up ridiculously early, and the damned Merlot order had gone round and round in her head, keeping her awake most of the night. Patrick was right. It was odd but she didn't have an answer. She *must* have done it. The fear she might end up where she'd been all those years ago tore at her. *But I'm not going to let it because I'm stronger this time.*

Patrick's phone buzzed with a message. Drowsily he snaked out a hand and grabbed it.

'Who's calling you at this hour?'

He sat up, rubbed sleep from his eyes to read the message. 'Shit, it's my agent. It's about those dates coming up.

He's wanting to confirm I'm available. The money is brilliant, much better than I thought.' He showed her the message. The money was indeed brilliant. 'It's because they want to start with little notice.'

'Great, well get back to him asap.' He got up and sat on the side of the bed, ready to jump in the shower. 'How long d'you think you'll be away?'

'I wasn't expecting anything that good in money terms. He said four to five days. I don't think there's anything in the diary for the dates he's mentioned.'

'Can't look a gift horse in the mouth, Patrick. We can really push the boat out on holiday with that.'

'I know, but after last night, are you sure you'll be all right if I'm away for that length of time?'

'I'll be fine. I've got work to do anyway. I was being a bit silly the other night. I'll get my head down. Probably better you're away anyway. No distractions. No sneaking off for afternoon sex.' She cuddled up to him, dragging him back into bed, snaking her body around his. They both laughed. Lizzie had nearly caught them the other afternoon. Not that it should be an issue, but teenagers didn't think parents had sex and if they did, they thought of it as ugh.

'We have time now, she's still asleep.' He began kissing her neck, sending wonderful chills down her spine.

'You have to go and shower and get those dates checked.' She pushed him away. He frowned.

She was uncomfortable him going but telling him to stay wasn't an option right now.

'Lizzie will be around, so you won't be alone. I'll only be a phone call away. It's only London. Oh, didn't she say she had a few festivals booked?' He climbed out of bed. 'Maybe I should—"

'She did, and it's not a problem, Patrick,' she cut him off. 'I'll be totally fine on my own.' She gave him her bravest smile, forcing it to reach her eyes. 'I don't want her to feel she has to stay in just because I've been a bit stressy. There's Pauline and Ralph too.' *The truth is I'm not looking forward to being alone this time.*

'Really? Ralph will probably go with her. You got pretty worked up last night after what Pauline said.'

'Jesus, Patrick, you make me sound so desperate all of a sudden. Stop worrying. Like you said, it was someone who was lost and Pauline egged it up. I'd forgotten about it until you mentioned it again.' She saw the look he gave her through the mirror on the wardrobe opposite the bed. 'What? What's that look for?'

'It's the drinking, Jane. I worry. I am worried you're drinking a lot and going to the island.' He walked to the shower. Naked. She couldn't but watch and smile to herself. She was only drinking to calm herself down.

Jasper jumped up on the bed, snuggling on the warm spot. He'd been a little odd since the other day with the mannequin. Hiding away upstairs a lot. It wasn't like him. She stroked his head and hoped it wasn't going to affect him permanently.

She lay staring at the ceiling, listening to the water running in the shower. She was pleased she and Patrick had reconnected, especially after last night's conversation. With the odd things happening, it didn't thrill her he was going away to be honest. There was nothing concrete to prove Murk had been near her. *Even though I think deep down I know it's him . . . I can't be sure . . . not one hundred percent.* Not really. Going to the police would be a waste of time. The newspaper had a perfectly good explanation, the neighbours often gave them to them, the teenagers with the mannequin, the lost man or the parent wanting to apologise. All had reasonable explanations. The reason she hadn't asked Pauline about the newspaper was simply because she didn't want her to start question why she was questioning it when it was a pretty regular occurrence. *Yes, but what I can't get out of my damned head is what if Murk had come to the house to see the lay of the land so he can come back and torment me? I can't stop these thoughts going round and round in my head.* She turned on her side, snuggling Jasper.

She must have drifted into sleep because the next thing she was awake with a start. Something had woken her. She turned to Patrick and found Jasper in his place — on high alert. She could hear Patrick still in the shower. She was heavy with tiredness having fallen into a deep catnap; it felt as if she'd slept hours when in fact it was just minutes.

'Patrick,' she whispered as she swung off the bed quietly and reached for her silk dressing gown on the armchair next to the bed. 'Patrick.' He didn't answer. The radio was on loud, the door semi-closed, and he was singing along. He must be shaving in the shower. Jasper looked at her for direction. She hushed with a finger to her lips and her palm face down in front of him. A signal to wait. He watched her, waiting for her release command. Nervously, she fastened her dressing gown and slipped on her slippers.

She strained to hear. She was sure she'd heard something. They both looked at the curtained window where a crack of daylight slipped through the join of the curtains. There was a thud downstairs. Heavy footsteps she didn't recognise across the kitchen floor. A tread on the stair, slow, then another, then nothing. She crept onto the landing to check Lizzie's room. Shit, she'd not come home. She could have sworn she heard her come in last night. Maybe that was a good thing. The fridge opened and closed. She leaned over the banister, to hear more. The keys jangled as if somebody was searching through them, looking for something. Someone was in the house. The back door opened and closed quietly. Not something Lizzie would do, if indeed it was her. She ought to fetch Patrick, but something stopped her. Footsteps on the gravel outside around the side of the house. She raced to the landing window. And thought she saw a lone figure slip into the foliage that ran down to the lake and towards the woods. Her heart pounded, sure it was going to burst from her chest. Trying to make sense if she had seen something go in the bushes or not.

'Heel,' she said to Jasper who came to her side. She checked the windows on their floor, the top lights were open for ventilation to keep the house from getting stuffy at night, all the while her heart hammered. The locking handles were all in place. Nobody could get in through the open space. Then she went downstairs and did the same. Jasper obediently stayed close. She checked the doors. Twice. Then looked around for signs of anything having been touched or moved. There seemed to be no signs of entry. But then as she moved away from the patio doors, she noticed one of her gardening shoes was askew. She'd paired them that evening and placed them neatly against the patio window well out of the way. No reason for her guests to go near them. Which meant whoever had been in her house had come in through the patio doors.

She glanced out to the garden. She would double-check the outside to do a proper job. She stepped out — it was already warm. She let Jasper out for a wee then promptly ran off towards the bushes sniffing.

She didn't venture far from the door, casting an eye over the garden.

Relieved, when Jasper came back several seconds later, she put her jitteriness down to having imagined the sounds and being half asleep when she woke from her doze. A sound outside had woken her and Jasper suddenly. It could have been anything. The patio doors had been locked and the key was still in the lock. She turned to go back inside and saw a bottle of Merlot on the counter. Open, and one wine glass next to it with a slither of red wine still in the bottom. She didn't use those wine glasses. They were antique and only for show, kept in her display cabinet in the kitchen by the walk-in pantry. And they'd tidied everything up before going to bed.

Prickling with fear, she picked up the glass, smelled the inside; it was definitely wine. Next, she picked up the bottle — it was nearly empty. She swore under her breath. *Who was doing this?* Her head snapped up to Jasper's sudden bark, compliantly still by her side, desperate to go to Patrick now standing at the kitchen door, watching her. A sickening comprehension hit her at how this would look to him. She, in the kitchen, alone, with a near empty bottle of Merlot and holding a glass with evidence of wine still inside. The full force of the realisation hit her. Alarm rang through her like church bells on a Sunday morning. This was deliberate bait, calculated to make her look culpable. Whoever had done this, were they still here? In the bushes? Watching her try to squirm out of this shameful situation? Her nerves failed her. *Christ. Fuck, fuck, fuck.* Jasper whined some more to be released. She gave him the signal as she put the bottle and glass down on the counter and tore past Patrick to escape his glare. The glass toppled, smashing on the granite; breaking glass echoed behind her. She sat on the stairs.

This was insane. She was going insane. *I am, I must be. I don't remember getting that bottle out.* She heard Patrick coming towards her. She didn't want to see him let alone speak with him. She lowered her head, wrapping her arms around it. *He* had done this. He was so good at manipulation. She had taken the bait just as he'd wanted. With her back pressed against the stairs, she sensed Patrick in front of her, then sitting next to her.

Then she did what only hours ago she thought was unthinkable.

She trembled as she turned to him, her face streaked with tears not of sadness but anger and frustration that she had been caught in Murk's net.

'Patrick. I need to tell you something.'

CHAPTER 9

'OK, Jane, it's OK, really. We'll get through whatever you're going through together.' She didn't think they would. If Murk didn't get her then her marriage wasn't going to stand up against all her deception. He got up and made her a cup of tea. 'Here, drink that and tell me. I won't interrupt. You just talk. Whatever it is, Jane, you must tell me. I'll help you, darling. With whatever is haunting you, causing you this pain, I'll help you, but you need to tell me.'

She sipped the incredibly sweet tea which nearly made her gag. After a few sips it did make her feel a little better. Warmed by the drink, she slowly stopped shaking. He'd think it was due to the drinking. *Jesus, fucking Christ. He'd think my shaking was to do with alcohol and that I'd sneaked down to have a secret drink.* How she loathed that was how he thought of her. What was her defence? She had none. He thought she drank too much. She denied it. Now he'd caught her red-handed. To protest when there was so much evidence against her was folly.

She looked into his eyes for a long moment. Wondering. *What are you thinking, Patrick? Do you really think I have a drink problem? Me? Jane? How can you believe it?* The simple answer was, he saw it with his own eyes. There was no clearer proof than that.

They used to be able to read each other in the early part of their relationship. She still felt they did but maybe not as clearly. There was too much going on in their lives these days. They had always been close.

She felt the pressure of needing to confess to him bearing down on her, and she began pulling the skin around her cuticles, a nasty old habit brought on by her anxiety that was resurfacing.

Patrick must sense her turmoil because he didn't push her to speak. Suddenly she wanted so badly to reveal it all that it made her laugh nervously instead, her anxiety pushing her to release the pressure building inside her like a pressure cooker ready to blow. Her head dropped into her hands before she blurted it out. She waited for Patrick to say something, to ask her a question, but he didn't, he sat waiting for her to speak. Her anxiety had flared many times throughout their marriage, but Patrick had always been able to help her though it. It never became unmanageable. He made her believe in herself, telling her the Franklin D. Roosevelt quote *the only thing we have to fear is fear itself.* Whenever her imagination took her off to dark unsettling places about her past, she tried to remember it.

Reality anesthetised her brain, part of it anyway. She swallowed down the emotions rising inside her, right now her reality was this: she was sat on the stairs with her husband who was convinced she had a drink problem and she had to clear that up.

'OK, well, OK, the thing is, right.' She shook her head; how truthful could she really be? She audibly exhaled. 'I don't know where to start, Patrick.' She flung her arms up, exasperated that the words wouldn't come. She tried to regulate her breathing to keep herself calm, but it sped up each time she tried to get the words out.

'Then just start at the beginning.'

She frowned. *The beginning. Right at the beginning, does he mean? No, because he doesn't know about the beginning.* He meant the beginning here, in their home, when she started drinking too much, allegedly.

91

'Jane, look, don't lie to me. We don't lie to each other. I can't continue like this with you keeping something that's making you sick all to yourself. We share everything.' He gripped her knee gently. This was the closest she'd *ever* been to talking about Murk.

'Patrick, it's not about the drinking — that's not the problem.' Maybe he was right and telling him would be all right.

'Then what is?'

Oh, for it to be so simple. She grappled with words to make sense of them and put them in a sentence that would make sense to him. Make him understand. She saw it all slipping further and further away from her. She tried to grab onto it but the fissure seemed to get bigger in front of her. 'What you saw just then wasn't what you think you saw. I found the bottle and glass there when I came down and . . .'

'OK. But I just want to help you. What's going on? Please just tell me. How hard can it be to tell me? I love you. I won't judge you, Jane.' He shook his head as if for her to think that was insane. His voice was gentle. He flashed her a warm smile. She wanted to. She really, really wanted to. As a child she'd had no parental anchor to grab onto to make her feel safe in times of need. The compulsion to tear the skin around my fingers with her teeth was virtually impossible to ignore so she clasped her hands, tightly in front of her around her mug.

'I, I, no, no, Patrick, I must clear it up first that I wasn't drinking. You have that wrong and you must believe me here when I tell you this.' He looked lost as if trying to find his way to her. 'I thought I heard a noise and came down to investigate. Then I saw the bottle on the table.' There was no choice but to tell the truth at this point; there were already too many lies floating around.

'What sort of noise?'

'I don't know, like there was someone in the house kind of noise. You were in the shower, so I came to check. I thought it was Lizzie but she's not back.'

'Did you find anything?'

92

'No, only the bottle of wine.' She saw the incredulous look on his face. His right eyebrow tugged a little. 'That I didn't open. It was open on the counter with the glass.'

'If not you then who else in this house opened and drank Merlot, Lizzie?'

'I don't know. It could have been Lizzie and Ralph, yes. That's what I'm trying to tell you. I didn't open it. I was looking at it and trying to figure out who had. I mean, don't you think I thought the same as you are right now? Nobody drinks Merlot in this house except me. Those were my thoughts when you walked in on me.'

'That's my point, Jane.'

His words stalled her. *What the hell is happening here?* She felt as if she was on a runaway train. 'Is that what you really believe?'

He sighed gently as if trying to get through to a recalcitrant teenager.

'Jane, I don't have to be a doctor to know you have a small drinking problem.' Well, she should be grateful that he thought it was only a *small* drinking problem. 'And if we don't get ahead of it, it could become a *big* problem.'

She gripped her mug so tightly that hot tea spilled over, burning her legs. He quickly grabbed the tea towel from the kitchen and mopped it up. She saw the look in his eyes as he watched her hands shaking as they grasped the mug.

Surrender was the only course of action, she realised. She knew how it looked to the outsider. Trying to say she wasn't a drunk when all the evidence lay scattered around her, was exactly what a drunk would say. She was snookered.

'OK, OK, Patrick, I don't want to argue with you about this because you won't believe me it seems.' *What was I thinking? To tell him the truth about Murk? The whole truth? That's the problem, he isn't thinking clearly. He won't believe it now anyway.* Looking up at him, into his worried and concerned eyes, she realised that if his reaction to her drinking was this blinkered how would he react to her telling him about Murk? She said with as much strength as she could muster, what he wanted to hear. 'What do you suggest we do?'

He tilted his head upwards to the ceiling. 'Well, I'd like to call a therapist. Someone who deals with alco — small drinking problems,' he corrected himself.

She jolted inside. He thought she was an alcoholic! *Dear God, the humiliation.* Lashed with fear of Lizzie and their friends finding out, she mumbled, 'Do we have to tell Lizzie?'

'No,' he said considerately. Then qualified it with, 'Well maybe we should. I mean tell her that you're off booze because—' She saw his face screw up trying to find a reason —'you have an ulcer and the doctors said no drinking.' He smiled turning his head to her as if he had found the cure for cancer. 'Maybe you'll find it easier to talk to someone about why you're drinking rather than me. But you can talk to me about it if you want. Only, sweetheart, I don't want to get into a battle with you. What do you think? You OK with that?' When she said nothing, he said, 'Please, Jane, let me help you.'

* * *

A few hours later, when they'd showered and dressed, and she'd walked around the garden with Jasper for a bit of exercise they sat in the kitchen having breakfast. Her phone rang. It was Suzanna.

'Hi, how are you, Jane?' There was an odd note to her voice.

'I'm well, thank you.' She was nervous the author might have rejected her work.

'Good, good, well, so, the concepts are great. The author loves them, and I was wondering if you were OK to finish the illustrations? She's made a few notes but it's not much. Do you think you can finish them in the next four weeks?'

This was great news. It would give her something to focus on. Patrick was going out for the day with Lizzie up to her university in York to bring back some stuff she didn't want and move her into a house share and out of student halls. And Jane could get on with the illustrations right away.

'I'll get on with them right away. And I'll send them back all together when they're done.'

'Good, great, so, how is everything?'

'Everything?' She scowled at Patrick who picked up his coffee and left the room. 'What do you mean?'

'I don't mean anything, darling. I was thinking about coming up to see you both like we discussed and the only weekend I have free is in September. How's that for you guys?'

'Text me the dates and I'll get back to you. We're still trying to book our holiday. I'll see if it clashes.'

'Okey-dokey, right, better get off. Hugs to you both. And don't forget to let me know about those dates.'

She sat quietly playing with her *pain au chocolat*. Patrick had gone to the local bakery as soon as they'd opened to get it especially for her. She felt invigorated by the positive news from Suzanna and relieved the author had liked her work. What did bother her was the conversation she and Patrick had had about a therapist.

* * *

It was six in the morning the following day. 'Right, we're ready to leave, darling,' he said, walking in to wash his hands after filling up the windscreen wiper fluid in the car. He'd been up a good half hour already as she walked into the kitchen yawning. 'I've put in the Ring doorbell I got. If you give me your phone, I'll set it up quickly before I go while we wait for Lizzie to get her act together and come down, and that way you can see if anyone comes to the door,' he said, standing in the hallway. 'She promised she'd be back for six this morning from Bev's. We must get off, it's a hell of a journey,' he said, irritated as he fiddled with her phone. 'Gordon's car's in the drive. Must have escaped for a day or so.'

'I thought this would happen when she text last night saying she'd stay over and be back at the crack of dawn but I thought she'd have a quick shower and be ready to go.' She peered at next door through the hall window. 'I bet he's zooming to his office in London shortly.'

'Good job he's got that studio apartment there otherwise it'd be a hell of a journey every day.' Patrick sighed. 'God knows what the hell she's doing up there. Come on, Lizzie, we have to go!' he shouted up the stairs.

'Thanks, Patrick. This is such a great idea. And you can see too if you loaded it onto your phone. I can't believe we didn't think of this earlier.'

'I know. Well, we've got it now. It works on Wi-Fi so don't turn it off. And I've rewired the old security cameras that came with the house. We're all up and running. Here's the code.' He passed her a piece of paper with six numbers written on it. 'Keep it safe in case you need to reboot the system. You know the signal here can be a bit ropey at times. I remember now why we stopped using it. If you remember it kept cutting out. If it becomes a nuisance, I've written down what to do to disconnect it. It might be more problematic than we remember. Sorry, I'm fussing — we'll be back late tonight.'

'Right, Patrick, got that. I'll keep the numbers safe, just in case. Stop stressing and drive carefully, please.' It was a hell of a drive for him. He'd insisted on doing it all in a day to get back home. But at least she'd made him promise he'd stop regularly and if he was tired to take a small nap at the services.

He kissed her goodbye. 'You'll be fine. Pauline and Tony are home if you need them. I've told them we're going to be out for the day. I think Ralph's around too. Take your mobile to the island, please—'

'I have that emergency one, remember?'

'Right, yes, I forgot. I know I'm being like a mother hen, but will you please tell Pauline if you do go over there?'

'Why have you done that? Oh, Patrick, she'll be over the moment you get down the lane.'

'She saw me fixing the doorbell and wanted to apologise for worrying us with that tale of the man coming to the house. As soon as she saw it, she thought it was because of what she'd said and felt bad. She's a sweetie really. She doesn't mean any harm.'

'I know she doesn't. I wouldn't put it past her to sit at her kitchen window and vet everyone who turns up, asking to see ID.' They laughed. It was good to laugh together.

'Maybe not a bad thing, hey?'

Jane rolled her eyes. She'd been joking. Imagine if she did do that?

'No, but . . . really, Patrick, I wish you hadn't said anything. You're making me sound like a fruit loop.'

He looked in the drawer for the car keys. 'Keys, Jane, where are they?'

'In the drawer as always.'

'But they're not. Any ideas?' He searched all the drawers in the kitchen.

'You opened the car to fill the screen wash up. I haven't touched them.'

'Well, they're not here now.' He was flustered. 'Lizzie, get down here right now or I won't take you,' he yelled once again.

'You'll have to take your car then,' she said. 'I've no idea where you've put them, Patrick. Stop blaming me, I've only just come down.'

'Jane, I can't. Mine's a small sports car. I need yours. It's a hatchback.'

Ten minutes later they found them inside the car. Thank God, for a moment there, Jane was beginning to believe she had mislaid them.

'See you later, Mum.' Lizzie bounded down the stairs with wet hair and grabbed a banana from the fruit bowl. 'What you doing today?' She asked, giving her a farewell hug. Jane looked her over, marvelling how well she looked, considering she suspected she and Bev had probably been up most of the night chatting after an evening of partying with their mates.

'I don't know. I've got quite a lot of work to get through. Suzanna has returned the approved pencil sketches with notes so I should really get to work on those and work them up into colour. But I'm tired. I might work this morning and have a lazy afternoon, chill out a bit, have a duvet afternoon watching telly and eating unhealthy food.' Lizzie laughed at her. She knew Jane didn't usually indulge in unhealthy food. Lizzie looked so like her dad it made Jane's heart swell. 'Have fun and keep me posted with what you're up to and your journey. Hope it goes well and there are no problems on the motorway.' Her new room in the house share was small from all accounts so there was very little she was keeping. Lizzie had told them all she wanted to do today was pack up the car, she'd already boxed everything, she'd done it before she broke up for summer. Then they were dropping it off at the new house. She was going to go up a few days before term started to unpack and settle in.

Jasper went to see them off, barking as they drove out of the close then ran back inside to nestle down beside her at the kitchen table. She rubbed her temples. Finishing her breakfast she opened her email from Suzanna. If she got to it right away, she wouldn't feel so bad taking the afternoon off.

CHAPTER 10

Later that afternoon, Jane settled down in the lounge to watch a film. Jasper sat with her, snuggled in close, his head on her lap. Flicking through Netflix she found an old Hitchcock film she hadn't seen in ages. She turned the volume off on her phone, sipped a Coke packed with ice and popped her hand into the bowl of nuts. She had the blinds down to keep out the heat. Dressed in a loose dress she still felt clammy and uncomfortable. Poor Jasper; even though he'd had a haircut recently, she felt sorry for him. He lolled on the sofa next to her.

This morning as Patrick had sorted the Ring app on her phone she'd poured all the wine in the house down the drain and made sure he saw the empty bottles go in the recycling bin He made her promise not to go out and buy any. She had no intention of doing so. She didn't have a drinking problem. She'd forgotten to ask Lizzie if they'd sneaked back to the house last night for any reason and had a drink. It must have been them although it was an odd thing to do. Neither of them particularly liked wine, being more into cocktails. But it could have been a bit of a lark.

She made a note in her calendar to search for a therapist as she'd promised.

Half an hour in there was a knock at the front door. Grumbling, she looked at the doorbell app and saw Ralph. Deliberately ignoring him, only because she didn't want company, she slid down the sofa, hoping he'd go away.

He didn't. *Of course not. He knows I'm here.*

She pressed pause on the remote and went to answer the door.

'Hi, Mrs C. I'm not bothering you, am I?' She shook her head. 'Only, I've left my car keys upstairs in Lizzie's room. She said it was OK for me to come over.'

'No problem. Go find what you're looking for.' His eyes locked on hers for a second or two too long and she pulled away first. 'Everything OK?'

'Oh, yeah, sure. I won't be here long, hopefully easily found.'

Jane walked back to the lounge where Jasper waited. As soon as he saw her, he closed his eyes, content all was good in his world again.

A short time later, Ralph came into the lounge. 'All done. Thanks, Mrs C.'

She paused the film. 'Got everything you wanted then?'

'Yeah thanks. What's that you're watching.'

'This? It's a Hitchcock film, *The Birds*. Have you ever seen it?' Old films, and domestic noir, kitchen sink dramas were her thing. Patrick wasn't much into them. She tended to watch them when she was alone.

'No, don't think I have.'

Her words came out before she had time to censor them. 'Join me if you want to.'

'Oh no, I don't want to intrude.' He smiled. He had a sweet smile which made it so easy to like him.

'You won't be. Sit down if you want to keep me company.' She'd said she didn't want company. She shrugged. Alone time wasn't all it was made out to be. She patted the seat next to her. He reached out and stroked Jasper. He snapped.

'Jasper!' she scolded. 'Sorry, Ralph. I don't know what got into him then. You might have frightened him. I think he was in a deep sleep.'

'It's OK, you're probably right. Nobody likes to be woken up from a deep sleep, do they?' He smiled.

She was struck by his words, not knowing why they felt odd to her. 'No, for sure. We, well I was woken early yesterday and this morning we were up early again with Patrick and Lizzie going up to York, so we're both pretty tired today.'

'Oh? Was it Jasper?'

'Jasper? What d'you mean?'

'You said you were woken up early yesterday?'

'No, I heard a noise in the house and had to go and investigate.'

'That must have been creepy. Did you find anything?'

'No, nothing. It was creepy though. I probably dreamt it. I've been a bit stressed these last few days. I've had a lot of work deadlines to deal with. Stress, it's not good for you.' She smiled warmly back at him 'I fancy a green tea, you want one?'

'I'll get it for you, Mrs C. You sit there and rest. You look so comfortable, and Jasper's nestled there with you. Best not to bother him again — let sleeping dogs lie and all that.' He chuckled. 'I know where it is. Lizzie drinks it all the time.' She certainly did, she was constantly having to buy it when her daughter was back home.

'You sure, Ralph? You don't have to.' But he was already on his way. She lay her head back and rested, closing her eyes and trying to clear her mind as she waited for him to return.

'Here you go,' said Ralph bringing her the green tea.

'So, how's the music going? You getting lots of help from Patrick?'

'Oh, yeah, he's great, so brilliant. All my mates are so jealous.'

'You enjoying your music course at uni?'

'Oh, yeah, so glad I made the move. Thanks for asking, Mrs C.'

Lizzie had come for a conspiratorial chat just the other day. 'Do you really think Dad likes him? Ralph doesn't want to be a burden. He's afraid Dad's just doing it because he's my mate. You don't think that's the case, do you? I mean he does like having him around, right?'

'I do, yes, he's a nice boy, and I don't think your dad would be doing this if he didn't like the lad. He's too busy to waste his time.' Her words had settled her.

Ralph adjusted his position on the sofa. 'You know, Mrs C, I'm really grateful for all that Mr C is doing for me. And I want to thank you for letting me spend so much time here with all of you.'

'That's OK, Ralph, you're Lizzie's friend, and our neighbour. You're more than welcome in our house. You know that.'

'Great that's great. I just, well, Mum said I spent too much time over here and to be careful not to outstay my welcome.'

'Oh, Pauline is an old hen. You tell her we don't have a problem with you being here. After all, it's only until you both go back after the summer break.'

He chuckled. 'Yeah, God, we're so lucky right now with this weather, aren't we? You need to get some AC into this house though, like you have in the studio. I know Lizzie's been banging on about it, but, really, I'm telling you, the difference it makes is massive.'

She grunted. 'Not that old chestnut. Has she put you up to this?'

'A bit, yeah,' he said shyly. 'Sorry. Anyways, I'm glad we've got this time to talk, just the two of us.'

'Is everything OK? You seem a little edgy.'

'Really? No, it's just after Mum said that about outstaying my welcome, I kind of thought, well that maybe you did feel that way. I'd hate it if I was intruding.' He laughed, standing up quickly. 'Like I am right now. God. Sorry, Mrs C, this is what Mum meant, I guess.'

'Sit down, it's fine. You said you'd never watched this film, and I want you to join me.'

A little while into the film she began to feel sleepy, her eyelids struggling to stay open. She yawned and stared at the TV screen trying to focus.

The next thing she jolted awake, her head woolly and feeling woozy. Had she fallen asleep? She must have. A hand touched her arm. She jerked away. It was Ralph. 'Oh Christ, sorry, I fell asleep, and you scared me. I thought I was alone.' Her memory was hazy.

'I thought it best if I stayed. You just zonked out like a light. And I wanted to watch the end of the film. It was great. I really enjoyed it.'

She frowned, feeling confused, trying to remember what had happened and why he was here with her. She remembered Patrick and Lizzie going and then sitting down to watch a film and Ralph coming over for something from Lizzie's room. She must have dropped off into a deep sleep.

Her mouth was paper dry. She reached for her mug. It was empty.

'You had green tea. Want me to make you some more?' Ralph's smile was expansive, lighting up his entire face. 'Lizzie said you'd been working long hours. Perhaps it's just catching up now. I should have left you a note and gone. But truthfully, I really did want to see the end of the film. I hope you don't mind.'

'Right, no that's OK. I'll get some water.' She hesitated because she badly wanted to know why she'd fallen asleep. She didn't think she'd been that tired. Yes, she'd been tired but not to the extent of zonking out like a drunk after a session. 'Where's Jasper?' She distinctly remembered he was with her.

'You put him in the garden.'

She did? 'I don't remember doing that. He was on the sofa with me. Why would I do that?'

He reddened. 'He snapped at me. I think you thought it best, just in case.' In case of what? Jasper would never hurt Ralph unless he provoked him. She didn't understand why she would have done that.

'But he knows you.' She remembered him snapping but not putting him outside. Then she heard him scratching at the back door. She hoped he was OK. Like all Jack Russells, he liked to chase things, and those squirrels were still out there.

'Sorry, Mrs C, I didn't want to let him back in in case, well you know, and I didn't want to wake you. He'll be OK though. Here, you wait here, and I'll go fetch him.' He strode out of the lounge. She badly wanted to be convinced that she was being overly concerned about her blackout. She retreated to safer ground and opened her arms wide to welcome a happy dog who scampered in and leapt onto her lap, licking her face all over. 'Sorry, darling, what a horrid Mummy.' She kissed him all over and scratched his head. 'Sorry, sorry, sweetie.'

A slow, low-level growl emanated from him; she could feel it and his sudden tension in her arms. He turned to look at Ralph approaching.

'See, he's got it in for me.'

'Rubbish, it's probably because he knew you wouldn't let him back in.' She laughed. She didn't want to sound overdramatic. But the fact was Jasper was never like this with anyone, and he'd not been this way with Ralph before, ever.

Awkward silence descended. They'd both ran out of conversation. 'So, what are you up to for the rest of the day?' Jane asked. 'Lizzie won't be back till late.'

'Yeah, I'm going into town to catch up with some mates.'

'That's good. Beer garden, no doubt. It's the weather for it.'

'Yeah, I'll get out of your hair, Mrs C. I've decanted what was left of the green tea and popped it in the fridge, I know you and Lizzie like drinking it with ice. I thought it was a waste to throw it down the drain. I made a small jugful for you. See you later and have a chilled day. Sorry to have monopolised some of it.'

She watched him leave through the back. He was so kind. It wasn't the first time she'd felt comforted that Lizzie and

Ralph were at the same uni. Then, with Jasper still in her arms, she walked into the kitchen to get some more iced tea.

It was then she thought about Jasper locked out. And how he would have barked to be let in. With all the windows open, that normally would have woken her. But it hadn't. *Why hadn't it?*

CHAPTER 11

'Helloo-oo,' a familiar voice rang through the kitchen some time later. She turned. Jasper trotted over to Pauline as she walked in. 'OK to come in? I'm here bearing gifts.' She held out a bowl of strawberries and a tub of cream. 'All organic. I thought we could have some strawberries and cream in the garden.' She gave a tinkly laugh. 'I must confess these aren't mine. I've run out for this year. I got these at Waitrose. Thought it'd be nice for us to have them with a lovely cup of tea. What d'you say, Jane? You game? Patrick told me you were alone today. Oh, you're busy, I don't want to be a bother,' she said on seeing her reaction. 'I can leave them here for you if you prefer.'

Jane was on her laptop at the kitchen table.

'Oh, no, nothing that can't wait. It's a great idea.'

Pauline drew up alongside, dragging over a chair. 'Shall I make the tea?'

'No, that's fine, I can do it. You can dish up the strawberries. Thanks, Pauline, this is kind of you.' She could really do without having to make polite conversation. Her head was still woozy from earlier. 'You know Ralph was round earlier. I was watching a film, and he joined me. The weirdest thing though, I fell asleep. I mean really asleep. I didn't even hear Jasper bark.'

Jane opened the overhead cupboard by the kettle.

'Oh, I wouldn't worry about that. I do it all the time. Oh, by the way,' Pauline said taking two bowls from Jane's hands, 'you know that fella that was around your house the other day? The one I said looked a little odd like he was snooping? Well, I saw him today.' Jane started. Pauline was quick to catch the mugs before they hit the floor. 'Gosh, Jane, I'm so sorry. I didn't mean to startle you like that. You know you really did get wound up the other night about that. I hadn't meant to frighten you. Me and my big mouth. You know I ought to think more before I go saying stuff.'

'No, it's fine. It was just a shock that a stranger was nosying around our house, that's all. And you say you saw him again, today? Where?' Pauline meant well, but really, she ought to think before she spoke.

'You know, someone sneaking around your house is scary, dear. You're bound to feel a little scared when you're alone here so much of the time, especially with Lizzie at uni.'

Why did she think telling her this was helping? 'Where did you see him? Not here, again, surely?' Her voice rose a little on the last word.

'Here? Oh, no, in town. By Boots. He had a Boots bag with him. He was sitting on the bench on the cobbles drinking a Nero. You know, I nearly went over to him. To ask him, you know about the other day. Well, I didn't. Of course, that could lead to all sorts of trouble. You know how touchy people are these days. You want me to pour the cream on your strawberries? Oh, is that green tea?' She watched Jane taking out the tea from the fridge from earlier. 'I'd like proper tea if that's OK. Ralph told me he made you some. I hope you don't think our little family is bombarding you.'

'No, of course not. I would never think that. It's too hot for me to have proper tea,' Jane said pouring out a glass of green tea and making Pauline proper tea. 'So, did you find out anything about this man?'

'Well, not really, but I did go to ask Jean, you know, in Boots. You know I know her — she used to bring her cats to the practice. Well, she said he'd bought some disposable gloves. Well, I never, whatever does he want with those? He didn't look the type to be bothered about getting his hands dirty. Mind you, Ralph was right, he is a big man. Hands like shovels. Would have had to buy the XXXL gloves.' She chuckled to herself. 'So. Strawberries and cream are ready — shall we go outside?'

The last thing she remembered was sitting in the garden on one of the cushioned chairs chatting with Pauline. Exactly where she was now. Only she was alone. So where was Pauline? She came to a little groggy. Just like earlier.

She spent the next few minutes trying to grasp what had happened to her. This was very peculiar. Where was Pauline for Chrissakes? Why did she feel so shit? Her mouth tasted sour. She picked up her empty glass, sniffed it. It smelled all right. Lizzie had brought the tea back with her from one of her trips out. She said she got it at a market. Jane wondered if they'd added something to it.

It felt as if there was a chunk of time missing just like before. It took her a few moments to come round, blinking in the bright sunlight that didn't do much for her head throbbing like a leftover hangover. Jasper whined next to her. She stroked him to reassure him. She felt woolly-headed like she'd had a shedload of alcohol. But all she'd drank was green tea.

The doorbell chimed. Pauline had mentioned seeing that stranger in the town that much she did remember. Was it him at the door? She looked for evidence of the strawberries and found none. Then walked slowly with heavy steps to the kitchen where she still found no evidence of Pauline ever being in her house. What was going on?

Jasper barked at the door. Had she dreamt Pauline being here? Had she dreamt Ralph, too? No, of course not. They had both been here. She wouldn't dream something like that up.

She made her way groggily to the front door, each step like dragging a block of cement. She stalled to balance herself against the wall in the hallway, breathing heavily. Had Lizzie bought some dodgy stuff at that market without knowing it? Then she remembered the box had been opened today. So maybe she had, and she was the first to try it. Her hand rested on the wall as she caught her breath. She suddenly didn't want to open the door, afraid who might be standing there. Then she remembered the Ring doorbell. Her phone. She turned, scouted the hall and what she could see of the kitchen and didn't see it. It must be in the garden. The sensible thing would have been to check that before coming all the way here. She wasn't used to it that was the problem. The doorbell chimed and her natural reaction was to open the door. She shuffled her way forwards to the door.

But as she tried to speak, to call out, to ask who it was, it was evident something was wrong. She struggled to call out, but her words were slurred, her tongue stuck to the roof of her mouth. The doorbell rang again. And again. And again, until she had to cover her ears with her hands before it rendered her deaf. But the ringing continued. The nerve-wracking sound was driving her mad. She leaned against the door, her hands over her ears feeling strangely out of control of her body. She strained to move, to call for help. It was no use, all she heard were slurs coming from her mouth. She started to panic. She had zero control of her body. *What did Lizzie buy and who from?* She sensed herself attempting to move and nothing happened. It was as if she was undergoing some kind of out-of-body experience. Her hands shook, reaching for the door handle. They fell away even though she willed them to grab and pull.

Then banging. Loud ferocious banging followed the ringing, reverberating through her back as she leaned against the door. 'STOP IT. STOP IT!' she yelled inside her head. She heard Jasper barking and whining next to her in a state of anxiety. The words sounded clear in her head. She desperately wanted to open the door. Finally, she managed to take hold of the handle. It wouldn't open. She tried and tried. Where was the key? It was always in the lock. Where was it? She swayed, putting a hand on the wall. *God, I'm going to collapse. What is happening to me?* She was terrified she was going to die. Jasper cried, seeing her state of anxiety. She had to get to him. She rested her head against the wall; it felt heavy. She managed to open the door a crack. Her heart thumped. Jasper whined some more. She peeked out. Nobody was there. She slowly grasped that the ringing and banging had stopped. Anxiety gripped her tightly in the chest, pressing harder and harder, making breathing virtually impossible. *Is he out there? Is he doing this to me?* Her chest hurt. As she gasped for breath a sheen of sweat coated her body and a long shadow covered her as she fell back against the wall, slowly sliding down until she was engulfed in a velvet darkness.

CHAPTER 12

Slumped on the floor, Jane frowned as she came round. Jasper leapt on her, licking her all over, delighted she was still alive. As was she. Her eyeline was focused on the kitchen. On her kitchen island. On a box wrapped in brown paper.

She managed to get herself, slowly to the kitchen and up on one of the stools.

She felt nauseous. She couldn't remember what had happened. Her breathing became ragged as she struggled to recall how she had ended up on the floor by the front door. *Don't break down. Don't cry.* Tears budded in her eyes. Tears of fear that she might have died. She blinked them back. Was she having some kind of mental breakdown? Was she sick?

Jasper barked around her feet, clearly concerned for her.

Fragments of thoughts flitted through her mind, pulling images from deep in her subconscious, making up scenes of her day. And none of them involved drinking alcohol, only green tea. Bad green tea that Lizzie had brought home.

She managed to get herself a glass of water, then another. Her mouth was dry and her tongue kept sticking to its roof. The water helped. She began to feel a little less groggy as she hydrated herself.

111

She sat in silence for a bit. Her head pounded. She sagged on the stool, spilling onto the worktop like a deflated balloon. Her body was completely unable to keep her upright, as if someone had stolen all her strength. Too many things rattled in her head for any to be heard. The gentle ticking of the wall clock just about audible was pretty much as much sound as she could tolerate right now.

The box stared at her from the counter. It was addressed to Janey. Reading the name made her heart accelerate.

Only *he* called her Janey. She didn't want to see what was inside. Jasper seemed agitated at her feet, sniffing the floor and barking. Was it possible that Murk had done something to her? Poisoned her somehow? But how? With the tea leaves? Had he been in the house the other night and put something in them? Made with a copy of her house key? *Stop it. Stop it, you're going to drive yourself mad thinking like this.* Then how else was he getting to her? It seemed too wild to think Lizzie bought contaminated green tea from a market. *You don't know that it is him.* No, no that was right, she didn't. But what if this was how he wanted her to think. Hadn't he done this before to her? *You're letting yourself get swept up in what ifs.* Yes, that was it, she was. It still didn't answer how she'd got into this state though.

She pushed the box away from her. Why was Murk sending her a gift? Or was there something inside there that would reveal who he was to everyone? Or was it something to threaten her with? Was that why he was playing games with her? Every fibre in her body told her it was from *him*. Because she was sure what was happening to her wasn't through her drinking or Lizzie buying dodgy tea.

She didn't want to open it.

It's only a box. What could happen? It's just a bloody box. Murk had the power to expose her. Was that what was inside the box?

There was absolutely no way she was going to look inside.

She was half brain-dead, and only working on auxiliary strength the likes of which was barely keeping her upright.

The painkillers she'd taken were struggling to combat her monstrous headache which felt like a heavy metal band had taken residency inside her head. Questions pulsed through her. Questions that needed answers.

She walked around the counter, unsteadily, and opened the box roughly. *You're not going to fucking scare me, Murk. Whatever you've sent me, you're not going to scare me. I know you. I won't let you hurt me or my family.* Inside was a huge candle with six wicks. Not what she'd expected at all! *What the hell is this? He wouldn't send me a frigging candle more like a grenade.* So, who sent it? She began to calm down a little. She'd overreacted. *Thank God.*

But then she flipped the lid back. The label read: *The Devonshire Candle Company.* She stood back as if her hand had been burnt. A greetings card lay inside, innocently staring back at her.

She turned it over with the tip of her nail, reluctant to touch any part of it. *Bideford* was scrawled in black ink. That was it. Nothing else. Where she'd grown up.

She blinked. A cold shiver ran down her back. *Oh, my God, it's him.* Floored, she reached to grab the edge of the counter as everything swayed in front of her. The devil on her shoulder whispered, *What you going to do now, Janey?*

CHAPTER 13

Patrick was back. Lizzie was raiding the fridge, and he was making himself a cup of tea. 'We got stuck on the motorway. They closed part of the M11 and we had a huge diversion. I'm so knackered and gasping for a drink.'

'Why didn't you call me?' she said, following them into the kitchen. She still felt out of sorts and exhausted from the day she'd had. She was pleased and relieved they were home. 'You should have stopped at the services for a drink.'

'I just wanted to get home, darling.' He blew her a kiss. 'And the phones died and neither of us had a charger. I left mine in my car.' She could believe that.

'Did you get everything done that you wanted?' Jane asked. 'What's the house like?'

'Great, Mum, I'm so excited. It's nice, isn't it, Dad? I have some photos I took to show you.' She took her phone from her back pocket and showed her.

'Lovely, looks cosy. Oh that's a small kitchen, will you manage.'

Lizzie laughed. 'I'm not going to be cooking much, Mum.'

'No, I guess not. What did you think of it, Patrick.' She saw him roll his eyes behind Lizzie.

'I liked it, small, but they won't notice. Your car is full of stuff that wouldn't fit. Clothes mostly. There's very little room in her bedroom.' That was nice of him. She was glad he didn't say he hated it because she knew from his expression that's what he thought.

'Well, then, I guess it'll all need washing and putting away in your room then, Lizzie. I'll wash them, you can do the rest. We'll start tomorrow.'

'Tomorrow!' she said as if she had an appointment with the King and couldn't postpone it.

'Yes, have you got something better to do? I don't want your dirty clothes littering the kitchen like they always do when you go away.'

Patrick drank his second glass of water and perched on the kitchen stool. 'How was your day, sweetheart?' He sipped the tea that she'd made him. 'God, I was desperate for a cup of tea.'

'It was OK. I got on with some work and then came in from the garden and watched an old film. Actually, Ralph came over and watched it with me. That was nice. He's a nice boy, but Jasper had a bit of a cob on him. He kept barking at him.'

'Ralph? Did you say Ralph came over?' chimed in Lizzie.

'Don't act so surprised. Yes, he came over for his car keys. He said he'd left them in your room and went to fetch them then joined me in the lounge and watched the film with me.'

'He couldn't have, Mum. He's been out with friends all day. I saw his posts.'

'But . . . really? Are you sure, Lizzie?'

She chuckled. 'Yes, I told you I saw his posts.'

What the hell is going on? She saw the look Patrick gave her and kept quiet knowing anything else would make it worse. She knew what he was thinking. She didn't want to go there. 'Right, OK, well, the thing is I had one of those green teas you brought back from that trip with Ralph, and it made me a little sick. Gave me a hell of a headache and wiped me out for hours. I must have dreamt it then. Wow, it seemed so real.'

'Well, it wasn't, Mum. He definitely wasn't around here.' Lizzie took a Coke from the fridge and poured it into a glass.

'How d'you feel now?' asked Patrick. 'Want a proper cup of tea? You do look peaky.'

'That'd be lovely, please.'

'Better throw those tea leaves away, Mum if they made you sick.' She went to the cupboard. 'Was it these?' Jane nodded. 'Right, let's get rid then. Sorry, Mum, the guy said they had healing properties in them.'

They had something for sure. What about the episode by the front door? Did that not happen either or Pauline bringing strawberries over? Best not to say too much right now. She took the proffered tea and looked around the kitchen.

'You lost something?' Patrick asked.

'Yes, we had a delivery. Someone dropped a parcel off. A candle. One of those huge ones. I left it here on the counter.'

'What candle?' asked Patrick.

'The one that came in the parcel. One of those huge, scented ones.'

'Where is it, Mum? Did you take it to the lounge or the pantry?' Lizzie went to look.

'I left it here on the counter . . .' There was no candle. Was she hallucinating all of this? Something happened for sure because she still felt crappy.

'Well, there's nothing here now. Who sent it?' Patrick asked, attentively watching her over the rim of his mug.

'I don't know, there was no card. It just came to me, to Janey.' Her voice sounded brittle. That name on her lips was like acid. 'It was an expensive candle.'

'Janey? Who's that?' asked Lizzie.

Flustered, she forced a small smile. 'Me, I imagine. It's a version of Jane, but nobody calls me that,' she explained wishing now that she hadn't mentioned the rotten candle in the first place.

'Are you sure, Lizzie, that Ralph was out all day?'

'Yes, look.' She showed her the photos posted on Instagram.

'But he might have come back at some point.'

'He didn't, I'm telling you.'

'So you are, but I am certain he was here with me. I can't have imagined it. He came for his car keys. Why would he lie about that?'

'Mum, will you just stop? For God's sake. Look, he had his car with him. He left not long after me. He texted me that he was on his way. Why are you being like this?'

'I'm not being like any way, Lizzie. But I can't believe he wasn't here. Because he was. What I don't get is why he's lying about it?'

'Right, well, you're wrong. I'm not talking about this anymore. I thought you liked him. Why are you being so horrible? You're so nasty sometimes. I'm going to my room.' She stormed off upstairs.

Jane stared after her, dumbfounded.

'What's going on, Jane?'

'What d'you mean? You heard. I know Ralph was here and what's more, Pauline came over with strawberries and cream and we ate them on the patio. I suppose she's going to deny that too,' she shot at him. 'And there was a candle delivered. I bloody remember. That green tea made me sick. I fell asleep with a raging headache. I know I didn't imagine any of this.'

'Right, well, I don't know what to say. Do you want me to call Pauline and ask her?'

'I don't, no. No. No don't do that.' She couldn't face another denial.

'Why? If you're certain she was here, then let's get it confirmed for you?'

She took in a deep breath. 'No, I mean what if she says she wasn't here? What then?'

He shrugged. 'I don't bloody know, Jane.' He was losing his patience. 'But you've just fallen out with Lizzie accusing Ralph of lying and now you say Pauline will lie too and there's no candle. No candle!' He stood up and paced. 'Maybe there was something in that tea. Maybe that guy on the market was selling doped-up tea, who the hell knows. You said the bloody candle was addressed to Janey. You said the name on the vanished mannequin was Janey. Who the hell calls you Janey?'

She played with her mug. She didn't want to talk about that. Maybe. Maybe she had imagined it all because she'd been drugged. And now Patrick was cross with her. She could see he didn't believe her. He was asking himself if she'd been drinking.

'I'm going to make a sandwich. Have you rung about a therapist yet? I bet you haven't bothered, have you?' He went into the pantry and was gone too long. Long enough for her to begin to panic that he had found something incriminating. She went rigid. What now? He walked out with the loaf of bread and a jar of piccalilli. 'Do you want to tell me why there are three bottles of Merlot in there? Or shall we just say that I'm lying too?'

He was coming for her.

She knew then she was in trouble.

Lizzie came back down; she'd clearly been crying. 'I can't believe you'd say those things about Ralph and what d'you mean about Pauline? I heard. Mum, she's your friend. He's my best friend. Why are you being so horrible about them?'

'Check the cameras. It'll all be on the recordings. You'll see I'm not lying,' she said, happy to have found proof that would show them she wasn't lying.

Stoney-faced, Patrick put down the bread and pickle. He opened the app on his phone. 'It's blank. You must have turned them off.'

'What! I didn't. I wouldn't. Why would I turn them off?' That was insane.

'I don't know. But they're turned off. Let me check the main control. Maybe there was a fault. If there was, it will show up.' He came back seconds later. 'It's all turned off at the main hub.'

'But I didn't turn it off! You have to believe me, Patrick,' she yelled. This was not happening. She stood up quickly, angry all this was happening to her. Still a little wobbly on her feet she went to look for herself.

'Darling,' Patrick called out, his own anger cooling. He ran a hand through his hair. 'Come back. Look, why don't we get away. You know, a weekend together just the two of us?'

'Yes, Mum that sounds like a good idea,' Lizzie snapped, angrily stomping out of the house. Jane saw her march over to Ralph's.

'I'm still sorting the long-haul holiday out but in the meantime something short may do you some good. Help you relax. Get away from it all for a bit.'

She watched his face as he struggled with what he thought was happening to her. The air vibrated around them. Her breathing came in shallow bursts. She felt the walls of the kitchen closing in around her. *Murk or someone is trying to tear my life apart.*

CHAPTER 14

Having allowed a long weekend in South Wales in a quaint little B&B by the sea to work its magic on them, things were looking up. Jane's head was feeling clearer. And she hadn't drunk a drop of alcohol. They'd had a wonderful time together. She couldn't believe how stressed she had been until she was away from it all and how de-stressed she felt since coming back.

She lay in the bath relaxing by candlelight. Candles dotted the room and the lights were off, the bathroom door slightly ajar. The blind was closed but the window was a little open. It was quiet, peaceful. She heard familiar noises coming from the kitchen; pots and pans, footsteps, cupboard doors opening and closing and some music playing she couldn't quite make out. Patrick was cooking for them, and Lizzie and Ralph were out. Things had calmed down with Lizzie after she apologised for what she'd said about Ralph. Having had time to reflect while away, maybe he didn't want to admit he'd sat and watched a film with her mum. Uncool or something like that. She rested her head back, letting the hot water and oils do their magic. She wasn't going to think about it anymore.

A sound beneath the window and a creak along the landing made her freeze and open her eyes. *Oh God, not again.* Was it starting again? Her stomach clenched. Shadows cast by the candles shifted in the hallway. It was nothing. The house creaked a lot with floorboards and expansion from the heat, noisy pipework through the partitioned walls. She sighed and breathed out slowly.

It was suddenly all quiet downstairs, not a sound, not even music. Where was Patrick? Footsteps crunched on the gravel outside the window. Another sound on the landing had her on alert, ready to climb out. *Ready to leap out more likely.* That wasn't the house creaking. Something caught her eye on the shelf. In front of the towels was the same snow globe that had been moved in her office. This wasn't by accident. She hadn't done this. Somebody had moved it deliberately. There was faint whispering outside the window. It was Pauline, she was sure of it but who was she whispering to and why? Her heart thumped. Patrick? Was it Patrick whispering with her? It couldn't be. But why? It sounded like him.

Footsteps rushing along the landing startled her. She almost broke her neck climbing out of the bath, grabbing her dressing gown and running downstairs. *Fuck. Someone is definitely in the house.*

'Patrick, where are you?' she yelled, bombing it down the stairs. The front door closed behind somebody. Patrick looked startled as she rushed into the kitchen. She almost skidded to a stop, not expecting to see him there. He was at the back door. 'Where have you been? Why didn't you answer me when I called you?'

'I didn't hear you. I was outside with Jasper. We went for a stroll down to the water, waiting for you. What's wrong?'

Jasper looked undisturbed, wagging his tail. Clearly it had to be somebody he knew. It must have been, or he'd have barked.

'I thought I heard somebody upstairs on the landing.'

'Really? Are you sure?' He looked concerned. 'I'll go check. You stay here.'

'I heard the front door close. Whoever it was isn't there anymore.'

'I'll go check anyway. You stay here with Jasper. I'm sure he would have barked if someone was here. Do you think the wind blew the door closed? There's always a bit of a through draft when the back and front doors are open.'

'But the front door wasn't open.'

'Aah, well, I watered the pots by the door and may not have closed it properly. It could have been that simple.'

He was right, Jasper would have barked, and he was right about the doors too. *Unless Jasper knew the person.* Patrick marched up the stairs, moments later returning. 'All clear, just the house stretching, I imagine. You know how creaky this place can be,' he said softly to reassure her. 'It was probably my fault not shutting the door properly. Calm down, there's nobody here. You're still worrying about that man Pauline mentioned, aren't you? It will have been the wind. It has picked up a bit tonight. Not a cool wind unfortunately.' She didn't miss the concerned look that passed over his face.

But somebody had been in her house and moved that snow globe. Maybe while she popped to the shops earlier. Only one person would know to move that *particular one.*

Jasper sat in front of his cupboard where she kept his treats, his tail wagging, his face turned towards her with pleading eyes. She handed him a small chew. He ran off to his basket with it clamped in his jaw.

'Patrick, will you check the cameras? My phone is on charge. It'll put my mind to rest.'

'If you want,' he said and opened the app on his phone. 'No, there's nothing there. I think there was another break in the Wi-Fi because I'm not on there either. I'll reboot it. Damned bloody nuisance living out here with crappy Wi-Fi. I'll go check outside and take Jasper with me. He'll let me know if anyone's been here.' He kissed her on the lips as he went back out. 'It'll be nothing, you'll see, just the wind. Come on, little fella.' Outside, the two of them walked the perimeter of the house. She heard him speaking to Jasper. 'Well, my lad, you find anything?' Jasper ran around happily before bringing his ball to him and waiting for him to throw it. 'I guess not. There's nothing troubling you tonight if you want to play.'

Jane went upstairs to dress, knowing they wouldn't find anything. There was no point waiting downstairs.

When Patrick returned she was sat at the table waiting for dinner. 'So, there was nothing outside that suggested anyone was around and Jasper didn't look concerned. You know what he's like when strangers come, always sniffing the floor. He did none of that. I bumped into Gordon while I was out there; he's just come back for a day before shooting off back to London. I felt awful, I was going to ask him to come in and join us, but it wouldn't work.' She was relieved, she liked Gordon, but this was their night.

'Another time, when they're both back from Wales after the holidays.'

'Yes, we must make a point of it. Anyway, as I said, Jasper didn't smell any strangers out there.'

'That's good to know.' She wasn't convinced. 'We can always rely on Jasper.' She smiled but her heart wasn't in it. She scratched Jasper's head to reassure him. He lay at her side, put his head on his paws and sighed contentedly. Candles on the table, best crystal glasses and china. Patrick had made a real effort tonight. It meant a lot to her. Maybe she was overreacting again.

'It's not amazing, I know but I hope you like it,' he said. 'Now, stop worrying about anything and let's enjoy this time together. We've had a great weekend, let's continue. I don't know what it is about this place that gets you so wound up at the moment.'

'It smelled divine upstairs. And you know I love Thai green curry. Thank you.' He was right, she had to stop this. She didn't want to talk about why she was wound up here; she hoped he thought it was the work she had to get through.

'I made it myself, not from a packet. It's a cheat one off the internet. We had all the ingredients in the cupboard, so I thought, why not.' He stirred the pan.

She watched the back of him, feeling her pulse quicken that she couldn't open up to him.

When they got married it was up in Scotland, a smallish affair of around fifty people. They'd struggled to find fifty people they wanted to invite.

When he slipped the gold band on her finger, she looked at his face, his eyes and felt so much love for him. She still felt the same level of love today. They'd not been bothered by the cold whistling through the ancient leaded windows, blowing against their backs as they sat at the top table of the three-hundred-year-old hotel. They chose December, because the hotel had offered a deal. Back then money had been tight, so it was a godsend. Marrying him was the best decision she'd ever made.

He'd set a cosy table for two, with candles and soft lighting. She did her best to not think about anything upsetting right now. She wanted to enjoy the evening he'd gone to so much trouble creating for her. He put on smooth jazz in the background. Patrick looked chilled. She couldn't stop thinking of the snow globe in the bathroom. 'Do you think we should change the locks?'

'What? Why?'

'Because what if someone has a key?'

'Jane, the back doors are open and the windows. Nobody has a key. I'm not giving into this neurosis of yours that someone was in the house. You really must stop winding yourself up over every little sound you hear and making it into a mountain.' He wasn't being mean, just stating the obvious.

He was in a good place, smiling warmly and humming to himself as he cooked, but she could tell she'd annoyed him asking. 'This is nice, isn't it?' he said, clearly not wanting to engage in her suggestion. 'There was nobody lurking outside, Jane, so just forget about it and relax.' He ran his finger up her arm, kissing her lightly on the lips and offered her the lick of the spoon. But she couldn't relax, not completely. She nodded anyway just to keep the peace.

They'd always had fun together, always done long romantic weekends. They got on great and were never shy of stopping in the street to have a little kiss. They held hands while out and rarely fell out. Which was why she was worried that what was happening to her right now was so unsettling for them. Her eyes darted away, unable to look at him, screwing them up to stop the tears. She willed the flashbacks away, trying to regroup and bring herself back to the present. Each day her secret weighted heavier. *I know how much he loves me; I do, I really do. But he doesn't know the half of what went on in my life before I met him. He'll pity me. I don't know if I could bear that. I glance at him and catch him smiling at me. I clasp my hands together in a bid to stop them shaking because I so want to believe he'll understand. The bitterness of my past swells in my guts. They say our past defines us. I don't really know what that means or if it's a good or bad thing.* She felt a horrible undercurrent of mistrust that he didn't believe her or thought she was going behind his back with the drink and that was threatening to destabilise what they had.

They had always been busy people; Patrick with his music, doing session work and going on tour as a stand-in drummer, her with all her illustrations. But they always found time for each other. If Patrick was away for more than a couple of weeks, she'd fly out to join him or drive to the nearest place he was playing. Outside forces could be destructive to a relationship if allowed to come between them. Up until now, they had managed to control all that.

Tonight, doing this for her and the way he looked at her made her understand that what they had was more powerful than anything. They just had to remember that and not lose sight of who they were together.

Patrick plated some chicken for Jasper.

Her family was everything to her. And she would fight for all of them.

He made them mocktails, which were delicious. She sipped hers.

'You OK?' Patrick said putting a plate of Thai green curry in front of her.

'Yes, I'm fine.' She wasn't going to let anything spoil tonight. She was starving. Patrick was by her side. She was in control of her life, despite what had been going on. She had to believe that. She wasn't going to let Murk ruin what she had. She wasn't going mad or drinking too much. Even if it looked like she was. She knew she wasn't.

She smiled at her husband. Jane Carmichael was not going to let anybody destroy her or her life. She held up her mocktail in salutation, they clinked glasses.

CHAPTER 15

Jane woke early the next morning, feeling revitalised after last night's wonderful meal and the sexy time they'd had afterwards. She stretched, feeling her muscles pop and give, releasing the tension they were holding on to. Turning over, Patrick was gone, already up. She swung her legs out of bed, smiling, remembering the lovely night. She saw a cup of tea on her bedside table. Patrick, what a cutie. She didn't want to lose all of this. They had a great partnership. She sipped and decided to sit back in bed and drink it before going downstairs. She let out a big sigh. It was a long time since she'd slept so well, and it made a world of difference to her wellbeing.

In the kitchen, she put her mug in the dishwasher and made herself scrambled eggs. Patrick had opened all the doors and windows to let out the stuffy air and dropped the blinds against the sun.

She really did have her appetite back. She smiled, remembering Patrick last night using his magic on her body.

'Hi, Mum, Dad said you were having a lie-in. It's not much of one though?' Lizzie strolled in, wearing a pair of new shorts and a crop top.

'No, I guess not, but I woke up and thought what a beautiful day it was. What a shame to waste it. It won't be long now before it all goes back to normal soggy days with intermittent sunshine.' For which she kind of longed but felt guilty voicing her thoughts on. 'I wasn't going to lounge in bed and waste it. Where you off to?'

'I'm going to Bev's. She wants to go shopping for the Horsham festival we're going to. Need more shorts and little tops. That looks yummy — are there any eggs left?'

'I'll make you some. Here, have mine. I haven't touched them yet and I'm not in a rush. I'll make some more. Is your dad in the studio?'

'No, he nipped out, said he was going for a loaf of sourdough.' Lizzie ate the eggs greedily and drank the orange juice she'd set on the table for herself. 'Right, thanks, you're the best, I'm off.'

'How are you getting there?'

'Walking to town and getting the bus. Don't fancy driving. It's so difficult to park near her house. You know she has a tiny drive. And we might go for a bite at the pub and have a little something, who knows.'

'See you later then,' Jane said, working on her second batch of scrambled eggs.

Jasper barked in the garden. Running back and forth along the fence, then into the shrubbery, popped out again and barked some more. Something was clearly bothering him. They hadn't done anything about the squirrels. A cat dropped from the willow tree. Jasper was instantly chasing it round the garden.

Patrick arrived as she was eating her breakfast, dropping the car keys on the island. 'Doesn't this smell good,' he said, holding out a loaf of fresh sourdough. 'Want a piece?'

'I'm fine thanks, I'm finishing-up scrambled eggs. Lizzie's gone to Bev's on the bus. They're going for cocktails and lunch too, so she didn't want to take the car.'

'Yeah, I saw her walking to the bus stop.'

'You sure you don't want a slice of toasted sourdough? Go on,' he asked as he popped two slices in the toaster.

'No, thanks, I'm good.'

'Sounds like Jasper has found something new to chase out there.'

'A cat,' she said watching the shenanigans as the cat outran Jasper and scrambled over the fence, much to his exasperation.

'There are some baby squirrels out there too. The parents can be vicious, if he gets near them.' Patrick pulled out the milk from the fridge. 'Want a coffee, darling?'

'Yes, please,' she said eating the last of her eggs.

Patrick made the coffees and took them outside. Jane joined him, loving the entertainment Jasper was providing — now chasing a butterfly. She couldn't help smiling; she felt so happy today and couldn't remember the last time she'd felt so light of heart. She leaned back, feeling the sun on her face.

A while later after they'd eaten their breakfast, Patrick asked, 'Did Lizzie say anything else to you about the other day?'

'You mean when I accused Ralph of lying?' She shook her head. 'No, but I have apologised so I think she's forgiven me. She was OK this morning, quite chatty actually. I think we're all good now.'

'Right, good, maybe not mention it again. She got quite upset, you know.'

She knew how upset Lizzie had got. That was why she'd gone and apologised. She'd given her the cold shoulder and Jane hated that. 'You know, having her home for the holidays is harder than I thought it would be. I think she's outgrown us — well, me — and sadly I've got used to the space and quiet when she's not around. Is that awful of me to say?'

He chuckled. 'No, she can be a bit of a tornado some-times and she's stronger-minded than she ever was. I just let her get on with it. Anything for a quiet life.'

'That's why she's a daddy's girl.' They laughed at the truth of her words.

Well, she felt crap thinking that way, as if it was wrong as a mother to admit she liked it when her daughter was away.

But they all fly the nest sooner or later. The nest becomes too small, and they need to spread their wings. It's the order of things. It's how it's meant to be. Still, she felt crap thinking it all the same. She didn't miss the mess, the arguments, the voracious appetite Lizzie had and worst of all, the buying of stuff for herself only to open the fridge or cupboard to find her daughter had eaten it.

'The thing is, she's asked me if there's something wrong. You know, like medically. She thought you might have cancer or something and that was why you were acting so weird at times and seemed so stressed recently,' Patrick said biting into his toast.

'What?' She couldn't believe she'd given off that impression. Now she felt doubly bad that her daughter was worried she might die. 'Why didn't you tell me this?'

'Because you'd get like you are now. Stressy. Relax, I've sorted it and told her there's nothing wrong with you.'

'OK, God, I can't believe she thought that.' What had he said *was* wrong with her then?

'Only because you've been doing random stuff and not remembering things. I don't want her to worry about the way you've been acting. You know she picks up on everything.'

'What did you tell her?' He should have told her. Discussed it with her as what they would say to stop her worrying. Patrick was like that at times, but this involved her, and he should have told her.

'That you were tired and stressed from work. What else could I say? It's the truth, isn't it?' That wasn't much of an explanation. If that worked, she'd go with it though. She really didn't want to get into it anyway. She didn't want to think about it today either. She had to control what she could when she could and worry about the rest when it happened.

'Shall we go out for the day?' Patrick suggested. 'Take Jasper and grab some lunch? Might be good to get out of the house. They said the temperature was going to hit thirty today. We could go to the beach. He loves having a good swim. It's only forty minutes in the car and a good walk along the beach will do us both good. I haven't done any proper exercise since I got back.' She worried the roads might be busy and they'd be stuck in the car for hours. She leaned in, kissing his lips. She couldn't let that stop them though.

'Great, let me do an hour or so of work and go before it gets too hot for him. Then he can chill at the pub under an umbrella.'

* * *

When they got back it was early evening. As predicted, the traffic had been awful so they'd pulled off in a nearby town to let it die down. Jane let Jasper out in the garden then hosed him down; he was covered in sand. As was the inside of the car.

'I'm surprised he's still got any energy left,' said Patrick walking into the kitchen and grabbing a beer from the fridge. 'I'm pooped.' He sank into the sofa, looking out at the garden watching him race around. 'Looks like he's picked up a scent again.'

'I'm going to shower. I feel I have sand everywhere.' Jane kicked off her trainers in the garden and shook them out.

'Want me to join you?' he said suggestively.

'Haha, I'm too tired. Besides, you could get his food out for him. I'm sure he's famished. Plus you said you were pooped.' He gave her a sad face. It was great getting back to some kind of normality even if it might just be temporary. She'd been a fool to let herself get so wound up. Although everything was still lurking at the back of her mind, she refused to give it credence as she watched Jasper so happy in the garden. If the dark clouds had blown away for the moment, she had to make the most of it. 'Maybe we should go to the beach with him more often now we've discovered that little cove. It's not too far.' They'd taken a wrong turn and literally driven over a dirt road which looked like it led nowhere and then quite by surprise they'd driven up to the most amazing little cove. With only half a dozen other cars there they suspected it was being kept a secret to stop the hordes descending on it.

'Let's take Lizzie and Ralph with us next time. He loves playing with Jasper.'

'I don't think we should take anyone with us.' Not to sound mean or selfish, she didn't want to share their new discovery.

'Oh, talk of the devil.'

'Hi,' Ralph said walking in through the back with Lizzie.

'Hi, Ralph picked me up from the bus stop.' She was laden with shopping bags. 'I got quite a bit and a backpack. Ralph thought I needed a bigger one.' She held up her Primark bags. 'There's a local open-air concert with tribute bands on at the weekend. Did I tell you?'

'Yes, several times actually,' Patrick said tongue in cheek.

'All right, Dad, I thought you'd be interested.' Patrick rolled his eyes.

'That sounds good,' Jane said thinking it didn't and the idea of it wasn't at all appealing to her.

'Who are the bands?' asked Patrick while Jane slipped out of the kitchen to shower. 'Your era, Dad. Bruce Springsteen, U2. I think they have tickets left if you and Mum want to go.'

'Nah, sweetheart, I wouldn't crash your day,' Jane heard him say as she left, feeling relieved that he wasn't going to try and persuade her.

'I wasn't suggesting you come with *us*,' she said, horrified at the thought of her parents tagging along.

Patrick rolled his eyes as if he didn't understand quite what she meant. Jasper ran in with his ball and dropped it at Ralph's feet. He went out to play with him. It seemed like Jasper had settled back down with him and stopped the barking.

When Jane came back down some twenty minutes or so, she was alone in the kitchen. She called Jasper but there was no answer. She checked his bowl. Dammit Patrick, he'd forgotten to feed him, and his water was low. He could be so gormless sometimes.

She opened a tin and banged the fork against it to call him inside. 'Jasper, come on, baby, dinner time.' She poured out the food and settled his bowl back on the floor, banging the tin again several more times. With no response she went outside to see what he was up to. Standing on the patio, she called out again. A gentle whining was coming from somewhere in the garden. Her instant thought was that one of the squirrels had got him and bitten him badly. She looked around but there was no sign of him, so she listened to see where the sound was coming from. 'Jasper? Come on, dinner's ready. Jasper.' Another little whine then a shriek of pain came from the bottom of the garden. The willow tree obstructed her view. Then silence. As she rushed towards the sound, past the tree, she caught a fleeting glimpse of a figure running away towards the shoreline and disappearing down the side towards the woods.

She came to an abrupt halt at seeing Jasper's lifeless body by the water's edge.

CHAPTER 16

It was one day since Jasper had drowned and she had fallen into a deep depression, not wanting to talk much to anyone. She'd spent the morning on the island, working on her illustrations, trying to focus but finding it hard through her grief. She put her pad and pencil down and stared into the middle distance.

She had put his collar in her bedside table drawer after they buried him under the willow tree. She'd wrapped it in a towel to keep his scent. This morning, when she'd gone to take it out and hold it, it wasn't there. She mentioned it to Patrick and managed to get herself worked up, but he convinced her it would turn up, that she might have put it somewhere else. Well, she had been in a state that was true; she could have put it somewhere else. But she was so sure she'd put it next to her bed. His smell comforted her when she wanted to feel close to him. The thought of it being lost pained her. What if she never remembered where she'd put it? Jane kept all her close possessions in her drawer. Why would she have put it somewhere else? It made no sense. Then again, she'd made no sense after she'd found him. She'd gone hysterical and frightened Patrick and Lizzie.

Patrick called her on her mobile, she'd taken it with her today, asking her to come back to the house. He sounded upset but said nothing about why he wanted her back just that she really ought to come back. She didn't want to. She was happy where she was. She didn't want to be around anyone right now.

'Jane, come home, please. There's something I need you to see.' She didn't like the idea of leaving her island and going back. Going back meant going back where Jasper had died. There was a growing sense of mistrust and insecurity as to who to trust right now. There had been nobody at the house but them when he died. She didn't believe Jasper just drowned like everyone said, even though that was the obvious reason. A dog didn't just drown like that. He was a good swimmer. He loved the water. She didn't believe it and she wasn't going to accept it either, besides what about the whining she'd heard and the little yelp before . . . That made it worse because now she was accusing someone of killing him, which hadn't gone down well. Either somebody had come to the house, like the figure she'd seen, or there was more to it. Patrick didn't want to entertain her ideas. But she had seen someone. She was certain of it. But without proof it was only her word that there'd been somebody else here. She used her binoculars to look at the house. The three of them stood by the water, waiting for her. What did they want that was so important that she needed to go back right now? She didn't like the look of that. She didn't like the look of it one bit.

* * *

The trip back to shore was unnerving. *Why are they waiting for me lined up like that?* She felt as if she was on her way to the gallows. The water was tranquil, another still windless day, warming up nicely to be another scorcher. The lake went on past their house around a small bend where it opened into a large expanse of water, on either side was woodland where she'd seen the figure run to. Patrick had put it down to grief and the simple fact that she couldn't handle that little Jasper had had an accident.

She slowed the boat down, coming to a gentle stop at the edge of the garden, averting her eyes from the spot where she'd found him. Patrick came over to help her tie the boat and help her out. Had something happened while she was on the island? He seemed really odd right now, and uneasy around her, which unsettled her no end. Maybe they'd found proof of the person she'd seen and were worried to tell her. She climbed out, holding his hand and glancing at his face. It was expressionless. Unnerving. Fear began to grow in her belly and rise up until it was around her throat, choking her, cutting off her airways. Was it someone they knew? Her family were all here, so nothing had happened to them. It could only be that they had proof of someone hurting Jasper.

'Jane? Are you OK? You've been out there since dawn and not eaten anything,' he asked taking her by the elbow. Hadn't she? She couldn't remember if she had or not. She wasn't hungry, that was for sure.

'I'm fine. I'm not hungry. I just need to be alone. I can't bear to be in the house without—' She burst into tears. She hadn't realised they were there but there they were pouring from her eyes, and she couldn't stop them. It cut her in two remembering how she'd found him.

'Oh, Mum, don't cry, you'll make me cry. It's so horrid. I can't believe it.' Jane gave Lizzie the best smile she could which wasn't much. Her grief hurt. It really hurt like nothing she'd experienced before. Her poor Jasper. Had he suffered? She couldn't bear to think that he had, and his whining told her he probably had. She felt bereft. She couldn't stop the feeling that it hadn't been an accident. Who had been on their property?

Patrick grabbed her hand. 'You need to eat something. This won't help, darling. It's awful what happened but you need to look after yourself too. We all miss him terribly.'

She didn't want to talk about it. It hurt too much. 'Why did you want me to come back? Have you found something? Did you check the woods? Was something there?'

'No, there wasn't.' He squeezed her hand. Lizzie sobbed behind her.

'Come into the house, Mum.' Lizzie walked on the other side of her, holding her other hand. Ralph quietly walked away back home; she was glad.

'What's going on? Have you found something?' she repeated. 'You're making me nervous.' Her breathing was shallow, her heart hammering against her chest wall. They were both worrying her by their behaviour. Had they found the person who'd done it? Were they in the house? Is that where they were taking her, to show her who had killed her Jasper? She couldn't bear it if that was the case.

'The thing is, Jane we think someone broke into the house this morning while you were on the island.'

She literally froze. No, she did. She stopped walking and stood as if rooted to the spot, unable to move a muscle. *They came back and broke into my house? But why would they do that?* It made no sense. 'Where were you?' she asked, horrified this was happening.

'In the studio. You know I can't hear anything with my headphones on and Lizzie was at Ralph's.'

'Did you catch them?' she asked hopefully, in the moment sure they'd also killed Jasper.

'No, no we didn't, we just saw what they did.'

What they did? *Dear God, what does that mean?* Her hands felt clammy, and chilled. Murk. It had to be him. Had he — had he — hurt Jasper? She couldn't say the other word, it was too ghastly. Fresh tears gathered and ran down her cheeks. 'Did the cameras catch them on there?' She sniffed, looking for her phone.

He shook his head. She saw the look pass between him and Lizzie. Nothing on the cameras? Like the last time? That was odd, surely he thought that was odd.

'There was nothing on there. Nobody came to the door and the cameras at the back as usual were rubbish. We can't rely on them. We'll have to forget them. They're a waste of time.'

'Have you called the police?'

'Not yet, no. We wanted to talk to you first.'

They walked into her bedroom. She stared around in disbelief.

The pillows from their bed were on the floor. The wardrobe doors wide open and the contents strewn all over the room. Everything was pulled out of drawers and on the floor. It was like a tornado had gone through the room. The shower was wet as if someone had showered recently, but nobody had done so since that morning. The medicine cabinet was emptied, all its contents in the basin and on the floor. Her hairdryer was out, so was her shower gel, make-up, hairbrush and the towels were in a pile on the floor.

'Oh my God,' she said horrified by the mess. 'Who did this? Did they do this? Is this what they did to our house? But why? What were they looking for?'

'So, you don't know what happened in here?' he asked, gently.

'Me?' she replied, shocked. *Why was he asking me?* 'I haven't been upstairs since I got up. Why are you asking me?'

'Well, who *did* do this? That's what I'm asking.' His voice was still calm, waiting for an answer.

'What? I'm sorry, I don't understand. You told me we'd been broken into, and this seems to me what they did. Why are you asking me if I know what the hell happened here?'

'We thought that at first, yes. Thought maybe they'd gone for your jewellery.'

She put her hands to her temples. 'Patrick, what the hell is going on? I don't understand. Either someone broke in or they didn't. I don't have anything worth nicking.'

He shook his head. Lizzie was by the window looking out as if she couldn't bear to look. Her arms folded tightly in front of her, almost as if she was holding in her frustration.

'The thing is, love, I heard you rummaging up here not an hour ago,' he said.

'No. I was on the island sketching. Didn't you check? Didn't you see the boat wasn't there?' *It must have been them.* 'I thought you said you were in the studio?'

'I was. I went to the kitchen for a drink. I didn't bother you. I knew you needed time to yourself.'

'What are you saying or trying to say, Patrick? That I did this? That I was so angry I lost my mind and trashed our bedroom?' It made no sense.

'Mum, you've been acting so strangely recently.' Her voice was laced with passive aggression.

Jane turned on her, angry with her and Patrick for even contemplating such a ludicrous suggestion. 'Like how?' she said pointedly knowing she'd struck the match to the tinder box.

Lizzie put her hands on her hips as if she'd been keeping all of what she wanted to say bottled up until now. 'Putting things in the wrong place. I mean you lost the car keys, then made up that ridiculous story of Ralph and Pauline coming to see you when they hadn't. And drinking!' Lizzie took a moment trying to rein in her temper. 'I'm, sorry, I know you're devastated about Jasper . . .' Her voice cracked. 'We all are. It's understandable if you did lose it. I mean were you looking for his collar? Was that what tipped you over the edge?' She looked around the room. 'We just want to help you that's all. We just want to make sure and not call the police saying we've been burgled when you did this.'

'You think *I* did this.' Some of her confidence faded that they actually believed she would do something like this. 'I didn't do this. And I have no idea if they took anything. I haven't anything to take.' The whole thing was preposterous. They were acting as if she was losing her mind.

Lizzie burst into tears. Her resolve vanished. 'Oh Mum, I know you miss him, we all do. But you've shut us out and we're worried that's all we're bothered about.'

'Jane, love, it was Lizzie who thought you might have been looking for his collar. We're not saying anything else. We're here to help you, you know that. But you need to talk to us.'

'I need time to grieve, Patrick, that's not a lot to ask. I'll be OK in a day or so but it's hard right now and I need time alone.' She knew she sounded irritated. She sniffed, wiping her tears with a screwed-up tissue.

She couldn't explain how much it was hurting to lose Jasper. The collar was hers to feel him close by. She had been afraid of losing it or losing his smell on it. And now it was gone.

Patrick came to stand between them. He rested his hands on her shoulders and looked calmly into her eyes. The gesture reminded her of how he'd calmed Lizzie as a baby, suffering from colic. Calming her down, making her feel safe in his arms. He was doing it to her now, to gain her trust and reassure her that he was on her side.

Lizzie moved away, back to the window and stared out.

'But I didn't do this, Patrick. I wasn't even here. I told you that.'

'Jane,' he said, 'When Ralph left this morning, he saw you in here when he walked past the room. Were you looking for his collar? You said you were when he asked you if he could help.'

'But I didn't,' she insisted. 'The collar was in the drawer, and I know it's missing. But I haven't been back since I left this morning.'

'He said he heard you muttering something about losing it. It's OK to admit that's why you turned the room upside down, because you were looking for it.'

'He said, he said! I wouldn't do this sort of thing. Besides, I haven't lost it. Ralph is lying. He must be. You said yourself I must have put it somewhere. I've accepted that.' Her voice dropped a decibel. 'I couldn't lose it. I've put it somewhere for safekeeping and I'm all over the place in grief that I can't bloody remember where that is.'

'Don't start all that again. Why would Ralph lie?' Lizzie shouted.

'OK, OK then, let's go with that,' Patrick said, trying to stop it escalating. 'So, you're saying someone did come in here and trash the room and took nothing.'

She laughed. 'There's nothing to take, and look, the iPad is still there. Whoever came in was looking for something specific. And Lizzie, I'm sorry but I know I wasn't here.'

'Really? Really? And you can be certain of that, can you?'

Her rebuke really hurt, shutting her up instantly.

She didn't remember talking to Ralph or seeing him this morning.

Her stomach churned. Patrick watched her carefully. He knew her too well. 'Jane, you've just said the iPad is still there and you have nothing to pinch. So, what's the point of any of this? Why would someone come in to trash your bedroom?'

She dropped onto the bed deflated. She had said that. So, what did that mean? She looked around devastated she'd done this and couldn't remember. *What the hell is happening to me?*

Patrick came to sit next to her.

What was happening was wearing her out. Losing Jasper had destroyed her. She still believed someone had killed him. She was confused and scared she was losing control over herself and her mind. *No, this is what he wants me to think*.

Patrick was so easy-going generally. But she sensed he was losing patience with her. And it scared her. *I can't blame him, either.*

He wrapped her up in his arms. But all she wanted to do was run and hide away. She thought she might never overcome what was happening to her. He hushed her quietly in her ear as if she was a damaged animal, and she supposed she was in a way. She needed this right now. She needed to feel he wasn't deserting her.

CHAPTER 17

Patrick and Lizzie decided to have a barbeque a few days later. It would be at the weekend, a small affair, he said. 'Let's take advantage of this weather. It won't be here forever so let's have some fun.' Lizzie had first suggested it as a way of getting her out of her depression. The one she'd sunk into after finding Jasper and couldn't pull herself out of especially since his collar hadn't turned up. Jane had to drink a little bit, despite Patrick's annoyance at it. But Christ, she needed a crutch. She just kept bursting into tears whenever she thought of him. 'I think we need something to take our minds off the dark cloud around us right now. It will do you good to have some distraction.' She hadn't replied. Secretly she didn't want to snap out of her mood. Because what if she started to forget him? 'Only the neighbours,' he said. 'I called Penny to see if they might be back but they're staying on at the caravan in Wales. So it's only going to be Pauline and Tony.' It would be beneficial for her to have company, apparently. 'Shame Gordon isn't doing one of his dashes back home for a day or so. He could have come over. I still feel bad about the other day.' Things were a little strained between them right now. Last night in front of the telly she'd had two small glasses, putting the bottle away after the second, and again felt rough this morning like all the other times she drank lately. Maybe it was her body telling her to quit. Patrick hadn't been happy.

It's only while I get over Jasper. I'm not addicted like they think. I can stop whenever. I only lost him a few days ago. What do they expect?

The hot water burned through her until she could stand it no more and switched off the shower. She wrapped a thick towel around herself. Now dressed, she made her way downstairs. The neighbours had arrived. She heard them through the open window and considered saying she wasn't feeling well and staying in bed instead. *What hellish surprises are waiting for me today?* It was how she was starting to think.

She didn't fancy being the subject of chatter today. She looked down at herself. She was dressed in jeans and a white shirt. It was what she wore yesterday. It smelt clean though; she shrugged not bothered. She simply had no interest in anything right now. She looked out the window and saw Ralph helping out. He was a liar, but why? He seemed so nice. Why would he lie about seeing her in the bedroom? *The same reason he lied about not watching the film with me.* There was no real reason for him to do so. She was wary of him now. Jasper had sensed something with him, too. *I can't bear to think he hurt him. And now he's here waltzing around my home, befriending Lizzie. My fingers rap on the windowsill quickly in another sign of my anxiety. I'm going to have to keep an eye on him from now on.*

She really didn't want to be social today either. With or without a drink. Definitely not without a drink. She grabbed a glass of Merlot from the kitchen before stepping out onto the patio. Ralph bumped into her, knocking her slightly off balance and grabbed her by the arms to stop her falling. 'Careful, Mrs C. Nearly poured your red wine over your lovely white shirt. I'm just fetching some more ice.' She didn't reply, not in the mood right now for niceties or to be bothered about his feelings even if it would upset Lizzie. She had to work out why he would lie in the first place.

Patrick strode over, smiling, putting on a brave face like everything was OK and clearly trying to encourage her to do the same. She painted on a smile to please him. It was half-hearted. 'How you feeling, sweetheart?' Taking her arm in a firm but gentle grip, he said, 'I've made some of my mocktails for us. I saw you looking at Ralph, Jane. Look, you must see how mad it is to think he lied. Why would he?'

'I don't know, that's the problem. Do you think I just forgot I trashed the room?' *I can't get my head around why he would lie, that was my problem.*

'Yes, you've been in such a funny mood, staring out into the distance, not paying attention to us. I just think you got into a state of grief and forgot.' That did make more sense than Ralph lying. She caught Ralph's eye and gave him a half-hearted smile. Maybe she was wrong. After all, it made no sense for him to lie. *I don't know what to believe.*

'So anyway, you said you felt rough after drinking last night so have one of the mocktails. Maybe stay off the booze today. It might help you feel a bit better.' It wasn't a suggestion. She didn't think it would for a second. She wasn't going to argue. She didn't have the energy. He would just have to understand how hard today was going to be for her with all the sodding questions Pauline and Tony were going to throw at her about Jasper.

'I know and I do, but, it's just the one. I can't face all the sad eyes and mournful faces when they say their condolences without a little Dutch courage.' She felt him stiffen slightly.

Smells from the barbeque drifted towards her. Despite her depressed state her stomach groaned with eagerness, surprising her. She heard the clink of wine glasses and saw that Ralph was on duty carrying trays of the jewelled liquid, keeping everyone topped up. Uplifting music was playing in the background. And the sun was out in the smooth, cloudless, corn blue sky. It was the picture of a perfect summer's afternoon. The one thing it lacked was her Jasper. The moment she thought of him she wanted to run back inside and curl up under her duvet. Patrick saw her look over to where they'd buried him under the willow and tightened his grip, bending down to her face. 'It'll be OK, Jane, I promise. After this one, it will get easier. Think of Jasper overseeing it all. I know it's hard. I can't bear the quiet in the house — it seems so empty. We have to move on. Please try to make an effort. He wouldn't want you to be sad. He was such a happy boy.'

She knew he was trying to make things better for her. She'd try. She really didn't want to fall out with him or argue. He was right. She had to snap out of it. It was nearly four days now. She took in a deep breath and put on her best smile. 'I will, you're right.' Plus, she hated how there was a gaping divide between them after she lost the collar and trashed their bedroom.

'Come on, let's go say hi to our guests,' he said with a smile. 'Give me your empty glass and take one of these mock-tails, I've made Margaritas. You like these, right?' She handed it over and took the brimming glass with the salted rim.

Pauline was a woman of many words and many opinions on just about everything happening in the world when she had a few drinks inside her and she was making a beeline for Jane. Jane eyed her suspiciously, wondering if she was going to start talking about Jasper. She couldn't cope with that. Well not without a drink anyway. Pauline was so kind-hearted. She just didn't know when to stop, that was her problem. She was going to have to be strong and not burst into tears.

Tony Jackson caught up with Patrick as he left Jane, heading for the barbecue to check on the food. He couldn't wait to grab some time with him to discuss music, any opportunity he got. As a secret KISS fan who dressed up as his idol to go to tribute concerts, it blew Tony's mind to find out Patrick played in the band years ago.

'I saw them live a few times you know. The last one in 2018 at the O2 Arena was part of their last ever tour, or so they said at the time,' Tony rattled on to Patrick who was only interested in keeping an eye on Jane. 'They're getting on a bit. I suppose they've had enough. I couldn't believe I wouldn't see them live again, and then they toured again,' Tony told

Patrick good-humouredly, plunging his hand into the bowl of Bombay mix.

The trestle table was laden with salads and breads, baps for the burgers and hotdog rolls, condiments and a huge bowl of fries and another of jacket potatoes — along with that Bombay mix. She had to hand it to Patrick and Lizzie, they'd put on a wonderful spread.

She glanced at the little mound nearby where Jasper lay; tears filled her eyes. She had to look away to stay in control because if she didn't, she'd be a blubbering mess. Pauline was talking to her about something or other, she couldn't remember. She was proud of herself for keeping it together when she'd mentioned him. But suddenly, seeing where his tiny body was buried, she needed a real drink and picked up a glass of Merlot from the table. She finished half the glass, feeling guilty. Not wanting Patrick or Lizzie to see her, she put it back down on the table. Then excused herself to bring over the large Laurent-Perrier ice bucket, pilfered from the hotel they married in — their excuse being the hotel had been too mean to put the heating on, so they deserved it as compensation.

'Let me help you with that, Jane.' Pauline was suddenly by her side as Jane tried to drag the full bucket out of the sun. 'You're such a little thing, you'll hurt yourself,' Pauline told her picking it up with a groan. 'You know, when I was working, I always picked up the big dogs and popped them on the examining table.' She gave a little laugh, her face turning pink as she tottered towards the trestle table. 'Everyone was surprised I was able to. I think they thought because I'm short I couldn't possibly be strong. I've always been strong. Even as a child. Where d'you want this?' she said, her voice straining. She probably wished she hadn't offered.

'Oh, sorry, Pauline, over here. Just pop it there under the trestle table.' Patrick scooted over quickly and gave Pauline a hand then meandered off again after replenishing Pauline's Prosecco and providing Jane with another mock margarita.

'Ooh, dearie me, that was heavier than I thought.' She fanned herself with her hand and dabbed her face with a tissue. 'Oh, I wish I could put our air conditioning out here in the garden. I won't lie, as much as I'm enjoying this weather, I can't wait for it to break. Shame Penny's still away. I think she said she was going to try and get back earlier this year, but you know how possessive her family is. She's the black sheep for leaving Wales, did she tell you?' Jane nodded; she knew the story. 'So, her guilt keeps her there. I can't remember the last time I felt I was able to breathe since we've had this heatwave.' She laughed taking a long drink of her Prosecco. 'You not drinking, dearie?'

'No, no, I've a bit of a headache and what with the sun and this heat, it's not a good idea.'

'Quite right, well, I hope that red you drank doesn't cause you a problem.'

'Oh, no, no it won't. It was only half a glass. That's fine.' She wished she'd get off the drink subject. 'So, are you going away anywhere this year?'

'Us? Not at the moment, no. There's some bits I need tidying up first, you know family stuff and then maybe, yes, maybe after that we will get away.'

'Great! Patrick is organising a trip for us somewhere in the Caribbean, I think. He's trying to sort dates.' She sighed; she could do with a trip right now. Far away with white sands and deep azure waters. Oh, it would be heavenly. Then she remembered Jasper and came back down with a bump. 'Lizzie was saying they were thinking of going to Wales, a bunch of them to a glamping site. Sounds like fun.' Jane couldn't think of anything worse, but then she wasn't Lizzie's age, and they'd have a fabulous time, she was sure of it.

'Look, tell me to mind my own business,' Pauline said. 'I won't be offended.' Jane didn't think she really meant that. 'But you will be careful, dear, over on your island — it's very overgrown. Ralph was telling me there are some pretty dense parts over there. I mean, if Jasper runs off and you go look—'

She cut herself short. 'Stupid, I'm so stupid,' she scolded herself. 'Sorry, dear, really, I am. I just didn't think.'

Jane welled up. *The woman is insufferable sometimes! Why doesn't she think before she speaks?* Jane pulled herself up at that. She meant well, really, Jane knew that. She was a sweet friend looking out for her, that's all.

'Here, have a tissue.' Pauline pulled a clean one from her pocket. 'I'm sorry, Jane. I just forgot.'

Patrick was over in a flash. 'Everything OK, Jane?' She wiped her eyes and smiled. It was easily done; no harm done. She hadn't expected it, that was all.

'It was me, Patrick. I forgot for a moment and made a silly comment about Jasper. I am sorry, Jane.'

'These things happen, Pauline. You OK, Jane?'

'Yes, I must expect people to mention him. It's just still very raw for me that's all.'

'Well, as I was saying, not that it will be a problem now — sorry, sorry, I'm doing it again, anyway, what I was getting at was that Ralph said that you can't hear anyone shouting from there, so make sure you have a full tank of fuel, won't you, and your phone.'

'Yes, I keep telling her this. She's naughty and doesn't like to take the phone.'

'I have a standby one I keep there all the time.'

'She likes the peace it gives her.' He gave her a *I've told you so* look.

'Well, there is that, but you need to in case you need help,' said Pauline surprised by this revelation. 'And that might lose charge so make sure it's topped up, Jane. I bet you've not bothered to check it.'

Parick gave her a look she knew too well.

'Stop fussing, the pair of you. I'll do it next time I'm over. And I will do as I am told, I promise.'

'I bet the two of you didn't know that from my house I can see onto the island. Sorry I just thought that might put your mind to rest. I mean if you did get stuck there.'

Jane was surprised. She thought the view from Bracken House was limited by the foliage and trees. They glanced over.

'Oh, I didn't know that, no.' That made her uncomfortable. She didn't think anyone could see her there. The idea she was totally on her own was what made it magical for her. How much could they actually see? She twitched at the thought of someone watching.

Lizzie came over with a tray of sausages and burgers. 'Ladies, you're so busy chatting I thought I'd bring the food to you.'

'That's very kind of you, Lizzie. Well, Jane, here goes my diet.' She took a plate from the trestle table and picked a couple of sausages and a burger. 'They look amazing. You can't be on a diet when you're invited to a barbecue, can you?' she said to Lizzie.

'Nope, help yourself to the rolls and salad behind you and come for more if you want. Dad bought loads.' Pauline chuckled as Lizzie walked away. Jane picked up a roll and slid her sausage between it. *God, that tasted so good.*

Pauline handed her a glass of cold champagne. 'Just the one, Jane, you have to have it. It's champagne, not Prosecco and tastes divine with a hotdog. Besides, I feel awful for earlier I do hope you forgive me. Let's drink to friendship.' Jane took the proffered glass and clinked it with hers. *Well, it would be rude not to accept champagne.* She knew a fact about champagne; the smaller the bubbles the better the quality. Her glass was bursting with tiny bubbles rushing to the surface. 'I just want you to know, Jane that I'm here if you need me. Anytime, just call.'

'I will, thanks, Pauline.' She put the glass down. Patrick would be proud of her. 'It's good to know, especially with Patrick going away for chunks of time. But I know that already. You've always been so kind in the time we've been here.'

'Well, you know me, I like to help where I can. I have loads more tomatoes if you need any. You not drinking your champagne? It really is delicious you know.'

'I always need tomatoes, thanks. No, I'll abstain but if you would pass me my mocktail margarita, thanks.' It was good to know that Pauline was there if she needed something. 'You know, Pauline, I think I owe you an apology. I know Ralph will have told you that I accused you of lying the other day when I thought you'd been round, and you hadn't. I mean with the strawberries. Well, I'm sorry, I've been going through some stuff lately. It's been stressful and, well I've not been myself.'

'Say no more, my dear. Ralph did say that you'd been a little stressed and Lizzie said you were forgetting little things. Stress can do that to you. I remember work stress too. I'm so glad I'm retired. That's a plus of growing old. There aren't many pluses but that's certainly one.' They both laughed. 'And, if you want to talk about little Jasper, I've a good ear. Whenever or if ever you need me.' She patted Jane on the shoulder. 'Now, I could do with another sausage. Oh, dear, my husband is chewing Patrick's ear off again.' She turned as she walked away. 'You know a funny thing that happened to me yesterday? I was waiting in the Costa in town in the queue. I called out your name, but you ignored me. I thought I'd upset you or something but then you turned around and of course it wasn't you at all, but Lizzie was there. I don't think she saw me. I'd already embarrassed myself calling your name, so I didn't want to make another fuss. I always have a Salted Caramel and Cream Frostino. I do like them. Have you tried them? You should you know, they're delicious. Not great for the waistline but one occasionally won't hurt, don't you agree? Well, as I was saying, I wasn't going to call out again until I saw Ralph. And then I was going to go over to them and say hello, but a man went over and started talking to them. He looked very similar to the man who'd come to your house the other day. The same man I saw in town with the Boots bag. So I stayed back to observe — see what it was all about, you know what I mean. I was a bit concerned he was going to try and scam them in some way.'

Instantly the hairs on the back of Jane's neck stood on end.

'They were talking to him for only a few minutes. Something about him didn't sit right and I couldn't work out what it was. Other than he'd been here looking at your house, I mean. I thought that was a real coincidence, don't you?'

Jane's heart raced. She was sure she'd heard correctly. She hadn't imagined it, had she?

Pauline gave a tiny chuckle. She wasn't looking at Jane but at Lizzie and Ralph. 'These youngsters have very busy lives, more so than we ever had — don't you think? But you never really know what's going on with them, do you? That's what I thought anyway. I mean, him coming here and then talking to them. I wasn't happy about it, I can tell you. So, after pondering over whether to tell you, I thought I really ought to. You know just in case anything *happened*.' She rested her hand on her heart. 'God forgive me if I hadn't told you about him and something did happen. Oh, don't look so worried. He left and that was that. I asked Ralph and he said he hadn't recognised him from the other day and didn't know him. He was asking for directions, I think. I thought that was odd, don't you? I mean, we all thought he was lost when he'd been here, or it could be a coincidence, of course. Anyway, the kids were OK about it. They thought I was being overly cautious.'

He was talking to her daughter? Why? What was he thinking? Jane looked at Pauline. Perhaps Murk knew Pauline was her neighbour and would report back. To frighten her. Well, he had. He'd terrified her. Her eyes instinctively went to Lizzie. *He's taunting me, like a cat with a mouse. Telling me he could do anything if he wanted to.* She began fiddling with the hangnail she had, pulling at the skin until it tore and stung. *Oh, I know you, Murk, you'd be thrilled to see my reaction right now.* She sucked her finger. She felt a stab of fear in her solar plexus. He was trying to erode her sanity by touching every part of her life. Would Patrick be next?

Did she come clean now with Patick and confide the truth? Or keep it where it's been hidden all these years? Locked away in the depths of her memory. She'd lived with these secrets most of her life and never once wanted to tell anyone until Patrick. She looked at Lizzie and her gut told her that if she mentioned this to Patrick now after he'd approached Lizzie, Patrick would never forgive her for keeping it from him. She justified to herself that not saying anything was not the same as lying. She felt Pauline's eyes upon her and then Patrick's as he instinctively turned towards her.

And there it was. Someone *other than her* had seen *him* up close. Here. In her town — talking to Lizzie and Ralph no less. It had to be him. It was too much of a coincidence for it not to be. And that meant . . . *Dear God, I'm not losing my mind!*

CHAPTER 18

A few hours later when the party was dying down and Jane had managed to get through the day without shedding too many tears, she sat down next to the barbecue to eat the last sausage; too well done and dried out like a husk. Ralph, in his blue shorts and ABBA Voyage T-shirt smiled, looking a little concerned as Jane looked over at him. He gave a little nod of acknowledgement. The truth was . . . what was the truth? She hadn't a clue anymore. No matter how many times she thought she was safe, nothing was going to stop him. She had to try and accept it was happening and stop it, instead of thinking it wasn't happening. Now he'd approached Lizzie that pressure was even more so. If that made any sense. She grabbed her mocktail and finished it off. It was warm and not very nice. She'd left it in the sun while Pauline talked.

She didn't feel well. The shock of what Pauline had said tormented her. Something told her Pauline wouldn't mention it to Patrick. She didn't know why she knew that, but she did. She felt a little unsteady, with a racing heart that made it difficult to catch her breath. She looked at the husk-like sausage in her hand then threw it back on the barbecue.

Pauline quickly took hold of her arm as she swayed, nearly falling off the chair. She staggered to her feet, lost her balance and banged into the table. Pauline guided her back to the chair. 'Jane, you look terrible. Are you OK?'

Her tongue felt fuzzy and large in her mouth; she was dizzy and disorientated. Not unlike how she'd felt the other day when the candle arrived — or not, as everyone kept telling her.

'You need to sit down and have some water. You might have overdone it with the wine. It's very hot today and that doesn't help.' Her head was banging, that was true. Maybe it was dehydration or a bit of sunstroke. She really didn't feel well.

The absolute last thing she wanted was to faint but that was how she was feeling right now as her heart hammered and sweat covered her skin. *How is this happening to me again?* She was not drunk and yet she felt and looked it; she was certain of it. Her thoughts stumbled — trying to remember what she was just thinking, her mind had gone blank. Her breathing was fast and shallow. She was scared, she realised. Scared at what was happening to her and how. Unable to calm herself, she felt herself on the verge of hysteria from fear at her loss of control.

She slumped backwards on the chair and took the glass of cool water that Pauline proffered. Her hand shook. 'My dear, you look as if you might be suffering from heatstroke.'

She looked for Patrick. He was on his way back to the garden with Tony. They must have been in his studio. Tony liked to have a go of the drums whenever he could. A slow melodic drumming at the back of her skull gradually began to crescendo. It was only a matter of time before he saw the state she was in. *He won't believe I've not been drinking!* Maybe she was having an aneurysm; her head was bursting and her vision distorted. *Please, please let me get myself right before Patrick sees me.* It might be heatstroke like Pauline said, or lack of food, or food poisoning. She'd only had a hotdog. But so had everyone else. Looking around there was no one else looking sick. She couldn't remember what else she'd had or what she'd drunk. It was all a blank. She put her hands to her temples, dropping the empty glass on the table which knocked over a bottle of wine which sloshed Merlot all over the gingham tablecloth and her white shirt. A huge red spot appeared above her breast, spreading through the cotton. *I look like I've been shot. Oh, God, what the hell is happening to me?*

'Jane? Jane! Are you OK?' cried Pauline in a worried high-pitched tone. She wished she wouldn't make so much noise about it.

Patrick couldn't see her like this . . . But he saw the commotion. He strode over. She looked at Pauline, making such a disturbance. *Why are you behaving like this?*

'She was OK then suddenly she wasn't. I think it could be sunstroke,' Pauline said to him and sighed as if in relief that he was there to help and take over. 'It's easily done, you know,' she whispered. 'She's had a bit to drink by the way but only a bit, but it is very hot today. I don't think she drank any water. She could be dehydrated.'

The drumming in her head built and built and finally climaxed in a crescendo of flashing lights behind her eyes then everything in her vision was soft and flowing. Voices gentle, colours so bright they were stunning and disturbing. She heard voices whispering around her. Ralph came over, his movements disjoint, his smile overgenerous. Lizzie, horror-struck behind him looking at her aghast. *They think I'm drunk!* She could see it in their faces. But she wasn't. She wasn't bloody drunk!

She knew that much. She *knew* that. She hadn't drunk enough for this sort of reaction. She'd only had half a glass. Or had she, she couldn't remember exactly. She wasn't drunk though. She absolutely *knew* she wasn't drunk. This was like the other times she'd had a little wine only she felt much worse today. Had someone spiked her drink? Was that it? *Has somebody been spiking my drinks? Is that the answer?*

Patrick checked her forehead, then wrapped some ice cubes in a tea towel and placed them against the back of her neck, holding them in place. He gave her another glass of water. 'You might be dehydrated,' he said giving her a look that suggested he thought she wasn't, and that she was just plain drunk. *Why don't you believe me after I promised I wouldn't?* Because of the way you look.

She turned to face him and nearly fell off the chair. He grabbed her. 'Come on, let's get you inside.' He supported her under the arms. 'Put your arm around my waist. Lizzie, will you take the other side.'

Her head dropped forward, too heavy to hold up. Her words wouldn't come out. She was mortified how everyone was looking at her.

'What the fuck have you taken, Jane?' He was losing patience with her, she heard it in his voice.

She shook her head, unable to get the words to flow.

Pauline, Tony and Ralph corralled around them. She felt hemmed in; it was still difficult to breathe but more so to get her words out. When they got to the back door, she managed to finally get some words out. 'I'm sorry, I didn't drink. I didn't.'

'Jane! Be quiet, you sound totally pissed. I can't believe you've got yourself into this state. What were you thinking? You promised.'

'But I didn't.'

'I can see that.'

'I didn't.'

Inside the kitchen he laid her on the sofa. 'Here, have more water.'

Lizzie had the foresight to fetch some the moment they got inside. Jane drank the glass. She was so thirsty. Her mouth felt like the inside of a sand bucket.

'Do you want something to eat?' he asked passing her a few small sausages Pauline carried in. He sounded stressed, worried, and angry all rolled into one. He was angry with her for drinking. She wished he wouldn't be. 'You didn't eat breakfast and if you had wine, it might have gone to your head too quickly, especially with this heat.' He was being kind, trying to be, anyway. She batted him away when he tried to force a sausage into her mouth.

'Look at her eyes, Mr C. She doesn't look right. They look weird.'

Everything looked so beautiful. The colours so bright. Why wasn't it like this all the time?

'What?' Patrick said, shocked and looked closely at her. 'I think she's got sunstroke.'

'Has she taken something?'

'Mum only takes paracetamol and ibuprofen. That wouldn't affect her if she had alcohol,' said Lizzie, defensively.

'I know, Lizzie, love,' said Pauline. 'Could she have got something from somewhere? Has she been to the doctors? She's been so low since Jasper died. Maybe she didn't want to tell you?'

'No, Jane wouldn't do that. She's not an idiot. Worst case is she's drunk too much, and the sun's got to her.' Patrick didn't sound convinced. 'Look, she'll be fine in a little while,' he tried to reassure them. 'She's got a touch of sunstroke. I'm sure that's all it is.'

'But her eyes, Mr C, look—'

'Will you shut up!' Patrick yelled at him.

'Yeah, shut up, Ralph. Shut the FUCK up.' Jane pointed her finger at him and laughed, pleased her words came out so clearly.

Lizzie gasped. 'Mum, shut up. Why would you say that?'

'Jane, please, shut up. Be quiet.' Patrick's voice was heavy with embarrassment. 'Sorry, Ralph.' He apologised for her as well as for himself. It made her sad he did that. He bent over so only she could hear him. 'Jane,' he said quietly almost a whisper, 'do I need to worry?'

She smiled and grinned like a fool, then reached up and stroked his face. 'Nah, I'm good. I feel great now.' She pointed at Ralph again, waggling her finger. Then she frowned. There was the possibility that she had it wrong and Ralph . . . Nah, she didn't. She wanted to pick the flowers — so pretty in the pots by the door. 'I want the flowers, darling. Let's go pick them together.' She struggled to stand up, but he pushed her back down. She crashed back onto the sofa and burst out laughing.

'Lizzie, come here and help me get your mum upstairs.'

'I'll help, Mr C.'

Jane laughed and wagged her finger at him, again and winked.

'What does that mean?' asked Lizzie annoyed. 'Why the hell is she winking at you? Ralph? Do you know?'

'How would I know?' he snapped making Patrick look at him severely. 'Sorry, Mr C. Come on, let's get her upstairs.'

'Dad—'

'Lizzie, be quiet. Just help me get her upstairs, get the bed ready, and take a glass of water up with you.'

He pulled her off the sofa. Pauline made herself scarce.

Not until they were upstairs in their bedroom alone, did he say another word. But before he did, he looked over at the bedside table. And there it was, waiting for him to find. The sheath of four tablets.

CHAPTER 19

The next morning, Jane woke with a thick head. She steadily sat up, finding Lizzie sat in the armchair by the window. 'Hey, morning.'

'Mum! How are you?' She sounded concerned but her words were cutting. In fact, she looked really pissed off with her. It tore at Jane's heart.

'I feel crap actually. What happened to me?' She grappled with the words inside her head that seemed to be slightly out of her reach and out of sync. She couldn't remember much if anything. She understood she'd embarrassed herself in front of her friends and Ralph's family, from the disappointment that flared in her daughter's face.

'You got drunk and embarrassed yourself. Luckily it was only Ralph's family who saw you.'

'Oh, right, I don't remember any of that.' Only keeling over and Patrick dragging her inside. *Is there more? Christ.*

'Probably better that way. There's some fresh water next to you.'

'Did you sleep there?' She pushed her fingers into her temples to ease the pain.

'No, Dad slept here. We were taking it in turns to watch you in case you choked on your own vomit.'

'Ewe, gross, Lizzie.' Was she kidding? Vomit?

'Well, that's what happens to drunks. Didn't you know?'

Wow the vitriol stung. 'But I didn't drink anything other than half a glass of wine so how could I have been drunk? Don't you think that somebody spiked my drink? Are there any painkillers about? Could you get me some?' Reaching over for the water, she saw the sheath of pills. 'What are these?'

'That's what we were wondering, Mum.'

'Lizzie don't say it like that. These aren't mine. I've never seen them before. What are they doing here?' She picked them up and looked them over. She'd never seen these before. Where had they come from? They had to belong to some-body in this house. 'Does Ralph take medication?' she asked. Lizzie scowled at her. She sounded accusatory and immedi-ately regretted her tone. But honestly that was how she felt right now having slept off whatever had been given her.

'Sorry? Why would you ask that? God, Mum, you really scared us!' she yelled. Jane winced at the volume. 'All we wanted was a nice barbecue. Everything turned out crap. You spoiled it all by getting sloshed and taking something. You promised you wouldn't drink, but no, it's too much for you to keep a promise, isn't it.' Her words sliced her in half. 'Are you actually suggesting he had something to do with how you behaved?' Lizzie put down her phone and stared at her as if she'd called him a paedophile. 'I had to put you to bed! Me! Your daughter putting her mother to bed. Have you any idea how crap that made me feel? And all because you were drunk.' Lizzie looked fit to burst.

'Lizzie, for goodness' sake, calm down. I was simply ask-ing a question. Can't I ask a question in my own house?' She felt beaten.

'You can but you can't imply stuff like that.'

For the love of God. 'I'd appreciate it if you would please give me the benefit of the doubt. I didn't drink yesterday and something else might be at play here. That isn't a lot to ask.'

Was Murk watching this? A game in which he controlled the players? Lizzie and Patrick — in denial that anything other than her own drinking was to blame. Ralph, Pauline and Tony — the lovingly kind neighbours. And she the schmuck, smack centre in his plans, too afraid to come clean with her husband. The veiled threat that he could control and destroy her life hovered over her.

'Oh, really? But we all *saw* you! Come on, let's hear your defence. I'm willing to hear anything you have to say, Mum. But suggesting Ralph did this is way off.' She sounded as if she wanted nothing more to do with it. It was cut and dry. Mum drank too much. End off.

There was a pause, and she sensed this was a fine line she was about to cross. Accusing a nineteen-year-old's best friend of harming her mother was going to alienate her daughter.

In the distance she heard Patrick talking with Ralph in the kitchen. She could see that Lizzie was rattled by her suspicions and waiting for an apology.

The words flew from her mouth with a snap. 'Lizzie, these aren't MINE. So, if they're not mine, whose are they?'

'And I want to know why you're asking me? Those are your pills, Mother. You have them by *your* bed.'

Christ. My daughter would be a crap detective. 'I simply asked you a question, Lizzie.' She had an overwhelming need to slap her right now. She reached for the painkillers she kept in the drawer; her head hurt. She didn't need this lambasting. 'Well? Is Ralph taking medication or not?' She swallowed two with half the glass of water.

Patrick arrived with tea. 'Morning.' His voice was kind, but she saw his unspoken concern in his eyes. 'I've put sugar in to give you energy. Fancy some food? Bacon sandwich? Everyone likes a good breakfast after a hangover.'

'Patrick—'

'Jane, just drink your tea for now. We'll talk about it when you're feeling more yourself.'

'She just accused Ralph of giving her those pills, Dad.' Lizzie waited for his reply and his support.

'I heard, that's why I went down to make the tea. Ralph came over to see how you were by the way. Pauline made you some kind of ugly-looking shake.' He pulled a face. 'She said it would help your head but I'm not so sure.'

Her lips twitched. She saw what he was doing, trying to bring down the tension in the room.

'So, what are you going to say about it, Dad?'

'Well, we have to look at every possibility, Lizzie—'

'What?'

'I'm not saying you're not drinking, Jane, because it's all I see. But I'm willing to think something else might be going on here.'

'Dad! I don't believe you're saying this.'

'It's not like your mum to be this way, is it? We know she's been out of sorts lately. Come on, Lizzie, think about it. I know it sounds outlandish, but we must at least hear what she is trying to tell us.'

He deflated her anger in an instant with his support. Thank God he was willing to listen to her.

'So, will you answer your mother's question, please? Is Ralph taking any medication?'

'No. No he doesn't take any *medication*,' Lizzie said, her wide-eyed look holding her mum's gaze. Jane knew that if Lizzie was certain of her answer, she would defend it with questions as to why they kept asking. But Lizzie said nothing. And that worried her, that she knew Ralph was taking something.

'You know what I think, Lizzie? I think you know that he is taking something but you're too afraid to admit it. What are these?' Jane held up the sheath of tablets. 'Are you taking them too?'

'What the fuck, Mum! No way. I do not do drugs and neither does he. How could you ask that?'

'The same way you ask it of me. By telling me not asking me. It's not nice, is it?' She was furious, and now convinced that somehow he — or someone — had spiked her drink. And angrier still that Lizzie wouldn't even consider the notion.

Lizzie blinked, dumbfounded. Jane saw the tears gathered in her eyes and suddenly thought she'd gone too far. *God. What kind of mother am I?*

'Calm down, Lizzie.' Patrick tried to stop the situation escalating. Lizzie batted away the tears. 'You know if he's taking drugs you have to tell us.'

Lizzie's confidence faltered. 'If you don't come clean, we're going to have to stop him coming over and tell his parents. And the police.'

Lizzie sniffed, wiped her nose with the back of her hand. She picked at a loose thread on the arm of the chair. 'OK, yes, he is, but they're not drugs as you think.' Her words made Jane flinch. She left the room, returning a few moments later.

'Sorry, Mum.' Lizzie sounded genuinely apologetic and took out a packet of tablets from her pocket and handed them over. On the label was Ralph's name. Jane couldn't pronounce the name of the tablet and googled it.

Bipolar medication. Mood stabilising medication to control manic or hypomanic episodes.

Jane took out the sheath inside — they were the same as the ones on her bedside.

'So, there you have it. He does not use recreational drugs,' Lizzie stated defiantly. 'He can't. It would really mess him up. I know he left them in the kitchen yesterday. He'd forgotten to take them in the morning. Pauline brought them over. He must have left them out to remember to take them home and you picked them up by mistake, thinking they were yours.'

Jane held the packet of pills. 'I picked them up? No, Lizzie I didn't, and why would I? I'm not taking any medication. Why would I think a sheath of tablets lying around was mine? That makes no sense.'

'She isn't, Lizzie,' Patrick confirmed. 'She isn't taking anything. How did they get here in your mum's bedroom?'

'It was you, Mum.' She laughed a little manically. 'It had to be you. Ralph didn't give them to you. Fuck, here you go again. Why on earth would he? That's what you're implying, isn't it?' She stormed out, calling from the door, 'I'm going over to his now. I'll see you later or I might stay over at Bev's.'

Patrick sighed deeply. 'Jane, I'm trying to understand what's going on, really, I am. I want to believe you. I just don't get how they got here? Ralph? Really? But why would he put them here? For what reason? You know him, we like him. There's no malice in the lad. I just don't understand. D'you think maybe he had them in his hand ready to take or to put them away in Lizzie's room to keep safe and — I'm fishing now, so hear me out, he got distracted, came in here . . .' He walked to the window. 'You can see the garden from here. What if he came in to look out the window, heard something and went to check it out. I don't know, I really don't know, I'm waffling, I know I am, love, but I just don't buy it that he deliberately put them down on your bedside table or even gave them to you. Jee-zus, I mean it could have killed you. No.' He shook his head. 'No, I don't buy it.'

'Huh! Neither do I, but what other way did they get here?' It felt awful to be blaming Ralph for this. She felt guilty and . . . For goodness' sake, what if somehow, fuck knows how, it had been her?

'But you definitely took something. I could see it in your eyes, babe. You know I see these musicians high all the time. I know the signs. I just didn't want to say in front of everyone.'

'I didn't take any pills, Patrick.'

She remembered what Pauline said about Lizzie and Ralph talking to Murk in Costa. It had to have been him. Her description of him was so like him and like the man who came to the house.

And then an idea struck. She'd seen the little boat a few times that she couldn't account for. What if it was him and he'd been in the house while they were in the garden and seen Ralph's tablets? And dropped one in the Merlot glass that now she remembered was conveniently placed on the kitchen table. She picked it up without thinking how or why it was there. What if? She was exhausted. She wanted to talk more, get to the bottom of what had happened to her, but she didn't have the energy right now. She needed to sleep.

CHAPTER 20

That evening, Lizzie found her mother in the lounge, munching on a bag of salt and vinegar crisps with a coffee resting on the arm of the sofa and surfing the channels on the TV.

Lizzie flopped down next to her. Jane muted the TV. Seeing Lizzie distressed and having no answers for her made Jane worry how far her daughter was going to take this rift between them.

'OK, so I think I ought to stay at Bev's for now. You know, until you get better. Pauline thinks it's a good idea. Anyway, so, that's it. I've told you now. I'm not going far. You know where she lives, and you have her number.' She sounded embarrassed saying it like she wasn't a hundred per cent sure about leaving but liked making a point about how cross she was with Jane.

'Look, there's no need for you to do this . . .' *Who is bloody Pauline to say it's a good idea!* She didn't share that thought aloud, knowing now was not the time to pick on that family.

'Are you kidding? Yes, there is, Mum. You clearly don't trust him, and I'm offended that you feel that way. He's my friend. Probably my best friend. Well kind of anyway, in boys, I mean.'

'You can't go and stay at Bev's. What will her mother think?'

'What will she think? Well, she's fine about it. And Pauline knows why because I told her what you said about Ralph. I could hardly not. It would make it difficult for Ralph having to lie to her when she asked him why I was staying at Bev's. He'd tell her anyway. Better to be upfront, I think.'

'Oh, Lizzie you didn't!'

'Ha, you thought I wouldn't? Why would you think that?' Lizzie shook her head in disbelief. 'I had to give her a reason and the truth was the best option. I don't like to *lie*, Mum.'

Patrick joined them with a coffee and sat in the armchair opposite.

'Lizzie, really, you don't need to move out,' Jane ventured again. 'This is your home.'

'Mum, stop, it's only Bev's house. Look, it will make things easier for you.'

'She's right, Jane. If you don't feel comfortable around Ralph and he's always coming and going it might be best for the time being.'

'Did you know about this?'

'We spoke about it just a little while ago. I told her she had to tell you herself.'

'So he won't be coming to the studio anymore?' She bet they hadn't thought of that.

'Ah, yes that might be a problem,' he said.

'Nope, he's thought of that. He'll call you, Dad, and he will knock on the door. He won't come over if you're not here. Is that OK with you, Mum?' She gave her a questioning look.

'But, Lizzie, I don't want you to think you have to go. It's a bit drastic, isn't it?' *God, teenagers*. She looked at Patrick for support. He gave her a nod of reassurance.

'Look, calm down, Jane. She's right, we can't stop her if that's what she wants to do. Let's just all take a breath here. We don't need to fall out about this.'

I don't want this. It feels like I'm driving Lizzie away.

'Mum you're making more of this than there needs to be. Stop being so dramatic.'

Patrick stood up and perched on the arm of the sofa next to her, taking her coffee and putting it safely on the coffee table. He leaned down to her as if to kiss her, then whispered, 'If you go in all heavy, she might not want to come back. Let's not make more of this than her needing some breathing space right now.'

'Right then.' Lizzie stood up. 'Ralph's upstairs helping me pack a few things so I'm not back and forth all the time.' She gave them a nervous grin. Her chagrin showed in her demeanour as she nibbled the skin around her fingernails. *Was this Ralph's suggestion?*

They watched the news on the telly waiting for Lizzie to come back downstairs but Jane wasn't really listening; she was too worried about what she was doing to her daughter.

'Well, I'm off. Ralph's waiting outside. I thought it best for him to stay out of your way, Mum'

'Lizzie, be careful will you.'

'Mum, Christ, don't you ever give up?' Her anger was instantly palpable around them.

'What? I only said be careful.'

'I know! But it's the way you said it, Mum — you need to hear yourself.' Lizzie shrugged shaking her head as if it was all too much. She grabbed her cardigan, hugged Patrick and waved at her. And it stung.

'Bye,' Jane said, but her daughter walked out without comment or turning back. Jane hurt inside like she'd been torn apart in two. Maybe this was the time to sort out a therapist like she'd promised Patrick she would. It felt like her world was crumbling.

The silence around her fell heavily on her chest. *What is happening to my family?*

Her phone pinged. Desolately she glanced at her phone screen. An email from Suzanna. What now? She couldn't take something going wrong with her work, too. She opened it. Then stared at it as if she'd misread.

'Everything OK?' asked Patrick.

'It's Suzanna. She says the illustrations I sent were incomplete, that only half the batch was attached. I don't understand. I had them in a file and saved under her name and date. I know I sent them all.' Her mood flared, unease posturing as anger. 'It's that damned computer! Something's up with it. I knew there was — only the other day something went wrong with my emails.'

'Go check on your desktop. Don't get all wired up. It's probably a mishap. You've been a bit off these last few days.' He didn't make eye contact when he said that. Annoyed by his inference she darted upstairs.

At her computer, Jane opened the relevant file. Patrick stood beside her. Suzanna was right. 'I don't understand. There's only half a dozen here.' She looked at the other files and found them saved in a different file marked last year.

He sighed. 'Well at least you've got them. Send them now and that's the end of it.'

But she knew she had put them all together. She'd checked and double-checked. 'I didn't make this mistake, Patrick.'

'Jane, it's easy enough to do.'

'But I didn't do it!' she snapped.

168

CHAPTER 21

The next morning, she woke early at 6.30 a.m. She reckoned she'd had three hours of sleep at most. She had to stop worrying about Lizzie. She was only at Bev's; she knew she was safe. Still, the whole thing had upset her.

She had a few new concepts to finish with a long deadline that she'd asked Suzanna to send to keep her mind busy. With no pressure of time, she felt she could relax doing them. And get on with her life and try to bring her family back together. What had happened she had no control over. Like the sense of dread she felt on waking these days.

Patrick was still asleep. Quietly, she opened her closet and pulled out a clean summer-weight dressing gown. It seemed to be a little cooler today. Jasper's bed that used to be in her bedroom, fell out, shocking her. She'd forgotten she'd put it there to stop it reminding her. She picked it up then saw a towel thrown in the back pushed down behind her shoes. Pulling it out she realised his collar was wrapped up inside it when it fell out. She smelt his odour then broke down into silent tears. She missed him so much. Careful not to wake Patrick, she walked softly out of the bedroom, holding the towel and collar close to her face.

In her office she tucked it safely into her bottom drawer. She would not have put it in her wardrobe, shoved behind her shoes. So, who had?

She sat at her desk in front of her PC monitor and opened her file. She spun around in her seat. She had an overwhelming sensation of being watched. Her hand automatically reached to the back of her neck. She rubbed the fizzing sensation to rid herself of the uncomfortable feeling. Was she feeling like this because she'd found the collar, and it brought back memories? Maybe.

Settling down to work, she found her thoughts wondering to the disappearance of the mannequin, the upheaval of her bedroom and the disappearance of Jasper's collar. Was there something linking them? She had a nagging feeling there was. There had only been the four of them on all four occasions. Wait, she remembered the day when they'd found her room in a mess. She tried to recall what it was that now bothered her about it. Something that morning had made her question something later. But in the chaos, she'd forgotten. God, what was it?

Then she remembered something else. Ralph had left them together and gone to make tea the day of the mannequin. Would that have given him time to run down to the water, maybe meet someone and help them take the mannequin away or did he do it himself? But why?

Her thoughts stacked up several possibilities.

She heard a bleep. Stopping what she was doing, she listened. There it was again. Her head swivelled to find the sound. It was in the room. *Bleep*. It came from her laptop on the chest of drawers. She'd left it there, charging, hoping she might Facetime Lizzie today. Rising from her chair she went towards it. She'd heard all about how laptop cameras got hacked. She reached over and pressed a key to wake it up. The battery warning light was on. She hadn't switched the wall socket on. Idiot. She closed it hurriedly. Anyone with some knowledge of IT could hack it. Had she been recorded all this time? If he was trying to drive her crazy, knowing her movements would be to his advantage, wouldn't they? He'd always be one step ahead of her.

Someone could be watching everything she did. A tiny camera slipped in somewhere or more than one. It would explain a lot. Patrick wouldn't go for it though and neither would the police. She had read online that these cameras could be so small and easily concealed in anything and impossible to detect without professional help. They would need the password for the Wi-Fi. That wouldn't be difficult, would it? It was written on the back of their router. Ralph knew it. And Pauline had asked for it too. Any of their friends who came, asked for the Wi-Fi code.

They could be watching her right now. It would account for the uncomfortable feeling she'd just had. And that sense of being watched in the house.

She scanned the room as a chill ran through her.

She searched on the top of the wardrobe, the paintings and photographs on the dresser and on the wall. Around lamps, coasters but found nothing. She opened her laptop and stuck Blu-Tac over the camera.

Then she sat back down, opened a browsing page, went to Facebook, and looked at Murk's page. She clicked photos and scanned through them. It was a waste of time; she had already done this. Nothing had jumped out at her before so why would it this time. This time she was looking with fresh eyes . . . Still nothing. About to close it down, her gaze fell on a photo of a lot of people gathered with him in a pub. It was taken ten years ago, the year he was sentenced. She didn't recognise anyone. But underneath was everyone's name. No one she had heard of. She took a photo of it on her phone, thinking it might come in handy later. Then she noticed the name of the Devonshire village on the wall where it had been taken. She knew why the Devon snow globe had been moved and why the candle had been sent from the Devonshire Candle Company. To remind her.

He was leaving her clues.

Letting her know it was him.

And he was closer than she thought.

Murk would know by now, if he was watching her, that she had worked out what he was up to. His intention to break up her life into small pieces.

But what if . . .

She headed downstairs, quickly, checking Patrick was still asleep as she passed the bedroom door. She went to open the front door, hesitated a moment, wondering if there might be somebody waiting for her on the other side, then pulled it wide. She let out a sigh of relief then checked the doorbell camera. That looked all right. She checked the other camera that didn't always work. No pulsing red light on the camera. It was off. But then it might have short-circuited again.

Looking out at Pauline's house, there were two cameras taking in their property. There was no way of knowing if there was a pulsing red light on theirs. If the angle of their camera was right, she was sure it would pick up her house.

After that dreadful day in London all those years ago, stumbling in on Murk killing that young lad with his bare hands, her guilt that she hadn't come forward at the time had been a heavy burden and was locked away in the dark corners of her mind — with all the other dark memories. But one day, not long after, while passing a police station she instead went in to make enquiries about the beaten-up man. But when the questions began towards her interest in the event, she'd clammed up in fear and left.

When he was finally sentenced, she believed it all to be over, for her anyway. She had followed the case in the news. There was never any mention of a witness. She was just relieved that he was locked up. But then she happened upon an article written in a newspaper some years later referring to Murk's case where it mentioned a witness had come forward whose identity was kept secret and whose testimony was what put him away. The day she read that drained the life from her.

He would think it was her. *He'd believe it was me.* She knew it as clearly as the sun rising each day. Now with everything happening to her getting worse, she knew she had to tell Patrick, or he would discover it some other way. She was sure Murk would enlighten him as to her past. How could he resist?

She had kept it a secret all this time because she was ashamed. He already knew she was keeping something from him. But he'd never imagine it would be anything close to the truth. Had she made an awful mistake in not coming clean from the beginning? She had dared to presume his reaction. What right had she to do that? Fear, she had been fearful he'd hate her. *And right now, I'm so confused as to what to do. Leaving it this long, lying to him, keeping the secret from him, knowing I had lied to him about who was behind everything that was happening to me, was much, much worse. I'm scared of which way to go. Christ, I'm damned if I do and damned if I don't.*

Was she a sitting duck?

She bolted the front door, walked back to the kitchen and made herself a strong coffee and some toast. She suddenly wanted to eat. Restless with nerves she paced the kitchen, trying to think what to do about Murk. She saw the bottle of Merlot, positioned behind the cushion on the armchair she always sat in. She had not put that there. There was no wine in the house. She'd been to the local Co-op yesterday afternoon and bought fruit and veg and no wine. She knew what Patrick would think if he saw it. Panicked, she poured it down the sink and buried the bottle in the bottom of the recycling bin.

CHAPTER 22

'I'm going to town, Jane. I'll see you later,' Patrick called from the hallway.

'OK, listen,' she called out from the top of the stairs, rushing out of her office to catch him. 'Any idea on these dates for the holiday? I need to put them in my diary and tell Suzanna.'

'Kind of, I've pencilled some in but I'm waiting for my agent to get back to me, he mentioned something about some possible work shortly and told me to hang fire, that I really wouldn't want to miss it.'

'Right, so when will you know?'

'I don't, I just have to wait. I guess in the next few days or so. If you're worrying that it's not going to happen, don't. I'll sort it asap as soon as I have word from him.'

She came downstairs. 'OK, well I have that counsellor meeting later this morning on Zoom, so be quiet when you get back, in case I'm still on it.'

'Will do, do you need anything?'

'No thanks.'

She took herself off to her office to work on her illustrations until it was time for her appointment.

When it was time, she clicked the link and waited for her host to open the meeting.

'Jane, hi. I'm Sarah, your counsellor. How are you today?' Sarah Livingston was a private practice counsellor. 'I know I said I wouldn't be able to meet with you for a few weeks, but one of my patients has cancelled and so I thought this was a perfect time for our introductory call.'

'I guess that's lucky for me. I had a devil of a time finding anyone with any availability.'

'Yes, it's very difficult to find someone quickly these days. So, let's see how we get on today. Anything you tell me is in confidence, and if by the end of the session you want to continue, then I have availability for you if you'd like more slots. Does that sound OK for you?'

'Yes, sure.' She was reassured that she didn't have to continue if she didn't want to. Although she had promised Patrick, she would see it though for a few sessions at least.

'OK, Jane. You start when you want to.'

Unsure how to begin, she thought it best to just go for it and get it out there. 'I'm really stressed right now and it's beginning to affect my life at home.'

'Do you know what's causing the stress?'

'Work, you know how it is, and I lost my dog.' She sighed. The mention of Jasper brought a lump to her throat. 'It's been hard. I . . . I've started drinking a bit too much and what I want is some coping mechanisms to help me when it all gets too much.'

'OK, well I can help with that. Is the drinking a problem do you think?'

'Oh, no, no, not at all. No. But I don't want it to become a problem, you see. So, is that something you can help me with?' God, she sounded in denial. She sensed Sarah suspected she was holding back, which she was, she wasn't ready to open up that wide just yet. This was a mistake. She was sure of it. She'd never be able to totally open up.

'Do you think you can stop drinking?'

'Oh, yes, for sure, definitely. I have actually. Stopped, that is. It would help, you know, if I have something I can do that can distract me when it all gets on top of me.' This was terrible, now she was talking to her, she knew she didn't want to discuss her life, and she sounded like an addict in denial. She was only doing this for Patrick. *I don't even have a bloody drinking problem. No, but I'm doing this for Partick. To show him I'm trying to help myself. I can do this for him, if it helps him.*

The session went on for another twenty minutes. Sarah tried to get her to open up more. She tried to go there. She just couldn't. No, no, to speak about *him* out in the open — she wasn't ready to do that — not yet. No, not yet. And to mention the random stuff happening around her? *That would sound mental!* She realised this wasn't going to work, that she was never going to open up. Coping skills for her stress would be great but there was no way she was going to tell this stranger anything more.

The meeting wrapped up and she did make another appointment, mostly to appease Patrick. To show willing. But if she was honest, she had kind of got a bit out of it. If nothing else, she'd see her again for her anxiety.

Afterwards she went out into the garden for a little pottering.

When Patrick got back, he found her deadheading her geraniums. She was in a good place. She felt happy; she had coping mechanisms that seemed to already work. Whenever she thought about Murk, she used the rubber band trick.

'You look happy — was the session that good?' He sat on one of the rattan chairs close to her.

'It helped, yes and she's given me coping mechanisms. I think it will do the trick to stop me getting too anxious.' She shied away from discussing it further. It wasn't a cure, just an aid to help her manage her anxiety and stop it escalating.

'Right, well I hope so. You really do need to try to stay in control.' He saw the look on her face. 'I didn't mean it like that. I just meant with the drinking and taking too much on.'

'Right, the drinking. God, Patrick, do you still think that I'm drinking too much? I thought you believed me when I told you I wasn't!'

'I do. I do. Look, I'm really trying to be on your side here, you know that. But you must see it from where I'm standing. If this, Sarah, can help you handle whatever is causing you this amount of anxiety then that's great. It really is.'

Something had changed with him. 'What's happened?'

'I don't know what you mean?'

'You. You seem . . . different, less tolerant.'

'No, I'm not. Well, the thing is, my agent got back to me and I've been given some work that I really want to do, but I have to go to London for a few days and—'

'You don't want to leave me alone. Is that it?' she said icily. 'You think I'll fall apart on my own because Lizzie isn't here either.'

There was a flinch, a tiny flicker of pain, in his face. 'I know you won't, but you're right, I worry. I know you're still grieving Jasper. It's only been a week. The last thing I need is for you to crumble while I'm away and get a phone call to rush back home. Sorry, that sounds selfish, I didn't mean it to come out like that.' Patrick stretched out on the garden sofa after putting up the umbrella, looking uncomfortable.

'I know. You have to go, though.' She didn't want to stop him going. 'Look, I have these new helping tools Sarah gave me, and they seem to do the job. I've work with no deadlines, well not close ones anyway. I won't come to any harm.' Jane knew this was the time to mention that her sessions with Sarah were a great help and she was going to continue to have her sessions to put his mind at ease. And that by saying Sarah was helping her see things more linear, hopefully he wouldn't feel too bad about leaving her.

'Look, the other day you unleashed some pretty combustible accusations. You need to promise me you won't hassle Lizzie about Ralph, right? We all know it was a silly mistake on your part, thinking anything other isn't helping anyone.'

She swallowed. 'But you said you believed me? I don't understand why you've changed your mind like this.' She stared at him, open-mouthed. *You believed me! What has changed?* She accepted that her behaviour was becoming hard on him, not to mention the worry of where it might lead. He didn't want to jeopardise his career, and she didn't want him to.

'I never actually said that I did. I said it was a possibility someone had tampered with your drink.'

'No, no, something has happened. What? Tell me. Tell me what's happened to make you change.'

'Look, it's Lizzie. She's upset and saying stuff like she might stay at Bev's until she has to go back to uni.' Jane's heart sank. 'I don't want there to be friction between us over this.' He looked sheepish. 'I'm thrilled you're getting help, sweetheart, really I am. But I still worry about leaving you alone.' He ran a hand over his face. She felt a little nervous, sensing an undercurrent about this conversation she didn't want to explore. 'Christ, this summer break isn't going quite as planned, is it? You have to admit it's all gone a bit tits up.'

It's all gone a bit tits up. Well, it probably had for him and Lizzie, she reflected as she tried to calm down and not reflect how the summer was going for her. She pinged her rubber band on her wrist. And she had to concede, she *was* the cause of the issues within the family. 'So, what then? You want me to apologise, again? You want me to go to Ralph and apologise on bended knee to make it all nice for everyone?'

'No, I don't, Jane. You and I both know something odd is going on here, but I feel like I'm standing on the outside. And for the record, you know I always stand by you. I would always, always support you. Put you first. Because I love you. But what bugs the hell out of me is that you are keeping something from me, and you know I would always take your side, always, but I feel you don't trust me enough to open up — I don't want you to shut me out like this. I've been patient but it's like it's the fucking Jane Carmichael show, and I have to stand by to jump in when you want me to.'

She stared at him. *Where the hell has all that come from?* She pinged the rubber band on her wrist frantically. 'I know it's been a shite summer and it's all gone a bit *tits up*. I can't help it if my anxiety has caused you so many problems.'

'It isn't your anxiety, love. It's what you're keeping from me that's causing this problem for me.'

'Actually, I think you're pissed off because you feel guilty leaving me and you really, really want to go play music with your musician friends in London — that's what I think.'

'What?' He stared at her as if he'd misheard.

'You know I'm right.' She turned and shoved the umbrella to give them more shade but pushed too hard and nearly toppled it. Patrick reached out, saving it from crashing to the ground. 'Oh, good save. You like saving things, don't you? Is that why you like saving me? Well, you don't bloody have to now. Bugger off to London. Go on.' Her blind fury wasn't allowing her any rationality, even if she knew she was totally in the wrong.

'Jane,' he began, 'stop this tirade. I love you, you know that. You have to see it from my side. I know you're going through a tough time. I know that. But you treat me like I don't matter. You demean me. You act like you're on your own dealing with whatever it is that's bothering you. It's breaking up our family. Don't you see that? I know you're stressed, upset and confused right now. But I am too. Have you ever considered how any of this is hurting me? Please, try to remember that I'm on your side. Always.'

Hearing his calm and astute reasoning removed the steel that had kept her upright and she crumbled, tears broke out into sobs, loud and crushing. She dropped onto the rattan chair next to him, catching her breath while he bent forward to calm her. Like he always did. And just like that she felt he was slipping away from her.

CHAPTER 23

Two days later, Patrick went to the studio in London, like he'd mentioned before their bust-up.

She planned to go into town, in a floral dress and sandals that made her feel carefree and brightened her mood from glum to glad. She also blow-dried her hair. The guilt and the disbursement of feelings they'd flung at one another a couple of days ago hit her hard in the chest when she recalled their words. She hadn't been nice. She grabbed her car keys and bag and drove the short distance, managing to find a parking space outside the quaint coffee shop that did great coffee.

She felt relief to be out of the house after virtually imprisoning herself there since the arrival of that damned letter. Well, no more. She pinged the rubber band on her wrist; just knowing it was there calmed her.

She wasn't going to let Murk paralyse her. And she'd show Patrick that she wasn't going to crumble if he wasn't around. She had to start pulling herself together; her behaviour was clearly rattling him. She didn't like the effect it was having on their relationship at all, especially since the barbecue.

She thought of Stephen King — that was Lizzie's fault. *The Shining* was one of his, as well as *The Mist* of course. *The*

Shining was a spine-chilling story of someone isolated within a building and what that did to the person. She couldn't erase the picture of Johnny smashing through the door with an axe, only in her mind Johnny was Murk. She would be alone tonight and for the next couple of days. She would lock up tight, ignore there might be cameras, make sure theirs were all functioning and take something to protect herself in bed — like Patrick's cricket bat. She already had it under the bed. She'd ordered more electric fans to help with the heat inside the house, knowing she was going to lock up both windows and doors. She was having them delivered to an Amazon Locker. She didn't want delivery men at her home right now.

She walked into the busy coffee shop, went to the counter and ordered a latte with oat milk and a croissant. They had the bi-fold windows open, so she sat close to them. She took her seat and waited. She logged onto the Wi-Fi and googled Curtis Murk, again. She needed to check if he was posting anything. Forearmed was forewarned. The more she knew, the better. Nothing but the crime and his prison sentence came up on Google. She clicked the article to reread. There in the small print as an aside was the mention of a last-minute witness, whose identity was secret and whose testimony had been conducive to putting him away. This was why he believed it was her. She thought of how angry he would have been thinking she had talked. She had a deep guttural feeling she was close to danger she wasn't ready for. She felt it keenly everywhere. She couldn't see in what format it would come, but now she sensed it all around. She pinged the rubber band as her heart rate increased and took the deep slow breaths Sarah had shown her would help, and they did. She felt the wormhole sweeping ever closer to suck her in, he was clever like that. She closed her eyes working on her breathing. This time she told herself, she could stop it. She had to stop it. This time she could do it. Everyone had a choice, and she wasn't going to choose to let him win and destroy her life a second time. *All I have to do is stop him, right? How difficult can it be?* He

181

was bound to make a mistake. After all he didn't really know her. Or what she was capable of. It was a very long time since he knew her. A lot had changed. She had changed.

Her coffee arrived. 'Thank you,' she said to the young girl. Slowly she tore her croissant into bite-sized pieces and, feeling calmer thanks to the exercises, she ate it, savouring the buttery taste and the fact that she was outside in the open away from home. And she was fine.

Jane left the coffee shop after promising herself that she would do this more often. She unlocked her car and climbed in. She started the engine, her hand crawling over her shoulder to ease that all too familiar sensation at the back of her neck. She turned around quickly, half expecting to find someone in the back. *Stupid. How could anyone get in? I locked it.*

She was going to take the opportunity while in town to do some shopping but first she drove to the lockers to collect the Amazon parcels. Then she parked near the market hall that hosted fresh vegetable stalls along with a delicatessen, fishmonger and butcher. She spoiled herself, filling her hessian bag until it was nearly too heavy to carry. It was time to start looking after herself, instead of cowering away, waiting.

On her way back to the car, she could feel someone staring at her from behind, their eyes burning a hole in her back; her desire was to drop her bag and rush to the car, but she didn't. She worked on her breathing as she walked and as her panic grew, she managed to control it. A shiver ran down her back then another that someone close by was going to harm her. She kept moving. Breathing in and out as Sarah had shown her. Footsteps behind her and the feeling of ants crawling over her skin made her shudder. Every instinct told her to drop the bag and bolt. She stopped suddenly, ready to face them and whipped around, forcing a teenage girl with earbuds in to slam into her.

'What the hell?' the girl yelped. 'What's wrong with you? Why did you stop like that?' she barked.

'I'm sorry, I, I forgot something. Are you OK? Did you hurt yourself?'

182

The girl shook her head, scowling. 'Wake up, Mrs.' She walked on. Jane pinged her rubber band until her wrist was red raw. Her mind was running away with her, again. She pinged some more. He was doing it to her without any effort. She hated the veiled power he had over her.

Fifteen minutes later she was home, slamming the front door behind her and bolting it. She dropped the food shopping on the kitchen island, bruising the fruit and losing two apples that rolled out of the bag and onto the floor. She switched on the kettle and made herself some Earl Grey. While she waited for it to cool down, she brought in the fans. She ran cold water over both the runaway apples and her red wrist. Even now, here in her home she could feel as if someone watched her. God! She was being silly again, she'd had no notification from her doorbell camera to make her feel that way, even so, she checked the other camera too. That seemed to be working fine. That made a change but at least nobody had been to the house. It probably felt worse because she knew she was alone. Still, she felt uneasy and couldn't shift the feeling. Until she'd unpackaged the fans, it was too hot at this time of day to keep the house locked up. The heat pent up inside escaped the moment the patio doors were flung open.

Only when she was able to breathe calmly did she sit down with her tea. The vibration of fear subsided. Idiotic to let her mind run away with itself like that. One little thing had built into a crescendo of anxiety. She needed to work harder on her new skills. All she'd wanted to do was get home. It had crossed her mind to drive to the park. To let the open space and wildlife sounds calm her but she'd worried she might not be able to get home if she left it too long. She didn't want to have to call Patrick in a state.

Had someone been watching me? That young girl? Paid to follow me?

To scare me.

She had to show him she wasn't going to be messed with. Tricks like that weren't going to work anymore. She told herself to build up her courage. She rolled her eyes at her big talk.

She had to. She wasn't going to let him destroy her. She had a wonderful life. And he wasn't going to mess it up.

A scream, raw and desperate ripped through the house, deafening her. She spilled her tea. Her gaze fixed to the window, expecting something to be there. Terror built inside her at a fantastic speed. She looked around, sure the sound came from inside the house. She waited for something to happen. For something or someone to appear. When nothing did, her ears strained to pick up any other sound in the house. She looked out of the window in case someone was in trouble. The sound seemed to come from all around.

The diabolical scream reverberated through the silence again, then stopped. She leapt up, her hands over her ears. Her eyes wide like sauces. She tried to pinpoint where the hell it was coming from. Was she still alone in the house? Was this in her mind? Was she imagining this?

The crescent was quiet. She walked to the lounge door, looked down the hall while telling herself to breathe in and out, in and out, slowly.

It was odd, but having the focus on her breathing sharpened her, made her more determined and less afraid. Or maybe it was the pep talk she'd given herself at the coffee shop that she wasn't willing to let him beat her at his stupid games. She brushed away thoughts of what Murk was capable of. What she had seen him do and what he had done. To get through this predicament, she had to start believing in herself.

Another heart-stopping scream bounced from the walls. It *was* coming from inside. She raced through the house, ready to meet whoever was doing this. In her bedroom she collected the cricket bat from under the bed and searched the house room by room. There was no one here.

She lingered on the landing, looking into her bedroom. Her fingers gripped the banister. She felt like prey being hunted. She didn't like where her thoughts were going. She longed to jump in the shower to cool down. The heat up here was oppressive. Her eyes flicked around the room. The front door handle rattled. She headed back downstairs, bat in hand, heart thumping. Laughter echoed through the house like at a party. She twirled like a ballerina to find the source. It was coming from the surround speakers. But that would imply someone *had been* in the house. The sound of breaking glass got her attention. Shaking, she tried to keep the rhythmic breathing going, but she was beyond that now, simply too frightened. She flicked the rubber band, frantically. She was better than this. This is what he wanted. Was he watching her right now? She had to show him he didn't scare her. Closing her eyes for a second, she forced her breathing to slow down. *I'm OK, I'm OK. This is not real, nothing is real. Breathe slow. Breathe slow.*

He was here.

He knew she was alone.

He had come for her. Oh God.

She grabbed her phone from her pocket about to call Patrick. A knee-jerk reaction. No. No, no, she wasn't going to do that. The police then. No. *Don't be ridiculous! And say what? That a weird sound is coming from her sound system?* Right, if he was here, she had to centre herself, not panic. If this was it, she needed to be in control.

He wasn't going to hurt her. Not straight away anyway. But she knew he wouldn't hurt her physically. He wanted to damage her for betraying him. A flashback of rubber-soled shoes squeaking on a linoleum floor jarred her. Made her catch her breath. This is what he wants. *He wants me to remember. He wants me to feel that way again.*

She wouldn't let him.

The horror of it got the better of her though and her thoughts began to spiral like before.

It all went quiet. The house was silent. She waited, looking around where the hidden speakers were. Nothing. Quiet as a graveyard.

She rang Pauline. Feeling awful that she hadn't spoken to her since Lizzie told her what she'd said about Ralph.

'Hello? Jane? Are you OK? You sound out of breath.' Pauline sounded surprised.

I'm surprised she's picked up the phone after what I said about Ralph.

She walked to the other side of the house and peered out the window but saw nobody then went back to the front where she looked over at Pauline's.

'I think there's someone prowling around the house. I heard a woman scream.' She screwed her eyes shut, ashamed of what she was saying. She knew there was no proof of that.

'I'm on my own. Tony's out. I'll come right over. Did you see anyone? Is he still there?' She spoke cautiously as if she didn't want to frighten her any more. 'Don't do anything stupid, Jane. Have you called the police? Should I?'

Maybe she should call. Pauline would think it strange if she said no.

'Yes, you call them.' She cringed at how this would look to them. *Maybe this is what Murk wants. To have it down on record that I'm hearing things, seeing things and perhaps unstable.*

'Not to worry, I'll do it now. You stay put, you hear me?'

A loud bang startled her. 'Oh, God I think they could still be here.' She nearly dropped the phone. Instantly glad Pauline was calling the police. What the hell was that? It sounded like something heavy thrown at the patio windows.

'Is the house locked up?' Pauline asked.

'No, it's roasting inside.' In a voice now almost a whisper, she said, 'I've checked everywhere. I think they've been inside while I was out.'

'What about Patrick?'

'No, I've not called him, he's in London. I don't want to disturb him.'

'I see, well if you're sure,' Pauline said sounding surprised. 'But—''

She cut her off. 'There's no point dragging him back. There's nothing to see. I think they've gone now.' She cringed at how ridiculous she sounded not wanting to call Patrick.

This is what he said he was worried about. Did Murk know he'd said that? Was this why he was playing this game? She bit her lip. 'Please don't call him, Pauline, it will only worry him. I'll call later. He's got an important session right now.' He'd have to pull out. They'd be cross with him. They may decide to go with someone else. He'd gain a terrible reputation. He'd walked out on a session recently because of her. No. She couldn't do it to him.

She knew if Murk wanted to harm her, he would just do it. This was him playing with her.

He was smart. A quick thinker. Hadn't he convinced the police of a huge injustice once before?

It wasn't long before Pauline arrived.

'Let's see if there's anyone outside,' she said authoritatively, walking in the front door. 'I'll go out the back. That is where you heard them, wasn't it?' she said getting straight to it. 'Give me that.' She had a no-nonsense way about her as she took the bat from her. 'What about your cameras, anything on them?'

Jane did a quick check on her phone. 'There's nothing. There's no connection.' She checked her Wi-Fi signal, it was gone. 'The Wi-Fi isn't on.' She rushed to the hallway where the router was. It was unplugged.

Jane grabbed Pauline's sleeve when she got back to the kitchen. 'Maybe you should wait for the police. I mean, he might be dangerous.' He wouldn't care who he hurt. He'd been in the house and unplugged the router. She didn't want Pauline going out there.

'He? Why d'you think it's only one person?'

Jane stalled. 'I . . . I don't, I don't know why I said that.'

'You made it sound as if you knew who it might be.'

'What? That's crazy. Of course I don't.'

'Right, so what about this scream you said you heard? I didn't hear anything. I was in the garden.'

'It was inside the house. I don't know how you didn't hear it. It was so loud. I had to cover my ears. I should come with you, Pauline. I don't like the idea of you out there alone.'

Pauline turned around. 'Inside? What do you mean? So, there was someone inside?'

'No, well not when I was here. I think they came in earlier. It was coming from the hidden speakers we have around the house. They played it through there.'

'Didn't your cameras show someone coming to the door?'

She shook her head. 'No, there was nothing there. I had no notification while I was out.'

'Huh. Really? That sounds very James Bond, my dear.' She fanned herself. 'I don't know how you can put up living here without air conditioning. Look, I'm not being condescending, but it does sound like a lot of trouble for a break in. Don't you think? I'll be quick out there. You pop the kettle on. I'm sure there'll be nobody here now. These sorts don't stay long. In out and grab what they can in a hurry. Has anything been taken?'

She hadn't checked. He wasn't there for theft. 'Not that I've noticed. Hopefully the police will be here soon.' A feeling of dread dumped itself in her stomach. *I am going to look so stupid when they question me.*

A few minutes later Pauline was back. 'Well, my dear, the back gate is locked and secure. I couldn't see any other way they could get in, only the front door and that was locked I presume.' Jane nodded. 'Of course, they could have come up the lake.'

That little boat, Jane thought.

And then she saw the snow globe on the kitchen table.

* * *

The officer, having checked the house and the garden and found nothing, asked her to tell him what had happened.

'I heard a scream,' she said putting her hands to her face, feeling ashamed that they were here and found nothing. *Silly. Silly. I shouldn't have called the police.* 'I thought it was in the house at first then realised it was coming from the speaker system we have.'

He looked at Pauline. 'And did you hear this scream?'

She looked embarrassed. 'No, sorry, I didn't.'

The officer pulled up a chair beside her. 'Mrs Carmichael, Pauline tells me you've been suffering from stress, lately. I believe your dog died recently.'

'Yes,' said Pauline coming to the rescue. 'Jasper, sweet little thing. He drowned. Jane's been very upset. She doesn't like to talk about it.'

'Thank you, can I ask Mrs Carmichael, please?' the officer said.

'Oh, right, yes of course.'

'Yes, he did. I have been upset that's right, but I know what I heard, officer,' she insisted.

'OK, now you said you'd been out shopping and came back and there was nothing that appeared out of the ordinary.'

'No, everything was as I left it.' *Except the snow globe. Better I don't mention that right now.*

'Have you been drinking, Mrs Carmichael?'

She flushed at the offence. 'No! I made myself a cup of tea. It's only three o'clock. Besides, I haven't been drinking lately.'

'Oh, is there a reason for that?'

God, that sounded bad. 'No, I have simply decided not to drink. It's not a crime, is it?'

'No, but Pauline mentioned there's an open bottle of wine in the kitchen and a glass partly drunk.'

Jane looked at her astonished. 'I'm so sorry, dear. I thought it was unusual, you know, at this time of day, so I mentioned it.' She dropped her eyes embarrassed. 'I only mentioned it because I thought it might help. I was trying to help, Jane. You do understand, don't you?' She gave her a weak smile.

'I know nothing of that, but—' She was about to mention the sudden appearance of wine that had been happening over the last couple of weeks, then thought better of it. 'But there was someone outside walking around my house and . . . well, the woman screaming.'

'Mrs Carmichael, can I suggest that perhaps you heard the noise then panicked and felt as if you heard something outside?'

'But there was a terrific bang in the kitchen.'

'That was a bird flying into the window. We found that, and we've removed it for you.'

'Oh.' Well that would explain it. 'But someone was in my house and somehow managed to put the sound of a woman screaming through our speaker system.' She saw his face and what it said.

'Do you know who would want to do that and why? Is there somebody who has threatened you in any way?'

If only you knew.

She shook her head. It all sounded so irrational. Just like he wanted it to.

'I heard breaking glass. Did you find anything?'

The officer stared at her a little too long to be comfortable. 'A wine bottle by the table on the patio.'

A bottle — but there are no fucking wine bottles in the house. Now there's one in the kitchen and one smashed on the patio?

Somebody had come into her house and put that snow globe in the kitchen; it hadn't walked there by itself. *Probably Murk or a henchman working for him.* And the bottle of wine. It had to have been while she was searching the house for the person putting the audio simulations through their media system and while distracted by the noise, unplugged the router and somehow deleted any footage. *But how is he doing this?* Someone young enough to escape by climbing over the locked wooden gate, perhaps. She glanced at Pauline, who smiled meekly back at her. *Why had she felt the need to mention the wine? Probably to get back at me for saying what I did about Ralph.*

'Here, Jane, have a drink of water. You're getting worked up. I'm sure there's a good explanation for the audio stuff, don't you think, officer?' She handed her the glass.

'There's no one threatening me, officer,' she said replying to his question. 'But how did the screams come through the media system — that's unusual, isn't it. It means someone was in the house, doesn't it?'

'We can assume that, yes, but maybe a simpler explanation is that you or your husband left something switched on, maybe a radio station, or some music and if it was on standby it simply switched itself back on.'

'It doesn't do that. It never has.' He didn't look convinced. She didn't like his patronising tone. 'That's not how it works. And what music could we be listening to that had that godawful screaming going on?' It was a pathetic suggestion, but she supposed he simply didn't know and didn't believe her. If she told them about Murk, then maybe they'd think differently. Then maybe not. *But that's not going to happen.*

'I don't know, Mrs Carmichael, but maybe your husband might understand it better than us. Why not wait for him to return and ask him?'

'Now, Jane I'll see the police out and come back.' When Pauline returned, she sat with her a while in the lounge. She took her hand in hers. 'Do you think you might have imagined it all?' She gave her hand a firm squeeze. 'I'm worried about you, my dear. I know you miss Jasper, but you must move on.'

Jane dredged up a smile and welled up just thinking about her little dog. Murk wouldn't have tried this on if her little dog was still around. Pauline didn't seem in a hurry to leave. *Maybe that's why he killed him.* And the temptation to confront Pauline as to why she'd felt she had to mention an open bottle of wine to the police crushed her right now. Jane had already upset her with what she'd said about Ralph. Wasn't she good enough to come over like she had? Best to leave that right now. She needed real proof and more information on how Murk was getting away with all of this so easily to prove she wasn't losing it. Patrick had already told her that her accusations about Ralph the day of the barbecue had upset Pauline a great deal.

'I have this terrible feeling deep inside something terrible might happen to Patrick,' she blurted out.

'Jane! My goodness, why would you say such a thing?'

She couldn't shake the irrational feeling. 'Sorry, Pauline, I'm just tired. I don't know why I said that.' She took a moment to gather herself. 'And I'm sorry about what I said about Ralph, truly I am. I wasn't myself; you know that. I'd hate for us to fall out over something said in haste.' *I still stand by everything I said actually.* Jane didn't want to fall out, that was true. It bothered her that Pauline might have mentioned the wine just to get back at her by letting the police know she was drinking too much at the moment.

Pauline's eyes swept over her. 'Maybe you should get some rest. Take a nap. You do look tired. I'll pop over later, check in on you.' *Wow, she's not even going to address what I said, she must really be annoyed with me.*

Jane saw her out then locked up the house and put on the new fans. She lay back on the sofa. She did feel overly tired. Maybe a catnap wouldn't be a bad idea. She could hardly keep her eyes open, strangely.

CHAPTER 24

Later after her little nap and alone in the house it seemed oddly quiet and stuffy, but she didn't want to open the patio doors. She had another headache, took some painkillers, and checked the time: five o'clock. Then remembered what had happened earlier. *Oh, God, I shouldn't have got Pauline to call the police.* It was so embarrassing.

She went upstairs for a quick shower to refresh and change into something more comfortable and cooler. On her way back downstairs, she walked into Lizzie's room. Looked around, running her finger over a satin shirt hanging from the door of her wardrobe. Then stopped when she saw it. Ralph's phone.

She was hungry and pulled out a ready-made fish pie from the fridge, sliding it into the oven. She plugged the phone into the charger. All she was doing was trying to find answers. When the pie was ready, she served it up on a plate, grabbed some cutlery, a glass of water and sat outside under the umbrella while she waited for the phone to charge. When she finished eating, she remembered the broken glass, got up to fetch the brush and pan, only there was nothing there. *I didn't clear that up, I'm absolutely certain I didn't.* Maybe Pauline did without her noticing. She was sure Ralph would have come looking for his phone, but he hadn't. That was odd. Who didn't miss their phone? And go into a tailspin if they lost it?

When she finished her food, she went back inside. The phone was charged . . . and the bottle of wine had vanished from the island. *I don't believe it. I didn't move that either. So where is it?* She checked the bins, found no trace of it. How odd. It had been there; she was certain of it. There was no wine glass out either.

Right, well, right now she was going to deal with the phone. But first she checked the house again and the outside and lastly the cameras. They were working. She checked the Wi-Fi signal on the app, there'd been a break in the signal while she'd slept. She went back indoors and locked the patio doors. Then she settled herself at the island in the kitchen. She had no clue how to go about doing this.

She had a sixth sense there was something on the phone that would help her find actual proof that something weird was going on and he was somehow involved.

Right. She had to ask herself several questions. First, she fetched a notepad and pen.

Why would Ralph be involved? She wrote down *Ralph*. Against his name she wrote: *Paid? Debt owed? Friend? Family? Forced to do it?* But what were the chances of him knowing Murk? Zero, in all honesty. And how would he anyway? The man had been in prison. The only reason she thought that way was because Pauline had mentioned seeing him and Lizzie talking to someone who resembled Murk. But it could have been anyone. That was something she was annoyed with herself at. Not asking Lizzie about him after Pauline had told her. Well, that would have gone down brilliantly, wouldn't it at the time when it had all kicked off at the barbecue. No, she didn't need any more fallings out with Lizzie. She'd have to work it out herself.

She wrote down *Surveillance* in a separate column. Had Murk been watching her from prison?

Ralph had been at Manchester Uni then. *Oh God! Is it a coincidence that Murk was in Strangeways?* But still, a young boy at university and a prisoner at Strangeways? How would they meet? What if there was a music programme at the prison or something? And what if the university worked with the prison to teach music to prisoners and the students had to volunteer to get points for working in the community? What if it was part of the syllabus that they had to give back their time helping others?

But if he *did* know Murk . . . what if he happened to mention them buying this house just in normal conversation? It wasn't implausible that he spoke about them. Ordinarily you wouldn't think much of it or even mention it, but he might have mentioned Patrick being a musician and that he'd played with famous bands as a topic of conversation. That could be credible. Ralph might have been excited because he was a musician himself. *Murk would know everything about me,* she was certain and then if he was told parole was likely he would stop at nothing to find out every detail of her life. Because he already had a plan. Maybe she thought she had evaded him all these years but in fact he had been keeping tabs on her.

This was the area they had wanted to live in, and they'd looked at tons of houses, never finding the right one. They wanted to be near water, thinking the chances of finding the right house with water close by and within their price range was a long shot.

And then she remembered someone Patrick knew, who told him about this house. They'd heard the sellers wanted a quiet sale without going on the open market. It seemed like a stroke of luck at the time. She did remember talking with Pauline and maybe Ralph had been around at the time they came to view. Either they told Pauline about Patrick's music career or Ralph had been there and heard it himself.

If Ralph was somehow in touch with Murk, and she still hadn't worked that bit out, he would and might have fed him information without realising he was.

She tapped the screen on the phone to wake it up. A password request came up. She stared at the screen. She had no clue what it could be. It hadn't occurred to her it might be passcode protected which was really rather stupid.

She fetched her laptop, opened Google and typed in *how to bypass locked iPhone*. Heaps of suggestions appeared. Several suggested going to YouTube. She dismissed them as poppycock after giving a couple of them all of two minutes of her time. The third video told her that attempting to bypass the code would delete all the information, taking it back to factory settings. Exactly what she didn't want to happen. There was still the possibility that Ralph might have already wiped the phone from his laptop when he found it missing. But it still had his screensaver of David Bowie. She had no idea if that would vanish too if the phone was wiped. She googled another idea. *How to open messages from locked iPhone on computer*. That was something she'd seen on TV. It mentioned retrieving from iCloud. But she still needed a password. None of this was going to plan. Then she read that to read iMessages when your iPhone had locked you out could be done on your computer. She looked for the iMessage symbol on her computer, only to realise it had to be Ralph's laptop not hers that she needed. She slapped the lid shut. And then a worm of an idea began. She had rarely seen Ralph on his laptop, but knew he had one, which meant he *might* not use it very much. She didn't think she'd seen him take it. If he was so remiss about his phone maybe he was the same about his laptop. He might not miss it as earnestly as Lizzie would hers now that he was on summer break. Or better still not register that someone could read his iMessages from it.

In Lizzie's room she searched for it. It was such a long shot, what were the chances? She looked around Lizzie's messy bedroom. *But where to look?* She didn't bother with the wardrobe. It had to be somewhere where he might just have left it. She looked at the piles of store bags shoved in the corner of the room. Her bedside table, under the bed. And she couldn't believe it. Her hand fell on what felt as if it might be a laptop.

She pulled it out quickly, opening the screen up. Darkness stared back at her.

She plugged it in to charge on the kitchen table next to the iPhone.

Soon it had enough charge to turn itself on. The little ball spun and spun until finally the Apple symbol appeared. At last, she might be getting somewhere. The desktop icons loaded. He must be signed in as there was no request for a password. She smiled, feeling good with herself. *About time something went in my favour.*

There wasn't much on the desktop. She clicked the iMessage icon and let out a little yelp of joy as all Ralph's iMessages loaded up in front of her eyes. *Whoa, amazing.*

She knew you could sign into your Apple account and delete a phone if you lost it. *Why hasn't he?* She sprang back from the laptop. *This is too easy, surely.*

A chain of messages rose up in front of her, and the temptation was too much. There were names she didn't recognise interspersed with messages from Lizzie. Looking for a recognisable name, preferably Curtis or Murk she kept scrolling. Message after message between him and Lizzie and a bunch of other friends. Some from Patrick.

She scrolled further down the timeline . . . to the day of Murk's release. There was a strange message from Ralph to someone called Jon.

Ralph: *Hey, sorry I can't make it today. I'll be there tomorrow. Mum asked if you have a place to stay.*

Jon: *I do. Thanks. Will text her soon tell her. Have you done your homework?*

Ralph: *It's done. Won't be a problem.*

Jon replied with a thumbs up and laughing emoji. The conversation continued.

Jon: *Meeting with the gang later when I get back. Will you join us at some point?*

Ralph: *Will do. Can Mum come?*

Jon: *Why not if she can face it.*

What might Pauline not be able to face? And why on earth would Ralph want Pauline to go with him? And what homework? Ralph was hardly of an age where adult interaction with homework was necessary. Maybe it referred to something else. Like what though?

Who was this Jon person? Was it a coincidence it was sent on that date? Or was she just putting two and two together and coming up with five? This Jon person wasn't mentioned anywhere else. Not before or after. She had a hunch and checked his contacts. There was a Jon with no surname only a mobile number. She didn't know why, but she thought it might be useful, so she added it to her phone: *Jon.*

She wrote on her pad, *Mum. Jon.* Why did it feel as if that message had a sense of urgency about it. And who was the gang Jon spoke about? People he worked with? Drinking buddies?

Nothing she read gave her any reassurance that this was or wasn't Murk. *Am I trying to make it fit my idea that I want Ralph to be involved with Murk, so I have someone to blame for all that is going on?* No. Because she was sure inside her gut that she was right.

CHAPTER 25

'Knock, knock,' Pauline called through the letterbox. 'Jane, my dear, it's only me come to check on you.'

Jane quickly closed the laptop and hid it under the sofa cushion and put Ralph's phone in her pocket. She checked the time: six o'clock.

'Just a sec,' she called back. She opened the door. 'Sorry, Pauline I was in the middle of something. Come in, you didn't have to come over again.'

'Oh, don't be silly. I'm just checking on you. How you feeling, dear? Have you spoken to Patrick? I came around the back, but you've still got the gate locked. Good call. I take it everything's been OK?' She fanned herself with a magazine she brought with her.

'No, he's probably still in the session. He'll call as soon as he gets a moment.' Guilt flooded her for hiding Ralph's stuff from her friend. She was his mother, after all. She was struggling with the knowledge that if he was in contact with a convict, his mother ought to know, shouldn't she? Pauline had told her about seeing Lizzie and Ralph talking with a stranger, aka, Murk in Costa because she feared it might have been important. And yet, as much as the guilt pulled at her, something told her that she should hold off for the time being. Better get her facts straight before ploughing ahead. *I've already accused him of feeding me pills and that was putting pressure on their friendship.* Pauline hadn't said she accepted her apology over that.

Pauline moved past her to sit on the sofa in the snug area of the kitchen. She let out a deep sigh. Jane felt herself redden. She felt Pauline's eyes upon her as if probing for something.

'You're probably right. Have you eaten, Jane? Tony and I were about to have an early dinner, nothing special, too hot for hot food, just a salad and cold chicken. Why not come over and join us? It will do you good and put my mind to rest that you're eating. And it's lovely and cool at ours — you'll feel wonderful there. Oh, Ralph's going to bunk at some friend's house near the trail he's going to walk tomorrow.' She chuckled. Jane lowered her eyes, aware that was probably aimed at her. 'It's been too hot to do it all in a day so he's going to do a shorter one tomorrow. So just Tony and me at home. How's Lizzie getting on at the festival?'

A stab of pain that Lizzie hadn't called and told her, hurt. It would explain why she hadn't heard from her, she guessed. No signal. She hoped that was why. 'I guess she's having a ball, she has no signal there I imagine so I've heard very little.' She didn't want to admit her daughter hadn't even bothered to tell he she was going to the festival this week. Although she knew she had tickets for Horsham festival, only had forgotten the dates. *It would have been nice of her to just drop me a text; it wouldn't have killed her, would it.*

'Oh, marvellous, right I'll text you, shall I, when it's ready?'

'Yes do. Looking forward to it. Can I bring anything?' It was good to have a friend so close by. She really did appreciate her kindness. Although she wasn't that hungry after her fish pie, she didn't want to upset her. Especially in light of what she'd done for her earlier.

'Of course not. Now just lock up the house before you come over. We don't want a repeat of earlier, do we?' She hauled herself out of the chair. 'About fifteen minutes max. It's all practically ready.'

'I'll go get cleaned up a bit. I might go to the island afterwards, so I won't stay long.'

'Do you think that's a good idea? I mean with Patrick away. It's only you who has a boat.'

'Yes, I'll be fine, Pauline, honestly. It doesn't start to get dark until about eight. I won't stay at yours too long. An hour over there will do me good.'

'Well, I'm not so sure you ought to go. Do you want me to come with you? I can bring my book, and you can get on with your drawings. I don't mind.'

It was a lovely gesture and kind of her. But she'd rather be on her own. She laughed. 'Pauline, I will be fine. I will have my mobile with me.'

'If you think so. Right, I'll get off. See you in about fifteen minutes.'

After Pauline left, she checked that the cameras were working and saw the Ring doorbell notification from when Pauline came over. That was comforting that it was working. The Wi-Fi icon in the bottom corner said that coverage was low. She frowned; it was usually very good. No matter, as long as it was working, they did get ups and downs with it sometimes. *I'm not going to read anything into that.*

Before she left, walking thought the kitchen after locking the doors, she thought about the bottle of wine that had appeared and then vanished. Had it though? Since she hadn't drunk any wine, she was much more clear-minded. Except for earlier after the police left. She'd felt tired and groggy but all she'd had was water. Maybe she'd been a little dehydrated.

At Pauline's she understood why Lizzie kept on at her about air conditioning. It was divine to walk into their cool house. Maybe Lizzie had asked Pauline to show her how wonderful it was, hence the invitation. Her house was sparse, with little in the way of ornaments or photographs. She'd noticed this before but strangely this time she felt it acutely odd. It was always something that surprised her. No family photos or holiday shots gracing any of the surfaces. There wasn't even a photo of Ralph. Unlike her home which was full of family photos.

They sat in the kitchen all lovely and cool.

'I know it's kind of sacrilege to eat indoors when it's so lovely out there, but it's too hot for me,' said Pauline.

'No, no don't worry about it. It makes a change to be able to escape it. I understand why Lizzie goes on about it so much.'

Pauline laughed. 'Yes, she's very taken with it.'

Tony brought out some Chardonnay. 'Lovely and crisp and cold, pass me your glass, Jane.'

She covered the top of the glass with her hand. 'Sorry, Tony. I don't wish to be rude but I'm off wine right now.'

'Oh!' He seemed hurt. 'Really? It's very good, you know.'

'Tony stop putting pressure on the girl, she said no. Pour me some and fetch some fizzy water or apple juice. What would you prefer, Jane, darling?'

'Water is fine, thank you.'

As they tucked into the chicken salad the conversation flowed and Jane began to relax. When she'd left her house to come over, she'd worried what she might find when she got back. But she'd locked the place up and made sure the cameras were all working. Not that they could rely at all on the one at the back. Often it said it was working but then would conk out, only to start up again later but with fuzzy recordings.

'So how are you coping without Jasper, Jane?' asked Tony dressed in his Bermuda shorts and tatty Led Zeppelin T-shirt that looked almost as old as he did.

'Tony!' scolded Pauline. 'Why are you always so blunt?'

Jane smiled, not offended at all. 'It's OK, Pauline, really. Well, I'm a lot better. It's been a struggle. We spent so much time together, you see. There's a void there that can't be filled by anything else but every day it's a little easier.'

'Yes, it's very difficult. We do understand, having lost dogs over the years ourselves,' said Pauline tucking into her food.

Tony drank his wine and dabbed his mouth with his serviette. 'It does get easier, Jane. Do you think you might get another dog?'

'Not right now, no. Maybe in the future. I can't think about that right now.'

With dinner finished, Pauline prepared coffee in the cafetière and poured some into each cup offering milk and sugar. Some wonderful sweet-looking dessert lay in front of her.

'This is a strawberry Vacherin — it's French. I learnt how to make it on one of our travels. You must taste it, Jane, it really is too nice not to. It's three layers of meringue, sand-wiching vanilla ice cream and strawberry sorbet.'

'Did you really make this?' she asked, holding out her plate for a portion.

'I did. It's one of our favourites. We love our desserts.'

That was true. She often dropped samples off. But she'd not had this one before.

'Well, you only live once, my darling,' said Tony. 'We've decided now we're retired, we're not going to deny ourselves anything.' They chortled.

The coffee was hot and strong. 'Can't wait to try it. This coffee is delicious too. French?'

Pauline raised her eyebrows. 'But of course.'

Tony, who left his dessert plate as clean as when it comes out of the dishwasher, cleared his throat. 'Did you get to the bottom of the scream business?'

She froze for a second and felt a little embarrassed by the whole ordeal now. 'No, but I suspect the police were right and it was something to do with the amp being left on. I don't know. When Patrick gets back, I'm sure he'll work it out.'

'But a scream, that sounds terrifying. Didn't you hear it, Pauline?'

'I already told everyone that I didn't.'

'You were in the garden, weren't you?'

'Yes, that's what I told them. I did tell you that didn't I, Jane?'

'You did.' A heavy awkward silence fell over them. She wondered why Pauline hadn't mentioned that to her husband. 'I'm not sure I did hear a scream. It might have been some high-pitched interference that sounded like a scream, I don't know for sure. I mean it was very loud whatever it was and I'm sure Pauline would have heard something like that if that's what it was.'

Tony frowned. 'Still, didn't you hear anything at all, Pauline?'

She wanted to get on safer ground, away from what might and might not have happened. She took a sip of her coffee. 'Can we change the subject?' she asked. She could see Pauline blushing a little. She wasn't sure from their facial expressions if they, meaning Tony, was completely satisfied with the answers. He was a curious man. 'Perhaps when Patrick returns, Tony, you can help him work it out?' she said.

'Oh, that's a splendid idea, don't you think, Pauline? We can get to the root of it.' She knew Tony liked to hang about with Patrick; it was like he hoped some of Patrick's stardust from meeting Tony's icons might rub off.

Raising all this again had made her anxious. She settled her hands on her lap and began pinging her rubber band. She finished her coffee and put her cup down. 'I ought to be getting back. Thank you for your hospitality.'

Pauline was the first one up and round the table. 'It was our pleasure. You do know you can come over whenever. You don't need an invitation. I don't know how many times I've told you this, my dear. Oh, before you go, let me cut you up a couple of slices of the Vacherin for you and Patrick. It can be a surprise for when he gets back.' She went to fetch some kitchen foil. Then handed her two small parcels of tin foil. 'Make sure you put these straight into the freezer.'

'Yes, I will. Patrick does have a sweet tooth. Thank you.' She hated leaving all the dishes on the table for her to do. 'Can I help you with those?'

'Oh no.' She tutted. 'I have all the time in the world to do them.'

She didn't want to offend by insisting. At the door, she kissed Pauline on the cheek, thanking her again for her kindness. But there was something about her demeanour, a cool reserve that made Jane think she'd done something wrong. *She's probably still starchy about the Ralph thing.* 'Oh, by the way, do you know someone called Jon? A friend of Ralph's?' she burst out, realising mentioning Ralph's name might displease her.

Pauline didn't blink, but smiled warmly. 'No dear, I don't think I do. Why do you ask? Do you need to contact this Jon?' Her tone was pleasant enough but with a slight onerous undercurrent.

'No, no, it's nothing like that. I don't know why I asked, not really. I just remembered him talking about him with Lizzie and thought I'd never heard him mentioned before.' An outright lie, of course. 'It just popped into my head. You know like those random sorts of things tend to do.' She could hardly tell her the real reason.

Pauline let out a burst of laughter and she didn't blame her. It was an odd thing to come out with. 'I don't know many of his friends, dear. He has so many. I imagine it's someone they both know at uni.'

'Yes, I imagine so.' She felt the collective eyes of Tony and Pauline on her. 'Well—' she swallowed — 'I had a lovely time and the food was amazing.' Even if she was stuffed to the gills. She let herself out the door. She felt more than a little sheepish remembering Ralph's laptop and phone at home.

Outside, the heat of the evening hit the moment she stepped out of Pauline's air-conditioned house. She began wandering back home. She turned to look over her shoulder; she wasn't that far away that she couldn't hear raised voices. She thought she heard her name but couldn't be sure. They were arguing about something. It bothered her that she might be the cause of their fighting.

CHAPTER 26

It was seven thirty in the evening and muggy. She had thought of going over to the island. She'd been excited about being away from the house for a few hours. It was one of the reasons she'd wanted to leave Pauline's. But something Pauline said made her stay home tonight. Maybe she and Patrick were right, and she shouldn't go over there right now, not when she was alone. She double-checked the doors and windows were still locked.

She stood by the kettle waiting for it to boil to make a camomile tea. She was proud of herself resisting the wine tonight. But then, she wasn't an alky so why wouldn't she find it easy to refuse. It was everyone else telling her she was drinking too much.

She brought the laptop into the kitchen, opened it back to the messages and noticed new ones had appeared. She stared at the screen in disbelief. These were sent today while she was at Pauline's.

Ralph: *The scream really got to her.*

Oh my God. Who told him about that? Jane's eyes opened wide as she read on. *Pauline must have called him but why would she bother?*

Ralph: *Did you mean it about the island?*

Jon: ☺ *Isn't it perfect? Janey even has a little boat.*

Ralph: *Isn't that going to be dangerous? What if they find DNA or something?*

Jon: *They won't.*

Ralph: *I don't know. What you're thinking about is huge. They investigate those things thoroughly.*

Jon: ☺ *Not this time. It won't look like that. Look, I know what I'm doing. This is something I must do.*

Ralph: *I'm scared. This is messed up. What if they find something and catch you? Or us?*

Jon: *They won't look that deeply.*

There were no more messages from Ralph.

And there didn't need to be. She knew enough.

Jon was Murk. They were discussing her, and it sounded like he planned on getting rid of her. All that talk about DNA and thorough investigations. What she couldn't understand was how Ralph was mixed up with him? Murk was a conniving hateful man, and he'd somehow got Ralph entangled in all this. Tears of angry frustration welled up. But unlike the last time that Murk got his own way, this time she was ready for him. This time she was angry not scared. *I will not let him control me.*

This time she wasn't going to take the fall.

This time he wasn't going to get away with it.

Murk had no idea how much she'd changed. If he was expecting that young girl, he was in for a hell of a surprise. She had too much to lose.

Jon: *Ralph. Where are you? Where've you gone?*

Jon: *Hello? Text me. What's happened? Are you still there?*

Jon: *What's going on? Where the hell are you? Are you OK.*

Jon: *Ralph????*

She wasn't a complete idiot. They knew she was looking at these. This was all part of their plan to drive her crazy, unbalance her. Ralph would have deleted his phone the moment he suspected it lost. This was staged for her. *Of course it was. I shake my head at my gullibility.* His laptop left here and his phone. Nobody left stuff like that for no reason.

God she was an idiot. She recalled praising herself at how smart she'd been, thinking she had one over on them. But how was Ralph sending these messages if she had the phone? Quickly she went to find it where she'd left it. It was gone. Of course it was. Why was she surprised? Somehow, they'd got in the house while she was at Pauline's. She glanced over at her house. *Had that invitation been a coincidence?*

No, Murk was writing to her. Showing her what he was going to do. He knew the messages were worthless to anyone. His number was probably a burner phone. Untraceable. It was all so cryptic.

He was baiting her.

And she had to take the bait to catch the monster.

Jane picked up her own phone. She waited until she'd calmed down, resting her head in her hands as she let the rising anger ebb a little. Then, with a pertness that was part annoyance and determination, she found Jon in her contacts. And sent him a message. Before she pressed send, she reread it several times trying to get the tone just right. She wanted him to know she was onto him in every way. She gave a sardonic laugh; simply sending the text was enough for that. She had been so obsessed with what he was going to do and waiting, letting his passive aggression get to her that she had played right into his cruel game.

Jane: *I know who you are, Jon.*

There was no going back now.

CHAPTER 27

The next morning as she woke to another day of sunshine and high temperatures, Jane remembered what she'd done the night before. The message sent. *Fuck him.* Although an overwhelming panic grew that she could disappear so easily, and no one would know where to look for her — a terrific feeling of control swept over her that it would have pissed him off *so* much. *This is my life, and I'm not going to wither and die because he terrifies me!* No. She might only be slight, but she was smart, and she knew him. She breathed in deep, closed her eyes and focused. Bring it on mother fucker because I am so ready for you. She wasn't, not really, she had to get herself ready.

Her eyes strayed to the lake through the bedroom window. It was deep. While she felt a renewed vigour that she now knew she wasn't going crazy and all that she believed was happening was true, she knew she couldn't afford to be distracted from what and who she was up against.

She threw off the sheet. By the time she padded into the kitchen and switched on the kettle, she was energised and ready to do what she had to do. Only when she walked down to the edge of the garden to look at her island did a weary acceptance of the possibilities replace her initial uplift. She had to stay strong. Focus and not be afraid of the fear.

It was time to make plans. She could get ahead of this, or she couldn't. And she wasn't about to fail herself. She made herself laugh at her build-up speech; she sounded like a right thug.

Suzanna would be impressed by her forthrightness and self-belief. Lizzie would howl and wonder who had abducted her mother and Patrick would smile and say, *Sweetheart, I love the new you.*

Thinking of her family did what no rallying speech could; it turned everything that was upside down back to where it should be. She was a good person. Bad things had happened to her. Bad things happen to good people.

She got a text from Patrick.

Morning, darling. I was up early and I'm in the studio, now. I'll call you later. I'll let you know where we're up to then. Love you.

She stared at the laptop when she was back in the kitchen as if there was something it was trying to tell her. She didn't trust it now that she knew she'd been set up.

To be honest, she was a little afraid of opening it after sending last night's text. She covered the camera so no one could see her — but what if they could hear her? Wasn't there a way to remotely access these things? She remembered seeing that in a film once and now it scared the life out of her how easily this could happen if you knew what you were doing.

She heard the back gate bang closed. It was closed. She hadn't opened it since Patrick had left. She looked along the wall where they kept their keys on hooks near the coats. The key for the gate was gone. She stood up slowly and walked to the window over the sink where she could see the gate. Her mind already whirred as to how it was open. She opened it slightly and peered, tentatively, out; the gate wasn't fully closed and swung gently in the temperate breeze, lock banging into latch. She was about to go outside through the patio doors when she heard voices and returned to the window close to the gate.

She blanched, backed away, goosebumps covered her skin. Her face turned to stone. Impossible to hear what they

211

were saying, she edged forward once more until she was able to hear Murk. He was raising his voice but still keeping it low. *Don't they know I'm right here? Who is with him?*

His voice was provocative to the other's agitation. She crept closer, stretching further over the sink to the open window, balancing on tiptoes, making sure to keep out of their eyeline. She saw him then as he moved. She nearly died on the spot at how close he was. His body language was anger and annoyance. His face twisted. The other person — it looked like a male figure, hidden behind the hedge — looked to stand his ground but she could see from where she was, he was uncomfortable by his stance; hands linked together around the back of his head then down to his sides, clenching and unclenching his fists like he wanted to land one on Murk. He'd be daft to try it though. She knew what Murk was capable of. It got more heated between them. She was about to pick up her mobile and call the police when they both laughed. She peered closer, her eyes narrowing. Murk pulled the man to him and into a bear hug. Everything was forgotten. Then Murk ruffled the man's hair, and he jokingly pushed him away. Murk was grinning at him. She imagined the other man grinning back, the pair of them acting like a couple of goons.

Jane's lips tightened into a hard line, her own fists into balls she wanted to use as weapons on them both as the other man moved and she saw his face. Whatever Murk was up to it looked like Ralph was a willing conspirator on a mission to harm her. *I just don't get it? What have I done to him?*

Murk was wrong if he thought she was on his hook, waiting for him to reel her in as and when he saw fit. Raw anger fizzed through her thinking of them plotting her downfall. But what was in it for Ralph? That was the part she didn't get. Did they think she was going to simply let them destroy her and her family? If looks could kill, they'd be struck down right now. Which one was it who killed Jasper? It had to be one of them.

She stayed quiet watching them. Where did they think she was? At that moment they both turned towards the kitchen. She held her breath. Like a crab she stealthily moved back to the kitchen island where she'd been when she first heard them. She'd make out like she hadn't heard anything. Sat down, her heart rapping a crazy rhythm, she picked up her phone, slid the laptop onto the other stool and pretended to be texting. Her hands shook. With her back to them she felt vulnerable.

Concentrating so hard on not flinching or turning around it was several minutes before she sensed they'd gone and it was safe to turn around. When she did, she was shaking like she had St. Vitus's dance. She glanced at the keys on the wall. It was back in place. They must have sneaked in the back door and replaced it. So stressed and with her blood rushing in her ears that they were going to harm her, she'd not heard a thing. Her wrist was raw from the number of times she pinged her rubber band.

When she stood up, she was weak. Her legs failed her initially. She went outside, holding the door frame for balance. What had they been doing in the garden? In *her* garden. This was *her* house. Damn them.

What are you plotting? This was Murk all over. He was taunting her. He knew she was there. He probably knew she'd been listening and that was his plan. To make her believe she was in control when in fact he was controlling everything. To fill her with a false sense of security and then BANG!

Fear and anger fizzed inside her. *You're wrong, Murk. You're so wrong about me.*

She'd channel it to strengthen her.

She marched over to the gate with the padlock. Checked it was secure then back inside she removed the keys and hid them. It was a small thing. No doubt they had a copy. *I know you, Curtis Murk. I know how you think.*

But you don't know how I do.

* * *

Exploiting her fear and rage, she opened the laptop to find everything had been erased. They'd done it remotely. Of course they had. It was only a matter of time. That performance in the garden was exactly that, a performance to scare her, to show her how easily he could get to her.

Now she had to wait for Jon to reply to her message. And he would. He'd make her sweat. But he would reply, of that she was certain. He wouldn't be able to resist.

She felt different now that she'd seen him here, close to her, plotting. It wasn't that she wasn't afraid how she would feel when he did respond. It was more how she would reply. She had to keep a clear mind and not alert him to her having seen him. Make him believe she was still this weak person that he was manipulating. He knew there was no clear course of action for her right now. Going to the police with no proof was pointless and telling Pauline, the same. Besides, she didn't want to bring up Ralph, again. She was her friend. She didn't have anything to do with this, she was sure of it, but then she remembered what Ralph had said in the messages. *Shall I bring Mum?* He couldn't have meant Pauline, surely? Could it be a name they called someone they knew? What her son did didn't reflect on her. Pauline would be mortified if she knew. To say something now with no proof would be pointless.

Annoyingly, when she looked out the lounge window, she saw Ralph's car on Pauline's drive with him sat in the driver's seat, Pauline talking with him. Where was he off to now and was Murk hiding in the back? Or long gone? Wasn't Ralph supposed to be doing some trail walk?

He'd know she'd been in their house last night and while she'd been there, they'd been getting into her house to pinch the key and open the back gate. Just to prove to her that he could have access to her whenever he wanted. Was that why Pauline had invited her over? No. No, that — no, Pauline? She couldn't believe that she was involved with Murk in any way. It had crossed her mind last night but, no, no, she was wrong there. How bloody brazen of them though. *Surprisingly* when she checked the cameras there was nothing on them; the Wi-Fi signal had failed. Of course, it had. *Quelle surprise.*

Where was Murk now anyway? Had Ralph brought him here? If so, where was he? Parked down the lane out of sight, no doubt. Didn't want any witnesses to his being here. Where was Ralph going? He waved Pauline goodbye and drove off. Where to? The pub to meet Murk to drink and make more plans? She pictured the pair of them shovelling fish and chips and drinking pints, laughing at her stupidity. She looked over at Penny's house, if only they'd come home from Wales early. She wouldn't feel as alone if they were there. Maybe she should phone and ask Penny when exactly they were coming back. She pulled her phone from her back pocket. No, that would be so rude.

She checked her phone to see if she had any missed calls or texts. Still no reply from Jon. Yeah, well, if he thought he was going to make her squirm by making her wait, and stop doing what she had to do, he was badly mistaken.

It was no use. She couldn't settle until she was certain Pauline was not involved in this.

She marched over to Pauline's. 'Hi,' she said in a tone that was confrontational rather than friendly and not at all how she wanted to come across.

'Hello, Jane, are you OK?' She stood in the doorway as if blocking her entrance. Very unusual.

'Yes, oh, yes, I'm fine, thanks. I saw Ralph, just now talking with you.'

Pauline looked at her, puzzlement creasing her forehead. 'Yes dear, that's right.'

She needed to choose her words carefully. She didn't want to get on the wrong side of her and cause friction if she was wrong. And she wanted to be wrong. 'Oh, right, when did he get back? Did he come alone?'

'Yes,' she conceded. 'He came back last night. Did you need to speak to him, dear?'

'I didn't see his car.'

'No, a friend dropped him off. He picked it up this morning. Do you need to speak with him?'

'Oh, no, not really, no. I wondered if he'd heard from Lizzie.' She thought this was a good opening gambit. 'I haven't heard a thing. I'm sure she's fine, you know no news is good news and all that. It's just, well, with it being a festival and all that. Lots of people. People you don't know. People taking drugs, that sort of thing. So, I was just wondering that's all.'

'Wondering what, dear?' she asked with the tiniest bit of impatience.

'If he'd heard anything, you know, to put my mind at ease, that's all.'

She shrugged. 'You know what they're like these youngsters. Don't let it upset you. I'm sure all is fine, but I'll ask him anyway when he gets back.'

'OK, right, well, yeah, that will be great if you could. Where's he gone?'

'Ralph?'

Jane stared at her. Of course, Ralph, who else were they talking about? 'Yes, has he gone somewhere nice?'

Pauline shook her head. 'I don't know, dear. Is it important to you where he's gone? I can phone him if it is and ask.'

That would be a bad idea. Pauline turned and picked up her mobile phone from the console table in the hall. 'Oh, my God, absolutely not. No need. I was just being nosy.'

'Right, are you OK, Jane? Is that what you came for?'

Normally, Pauline suggested she come inside but not today. 'Actually, yes, I can't find my mobile, and thought I might have left it here last night. Can I come in and look for it? I realised I couldn't find it when I went to check if Lizzie had been in touch.'

'Really? Well, I haven't seen it. I'll have a little look around and if I find it I'll bring it over to you. Is that OK?'

'Yes, of course, thanks, sorry to bother you. It's probably in my house somewhere. I just forgot where I've put it. Silly. I'm sure it'll turn up.' *Why won't she let me look for it? That's odd.*

Pauline was always happy and encouraging for her to come to her house. Was Murk inside? Was that why she was being evasive? Was he listening to them right now?

She wiped her hand across her sweaty forehead as she got back to her house and took a bottle of cold water from the fridge. She had to get Murk out of hiding. They had to talk eye to eye, but she had to be ready to protect herself if he didn't believe that she wasn't the witness who put him away. The best place for that was the island.

Her phone on the kitchen island pinged. She swiped it open. Her eyes widened in surprise and she almost dropped it. She was right. They'd known all along she was reading the messages. His reply floored her.

Jon: *I know.* ☺

CHAPTER 28

The next morning, she was up early, she'd put in a food order with Sainsbury's last night so checked again when it was due — she fancied going to her favourite café for croissant and coffee and didn't want to miss it. The weather report said the heatwave was going to break over the next couple of days and they were in for thundery showers and lightning. She couldn't wait for a cool night's sleep. The fan she had in the bedroom was OK, but it didn't match a drop in temperature.

By the time she got home she was itching to get to her island. She had ideas jumping in her head how to handle Murk and wanted to get it down on paper. Ideally, she'd like to sort it before Patrick got back. He was going to tell her today when that was. He'd already told her he was staying another day. With Murk's reply yesterday, she had to think fast.

As she pulled into the crescent, she saw Pauline and Penny talking in front of her house.

Once she parked up, she opened the front door. 'How lovely to see you, Penny! How was the trip? I just have to open up the place. It gets so stuffy so quickly.' *I'm so thrilled she's back and immediately feel better there's going to be someone else around.*

'Difficult, when you have two youngsters under the age of five. But I moan too much, we loved it.'

'Did Gordon manage to relax?' Gordon was a workaholic. 'Did you get him to switch off?' Jane said.

'A bit, but you know what he's like. The office phoned several times. It's not fair, really it's not. Anyway, how's your summer going?' She let out a huge sigh. 'I'm so glad to be away from my family. They're so stifling when we all get together.'

'Yes, great thanks. Lizzie's been busy going out with friends and Ralph and right now she's at Horsham festival. Patrick's away in London and I'm roasting in this house.'

'It was awfully hot in Mumbles; the caravan was so hot it was like torture. And the girls, well I won't get started on that, but you can imagine, right?' They laughed together. Jane had always liked the look of their static caravan.

The Sainsbury's delivery arrived.

'Give me a hand, ladies, would you? Why were you waiting outside my house? Are we supposed to be doing something that I've forgotten?'

Pauline dropped a crate on the floor by the fridge, lifted out its contents and handed it back to the driver. 'Penny came over this morning,' she said, 'and I thought seeing as the weather's going to break in the next day or so that it would be nice to have a picnic on your island. What do you say, Jane?'

Jane laughed. 'I'm thinking of calling it Jane's Island. It's not mine legally, Pauline.' Her spirits were high today, having her friends around her was bolstering. She had plans for Murk going around in her head that were beginning to show promise and she felt in control and plus she'd missed Penny; it was nice to have her back. Penny was creative like her, and closer in age too. She bought old bits of furniture from car boots and turned them into stunning pieces she sold on the internet. Not that she needed the money — she just loved doing it. She said it calmed her mind and she fitted it in when the girls were occupied or at play school.

'You might as well,' said Penny. 'You're the only one who goes there, and I don't think, apart from the three of us, that any of the others along the lake can see what you've done.'

'That was the idea.' She sighed. 'Well, I can rustle up some sandwiches and bits if that's what you want.' Jane signed for the delivery. She heard the van start up and drive away.

Pauline held up her hands. 'Stop right there. I've got it in hand. I made Tony pull the hamper from the garage. So, what do you say? Is one hour time enough for you, Jane?'

'Well, yes, but Penny, will you bring the kids?'

'No, Gordon's taken them to the swimming baths. They learnt to swim while we were away and that's all they want to do.' She wrinkled her nose. 'They wanted to go in the lake but I'm not keen.'

'Are you sure you're OK with this, Penny? You don't like camping and bugs,' said Jane, remembering how squeamish she was in the garden. 'How do you cope in that caravan?'

'No, you're right. Caravans are as far as I like to go in terms of camping and only static ones at that.' She giggled. 'Well, Pauline convinced me it would be OK with the blankets and deck chairs. And apparently, you've been a little under the weather, so I'll rough it for you.' She gave Jane a hug. 'I've missed you so much.' Jane was pleased no more explanations were needed about her feeling under the weather.

One hour later Pauline was back with the hamper as promised.

'You are good, Pauline,' she said opening the front door to her. 'Penny didn't go back so we've been catching up on Mumbles.' Pauline was all smiles and back to her normal self, making Jane feel crap after the last time they'd spoken and the way she'd thought of her in cahoots with Murk. Ludicrous.

'Marvellous. Here we go,' she said plopping the hamper on the kitchen island. 'I think I have enough to feed an army in there. I thought we could stay for hours that way.' She gave a conspiratorial grin to them. 'So how was your family in Wales — nice to catch up?'

'Yes, I do miss them. It's so far away. But you know family, after a while it can get a bit claustrophobic. Well with my family it can, there's so many of them. It's a four and a half hour journey each way. That's why we go really early or late at night to miss the traffic. They're rotten though, they never make the journey here to visit us. It's always us having to go to them.' They'd been away since the beginning of August. 'I think Gordon likes that he can dip in and out and not stay the duration. It's good they all have their own caravans, and we're not cramped. You'd be amazed how roomy ours is. You're both welcome to use it when we're not there.' Penny had offered this on many occasions.

'You do it for the kids though, and soon enough they'll be grown up and you'll wonder where the time has gone. So don't wish it away.'

Penny sighed. 'I know and I don't, only when they have meltdowns because they're overtired. I tell you, living near the lake gives me a headache, too. The girls always want to be in it.'

Jane wrinkled her nose. 'I'm with you, Penny. I don't much fancy the idea either. I guess by the edge it's OK for paddling though. Now they can swim you'll have to keep a sharp eye on them. How about you, Pauline?'

'What's that, dear?'

'Ever fancy a swim in the lake?'

She blanched. 'No. Never.' Pauline turned away.

'Clearly not a fan either,' said Penny to Jane.

Jane took them over in her boat. She hadn't been across for a few days and had missed the peace and serenity.

After disembarking and tying the boat back up, they sat down on the deck chairs, Jane spread a blanket beneath for Penny in case anything should crawl up her leg. Pauline laid out another blanket, and emptied the hamper. She handed out paper plates. 'Dig in, ladies.'

'You said you could see me from your house, Pauline. How much can you see?' Jane had been meaning to ask since Pauline had told her.

'Oh, not a lot. I can see you sat here but that's about it. Don't worry about it.'

But she did worry about it. If she had binoculars, she'd be able to see very clearly indeed and that made her uncomfortable.

Jane looked over at her house. 'I can't imagine you can see that much, really, can you? It's quite far away. You'd need binoculars to see clearly.'

Pauline laughed. 'I know that, but I also know you and Patrick come over here occasionally.' She grinned cheekily. 'I just wanted you to know in case . . . well, you know, the moment took you?' The three of them burst out laughing and Jane blushed. She had a point.

'I'm sorry about Jasper, Jane,' said Penny. 'You must miss him terribly. I was looking for him when I came over. Pauline told me the sad news. The girls will be so upset.'

Jane's chest tightened. 'Yes, well, let's not talk about it, please or I'll start blubbering.' Penny laid a hand on her leg.

She opened the flask Pauline had brought and poured out rich dark hot chocolate into clean mugs to change the subject. 'Ooh, this looks delicious. Did you make it yourself with proper chocolate? I was expecting something cooling.'

'I know and I was going to do that. In fact I have got some of that too, but I wanted you girls to try this. It's so divine that once you do you'll get addicted like me.' Pauline took a sip of the rich velvety drink, closing her eyes in joy and sighing with pleasure. 'I added brandy too.'

'Brandy! But it's still early!' squealed Penny taking a long-contented sip. 'It is yummy, Jane. You must try it.'

'The chocolate is from France,' continued Pauline. 'It's only a drop of brandy, Jane nothing that's going to make you drunk in control of a boat.' The three of them giggled. 'We brought a few tins of the chocolate back with us. We only use it sparingly. It's so expensive and we don't want to run out before we go back.' Jane couldn't resist, and Pauline was right; she could hardly taste the brandy, but it made all the difference to the flavour.

'We're honoured you're sharing it with us.' Jane pulled out a packet of biscuits from the hamper that Pauline had left in there. 'Can we have one of these? You can't have hot chocolate without a digestive,' she said cheekily. They all smiled as she passed the packet around.

'Oh, well spotted. I completely forgot I'd put them in.'

'Ooh, how fab,' said Penny. 'Chocolate digestives.' She took one greedily. 'I'm lucky to get a look in with these when the kids are around.'

Penny tilted her head. 'Was that your phone or mine that pinged?'

They both looked at their phones. 'Mine,' said Jane, quickly flicking to her emails to see what had come in. A notification that someone had tried to access her emails. She'd changed her password after the debacle with Suzanna's illustrations. Her heart pounded, knowing who it would be. She felt relief that he'd been unsuccessful and how angry that would make him.

Each time she thought about him, it made her sick.

'No major problems you need to get home for?' asked Pauline.

'No, just an email I can deal with later.'

'Jane, Pauline said you thought you heard a woman scream the other day, is that right?'

'Yes,' she replied.

'And you didn't find out who it was?'

'That's right. Nobody else heard it apparently.' She looked at Pauline who raised an eyebrow. 'Pauline was wonderful. She came right over because I also thought someone was trying to break in.'

'How scary for you. Was there?'

She smiled timidly. 'No, turned out there wasn't and there wasn't any sign of anyone. We called the police. They came but couldn't find any evidence that anyone had been there.' She shrugged not really wanting to remember that day.

Penny looked down at the ground as if finding the dirt beneath her shoes fascinating. 'Pauline said she didn't hear anything, but you maintained it was deafening.'

'Why, Penny? Why do you ask?'

'She said it was Thursday late afternoon.'

Jane sat up a little straighter. *What does Penny know?* 'It was, that's right. Why? You weren't here.'

'I was actually. I'd come up that day very early to see Gordon's mum in the care home in Horsham. He got the call in the early hours while he was at Heathrow waiting to catch a flight to Amsterdam. She had some sort of episode, and he couldn't cope, the meeting he was flying out to he couldn't miss, so I had to catch the first train up here. I went straight to the home. I was there hours and didn't come back here till mid-afternoon. I got a taxi here to freshen up and collect some extra things for the girls. That's when I heard it.'

'Really? You *heard* it? Are you sure?' asked Jane excitedly. 'But why didn't you come over? I've been going out of my mind. Did I hear it, didn't I hear it. Where did it come from?'

'Oh, Jane I feel so bad now. I should have. I know that now. But the taxi arrived. I had to get to the station, or I'd miss my train and there wasn't another one until the next day. There was so much going on at the caravan, the girls were playing up. My sisters were insisting I get back as quickly as I could. I thought it was someone with the TV on really loud or listening to some weird music. Maybe those teenagers larking about who sometimes go up and down the lake on that little boat. I wasn't really thinking too much about it if I'm honest.' So she'd known about the teenagers too? *How was I the only one who'd never seen them when I'm the one most on the lake?* 'You know there are some teenagers that come up the lake sometimes, don't you?' she asked, seeing my look of surprise. 'I thought it was them messing about. I didn't actually think it was real or sinister, so I dismissed it. I'm so sorry.'

Jane didn't know what to say and simply shook her head as she attempted to digest Penny's news and its implications.

'I don't understand. Pauline, you said you didn't hear it, and you were in the garden. Sorry, I'm confused. How did Penny hear it, and you didn't?'

'Gordon told me it was probably a fox in heat when I told him. He said they can sound very human,' said Penny.

'Hang on, hang on,' said Pauline turning to Penny. 'It might have been a fox, but really, I don't think so, the police and Jane at the time thought it came from their sound system. Didn't you Jane? You said it sounded like it came from inside the house. Gordon is right. They do sound like a woman in pain. I mean it could be a fox of course, but you insisted it came from inside your house, all around the house, you said. So I'm more inclined to think it was a fault on the music system, don't you, Jane? No disrespect, Jane, dear, but you were adamant it came from inside your house.'

'Well, I suppose you're right, Pauline, if Jane said it came from inside the house. Maybe it's some faulty electrical thing that set the system off. I don't know, Jane, maybe it was, it could be the Wi-Fi cutting in and out. It is rubbish at times round here. What does Patrick say?' asked Penny.

'He's been away, I haven't asked him yet,' Jane said.

'Huh,' said Penny.

Pauline looked at Jane sadly. 'Oh, Jane, really, I thought we'd come to terms with that day. You heard what the police said. My dear, don't get yourself in a state again, really it won't do you any good. I know you think it strange I didn't hear it. But I didn't, I don't know how else to tell you this.'

Jane shook her head. 'I just think it's odd that Penny heard, and you didn't, that's all.'

'Jane, darling, please stop thinking like this,' Pauline continued. 'Can we please drop it now? It's so lovely being here just the three of us. Let's not fall out over this. When Patrick gets back, I'm sure he'll be able to clear it up.'

Why? Patrick won't be able to clear it up because he won't find anything. Somehow Murk controlled it remotely, I'm sure of it now. But it was a woman screaming even if it was coming through the sound system.

The only reason the sound system was mentioned as a cause was because nobody else appeared to have heard the noise.

'The police didn't say categorically that it was the sound system, Pauline,' Jane said. Penny looked uncomfortable now they seemed to be arguing.

'No, they didn't but they couldn't find any other reason for the noise. But Jane, darling, you also thought someone was breaking in.' Jane rustled up a smile. She remembered Ralph and Murk in her garden. *What if they took a copy of the key for the padlock?* It would make sense then how they might be coming and going. Good job she'd changed the padlock. The doorbell didn't capture the side of the house, and that useless security camera might as well not be there for all the good it did. She felt her resolve strengthen.

'Pauline, why can't you consider that you might be wrong? After all, the two of us heard it. It was a woman screaming,' Penny said. Pauline's face was crimson.

If Pauline thought it a strange question, she didn't say. Pauline placed her hands flat on her knees thinking how to reply. 'Jane, my dear.' Her voice was full of concern. 'I am not disputing it out of hand, you must believe me. But I have seen you . . . a little erratic. I'm worried about you.'

'I know you care about me, Pauline.' Jane chuckled to try and calm the situation down she saw might get out of hand. 'That's not what this is about.'

'Then what is it about?'

'I just want you to acknowledge that there was a sound that day whether it was a scream or a fox or the sound system being faulty, Penny and I heard something, the same thing. Where it came from who knows. I just want you to accept that we did hear something we both think sounded like a scream, and I did not imagine it.'

Pauline smiled. 'Then I will, if it will make you happy.'

'It will.' Jane wanted to say that there was much more to it. But it was best to keep her own counsel for now.

'That's settled,' said Penny reaching for the flask. 'Let's have some more of that delicious hot chocolate and not talk about it anymore.'

The snap of a twig close by made Jane jerk her head to the side. 'Did you hear that?'

'What?' asked Penny panicked.

'It's just a twig snapping. Probably a water rat or a vole, nothing to worry about,' said Pauline.

'A rat! Christ!' Penny quickly tucked her feet under her.

'Penny, you look rattled, my dear. It won't hurt you. It's probably more scared of you than the other way around,' assured Pauline.

'Jane! Can we go? Please? I hate rats or voles or anything like that.'

Jane turned towards the sound; it had been a very sharp snap, she'd heard something like that before and it had unsettled her then. She wanted to stand up, demand whoever was hiding in the undergrowth to show themselves. But then she really would come across as weird.

She was taken aback by the quickness of Pauline's appearance at her side; her hand squeezed Jane's shoulder gently before she could voice her concerns. 'Calm down, dear. You know there are water rats here and they're harmless if you leave them alone.' She knew that. *Why are you saying that to me?* 'You're frightening Penny,' Pauline now whispered to keep Penny from hearing. 'She'll never come here again if you spook her.'

Then her phone buzzed. Jane looked at the screen. A message from Jon.

Jane didn't want to read it. She was about to delete it off the screen, but she couldn't. She had to know what it said.

Jon: *Nice day for brandy and hot chocolate, wouldn't you say?*

She whirled around looking for him. Was it him in the bushes? She waited, feeling foolish. She wasn't alone here. She had her friends. And yet she waited as if something was going to pounce. She looked down; the earth behind them from where the sound had come looked disturbed. It had been so dry lately that the twigs and sandy earth showed signs that something large had walked upon it, disturbing the symmetry. It was so dark inside the bushes. Anyone could be hiding.

She stood up quickly, stepped back and stumbled over Pauline's feet. 'Careful dear, you'll hurt yourself if you're not careful.' Her phone went flying, landing face down near the dark opening into the bushes. She swallowed down her fear, bent down and reached forward to pick it up.

She looked once again at her phone. Reread the message. Three grey dots pulsed.

Are you here? Watching? She looked up at Pauline smiling benignly at her, sipping her hot chocolate.

She looked at the phone.

The grey dots still pulsed. Waiting.

She closed the screen and dropped the phone into her pocket.

* * *

As they tidied everything away and loaded the hamper back in the boat, Jane tried not to think about what that text had meant. Had it meant that he was on the island watching her or was he watching her from somewhere else? She looked up at her house. *Are you there? Inside? Waiting?*

'You're pretty exposed out here, wouldn't you say?' Pauline crept up behind her making her start.

'Christ, Pauline, don't do that. You scared me half to death.'

'Oh, I'm sorry. You see that's why you should always bring your phone. If it was a water rat, and it bit you, you'd need to call someone.'

'Yes, I do bring it with me. Stop worrying and don't say stuff like that. It's horrible.'

'I'm sorry to spoil the moment, Jane, but the mention of that rat and I just couldn't relax. You really don't mind going back, do you?' said Penny putting the last blanket in the box.

'No, don't be silly. Besides, all the yummy hot chocolate's gone now so it's not the same.' She tried not to show she was rattled but her voice had a bit of a quiver.

Pauline climbed in first. 'I know you love it here, Jane, but doesn't it bother you when you stay here until it's dark? I don't think I could do it. What about you, Penny?'

'Oh, Jane, you don't! Do you?' asked Penny in shock. 'I couldn't, no. And as for the rats . . .' Penny shuddered dramatically.

'Not often and only generally when Patrick's home. I was here when that heavy mist came down. Now *that* was creepy.'

Penny shivered. 'We heard about that. So glad we weren't here.'

'It didn't help when Lizzie mentioned Stephen King and his creepy books.' She shivered herself, just remembering what had happened that night.

'Oh my God, my dear that's not good, especially when it's dark. Tony loves his books.'

'Ooh, too creepy for me,' said Penny.

Jane turned, looked back at the bushes and her chest tightened as she pushed away and started the engine.

'Have you seen any of those horrid water rats for real?' asked Penny.

'No, I've never bothered to look. I say rats but it's probably voles or badgers or the like. Mind you, Jasper went barmy one day when we heard something moving about in there. It was the night of the mist, and he wouldn't come back out.'

'Did you go and check if he was OK?' asked Pauline.

'Ashamed to say I didn't. It was too creepy and besides, it's horrible in there. I was terrified of getting tangled up and being trapped.'

'Goodness, well it's a good job nobody around here has a boat, otherwise I'd be concerned for you, my dear.'

'Not so, the teenagers who occasionally sail out have one,' reminded Penny.

Jane remembered the little boat she'd seen with the single person inside. 'Are you sure nobody else has one?'

'I don't think so. I've never seen anyone over there but you,' said Pauline. 'Why do you ask?' She dragged her hand in the water.

'Oh, nothing really. I thought I saw one. Actually, I think I've seen one a couple of times.'

'No!' said Pauline with great exaggeration.

'Pauline, stop it. Are you trying to scare me?'

Pauline laughed, flicking water up at her. 'No, sorry. Why would I want to do that? Are you being serious, Jane? That you saw another boat?'

'Yes.' Then she realised she hadn't mentioned this to Patrick.

'Could have been the teenagers or one of them,' said Penny.

'Maybe. What does Patrick think to that?' Pauline asked.

She shrugged. 'I haven't told him so don't you. He'll only worry when he's not here and insist I don't come out here.' *It wasn't teenagers that I saw.*

'No, of course I won't. But Jane, I've never seen anyone with a boat around here, and I know most of the people up and down the lake. They don't have a boat.'

'Where do the teenagers come from then?' asked Penny.

'You and your teenagers, Penny. I don't know of any near to us but of course they might sail up from further up. Maybe that's why we rarely see them.'

'Maybe, you have a point,' said Penny.

She wished Pauline hadn't said that about nobody close by having a boat. 'Well, you know, maybe somebody comes fishing that doesn't live along here.'

CHAPTER 29

Later that afternoon, Jane settled down to work. Focusing her mind on her illustrations stopped her from thinking about Murk. However, after about half an hour her thoughts started drifting. How could they not?

What played on her mind was Pauline. Unable to get back to her work, she opened a new Google tab.

Jackson's Veterinary Clinic, Ridgemont Park, came up. That wasn't far from here.

She clicked on other links about the sale of the business. Pauline Jackson had indeed been the owner. There was even a thumbnail photo of her. She clicked link after link, taking her further away from the vet that she was to reviews she'd left on Google from places, restaurants, and holidays she'd been to here and abroad. More links. And then nothing. *How frustrating.* She slammed the laptop closed.

Something bothered her. She couldn't put her finger on what it was.

She went downstairs to check the back gate was still locked; she double-checked. She'd hidden the new key and didn't think anyone would be able to find it. The only other way in was over the gate. Ralph might be able to, but she doubted Murk would.

Although she sneered at the strength of her security measures, she couldn't help checking the key was still where she'd left it. There wasn't anywhere lockable in the house, so she'd sunk it into the soil of the orchid on the dresser in the kitchen. It was.

Patrick called her not long after. She'd been waiting to talk to him all day.

'Hi, how's it going?' she said excitedly, having waited hours for this call.

'Hey, sweetheart, it's going great. How are you? Everything OK at home?'

'Oh, yes, yes. I saw Penny earlier. They're both now back from Wales. We went over to the island with Pauline for a bit of a picnic. It was nice.'

'That's nice. Did they enjoy Wales?'

'Hectic, I think. When d'you think you'll be back?'

'Look, I'm sorry.' He sounded exhausted. 'I couldn't call before. We've been rehearsing for hours, and you texted last night that you were having an early night. We were at it really early this morning, too.'

'I can tell you're loving it.' She heard the smile in his voice coming through. 'Any idea when you'll be back?' She sensed what he was going to say before he said it.

'Sorry, darling. I know I said this was only for a few days, but it might be another couple. Are you sure everything's all right there?'

She sighed, feeling let down. She wanted him back . . . *But I need to do something about Murk* . . . 'Oh, fine, yes, I'm fine. I've not drunk anything if that's what you're trying to establish.' She gave a faux laugh and thought about the delivery of wine earlier which she still hadn't managed to get around to investigating. 'It's great having Penny and Gordon back.'

'That picnic sounds like it was fun. Have you heard from Lizzie?'

'No, I think she's making me sweat. I asked Pauline if Ralph had heard from her and she's going to ask him. Have you heard? It might be there's no signal there or her phone's run out of battery.' She was making excuses, not wanting to believe she was still giving her the cold shoulder.

'She was upset, darling. She texted me, yes. She's doing fine, having a fun time.'

She pulled a fed-up face. She wouldn't deny this hurt. 'I know, but come on, she's dragging it out a bit, don't you think?' She heard him sigh. 'I'm not going to do anything about it,' she continued. 'I promise. She's old enough to look after herself. She'll come back when she's cooled off I'm sure.'

'It must be killing you. I'm sorry, but if I tell her to contact you, she might stop texting me and at least this way we have some contact with her. She'll come round in her own time.'

'I know, I know. Well, the end's in sight to get my work completed so that's a relief.' She felt herself begin to crumble a little and didn't want him to hear it in her voice. 'Oh, I'd better go. I've something in the oven and—' She didn't have anything in the oven. He'd know that. She never cooked 'oveny' things when she was alone.

'Jane? Don't rush off . . .'

'I have to. Call me later, darling. We can catch up then for longer.' She rang off, feeling horrible for pushing him away when he wanted to talk.

To be honest, she was struggling with the guilt of not telling him all that was going on, and anxiety at the sudden realisation that she only had a few days to sort this whole bloody mess out. But it was Lizzie being so cruel that truly hurt. She pulled at the rubber band several times until she felt herself begin to calm down a little. She hoped telling him she was feeling better and not drinking, would settle his worry about leaving her here alone. If he sensed she wasn't OK, she was sure he'd pack up and come home. She'd ended the call before that could happen.

She put the radio on and made herself a sandwich. The background noise and chatter helped fill the quiet spaces.

Looking at the weather app on her phone, she saw the storm heading their way.

She ate her sandwich outside enjoying the cool breeze that had picked up after checking the gate was still locked. It was. The air was still thick like treacle. They were ready for a monster storm. It would be spectacular when it came. The hosepipe ban wasn't helping her lawn which resembled a field of straw.

As her mind drifted, she couldn't shake the feeling that there'd been something strange about Pauline's behaviour earlier. And she'd kept on about there being no possibility of another boat as if she was almost trying to sow that seed in her mind. But she'd definitely seen another boat. Was it possible that she really knew nothing of what Ralph was up to?

There was still the *why* as to how Ralph knew Murk. Surely, Pauline would not let him fraternise with an ex-con?

No matter how many ways she thought about it, she couldn't come to an answer as to how the connection between them came about. He was a bad person. So why?

Exasperated, she dropped what was left of her sandwich on her plate and leaned back, resting her head on the cushion.

He wasn't going to leave her alone. But first, he would want to know what she had done with the information she'd found on Ralph's phone and laptop. They didn't know she might have taken photos of it. If something happened to her it could lead back to him.

She dropped her plate in the kitchen sink then went back upstairs for a shower; she was feeling sticky and uncomfortable. When she was finished, the light was beginning to fade. She sat at her desk answering emails and trying to think of a way of stopping Murk.

This was ridiculous, she told herself.

Then everything electrical went off. She waited, expecting something to go BANG. When it didn't, she expected someone to jump out at her. She reached for her phone, turned on the torch app. The fuse box was in the walk-in pantry at the back of the kitchen. There was still some daylight coming through the windows. Shadows played on the walls. She pressed her lips together. He was trying to scare her. But she could do this.

Slowly, shining the torch, she made her way along the landing. She swivelled it to take in all corners and sides of the walls. Heading to the top of the stairs was a black spot where anyone could be waiting. She hadn't prepared for him suddenly appearing. She'd locked up before coming upstairs. So far, she hadn't heard another sound so it was most likely the fuse box. Simple, something had just tripped. She would keep telling herself that.

Standing at the top of the stairs, she aimed the beam downwards; the stairs were clear and the immediate area in the hall visible. Beyond that and into the kitchen where she had to get to to gain access into the walk-in pantry, was shrouded in semi-darkness. She went down the stairs, slipping on one but regaining her balance. Her hand holding the phone shook. *It's a simple fuse problem. He won't be waiting for me in the pantry.*

A distant familiar clank of metal on metal from the gate latch made her heart sink. The patio doors were open . . . but she knew she'd closed them. The wind had picked up and was blowing the lace curtains she had drawn across the doors and which she used as a fly screen, inwards, fluttering them in the air. The storm that was predicted was on its way. She pulled the doors closed and locked them. She turned. The padlock was on the kitchen island. She dropped her phone with a loud crack. Gingerly she picked it up. Luckily it hadn't fallen face-down to damage the glass and the torch still worked. So, he'd found the key. But how? She'd hidden it so well. How was that possible?

It was futile for her to think they weren't watching her. They had to be. A cloud covered the sky, dropping the house into heavy darkness. She shone the torch around the kitchen looking for hidden bodies in the corners of the room.

She ignored that her chest felt like her skin was being stretched by a mangle. What were the chances it was a fuse now?

She made her way to the back of the kitchen, to the walk-in pantry that led off the back of the kitchen and to the back door. She shone a shaking beam of light around the room.

She should call Pauline or Penny. *No. He's just trying to put the fear of God into me.* She had to do this by herself.

Why couldn't he just get on with his life and draw a line under what had happened? He'd got out early. He had the rest of his life ahead of him. Why did he want to do this and maybe end up back inside? It made no sense. He thought he knew the truth about the trial. He ought to live with it then. Move on. Why wouldn't he just let her go. Why did he feel he had to torment her like this. Hadn't he destroyed her life once already?

But only I know the real truth.

Her phone pinged with a message . . . and lit up with a name. She leapt backwards. She screamed.

Jon: *BOO!*

CHAPTER 30

The following day was Sunday, two days after she and Penny had heard the scream. Patrick was due back today, but it looked like he was going to be delayed after their last conversation. She had to sort out what she was going to do and how before he got home. In her mind she had gone over various ideas about how to stop Murk. Lure him to the island, club him on the head and throw him in the lake to drown. Convince him to leave her alone. Pay him off. All stupid, dangerous and ridiculous. Finally, she thought the best way was to talk with him. Face to face. Tell him the truth and find out why he was so bent on destroying her. And then what? *I just don't know, that's the problem.* She wasn't a criminal or a violent person, despite what Murk said about her. He was a liar.

Jane was in her office scanning in some new illustrations for Suzanna. Yesterday's debacle with the lights seemed to have been caused by the main switch being pulled or something had blown but when she'd checked she'd found nothing wrong.

The doorbell rang. Still jumpy and exhausted from lack of sleep, she peered out the window. *Oh my God, yes — Patrick!* She raced down the stairs.

She'd missed Patrick's call last night — he must have called to say he was coming home. With the power down, the doorbell camera hadn't been working on the app and she still had the phone on charge.

As she rushed through the hall, she caught a glimpse of him through the narrow side window beside the downstairs loo, talking with Pauline. Something stopped her from charging outside. Her hand reached back to stroke the uncomfortable sensation along the back of her neck. His early return was of course going to cause some problem with her plan. She'd been planning on the extra couple of days he said he'd be away.

She had been about to tell him about last night and the lights. But something stopped her now.

They turned their backs to the house. She couldn't see their expressions. Was Pauline telling him about what had gone on at the island? How Penny had agreed there had been a freakish scream on Thursday but she thought it was nonsense, just the sound system playing up? How was she retelling that story though? Was she getting the first word in to control the narrative? She realised Pauline always seemed to do this. It was her MO — how had she not picked up on it before?

She thought of how threatening Pauline had made the little boat Jane had said she'd seen appear. Was she telling Patrick that too? And how was she telling it to him, with a twist? Pauline had unsettled her on the island being so bullish about what she and Penny had heard. And now, she felt unsettled again by the way she'd cornered Patrick and seemed to be talking to him conspiratorially.

She pulled open the door and suppressed the uneasy feeling brewing inside, knowing that Murk had been in her house and she'd yet to discover, doing what? Other than possibly messing with the main switch. But what disturbed her the most was how he had known where the new key to the padlock was hidden. Patrick arriving early was going to be a big, big problem.

'Patrick, hi.' Her voice was genuinely full of happiness to see him.

They both turned, surprised. Why were they surprised? She did live here. He smiled, quickly leaving Pauline and wrapping her in a huge bear hug. She buried her face in his chest, loving his smell. 'God, I've missed you, Jane.' Then he kissed her long and deep.

When they parted, she smiled brightly up into his face, not wanting to show any signs of the stress she was feeling.

They waved Pauline goodbye and walked to the door. On the mat was a Jiffy envelope face down. She must have trodden on it in her haste to get to him and not noticed. Patrick bent and picked it up then handed it to her without looking who it was for in his haste to get inside. She turned it over. Scrawled across the front in black Sharpie was the name *Janey*. She couldn't stop her eyes sliding over to Pauline. This was a hand delivery. Had it been delivered today or last night when the lights and cameras were out? Pauline turned and smiled at her warmly, giving her a little wave. Jane returned the gesture.

'You hungry?' she asked as they walked through to the kitchen. She dumped the envelope among the detritus on the island that she had piled up with every intention of going through at some point, hoping Patrick wouldn't ask about it.

He put his bag in the utility. 'Starving. Do we have eggs? I'd love eggs, bacon and baked beans with some of that sourdough toast,' he called as he nipped into the downstairs loo.

She quickly checked the phone app for this morning. There was nothing on it apart from Patrick arriving and Pauline coming to meet him.

She sat in the kitchen on one of the high stools, picking up the Jiffy envelope again and holding it, trying to weigh up what was inside. She looked out the window towards Pauline's. She was seeing everyone now as complicit.

She spotted the glass of Merlot by the sink as she heard the loo flush and the taps running. That was not hers. But that was the thing; there was no Merlot in the cupboard. If Patrick saw it, which he would, he'd think she'd been lying about her drinking. But there was. The few bottles that had arrived with her order the day of the picnic. She had not opened a single bottle and put them in the walk-in pantry out of the way. She still had to address that issue but frankly, she didn't think she had the wherewithal to handle an altercation with Sainsbury's when she wasn't even sure if she hadn't ordered it by mistake or not. She shot off the stool, grabbed the glass, quickly rinsed it, dried it, put it back in the cupboard with the others. Hurriedly, she checked around for a bottle. There was none.

She was making the breakfast for him when he reappeared.

'It's so nice to be back home.' He put on the coffee machine.

'And early too! You said you were going to be a couple more days.'

'Yeah, we got through what we had to a lot quicker than anticipated.' There was a long pause. 'Listen, Jane, I have to go away again in a day or so if they need some remixing. I want you to know now and not spring it on you. It'll be extra money for our holiday.'

She chuckled. 'That holiday that never seems to get booked.'

'I know, I know, but I promise I'll get to it. I have sent you some hotels to choose and you haven't even got back to me which you prefer.'

'Ah, yeah, I think I lost that email. Send it again and I'll have look through it. So how long d'you think you might be away this time?'

'Two, three at the most.' She smiled. That would work out great for her. A plan was beginning to take shape in her mind of how she was going to get Murk over here to talk without him wanting to harm her. But she needed a backup plan if he didn't go for it and that wasn't easy to formulate. How do you get rid of a person that doesn't want to be got rid of? 'That's OK, do what you have to. Then we're free to go on holiday.'

'You OK if I go take a quick shower before I eat?'

'Sure, I'll slow the food down.'

He kissed her on the top of the head. 'I'll only be a flash. Then you can tell me what's gone on while I've been away.' He was gone and she stared at the Jiffy envelope like it was calling to her, suspicious why he'd said what he had. Had it something to do with whatever Pauline had said to him? She didn't want to open it. But neither did she want Patrick to ask her to open it in front of him.

She stopped whisking the eggs, put down the bowl and picked it up.

She squeezed it. Something small was inside. She tore it open. A flash drive dropped out. Scared the flash drive might have some kind of virus to corrupt her laptop and spy on her, she didn't much feel like plugging it in. But she had to see what was on it. She raced upstairs. Opening up her laptop she inserted the drive and clicked the mouse to do the necessary. There was only one file on the stick — imaginatively named *File 1*. Did that suggest there might be more? It was a recording. She listened to the shower still running and pressed the space bar to play. It looked like it was a video taken on a phone. There was darkness and movement. Light footsteps like bare feet on carpet. A door opening then someone used the toilet. She clutched the flesh of her neck, cringing as she recognised where this was. The toilet flushed. More footsteps. The time jumped. Now there was delicate snoring. That was her. Gentle murmuring and shuffling of bedclothes followed by a groan. She slammed the lid down hard and yanked out the drive with fierce anger. The date stamp was last night.

It must have been the only time she'd slept because the rest of the night she'd stayed awake with a sense she was not alone and terrified. This was why. She'd been right.

He'd been in the house with her. Watching. Recording.

How long did he stay in my bedroom?

In my house!

Alone with me.

He spied on me and I didn't know he was there!

This had to stop. She couldn't go on any longer; she was at her wits end.

He was everywhere. Watching every move she made. Her skin crawled with the thought of it. Her wrist hurt, she felt it wet. She looked down and saw she'd broken the skin with the rubber band.

He was watching her right now. Laughing at how he was making her feel. She turned around three hundred and sixty degrees and shouted out, 'FUCK YOU!'

And just like that she was face to face with Patrick coming into her office to find her.

CHAPTER 31

Back in the kitchen, she only just caught the bacon before it incinerated. *Damn it!* She cut a couple of slices of the sourdough, slid them into the toaster as Patrick came down the stairs. She was at sixes and sevens, unable to co-ordinate her thoughts and her hands, knowing Murk had been there, watching her last night. It was taking a few minutes to calm herself down.

'That feels better. Want to tell me why you shouted *fuck you* up there just now and ran away?'

'I didn't shout that at you, silly. I shouted it at the computer, which is still playing up and driving me insane. You know I'm not techie with all this stuff when it doesn't work.' That had been a very awkward moment.

He smiled. 'Thank God for that. For a minute there I thought I was in trouble.' He walked over to the patio doors to open them. 'It's stuffy in here.'

She sighed with relief he wasn't going to make more of it. 'Come on, food is ready.'

'You can sense the weather's on the turn,' he said, leaning against the island and drinking from his glass of orange juice. 'They said on the radio that we're in for some big storms. I hope it's not when I'm heading back to London. I hate driving in that weather. Mmm, that smells amazing.' He wrapped his arms around her waist. 'Thanks, babe.'

She shivered, wondering what else Murk had done last night.

'You cold?'

'No, I think someone just walked over my grave.' She laughed, shocked at her own words.

'Don't say stuff like that. Maybe it's anticipation now that I'm home.' He gave her a cheeky laugh. 'I do appreciate you cooking this.' He pinched a rasher of bacon and ate it.

'My pleasure. I've not had a cooked breakfast in ages so I'm really looking forward to it too.' She plated up and they sat down companionably. 'This is nice,' she said, sliding scrambled eggs onto her fork. 'I've missed you.' She paused. 'Did Pauline tell you Penny came over? She's back from Mumbles. Oh, I told you that on the phone, sorry, forgot. What was she saying to you earlier? It looked intense?' She tried to look relaxed.

He smiled back. 'Oh, not much, you know Pauline's always chatting. I switch off half the time. I wanted to get in and see you.'

'Yes, she is that. So, what did she say?'

He buttered his toast. 'Not much. She was worried I might be a bit off with Ralph, you know after the words you had with him.' He looked up from his plate. 'She just wanted to know if he was still welcome to come to the studio. And about London, how it had all gone, that sort of thing.'

'Nothing else?'

'Well, no love. She was asking if I was going to London again before we went away. I told her we didn't have dates yet and that I had to get this work out of the way before booking anything.'

'I see. Not like Pauline not to give you up-to-date information on what she's been up to.' Every part of her worried he was keeping something back.

'I think she wanted to.' He chuckled. 'I'm sure she'll be over shortly and no doubt Tony too. He'll want to know how I got on. He's fascinated with it all. You know his dream was to have been a musician.' He grinned and shook his head. 'He's totally tone-deaf — can't hear a note if it hit him in the face. Listen, do you want to do something today? Go out somewhere?'

'That'd be nice. Yes, great idea. What you thinking? Not the beach, please. I can't go back there. Too many memories.' He gave her a lopsided smile. She wasn't sure she'd ever be able to go back to that beach again without Jasper.

'I'll have a think on it,' Patrick said, in answer to where they should go for the day. 'Not too far a drive as I'm still exhausted. Are you up to speed with work by the way?' She detected some concern there.

'All sorted, just some finishing touches and then I'm done. And don't worry about going out far, let's stick to town. Why not go out for a long lunch? There's that lovely Italian that's opened. We keep saying we'll go.' She smoothed the back of her neck and looked around, her eyes focusing on the garden and beyond.

'That's great, good idea. I'll call and book a table when they open, and the counsellor? Sarah, was it? Have you seen her this week?' He noticed her looking at the garden.

She blushed. 'No, no.' She turned back to face him. 'Well, we had an appointment booked. But she cancelled. I have made another appointment for another session next week. But the coping skills are a real help.' She hid her sore wrist.

He looked serious. 'Jane, you promised you would continue seeing her. It wasn't you who cancelled was it?'

'No! And I will. I fully intend to. I told you she was great.'

'And your drinking? Have you really stopped?' He watched her carefully.

She frowned. He knew she had. She'd not been responsible for any wine coming into the house — and what was delivered in that blessed Sainsbury's delivery was now in the back of the walk-in pantry, hidden behind the vegetable rack. He wanted to say more, she sensed it. Something was holding him back. 'Why do you say it like that? I told you I had. And I have. You do believe me, don't you?' Clearly from his look he wasn't sure. 'Patrick, I haven't touched a drop since I spoke to Sarah. I'm not lying.'

He put his knife and fork down and pushed his plate away. 'I want to believe you, Jane, but Pauline . . .'

'Pauline! What has she been saying?' Her tone was definitely salty this time.

Talk of the devil and he shall appear.

'Helloo, it's only me, dearies.' Pauline practically waltzed in through the patio doors. 'Your gate is unlocked, did you know?' Jane scowled at her disingenuous affability.

'Why was it unlocked?' asked Patrick, puzzled. 'You like to keep it locked.'

'I thought I had locked it,' she snapped, irritated. Realising that Murk must have left last night through the gate, she put her cutlery down with a clank. After the power was restored last night, and she *thought* her house was clear of any imposter she did lock it.

'Aha, right. OK, I was only asking,' he said backtracking but looking at her, evidently surprised by her sharpness.

'Oops, have I come at a bad time? Now, now, you love-lies, I have come bearing some brownies I baked and there's too many for us. These are for you, Patrick. I know how much you love them. They're to welcome you home, they're still warm.' She turned to Jane. 'I wasn't sure if you liked them, I couldn't remember, so I took it upon myself to bring a few extras knowing most people do. I'll pop the lot in the fridge, shall I? Or do you want a warm one now, Patrick?' What was she up to now?

He shook his head. 'No thanks, not after my breakfast. I'll have one later. Thanks though, that's very kind of you Pauline.'

She opened the fridge and slid the plate of brownies on a shelf. 'I don't want to leave them out in this heat.'

What exactly did you say to Patrick? She didn't want to just fire off what she thought she might have said and be wrong. But she clearly had said something for him to doubt she'd stopped drinking.

'Pauline, what did you tell Patrick this morning?' Best to come right out and ask. She didn't have the time nor the patience right now to skirt around.

'This morning, dear? Oh, not much, not much at all.' There was a glint in her eyes as she smiled sweetly and turned to Patrick. 'But aside from that, have you seen the local paper?' She put the newspaper in front of Patrick. 'Terrible isn't it? I don't know what the world is coming to, really, I don't. Don't you agree, so much violence around today.' Then she turned and looked at Jane. 'It's such uncertain times we live in. Don't you agree, Jane?' She kept her eyes on her long enough to make her uncomfortable.

'You always get the newspapers, don't you? I mean the actual papers,' Jane asked.

'Yes, I can't stand reading it on the iPad or the phone like Ralph does. He does everything on that contraption. Tony and I like a real paper to hold and turn the pages. But you know that, dear, I give them to you for the log fire.'

'I used to think that way,' said Patrick, 'but I've got used to it.'

Jane didn't take her eyes off Pauline, watching her warily. She was sure Penny and Gordon read theirs on their phones, being younger than them. But they did sometimes get the papers, Gordon liked the FT. Did they get others? Maybe the local paper to know what was happening locally for events for the kids and all that. One of them left them that day on her doorstep. Now, Penny's were usually covered in paint or glue, but the one that was left the other day wasn't. So, it must have been Pauline who left it. Her or Murk. She began to suspect her neighbour. But why were they associated with him? It made no sense at all, and it was really doing her nut in right now.

Patrick picked up the paper and read the article Pauline was referring to. 'Dreadful, you're right. And he's settled in the Sussex area for some reason. You'd think someone like that would want to be in London.'

It was as if Murk was invading her home. She saw his name in capital letters on the page. He had dropped himself right into her life like a ruddy red pin on a map.

She tried to keep her voice steady. 'Let me see.' She stretched out her hand for the paper.

'Wouldn't want to meet him in a dark alley,' said Pauline, looking at the picture. 'Shall I read it to you, dear?'

Jane heard the stirring of Patrick's tea, the clink, clink of the teaspoon against the sides of the china mug, so loud in the quiet of the kitchen as they listened to Pauline. Her fingers pinged her rubber band under the table.

Pauline read aloud.

Hardened criminal Curtis Murk said of the young man beaten to death because he dared talk back to him: "He caught me on a bad day." Murk was convicted of manslaughter charges and imprisoned for fifteen years. Murk's barrister, Peter Longbody, known in the underworld as Mr Fix It, managed to get him parole after ten. Murk is now living in the Sussex area.

Jane sat back. He'd only served nine years, having waited twelve months for the case to come to trial. A headache was growing behind her eyes, slow and discordant. He'd deserved a full life sentence. The face of the poor boy appeared before her. Murk was an animal.

'Bloody hell, can you imagine knowing a bloke like that? There's some real nut jobs out there. We don't know the half of what goes on in this world and I don't want to either,' said Patrick in disgust.

There was real fear in her thoughts. It felt weird that Patrick now knew of Murk. Spoke about him. Murk's omnipresence hung in the air like a thick black cloud.

Remembering that awful day made her visibly wince as if Murk had reached out of the ether and touched her.

'Is something bothering you, Jane?' asked Pauline. 'I'm sorry, my dear, to upset you.' There was something about the calm way she spoke that sent a shiver through her.

Jane walked to the dresser, opened the drawer and swallowed a couple of paracetamols with fresh water from the tap. She touched the back of her neck, feeling vulnerable. And that all too familiar feeling of being watched. She saw a loose piece of paper inside the drawer next to the pills. On it were words typed in heavy black ink. *Be very careful.*

What did *that* mean? Be very careful of what? What she did? Who she opened the door to? That she didn't burn herself on the hob? What? She wanted to scream. She wanted to suddenly lose control and smash everything up. *HOW ARE YOU DOING THIS?*

'Jane?' asked Pauline, sounding concerned.

'No, sorry, I've a headache, it's so muggy today. I think it's the tension in the air with the storm brewing. I can't wait for this heatwave to break.' There was strength in her words. She was finding it hard to square up the two versions of Pauline in her head. What did she have to gain from bringing this article to their attention? That's what didn't make any sense.

249

CHAPTER 32

Patrick had booked the restaurant for 1.00 p.m. The thought of going out into the town and escaping the house was a wonderful one and she felt the relief as he parked the car in the supermarket long stay car park. They walked the short distance to the restaurant.

Her phone vibrated in her back pocket. She pulled it out and read the message.

Jon: *You're looking tired, Janey.* ☺

The smiling emoji creeped her out. She turned around. Could he see her?

'All right? What's up — you seen someone you know?' Patrick turned to look with her.

'No, no one. I thought I heard a familiar voice.'

'Oh right. I hope it's not too hot to sit in the garden. They said that was all they had. Most people want the air conditioning.'

'Are you hungry?' she asked. 'I'm not much. Maybe I'll just have a salad.' The text and the newspaper article and Pauline had taken the edge off her appetite.

'That breakfast certainly filled a hole. They didn't have any other times available. Do you want to cancel and go somewhere else?'

'No, it'll be fine. It's a lovely idea.' She took his hand in hers as they crossed the road.

They were sat under a huge umbrella in the outdoor seating. It was a little cooler but not much. She was sick of this weather now and desperate for it to end.

Patrick poured out some sparkling water for them. 'Listen, I'm sorry I had a go at you earlier about the counsellor. I don't want to interfere. I know you know what you're doing and if you think these coping things will help then I'm right by your side.'

She nearly burst into tears. 'Thank you. I know how you worry. Do you believe that I haven't drunk while you've been away?'

'I do. But I do have a small concern, and I don't want you to jump down my throat when I ask.'

She took a sip of her drink. This was it then. Pauline had filled his head, clearly, with everything she thought wasn't real. 'Go on then, what is it?'

'Pauline mentioned you'd seen a man in a boat on the lake. And that she thought she'd heard someone *might* have bought a small fishing boat, but she wasn't sure.'

'Why didn't she tell me then?'

He shrugged. 'Let's change the subject. Have you seen Ralph since I've been away?'

'Not exactly, no.' Her stomach churned at the mention of his name and her face hardened, remembering him with Murk.

'Right, well look, from what I've garnered from Lizzie, is that she wants you to apologise to Ralph for what you accused him off.' She looked startled at him. 'You saying he drugged your drink at the barbecue,' he reminded her, as if she'd forgotten.

'Right, I see. Just be clear with me, Patrick. What are you actually asking of me?'

251

'Well, Lizzie is concerned that her friendship with Ralph will be damaged if you carry on accusing him and she wants you to apologise.'

'And what do you think I should do?' She pinged her rubber band. 'D'you think I should do that?' *I am not doing that.*

'The thing is, darling, Lizzie is being stubborn about this and what I don't want is for it to damage your closeness. She isn't happy. I thought you might have figured that out by now.' He drank his water, put the glass down on the table. 'She hasn't been in touch with you since she left for Bev's.'

'So don't you believe he did it?'

'I don't know, in the heat of the moment . . . I'm not sure.'

Their food arrived. She dug into her salad. 'You're saying I should apologise, to make life easier for them, is that right?'

'And for you, too, darling. Lizzie is still at Bev's. She's back from the festival and won't come back until you do. I want us to enjoy what's left of her summer break as a family before she goes back.'

Jane's phone, lying on the table, vibrated. She hesitated. Patrick noticed.

'You can take a look, you know.' He laughed at her hesitancy.

'It'll be nothing. I'll look later.' Her hands felt clammy. She knew who it was, she had such a strong feeling she was being watched it took all her strength not to look about.

'I know you. You won't settle, go on.'

She picked up the phone, turned it to face her and read the message.

Jon: *How's the salad?* ☺

She took a deep breath, told herself she had to stay calm; Patrick was watching her. To not look shocked or to look around. What if he kept texting her? In a knee-jerk reaction, she texted back, hoping it would stop him if she acknowledged him.

Jane: *Hello, Curtis.*

He'd had all that time in prison to plan how to kill and punish her, under the false belief that she was the witness who put him away. The mind could create wondrous detailed outcomes when left to play for years. He'd had time to plan everything to the very last detail.

She didn't want any more surprises.

'Jane?' She looked up. 'So, are you going to sort this situation out with Ralph?'

'What?' His question threw her. 'No! Sorry, Patrick, no I'm not, not yet.' She silently cursed. 'I'm not going to pretend I'm OK with him.' She closed her eyes. 'I need more time to think about it.'

'Think about it?'

'Yes, look, please, darling, this is supposed to be a lovely day out for the two of us. Can we just enjoy it? And deal with all the crap when we get back home?'

He smiled, cut a strip of steak and popped it into his mouth. 'You're right. Well, remember I said the studio would be in touch if any remixing needed doing? Well, they have — I've just seen the email. They need me to go back.'

Her phone vibrated again. Patrick stopped chewing and looked at it. 'Who is bothering you that much?'

She felt herself redden. Picked up the phone and wished she hadn't.

Jon: *Oh dear, oh dear, squabbling? I hope it's not over me, Janey.* ☺

* * *

She wished there was some way of finding out just where Murk was.

When they got back from lunch, she shot upstairs on the pretext she had emails to deal with. Which she did but after opening them up, the thought of dealing with them was too much. How was she to concentrate on anything right now.

She knew Patrick would want to discuss the Ralph issue again at some point.

While she had a plan formulating in her head, it was a long way from complete. As to what to do? The one thing she knew for certain was that she couldn't go on like this. Her nerves were shot and if she pinged her bloody rubber band any more it was going to sever her veins. She had to think. Really focus her mind. Patrick returning to London was her opportunity. No time to waste.

She heard Patrick open and close the back door, his footsteps on the gravel path, talking to somebody. She leaned out the window; it was Tony. Then they were both gone inside the studio.

She pushed down the fear threatening to rise up and consume her. She looked at the messages once more. They made her shiver. And what was it with the emojis? They creeped her out more than anything. What was he planning for her? He knew everything she did. She was a sitting duck. She had to find a way of getting ahead of this.

He had to come to the house to get her, that was the first thing. She had the advantage of knowing her house and the island inside out.

Frustrated, she stood up so quickly her office chair flew back, crashing into the wall. *Damn. I don't have a clue how to protect myself.* Not really. She paced, finishing by the window.

She had a good view right into Pauline's kitchen from here. But from her bedroom she had a better one. She threw open the doors of her wardrobe and searched for the pair of binoculars she knew was in there. *Yes!* Patrick had bought them for her to use on the island, but they were too expensive and she'd never used them, afraid of losing them; she'd bought some cheap ones that she kept there instead. She pulled the chair she usually dumped her clothes on nearer the window and moved the chest of drawers slightly to lean on while she kept a check on the time. The last thing she needed was to get swallowed up in her surveillance, lose track of time, and have Patrick find her this way.

A car pulled up. She tensed. Two men got out, both dressed in dark hoodies, heads covered. Unusual in this heat. They clearly didn't want to be recognised. Now that *was* odd. She turned the swivel on the lens to max. Wow. Every detail was so clear. These things were amazing. She knew the body shape of one of them. It had to be Ralph. The front door opened. The large man walked in first, taking his hood off. He was followed by the other slimmer one; just as he stepped inside, he turned, took off his hood and looked right at her as if he knew she was watching. She gasped. *Ralph. She knew it!* She almost dropped the binoculars. She backed up as if they could reach out and touch her. Murk was there too. He had to be the other one. But what connection did they have with him? God, it was driving her mad not knowing. She was certain the other man was him. Absolutely certain.

She caught sight of herself in the mirrored wardrobe, her eyes wild, her lips tightly pinched. What to do. *God. This is real.* She couldn't breathe. This was it. She knelt on the carpet, focusing, breathing slowly in and slowly out. She emptied her mind. Closed her eyes, thought of nothing but an empty space and breathed in and out, slowly. It took longer than usual but it worked. Several minutes later, she was calmer, able to open her eyes and stand up.

She fought her way past the muddled thoughts racing through her mind, all trying to outdo one another.

If they had access to her home and her email account, what else had they been doing that she wasn't aware of? But wait, she'd changed her email password. Surely, they hadn't worked that out too. She was their puppet. The forgotten phone and laptop. The easily accessible messages for her to read. The spying on her. They were playing with her.

She had to think like them or at least like Murk. Her phone vibrated.

Jon: *You have mail!* ☺

She fumbled for her phone. There was an email from jon52C@aol.com and it had an attachment. Her hand flattened against her mouth to stop herself crying out when she opened it. There were photos, short videos of her in the kitchen. Getting ready in the morning wrapped in a towel. Drinking wine alone. Lots of her drinking wine alone. Staggering around the house. She checked the date and time stamp. Two days ago, while Patrick was away. How was that possible? She hadn't drunk. SHE HADN'T. They were fake. They had manipulated them. They could do anything they liked with these! Oh God. If they sent them to Patrick, he'd never believe they were fake.

She quickly went to her emails sent folder with a bone-crushing fear. There were emails to Lizzie that she'd never sent. Hesitantly, she opened one and read it. It was awful. Nasty. All about Ralph and how she really felt about him and how she'd only agree to allowing him back in the house to please Patrick. The words hung in the air, strange and scary. No wonder Lizzie hadn't been in touch if she thought she'd sent this poison pen email. She must have been devastated reading them.

What she didn't understand was why Lizzie hadn't told Patrick. He would have blown his top at her if only to ask her why she'd sent them. At least then she'd have known about them. Why hadn't she told him? Ralph must have stopped her. Of course, that way they manipulated her. And now they were manipulating Jane. Clever.

There were more that she didn't dare open, terrified at what she would read. Oh, God. Some had been sent to friends. She braced herself . . . and her freelance clients. Panic set her nerves alight. The instinct was to move, to run and hide. He was simultaneously destroying her while not physically laying a hand on her. In a moment of clarity, she sent a round robin email to all her contacts in her VIP account telling them she'd been hacked and to ignore all emails. The ones who had replied, she ignored and deleted hoping her new email would clarify her situation. Then she changed her email password, again. *How are they working it out so easily?*

She rushed downstairs as a thought struck her. In the utility she pulled off the cover of the alarm system to check it was working. The green light was on. Then she opened her app on her phone and saw instantly the front of the house, the sides and the back. Her app was switched to *no notifications*. Confused, she thought for a moment. Had he turned it off when he was in the house? In her bedroom? She shivered that he got that close to her, and she didn't even know it. She went straight into *history* and saw that all the files were date-stamped. She tapped through until she found what she was looking for. Then went into the time of day. Night. It would be the only time they would have been able to enter the property without being seen. She clicked one of the videos and pressed playback. She sped through, moving the time bar along the bottom with her finger. She stopped when she saw a figure outside the house. Pressed pause. 03.00 a.m. She pressed play and watched.

Her gaze flicked over the single person, dressed in black, wearing a hoodie and walking from Pauline's house to hers. She knew that person.

She pinched the screen, bringing into focus the grey Golf; the same car that was now parked on Pauline's drive.

She flicked through other recordings. All the same. All at the same time. On all of them the front door was opened very slowly; they clearly had a key.

She flicked through all the recordings. On one occasion the figure coming into her home wasn't alone. The other person was also in a hoodie and tilted their head upwards, looking up to check the camera above the front door. It was only a quick glimpse of their face but enough for her to know it was Ralph — well, it looked very much like him. What were the chances it was someone who looked like him? *Pretty small*, she thought.

If they knew they were being recorded, why not delete it all from the app? They clearly had access to her phone and the home security app. Her breath snagged in her throat. They wanted her to see it. Oh, God.

But how had they got into her phone? It would take some doing to work out her passcode. But easy if they were watching her and saw her tap out the code. She cringed. Or put it close to her face when she was asleep. *So easy. Why didn't I think of that?* She was so annoyed with herself.

She was about to send to herself by email the security recordings — but if they had access to her email what was the point? She opened the app again and suddenly — it was all gone. Everything. There were no more recordings. She reloaded the app. Nothing there. She turned her phone off and back on then opened the app, again. Nothing, all gone. Quickly she spun around, looking upwards along the walls, the shelves, the paintings anywhere where a camera could be sited. It could be anywhere. She'd have to tear the whole place apart and that would not be a great look. Consumed with frustration, she flung her phone to the floor. Devastated.

CHAPTER 33

'Wow, what happened?' said Patrick walking in right at that very moment. 'You've probably smashed that. Why did you do it?'

She said nothing, holding back her rage, bent down and picked it up. 'I have a screen protector on, it's OK,' she muttered. 'It was an accident it just slipped out of my hand.'

'Lucky for you it landed on Jasper's bed. Good job you hadn't moved it. What was that about, Jane? What's happened?' The room filled with silence. She felt swamped by it and the guilt of not being honest with him. 'I don't know, I just, I felt something on my hand and thought it was a spider. Way too dramatic, I know.'

She didn't know what else to say. What could she say? It was there, then it wasn't? She wanted to tell him. She really did. But she had no evidence of any of it. If she told him with no proof, what would he think? She was driving a wedge between them, she knew it, he knew it. Only he was trying so hard to keep it together but if she told him . . . what could she expect him to think?

'I don't know how to say it,' she said mustering the courage to confess to him.

'Say what?' He looked baffled.

She looked around, biting the inside of her lip, paranoid Murk was watching and listening. Would he send the images if he knew she'd confessed to Patrick to spite her? She didn't know which way to jump. She grabbed his hand and dragged him into the walk-in pantry behind her. And then a thought struck. 'Wait a second.' She turned away from him to open her email account on her phone. She went to the sent folders and looked at the emails she'd sent to Lizzie. She tapped the email then the email address; she knew something had looked a little odd. It was virtually the same but only different by one digit. He hadn't really sent them. He was playing with her. Bastard.

'Jane? What's going on? Why are we hiding in the pantry?'

'It's the safest place. I don't think they can hear or see us in here?'

'Jane? What are you talking about? And who are *they?*'

They were silent for several moments as she let his words settle and what the implications were for her if she didn't tell him the whole truth. He thought she was nuts, she saw it in his eyes; the fear that she had lost the plot.

'That didn't come out right. I have to tell you something and I should have told you ages ago.'

'OK,' he said very slowly. 'And that is?'

'Before I do, please, please don't be angry with me. I have good reason why I didn't, even if I might not articulate it the right way.'

'OK, but Jane, you are really frightening me right now.' He looked around the pantry.

'Oh, stop looking where we are. This is the least of the problem. Don't look at me like that. I can't tell you if you are already closed off to hearing me.'

'I'm not. Really, I'm all ears. Go on, tell me.'

'Ten years ago, I — no wait, better still, please listen to everything I have to say without interrupting.' He nodded with eyes like saucers. 'You know that newspaper article

260

Pauline brought over? Well, the thing is, I mean, what I'm trying to say—' Patrick's phone rang. 'Don't answer that!' she snapped. His hand froze mid-air.

'What?'

'Don't answer that.' He looked at his phone; his eyes grew bigger.

'Wait, wait, what the hell are you talking about? You sound like you've—'

'Lost my mind?'

'No, actually, I was going to say you sound like you've dropped into a spy novel. What the hell has got into you?'

'I know how mad it all sounds. Just let me talk, please. I must get this out now.' He nodded, stunned. Confused. 'That article in the newspaper, well, oh shit, here goes nothing. I know him.' His eyes opened so wide she wondered if they'd fall out. 'I was there, Patrick, when he killed that boy.' His mouth made an O shape. 'I literally fell into the pub on my way home, desperate for the loo that day.' He mouthed *what?* 'He threatened me if I went to the police, he'd find me and kill me.'

'What did you do?'

'I didn't go, obviously. I ran away. I feel awful and guilty and all that shedload of guilty shit that goes with doing the wrong thing. But I was afraid. But you see, someone else saw it and went to the police. Somebody gave evidence against him behind protection.'

'And what? He thinks it was you. Is that what you're saying?'

She nodded. That sounded as if he believed her. She looked at him pleadingly to believe what she was saying was the truth. It was a big ask, she knew that.

She should have told him all about Murk at the beginning of all this. She should have trusted him to understand.

'Why didn't you tell me about him, about what you witnessed?! Jane! I can't believe you kept this from me. Jee-ZUS! Is this for real? I mean this isn't something—'

'What, something I made up? No. It bloody isn't, Patrick. It's real. Very real.'

He brushed his fingers through his hair. 'Real? So, you witnessed this thug beat some kid up, no, no, kill him and you walked away?'

Shame engulfed her. To tell him everything wasn't a choice. She wasn't going to do that. He just needed to know about that day. 'Yes. I did. I'm not proud of it. But I was scared. Christ, look what's happening now?'

'What is happening now, Jane?'

She stumbled over her next words. Of course, he hadn't seen any of it, only what she'd said had happened. She could have made it all up. That was more plausible than the truth. 'You don't believe me, do you?'

'I didn't say that.'

'You didn't have to. You implied it.'

'Can we get out of here and sit down?'

'No! He will see us together and he might be able to hear us out there. He has cameras in the house, it's the only way he can have done what he has and known all my movements. When you leave. When I'm alone in the house.'

'Jane, calm down, please.' He was beginning to lose patience. 'I hate to say it but listen to yourself.' He took her hand. 'Please, darling. You sound . . . come on, let's sit down with a cup of tea and see what we can do.'

'No, Patrick. No!' She yanked free. 'I don't need a cup of ruddy tea. I need you to listen to me and believe me. I am not nuts. This is very real and you have to believe me.' With every word she said she heard how unstable she sounded.

He turned back around. 'OK, OK, tell me everything. I'm listening.' She felt he wasn't at all, just trying to keep her calm. 'Just tell me why you are telling me now and not when it started.'

'I thought I could handle it. I didn't think he'd go this far.' Her words were said with half-hearted sincerity.

'He killed someone, and you didn't think he was *dangerous*?' he snapped. Then shook his head. 'Sorry, sorry, carry on.

No, wait, Jane, just tell me, didn't you think that you'd put us all in danger by not going to the police?' He rubbed his face and groaned as if the burden of the world had dropped on him. 'I don't understand any of this. Wait, hold on. So, are you saying that what you saw by the lake, the mannequin, the delivery of the candle, even the wine you're drinking . . .' He took hold of her gently by the shoulders. 'Are you telling me that you believe that was really him doing those things?'

'Yes, and I'm not making this up. This is the truth, I promise you. I know how crazy it sounds, Patrick.'

'Honestly, Jane, I'm trying to believe you. But there's nothing to show me it was real. You should have gone to the police when this all started. But why didn't you tell me about this right at the start?'

'Because I was trying to do the right thing and not worry you. I'm sorry. I thought I could handle it and . . .' Her words stuck in her throat. It was in that moment that she realised how wrong she'd got it.

She couldn't bear to look at him and see the confusion and hurt in his eyes. She reached for his hand. 'He's hacked my emails, twice. That's why I want to talk in here. I don't think he has any surveillance in here. It's the only way he could have seen me change my passwords. He messed with my work, changed file contents, Suzanna questioned me when I sent her work with nothing in the files. That's when I knew I'd been hacked.'

'But why would he bother doing that? If he wanted to hurt you . . .'

'He wants to drive me crazy, so I don't know which way is up.'

'But why? A man like that, surely, he'd just want to physically hurt you. He doesn't strike me as someone with much upstairs, just in his fists.' There was a pause during which he looked uncomfortable with what he was going to say next.

She groaned. 'Patrick, you must believe me now. I can't prove any of it. That's my problem. You must believe in me, Patrick. You have to believe I'm telling you the truth. Please.'

'Jane, what did you think I would do if you'd told me?'

Remorse crippled her. What was there to say? She hadn't trusted him. 'I don't know, I wasn't thinking. I thought I could handle it myself and he would go away. I didn't think it was him at first. Honestly, in the beginning I doubted myself. He's trying to destroy my life, my family. I guess he thinks because I destroyed his he'd do the same to me.'

He didn't look at her when he spoke. 'Is that everything?' He saw the slight hesitation in her. 'Please tell me everything, whatever it is just tell me. Let's get it all out there, please. I can't believe after all these years and everything we've gone through that you didn't trust me to support you.' She couldn't tell whether he believed her or not or was just placating. The anger was bubbling under his words as he tried to hold on to it. The tears came out of frustration more than anything. He hugged her but he was tense. She held on tightly, taking in a huge breath, preparing to tell him who Murk really was, but she couldn't do it. She clung on tighter, burying her face in his chest. 'I don't know what to do next.'

'But what made you believe it was him in the first place?'

'That letter I got that day you returned from the tour. It was from the victim support organisation, telling me he was let out early on parole.'

'Why would they contact you?'

'Because . . . because . . .' *Fuck. Fuck. Fuck.* The lies were getting messed up in her head. She couldn't explain about the letter to him.

'But you said nobody knew you were a witness.'

She stumbled on her reply. 'Well yes, I didn't come forward, to the police I mean, I wouldn't testify, I mean.' She couldn't tell Patrick why. So she faked it; there was no other way of getting around it right now. 'I asked to be informed if he ever got parole.'

He frowned, shaking his head. 'The first thing we must do is call the police, Jane. What this man is doing is harassment and you said you feared for your safety. We must call them. They're looking for him, aren't they?'

'No.' Panic engulfed her. 'That's not a good idea. I can't prove any of it. Not one single thing. So, what can they do? And then there's Ralph and Lizzie.' Her anxiety began to escalate that he'd call the police, regardless.

'Look, we'll deal with Lizzie later. We'll tell her to stay at Bev's until it's safe, but for now we need to call the police and tell them about Murk. He needs locking back up for fuck's sake.'

'No, please, they can't do anything, you know that's true, and I can't bear the pain this will bring Lizzie if she finds out.'

He pulled away. 'What does that mean?'

'Ralph! He's involved in this too. I've seen him. I saw him come to the house and take the key for the back gate with Murk.' Stunned, Patrick stared wide-eyed at her. He took a step back. 'He did, I didn't do anything. I was afraid and what could I prove anyway? My word against his? Oh, and they've got into the doorbell app, and removed the footage. That's what I'm saying, they've logged in with my details. They can see everything I do. . .'

'Whoa, Jane, are you being serious? You think Ralph is out to hurt you, for real?'

'Yes, I'm sure of it.'

'Are you listening to yourself?' He finally lost it. She'd seen it brewing in his eyes but until this moment he'd contained it. 'Jane. If you think Ralph is involved and I've no idea how you think he knows this thug, but if he is, why haven't you been over there and spoken to Pauline?'

She laughed bitterly. 'You think she'd believe me? What would I say?' He looked bewildered. 'What?'

'What fucking difference does it make? Tell her what you've just told me!' he yelled incredulously.

'Don't yell at me. You know how mad it sounds yourself. You think she'd believe me? And I'm not so sure she doesn't already know about him anyway?'

'What?'

'What! She looks so innocent and kind. People can, you know, if they're up to something.'

'You're in— and that's another sodding thing.' He cut himself short of calling her insane. It wound her up. 'Have you thought about how Lizzie and I might be in danger? What if he decides to get to you through her?' He tensed up. His body rigid. It hadn't crossed her mind. Would Murk do that? 'I'm sorry, we need to call the police and if you don't then I will.'

She couldn't cope with the police. They would do some digging and then the whole truth would come out. 'No!' she yelled. 'Patrick, listen to yourself, I have zero proof, and they can't and won't do anything. They won't understand why he's coming for me.'

'You just said he thought you were the witness in his case.'

'I know. But I wasn't, and they will want to know why he would think that?'

'And?' He shrugged. 'Who gives a damn why he thinks it? You believe he does so it's a possibility.'

'Don't please. I think it could do more harm than good.'

'Jane, I can't just not call them. That's our daughter who might be in danger.'

'I know that. But listen to us. If the police come over with zero proof, what will they think? I don't like the situation, but it could make it all worse.'

He shook his head. The logic of the situation becoming clear. 'I don't know how the fuck you've come to that conclusion. I don't like this. So let me speak to Ralph then. If I put the fear of God into him . . . *what*? Why are you looking at me like that?'

'Patrick, you couldn't put the fear of God into anyone. And besides, it will only irate Murk and he might come after you.'

'Better me than you. And how do you know that?'

'I don't. I think it that's all. No. He won't substitute you for me.'

'How do you know so much about this thug if you didn't even play witness?'

'I followed the trial and read everything I could about him. I told you, I felt awful about not coming forward.'

'OK, well . . .' He seemed to accept that, kind of. 'But how does Ralph know him?'

'I don't know. He was at uni in Manchester. Murk was in Strangeways. I don't know, that's the only connection I have. Maybe he did some day release at the prison for music therapy or something like that and got to know him.'

'Yeah, no, that makes no sense. Have you asked him?'

'No!' she wailed. 'He's hardly going to tell me, is he?'

'I don't know how I'm going to handle Ralph. He's been texting me while I was away. I don't want to speak with him now. I still can't believe he's involved. Why? That's what's bothering me. Why is he involved with this Murk bloke? Maybe because he trusts me, I can get something out of him.'

'I don't know. I don't think so. You shouldn't do that. No. And Pauline's been a little odd. I think she does know what Ralph's been up to. The more I think about her behaviour since that letter arrived, the more the pieces fit that she must be somehow involved. I mean, why bring that newspaper over? What was the reason for that? Ask yourself — you didn't think that was a bit weird?'

'I just don't understand why this Murk person is playing these games with you and doesn't just show himself?' Patrick said. She knew why. But that wasn't something she thought she ought to voice right now. 'And don't you think it's a weird coincidence Ralph living next door and knowing him?' Then it all seemed to get to him all at once and he exploded like a volcano. 'God, what the hell is going on here, Jane? What are you not telling me? It just makes no sense. There must be something more. It doesn't add up.'

'I don't have the answers. Please stop asking so many questions. I've told you everything I know.'

Jane remembered the strange comments Pauline made about the man in the boat.

'Pauline's spoken to you quite a bit when I wasn't around. I've seen the two of you gassing. What did she say to you?' she said.

'What are you suggesting? That I'm in on it with her, for God's sake?' He laughed at the ridiculousness of her suggestion. His voice was stern and harsh.

'No! Don't be an idiot. I was just saying.'

'Well don't. It sounds too much like you are calling me a liar.'

* * *

When they finally came out of the walk-in pantry, he'd calmed a little. She acted as normal as possible, aware Murk would be watching them. Sensing Patrick didn't believe a word she'd said, she saw him looking around the room to find the cameras. She whispered, 'You look suspicious. You can't act that way. Besides, I've tried to find them and failed.'

She had to get him to go to London. And not think of cancelling and staying here. That wasn't going to be easy in the circumstances.

'When do you need to go back to London for the remix?'

'How the hell can I go now after what you've told me, Jane? If any of it is true even,' he reproached angrily. She hushed him with a stern look.

'But you can't *not* go.' There was a terrible pleading tone in her voice. 'They're expecting you. How bad would that be, Patrick? You've done all the work. You must go.'

'Don't you think I know that? Christ. Fuck, Jane, this is such an opportunity for me.' She hushed him again. Frustrated he grabbed her by the arm, dragging her outside. 'If I fuck up now and don't do the remix on the tracks they need doing, my name will be shit in the industry. I'd be lucky to work again. Have you any idea who I was working with?' She shook her head, tears budding her eyes at what she had done to him. She never should have told him. She'd known right from the start doing so was a mistake. 'Only *the* sodding biggest band in the frigging world . . . who need a bloody drummer!' Her eyes bulged instantly in comprehension.

'No! Really? But that's been your dream, Patrick.'

'Humph.'

'You must go. You *must*. Why didn't you tell me? This is massive, darling.'

'I don't like to boast. You know me, low key. And I was afraid I'd get there and not get the gig or they'd change their mind about me.'

If he'd told her she wouldn't have said anything to him until he'd done the work.

'I don't think I can go, Jane. I can't leave you here with you believing this nutter is chasing you.' He paused and glanced around. She wasn't sure he believed her. 'The thing is, I've turned down a lot of jobs recently and you know this business and how fickle it can be. People get fed up and then start looking elsewhere. The reason I took it was that the money is great and with that holiday looming I wanted to work as much as possible. I didn't know it was for them when I went for the audition. It was all hush-hush, but I'd heard a rumour — you can't keep things quiet in this industry. That was why I was there longer than anticipated. We started work straight away.'

Her heart ached for him. This was her doing. 'Why didn't you let me in on it?' she asked.

'Why? Would you have told me what you've just told me if you knew?'

'Probably not.'

'I can't take this in. I'm sorry. I really am. It's all so far-fetched. I think you're having a breakdown.' There was sadness in his eyes that all this was his fault.

'I knew you wouldn't believe me,' she said sadly but what was she expecting?

'I'm not going, Jane. There's no way I'm leaving you here alone. You're not well. Come with me? Spend time in London. Shop. Go for lunch. That way I can keep an eye on you.'

'On my own?' She couldn't think of anything worse. She hated London. 'I — no, I don't like London, you know that. And it won't be much fun for me, on my own.' She thought quickly. He thought she was ill. 'I could ask Penny if I can go to her caravan for a few days if that would make you happier.' That might work, if she could persuade him that maybe she was overworked and just needed time alone away from everyone. But what about what she'd told him about Murk? Backtrack? 'Maybe you're right.' She sat on the grass. 'Maybe this isolation has something to do with it. Maybe I've imagined it all and I do need to get some help.' She put her hands to her head, trying to make it look like she believed what she said.

'But that's miles away. I don't like the idea of you on your own right now. I'm not leaving you like this.' He sat with her and took her hand in his. 'D'you think reading that newspaper article has something to do with this? I mean, like it could have triggered something inside your head? Then all that time alone and maybe the drinking hasn't helped?'

'I guess so.' She cringed that he still thought she had a drinking problem. 'Let me ask Penny. Don't you think getting away from here might be good for me?' He shrugged. 'If I go there, and check Lizzie is good to stay at Bev's, will you go to London?' She had zero intention of going anywhere. This was her opportunity with him out of the house to finally get shot of Murk once and for all. He didn't believe any of what she'd said, that much was clear. Who would? *I know I sound completely out of my mind.* 'Maybe you're right. Maybe I am ill.'

'I don't know, I don't like the idea of leaving you like this.'

She could tell he was being pulled to do the right thing. She saw it wasn't working, he wasn't going to go.

'Jane, no, I just . . .'

Then she had an idea. 'Wait, what if I speak to Penny? Her family are still there on the site, I could stay in Penny's caravan, but her sisters are next door. I won't be alone then.' She saw he wasn't buying it. 'Maybe I can ask Penny if she fancies a long weekend, one last one before the kids go back and I'll go with her.'

'You really scared me in there just then. I mean, d'you know how crazy you sounded?'

'I do now, yes, saying it aloud, yes it sounded mad. I'm sorry. I should have listened to you sooner and got professional help. I just didn't know it wasn't real.' He still looked at her as if she was having a breakdown. And maybe that was how she should let him think for now. It would be kinder.

'Look, I realise now I need to do something about how I'm feeling. But I can't let you miss this opportunity in London.' *Oh God, if he doesn't go, I'm in a mess.*

'Will you honestly go to Penny's place and not just say you will if I do go?' There was so much hope in his voice it hurt. 'I'm really not comfortable with this, Jane.'

'Yes. I promise.' This seemed to appease him a little. She crossed her fingers behind her back. *Please, please go. Say yes.* 'You have to finish this work, Patrick. I won't let you miss this opportunity.'

'I do believe that you believe what you told me was true. But you must understand how it sounds to me, Jane.' He took a deep breath, exhaled and shook his head. Looked unsure. 'If I do go it'll only be for a couple of days, three at most. It could run on, but I don't think it will. I don't want to leave you on your own any longer than I have to, Jane.' He looked pained. His internal struggle clear on his face. 'Call Penny,' he said.

'OK,' she said, dialling Penny on her mobile. She picked up after a couple of rings. 'Hi, Penny, hi, how are you? Great, listen I want to ask you a huge favour. Sure, sure, I just don't want to put you out. That's great, well, the thing is Patrick's going back to London and I fancied a break and wondered if I could go and stay at the caravan for a couple of days, or maybe three. Maybe you fancy a long weekend with the girls too before the end of summer? Really? That's great,' she nodded to Patrick. 'OK, hang on.' She turned to Patrick, 'When are you going?'

'Tomorrow?'

'Hi Penny, he's going tomorrow so maybe the day after? Brill, OK, yeah, I'll speak to you tomorrow then, bye.' She hung up. 'So that's sorted. I'll go there when you go, well the day after. It's only a four-hour drive and we'll break it up. It'll be lovely and good to get away. And I won't be on my own.'

He took a deep breath.

'I really think it will do me good. Getting away from here. A new place. Maybe that's what I need.'

'I thought you loved it here, alone.'

'I do. I really do. But I, I don't have the answer as to why I've flipped like this. I'm not going to start thinking about it either, not right now. I'm sorry, Patrick. I don't know what to say to you. I—' He looked doubtful. Worried, and why wouldn't he after what she'd said to him. She was a fool to have said anything. 'I think you're definitely right. I need to get away and then see someone when you get back. We'll go together.' He nodded, looking at her sadly. 'As soon as you've finished, we have to book that holiday.' He nodded, not looking convinced.

'Right,' he said looking sceptical.

'Oh, remember the signal there isn't very good, according to Penny, so don't worry if you can't get hold of me. I might have to find signal to text you.'

CHAPTER 34

Patrick left early the next day. And suddenly the house was silent, filled with both anticipation and dread. The idea was not to tell anyone he was away apart from Penny, who already knew. She made sure the cameras were all disabled and hoped Murk could only see what went on inside the house. She had never minded being on her own. In fact, she liked it, no, she loved her own company. Well, before all this happened, she did. Now each new sound or old sound for that matter that creaked, rattled, or clicked gave her a minor heart attack.

Hating that she had lied to Patrick, but knowing it was necessary, she went over to Penny's soon after he left, telling her she wasn't sure about going today and could they go tomorrow, she had last-minute work she had to finish and needed time alone. She hoped it would all be over by then and Penny wouldn't come over.

'Oh, that's fine, no problem; gives me time to wash another load. I'll speak to you in the morning. We can go in my car and share the driving if you're OK with that.'

'Fine, great, tomorrow then.' They hugged and she went home to make her plans.

She didn't want to wait so she texted Jon.

Jane: *I know you have been coming into my house. I know Ralph is helping you. All the information from your phone and laptop I have on a flash drive, and I am going to the police with everything. I also have the recordings from our security cameras — you were too slow deleting them.*

A few moments later he replied.

Jon: ☺ ☺ ☺ ☺

She saw through the lounge window something going on at Pauline's. Tony left in his car, slamming the door; he didn't look happy. A few minutes later the car from the other night pulled up and the same two men climbed out and entered the house. She made herself a camomile tea.

This wasn't good. Murk, she was sure, was now in Pauline's house.

She raced upstairs and grabbed the binoculars. What were they doing?

She guessed Pauline knew Patrick had gone away, and that whatever they were planning would happen in the next day or so. She had to make it happen today.

A Sainsbury's van pulled up on her drive with some essentials and bits to take with her to the caravan. She dropped the binoculars and breathed. In out, in out, slowly. This was it then. He was planning, she knew it. Her wrist had a red welt forming.

She opened the door.

Her mouth watered at the sight of a jar of olives and a packet of cured meats. The first thing she did was open the jar of olives. Mmm, delicious. She checked the order for added wine. Thankfully there was none this time. The last lot was still hidden in the walk-in pantry, knowing if Patrick had found it — well, she didn't want to go there right now. She had more than enough rattling in her brain to reflect on how that might have gone down.

274

Her phone rang: *caller unknown*. Her heart skipped a beat. Was this it? Was this how it was to begin? A phone call? She answered, hesitantly.

'Hey, Jane, how are you?'

'Suzanna?'

'Yes, of course it's me. Didn't my name flag up?'

'No, actually, I wasn't going to answer. I don't tend to answer unknown numbers.'

'Oh, damn it. I had to make a call and hid my number. I hate unsolicited calls too. I'll pop it back on after our conversation. So, those illustrations were awesome by the way. I just had to call you and tell you. Great idea about texting and calling while your emails are playing up. Have you not got to the bottom of it yet?'

'No, nightmare, Suzanna. I seem able to send but I don't always receive, so for now if you don't mind calling or texting?'

'OK, let me know when you're back up and running. How's Patrick? He told me last time I spoke he was getting lots of work.'

'Yes, he's quite in demand now. So, we're taking advantage. Hey ho, make hay while the sun shines as the saying goes.' She picked up her tea and a jar of roasted red peppers, making her way to the window to see Pauline's house.

'Absolutely. Yeah, so, remember how I said I'd come over?'

Christ, no, please God, don't tell me she's coming over soon! 'Oh yes, what of it?' she said breezily.

'I'm coming to see you both. Flying visit, but better than nothing. So, I can surprise Patrick. He won't believe it.'

'When are you thinking of?' She crossed her fingers and her arms that it wasn't in the next few days.

'Oh, well the earliest I can do is late September. Is that OK?'

'I imagine so, but we're going away around that time. We'll know for sure when Patrick gets back from this last London trip. We've still not booked the holiday.'

'OK, great, sounds amazing. So, I have just a few final changes on the illustrations. Only a few, if you could let me have them back asap that would be great. It's only teeny changes, if you wouldn't mind.'

Jane checked her emails on her phone; thankfully there it was. 'I'll take a look shortly and give you a timeframe once I see what you want doing.'

'Right, have to fly. Keep in touch.'

She twisted the lid off the jar to stop her stomach groaning. It released with a pop. She pinched one with her fingers and popped it in her mouth. One was never enough.

Taking the jar of peppers with her she went back to the lounge window. Murk was talking to Pauline in the kitchen. What was he saying to her? She must find him creepy. And then they were out of sight.

She picked out another pepper, eating it as she watched. The sooner this was over the better. She picked up her binoculars, watching the house, searching the windows. Everything seemed quiet. *Where are they?*

A face appeared at the window, staring right back at her with binoculars. She stepped back, dropping hers.

Fuck!

CHAPTER 35

Tossing and turning, she checked the time on her phone. Her mind was alight with ideas, worries, fears and her stomach felt as if all it wanted to do was barf. Exhausted, she turned over and fluffed her pillow for the millionth time to try and find sleep. She hadn't come to any firm idea of how to deal with Murk. She'd actually thought he'd come to her as soon as he read her text. She'd gone to bed frustrated and fed up waiting for him.

The sound burst through her consciousness like a firework ripping through the quiet night. Disorientated, she started out of her bed, sitting on the edge, ready for something to happen. Confused by what had made her start that way, she blinked, trying to make sense of the sound and where it had come from. Her heart rate ascended dangerously. She looked afresh at the time on her phone. 3.00 a.m.

It came again. A woman screaming. The hairs on the back of her neck rose, as a clammy sweat covered her body. She squeezed her eyes shut. Her nails dug into her palms. And just like the last time, fear tore at her, almost paralysing her. Patrick had disconnected the sound system. It couldn't be that.

Grabbing her phone off the bedside table, she called Penny. It went to voicemail. She must have it switched off.

Hesitantly, she climbed out of bed, went to the window and looked at Pauline's house. The sound seemed to emanate from there. The kitchen lights were on. A figure resembling Murk stood with Pauline, framed in the kitchen window. At this time in the morning? What was going on? Tony's car was back. She kept her eyes fixed on them. Shouting streamed out through the open window, loud and angry. Too far away to hear what was being said, all she could do was stare. Like a snake, Murk's hand, without warning, latched around Pauline's neck . . . Jane gasped. Murk was strangling her! Oh God, had Pauline questioned him? She must have been concerned, recognised him from the paper and told him to leave. Maybe even threatened to call the police. She gasped for air as everything around began closing in. And now he was trying to get rid of her. Where were Tony and Ralph?

I don't know what to do. Oh God, not again. No. She couldn't be a witness a second time. She looked out at Penny's house, saw Gordon's car not there; he must be staying in London. Penny always said she slept like the dead, how had she not heard this, though?

Pauline collapsed onto her knees as he squeezed the life from her. Jane grabbed her binoculars. It looked so real. Pauline's hands tried to pull him off her neck, but like a cobra it was impossible to free herself. Was it another of his tricks? But Pauline? Was she not involved? Was she just a nosy person, a gossip who would never be involved with someone as dangerous as Murk? *I have to do something. Don't I?*

She snatched at her phone, but it slipped from her clammy hand, bounced on the bed and fell to the floor. Cursing, she fumbled for it blindly, not wanting to take her eyes away from the window. Finally latching onto it, she dialled 999.

'Hello? Police? Emergency. Someone is trying to kill my neighbour.' She rattled off the address. 'Jane Carmichael. I'm watching it now. He's strangling her. Come quick.' Jane screamed, covering her face with her hands as Pauline fell to the floor in a heap. The phone toppled from her hand with the operator still talking. She picked it up, racing downstairs. 'I'm going over there. I have to help her.' She flung open the front door, the phone shooting from her hand in her haste.

She dashed over the gravel in the dark and noticed how quiet it had gone. None of the security lights came on. She came to an abrupt halt, skidding on the stones, losing her balance, falling to her knees. Something was wrong. She sensed it at once. Her instincts pushed her to stand up. The gravel had cut through her pyjamas, the sharp stones digging into her knees and she felt the trickle of blood running down her shin. All the lights were off in Pauline's house. She blinked. *What the fuck is going on?* She could hear her blood rushing through her ears. Her body went into survival mode, moving her legs back towards her house. Something told her not to go to Pauline's. Were they watching, laughing at her? She looked at the house in darkness. It was impossible to see if anyone was there. She took another step back, then another. Shadows around her moved. A scream jammed in her throat. Adrenaline soared through her. Her bowels cramped with terror of the unknown in the darkness surrounding her. No, Pauline wouldn't do this to her. *Oh, Christ, is she dead? Had he run off?* She stumbled on an uneven stone but kept on her feet . . . then heard the crunch of gravel and footsteps in front of her . . . somebody was coming towards her. She didn't want to look. She fought the fear and made herself lift her head. She knew who was coming. She swallowed to rid herself of the lump jammed in the back of her throat. As the footsteps came closer, she stopped backing up. Waited. A body came into view. Large. Tall. Wide and chillingly all too familiar. Like an alarm system being tripped, her entire body went into shock, violently, tugging at her to run. *RUN*, every sense inside her yelled.

She stood her ground to face him. He walked up to her. Towering over her he bent low, right in her face. She held her breath. Forced herself to face him.

'BOO, Janey,' he said roaring with laughter and then he vanished into the darkness, leaving her there on the drive. Moments later the police pulled up, flashing blue lights and sirens blaring.

She watched in horror as the police and paramedics banged on the front door which swiftly opened. A female police officer stood with her, taking her to the back of the ambulance to sit down. The emergency services rushed inside, only to re-emerge a few minutes later . . . with Pauline. Uniforms moved about the front lawn and the crescent. Lights went on over at Penny's house. Pauline came out of the house with Tony, both in their pyjamas.

Voices grew louder and clearer. In shock, she sat and stared at Pauline and sensed bodies approaching. She twisted her head in their direction. Two officers advanced, one talking into a radio. A wave of horror wrapped around her. She'd been set up.

DI Saint spoke to her. 'Mrs Carmichael, can you hear what I'm saying to you?' He had sad, serious eyes. She nodded. 'You called the police saying that you were witnessing your neighbour being strangled. Do you remember making that call?'

'Yes,' she said unable to remove her eyes from Pauline.

'Mrs Carmichael, can I ask you if you'd been drinking tonight? As you can see your neighbour is unharmed and knows nothing about what you say you saw.'

A warm hand caressed her back, gently. Penny was by her side. 'Jane, are you OK? I heard the police and thought something terrible had happened when I saw you outside.'

'Could I ask who you are?' asked DI Saint.

'The other neighbour, Penny Hill. Gordon and I live there with our two little girls.' She pointed to their house. 'I heard the emergency services. I've come to see if Jane is OK. What happened?'

'Mrs Carmichael called us saying she saw your other neighbour, Pauline Jackson, being strangled in her kitchen.'

Penny gasped. 'What!' She instinctively looked at Pauline's house and saw her standing at the front door. 'But . . .'

'You don't need to say anything, Penny,' Jane said. 'I take it you heard nothing tonight before the police arrived?'

'No, sorry, Jane. I didn't, but I noticed your missed call when I woke. I turn off my phone when we go to bed.'

She remembered her telling her that.

DI Saint looked a little confused. 'Can you confirm if you had been drinking or not, Mrs Carmichael or if you're on any medication?'

'No, I hadn't. And no, I'm not on any medication.'

Penny sensed the tension immediately and was about to say something, but Jane squeezed her hand which was now in hers. 'Maybe she had a bad dream. You can have them sometimes when everything looks real and when you wake up, you're convinced it happened,' she said nervously.

'So, I believe, Mrs Hill. Is that what happened, Mrs Carmichael? You have in fact called us once before, insisting you had a prowler.'

Penny squeezed her hand. 'I heard the same sound, but I had to rush off to an emergency. I wasn't sure what it was. But I heard it.'

'I think we concluded it was a fault with the sound system, is that right, Mrs Carmichael? Did you husband find the cause?'

She nodded, not wanting to talk about it.

'Yes, I did, you're right,' Jane replied to his question. 'I don't know what happened tonight. I was convinced what I saw was true and before you ask, again, no, I haven't taken any medication. I was asleep when I was woken up by Pauline screaming. Then I saw her arguing in her kitchen and the man trying to strangle her.' She looked up towards Pauline, talking to a policewoman. Their eyes locked. 'Clearly, I must have been dreaming, like Penny said. I'm sorry for calling you out. I don't know what else to say.' She wanted them all to go and let her back into her house.

'The paramedics will do a quick check to make sure you are all right before they go. Is there anything else you want to tell us, Mrs Carmichael? Will you be OK here by yourself? Mrs Jackson told us your husband was away in London. Would you like us to contact him?'

So, Pauline and Murk knew Patrick had gone to London. It didn't surprise her. 'No thank you, that won't be necessary.' She couldn't look at Pauline anymore. Why had she done such a heinous thing to her? And being in league with Murk? She didn't get it.

The realisation that he would go to any lengths to have her certified, burned through her. Was that what he was trying to achieve? Well, he certainly had form.

In the stillness of her house that followed, alone and scared, she thought carefully about her next steps. Maybe telling people what was happening was the wrong thing to do. Maybe that was playing into his hands. After all, if she didn't tell anyone then his plan would come away at the seams for sure. But she'd made the call to the emergency services. She'd said Pauline was being strangled. How the hell was she going to get herself out of that? She had her own plans on how to deal with him.

* * *

A few hours later, she watched the sunrise from her kitchen. She was exhausted physically and mentally. Now on her third coffee, she paced the floor. With no sleep, her mind was going over and over what had happened. She texted Penny to say she wasn't up to going today and could they go tomorrow.

'Oh, Jane, I do understand but I don't mind driving, you can sleep if you want.'

'That's so kind but I'm really not up for travelling. I'm sorry to mess you about, really, I am.'

'Don't worry; luckily, I haven't told the girls yet, it was going to be a surprise. But Gordon is coming back about ten this morning. He stayed over an extra day in London.'

She felt rotten. 'Oh, Penny, I'm so sorry. I'm messing you all about.'

'It's no bother but if we don't go tomorrow, it won't be worth it. Listen, if you don't want to, we don't have to. It was a lovely idea but if you're not up to it . . .'

'I'm sure tomorrow will be fine.'

She had to implement her plan now. She couldn't wait any longer. She'd send Patrick a cursory text a little later, just to let him know she'd arrived in Mumbles and the signal was dire, but she was OK and the journey relatively quiet. She couldn't tell him she was still at home.

It was so hard to believe that Ralph had seemed so innocent and loving towards them. How wrong she had been. Why was he even getting himself involved with Murk? You'd think, being a talented musician, he would want to make his career his focus. But then, maybe he hadn't had a choice. Maybe he didn't know how to get himself out of the situation. Maybe Murk was blackmailing the two of them? That was a possibility. But how and why? They could be too afraid to say no. Or they hadn't had a choice. That would make more sense. She was giving herself a headache. She knew only too well how controlling Murk could be.

She now sat in her garden, looking out at her island. Would that be where he killed her, leaving her there for days only to be found bloated and unrecognisable, animals having mauled her face? Would that be the first place to look for her when she disappeared? Or would they not think of it for days? And then by chance, Patrick or Penny or even Lizzie would come up with the suggestion.

Before she could change her mind, she sent a text.

Jane: *I'm ready for you. Do you have the guts to face me for real this time and not just skulk off into the night?*

It was a leap, but she was sure he would be pissed off with that text. She hoped so. She had to give him no excuse but to come to her.

She stared at the text as the delivery acknowledgement appeared. She told herself that he probably wouldn't reply, and if he did, he might not tell her anything. So she had to be ready for him. He was hardly going to put anything in writing. She realised then that she shouldn't have sent that text before implementing her plan. To take him to the island, attack him by taking him by surprise then dumping him in the lake. Simple enough. She could if she got the advantage.

And then she saw the three tiny dots flash on the screen. Her heart jolted like she'd been shocked with a defibrillator. They stopped. She let out her breath. They appeared again. She waited. Her eyes glued to the screen.

Jon: *I knew you'd be missing me* ☺ *When and where?*

This was it then. As a precaution, she screen shot all their correspondence. It would go up to the cloud. It was her security.

CHAPTER 36

It was 8.30 in the morning and felt like the middle of the night to Jane's body clock. She found herself thinking she needed a weapon to protect herself when she met up with Murk. Like a gun. No, not like a gun at all. And where was she going to get a gun from? This wasn't America, where you could pick one up easily. No. Something like a cricket bat or a knife. But then wouldn't that be called premeditated? Of course, it would. It had to look as if it was all spontaneous.

She was out of her league with Murk, she knew that. She wasn't insane, although some people might agree to differ. She could handle this. She knew all about him. A frown creased her brow. She had to be unpredictable. He would anticipate how she'd act and what she might do. She couldn't afford to be predictable.

Murk hated her. She didn't doubt that. He wanted to destroy all that was hers, so convinced that she was the witness. Telling him he was wrong wasn't going to work. The witness was protected, and he believed what he wanted.

Murk was not like normal people; he saw the world differently. Maybe Ralph was forced to do the same? Or maybe he wanted to, who knew.

She knew she was in real danger, and how it could escalate. First, she had to find the cameras. She began systematically taking the pictures down off the walls, properly searching every nook and cranny this time and then she stopped, looked up at the TV and cursed. How utterly mental was she! Why hadn't it occurred to her that that would be the logical place, just like her laptop. She yanked the cables out of the back and threw a blanket over the front.

As she stood and stared, she heard her phone vibrate.

Jon: *Clever girl. I knew you were smart.* ☺

Desperate to reply, she controlled herself. Not yet. About to put the phone back in her pocket, it vibrated again.

Jon: *Tick-tock, times running out, Janey. If you don't suggest a meetup, then I will have to come for you.*

He could already be here — in the house or close by or even . . . on the island . . . watching her through binoculars. She drew the curtains, pulled down the blinds. Locked the front door. Locking herself in completely was a bad idea. It was daytime and hot. Even with the fans running it was suffocating.

She needed a weapon to protect herself . . . not to kill him, but to help give her time to call the police. If it got that far. If she killed him then she was no better than him. And that was abhorrent to her.

On top of the wall cupboards in the utility, in a wicker basket. She was sure she'd put it there after buying it online for her own peace of mind ages ago, long before Murk came on the scene. She stood on the stool to reach it. The Farb-Gel defence dye spray singularly stood out among the myriad of pens, Sellotape, brown tape, superglue and various colours of plastic paperclips. Like most things, she'd bought it for when she'd lived in London but then forgot she had it. Out of sight out of mind.

It was perfectly legal. And she had reason to have it, seeing as she spent long times on her own here and on the island.

She had always thought she would live a mundane sort of life with little if any out-of-the-ordinary drama. That was until she walked in on Murk in the pub that day. It was remarkable how one wrong decision could effectively change your whole life. Since that day, her life had been anything but ordinary. But what never occurred to her was that, while nothing ordinary would ever be a part of her life again, she would ever contemplate having to kill another person to save herself. She'd always entrusted the law. Of course, that was before she was in the epicentre of such a situation.

She stored the mini spray in the pocket of her jeans. She grabbed a baggy jumper from the washing basket and put it on to disguise the bulge. She looked in the mirror. That would do nicely. Now all she had to do was text him with the time and place.

Jon: *Changed my mind as you can't make a decision so I'm calling it. The island, tonight at nine.*

Jane: *Come alone. If I see anyone else, I'll call the police.*

Jon: *How do I know you won't anyway?*

Jane: *You don't but neither of us want the police involved, do we?*

She squeezed the Farb-Gel tightly and threw up a little bit in her mouth.

She tried not to think what Murk had planned; it was better that way. It would be dark at nine, certainly on the island and with the cloud cover today there would be little moonlight.

All she could think of was what if it all went wrong, what would Patrick think when he got home and found her not here. If he never saw her again. If they never found her. For the rest of the day, she paced. Thought her plan through. First, talk him round. Second, if that failed, plead for her life. Third, because she knew neither of those was going to work, record the conversation, call the police and tell them that he was there, and she was in danger. Crap plans. It was all she'd been able to come up with. It was going to come down to him or her, she knew it, deep down. She knew Murk much better than he knew her, she was sure. She was sure he hadn't changed. She was banking on it. But he didn't know her, not the new her. If she had to . . . she would *do it*. She would kill him.

* * *

Outside in the intimidating oncoming darkness, she checked the time: just before nine. The sky was cloudless, which she hadn't thought would be the case, and the stars looked down like millions of eyes watching. Was that God keeping an eye on her or the millions of souls that had gone before her? There was one light on at Pauline's house and the same car that was there yesterday was on the drive. Penny was in with Gordon, who'd arrived earlier today, and the kids. She wondered if Pauline knew what was happening tonight. But she suspected Murk wanted this all-kept secret. However, she was the only other person around here with a boat. He was going to surprise her of that she was certain.

She landed on the island, killed the engine and tied her boat in a different part to her usual mooring. A little further away and easier to conceal. She checked her Farb-Gel was safe in the pocket of her jacket — easier to access there than in her jeans. Her phone was in the inside of her jacket, zipped up. She had no intention of being a hero. If the situation got out of hand, she was quite prepared to call the police; the number was on speed dial. Then she pulled it out again, opened the voice memo app, set it to record and popped it back in the pocket.

Time passed slowly; her stomach was so tight she had little cramps going on. Sitting waiting wasn't an option so she paced. Her ears primed for any noise on the water. It was much darker here. Her eyes grew accustomed to the little light. She was pitched to hear little splashes of water as oars dipped in and out, bringing him closer to her; he would use a rowing boat to be as quiet as possible.

She didn't dare check the time on her phone, knowing the small illumination from her screen would identify where she was.

Then she heard it.

Tiny sounds of surface water breaking. Focused, she listened as the sounds grew louder, the closer he came.

There could be anyone already on the island. It wasn't something she wouldn't put past him to have one of his thugs go on ahead. They could be watching right now through the trees and thick foliage, and she wouldn't be any the wiser.

His arrival was painfully slow. Finally, he stepped out of the boat, his foot squelching in the muddy water as he hauled his bulk onto firm ground. He didn't look around. He probably already knew where she was. He dragged the boat further up onto the land to keep it from floating away. There was nothing for him to tie the rope to, so he left it snaked on the muddy bank. She looked back at Pauline's, wondering if someone had binoculars focused on them.

She didn't think he would be expecting anything from her but pleading and grovelling.

He made his way onto firmer ground where he stopped and looked around. She wasn't visible to him yet. She turned, looked back at the two houses and when she turned back, he was gone. There was only blackness and quiet. So much quiet it hurt her ears. She strained to make out noises that might alert her to his whereabouts. For a man of that size, he was uncannily light on his feet.

She paused when she heard the snap of a twig. Shocked it was so close, she moved slowly to the edge of one of the bushes and looked out into the inky darkness that now had fallen all around the island.

She cursed herself for losing sight of him so easily.

She thought of staying where she was until she could pinpoint his whereabouts then reflected it might be prudent to go look for him. She didn't want to be a sitting duck. She moved slightly, only for a sharp branch to catch her on the leg, penetrating her jeans and no doubt cutting her flesh. She drew in her breath to stop crying out. She made herself re-focus away from the pain. She mustn't let anything distract her now. Moving a little further from the safety of the bush, she found herself framed in the moonlight, immobilised, knowing how visible she must be to anyone watching.

In the distance, a hushed voice called her name, making her snap back. She turned to see him a few yards in front of her, looming out of the foliage like a dinosaur. Her instant reaction was to cut and run. But she didn't. She knew this was their final destination. Only one of them was coming out alive.

'Hello, sis.'

CHAPTER 37

She stepped back a little, not taking her eye off him for a second in case he charged. The darkness swallowed him up, but she knew she was still illuminated in the beam of moonlight. Then he was gone. Quickly and with trembling fingers, she pressed the record button on her phone.

The sounds around her amplified. Her senses instantly heightened. She reminded herself why she was here and felt for the Farb-Gel. The rushing of adrenaline was like a drug hit and had her instantly alert, aware of everything around her to the point of painful accuracy.

She unzipped her jacket, ready. Her breath came quick and fast. She settled it down by doing her slow breathing, in out, in out and not allowing her mind to roam, to panic. She had to stay focused.

Where was he? She turned her head left to right. Turned in a circle. No sign of life. And yet, she felt him close by. Sensed him like an evil spirit, lurking, waiting to find her weak spot.

She let her mind work with the idea that he wasn't alone. That way she was prepared for any surprise. She'd be surprised if he was alone. He agreed he would be. But did she trust the word of a killer? Not likely. She let her mind wander, colouring in all the possibilities that yet again, she had walked into his trap.

'So, Janey. We are here. On your island. Together again. Now what?' He stepped out of the darkness.

She spun quickly at the sound of his voice right behind her.

Everything inside her screamed that this was a mistake. She waited for her nerves to subside a little so she could actually swallow. They didn't.

She wasn't going to freak out. She wasn't going to show she was intimidated. But seeing him in front of her was hard.

His face was threatening. There was nothing friendly about him. He oozed menace. Her stomach flipped. The man she had dreaded to meet after all this time watched her. The man of her nightmares. The man whom she thought would never see the light of day again. Curtis Murk. She stopped herself recoiling and bringing up what little food she'd eaten.

Wordlessly she looked back at him. The taste of vomit, sour in her mouth.

He smiled at her. A gesture that made her wince inwardly. She tried to relax, letting her shoulders loosen. But she was too tense, her rigidness giving her a statue-like quality. She studied him, the man she had doggedly been trying to entrap only to fail miserably. She knew right now, she stood no chance against this monster.

'So,' he said, 'here we are . . . Janey.' The sound of her name on his lips was like a blow to the face. 'It's been a long time.'

She nodded. The movement almost imperceptible. 'You changed your name.'

'I did. I wanted to distance myself from the horror of our past.'

'The horror you ran away from, leaving me behind,' she scorned.

'And now we're here, together, again. Finally. Face to face after all these years. So what now?' he asked.

'Can't you guess?'

'No. Not really.' He was flippant. A tactic to unsettle her.

'I would have thought you'd know what I wanted to meet you for.'

He shrugged. 'No idea. I am surprised though. I didn't think you wanted to ever see me again. I took the initiative for tonight. Didn't want you planning some kind of trap for me.' He made spooky sounds, mocking her. Of course he would have known her moves. 'Don't tell me you've softened in all these years towards your dear brother. So, come on, tell me why. Spell it out to me . . . Janey.'

'Why? You have to ask why?'

He'd gone grey since the last time she'd seen him. The moonlight picked out the silver in his hair. His face was heavily lined with a deep crease between his eyes but all that was superimposed over the killer that he was.

'Because you're terrified of me—'

'You're so full of shit,' she snapped irritated he could see that in her.

'Must be because you missed me then . . . because you want to mend bridges?'

'You're still as fucked up.'

'Aren't you?' He laughed. 'You're really fucked up from what I've seen. What's up, Janey, cat got your tongue? Where's the feisty cat that had claws?' He pulled a sad face. 'Did they snip them off in the hospital? Boo hoo.' He rubbed his eyes in a crying gesture.

She wanted to yell and scream at him and if she could punch his condescending face, she would. Once, long before he became Curtis Murk, killer, he was her brother who took her to school and made sure she didn't get into trouble for being late. She knew the day she walked into that pub and saw him covered in blood, holding the body of that boy, that he was a monster.

'If you think you scare me. You don't. I want you to leave me alone and believe me when I tell you I wasn't the witness.'

Her voice was serrated with fear, not wanting to turn back time. She had managed to close that door. To put it all behind her. She had created a new world for herself where her past was as she had created it. Decent. Normal with zero violence. Her immediate instinct on seeing him was to fold into herself and try to disappear.

'I know that's a lie, Janey. Your fear is so powerful it controls you — we both know that. It makes you . . . delusional. It's always been that way. Have you forgotten?'

Her anxiety grew like an oil slick in the ocean.

'Why didn't you show yourself at the trial?' He snorted. 'Hiding? Scared to show your face?'

'I wasn't there.'

Murk nodded. 'Don't lie to me.' He let out a long breath. 'I know it was you who gave evidence. It could only have been you.'

She cleared her throat. 'It wasn't me.'

'Clever to try and convince me of that,' Murk said. 'But there was no one else that would have grassed me up. I trusted *them*. I didn't trust you, though. I still don't. I thought you might think you wanted payback. Tell me how you knew so quickly it was me watching you?'

'I got a letter from Victim Support, telling me you were out. I requested it, as family.'

'I see, so really you did want to know how I was, was that it?'

'Don't kid yourself. I don't know what to say to convince you, I wasn't the witness. You seem confident it was me. No point in me trying to change that. I know how stubborn you can be.'

'If not you then why not you? I mean, come on, Janey that was your opportunity to stick it to me. Don't tell me it didn't cross your mind. I had you stitched up for something I did.'

'It didn't,' she said.

'When you left the pub that day, what did you think of doing right then at that moment? I bet it was to call the cops.'

She swallowed. 'It was.' She shifted. Her throat, dry, her words caught in their confusion of what order to set themselves free. 'But I didn't. I walked to the train station. Got on the train and tried to forget.'

She recalled the memory of the tangle of thoughts she'd had that day. The pull of doing the right thing for that boy and the need to survive. Ashamed that it hadn't been that difficult to walk away and do nothing. On that journey home she had gone over what she *should* do and what she *could* do. The sentences running into each other, crashing against one another like a train wreck. Her treacherous mind wanting to open that door and slide back inside — to remember the past she had so firmly locked away.

'So, the question is . . . what happens now, Janey?'

She backed away, sensing something change in his manner. He lashed out, grabbing her wrist viciously, dragging her towards the edge of the water. His assault took her breath away. Unable to stop the momentum, she went with it, fearing if she didn't, he would drag her along the ground. He edged along the fringe of the water towards her boat. She steadied herself against a thick root so as not to fall over.

'I need to tell you why you should have listened to me and not talked. You didn't listen to all the warnings I sent. You only listened to yourself.' Her stomach lurched. *This is it. Yet again, he's taken me by surprise and gained the upper hand. He's going to kill me now.* In her boat. And throw her overboard. Her phone and her Farb-Gel would follow her to the bottom of the lake. There would be no proof he did anything. 'You only knew what you *thought* you saw that day. Which is not the same as what really happened. That boy was the son of someone close to me. And someone I would never hurt.' He turned to face her; in the low light she saw his face had softened, together with his eyes — no longer the hard, angry, terrifying face she knew. 'I loved that boy like my own.' He stopped and looked up at the sky as if searching for something. 'Get in the boat. You need to know the real truth.'

An image of them in the middle of the lake flashed through her mind. Him pulling a knife telling her she destroyed his life because she was too selfish to see another side to what happened that day. Too blinkered. Too consumed with thinking she was right and refusing to see or listen to anything different. *Oh God.*

'How was I supposed to know any of this?' she snapped.

'I know they told you who that boy was. I know they told you that I would be telling the court what I'm telling you now because it was the truth. I had just arrived at the pub, moments before you, when he walked in, bruised and battered. They just didn't want *you* to know the truth. They wanted me behind bars. They'd been trying a long time to pin something on me, and this was too perfect for them to lose you as a witness.'

'Who are they?'

'The people you trust to protect you.'

'The police?' Her thoughts raced. 'But I keep telling you I didn't speak to anyone about what I saw. If they told you I did, they lied. Nobody knew I was there. They must have had another witness.'

Was this Murk's way of muddying the waters to confuse her even more so she would believe whatever tale he was going to spin her? But sometimes the truth was stranger than fiction; wasn't that how the saying went?

As if she could trust anything her brother said. She narrowed her eyes; he was trying to make her question everything.

He held her gaze. 'Get in the boat,' he insisted.

'Why are you lying to me?' she said.

'I'm not.'

'Yes, you are! And why couldn't there have been another witness. Why are you so set on it being me?'

He laughed as though she was pathetic and wasting his time. 'Revenge is sweet and best served cold, dear sister. You couldn't resist getting your own back. It's logical. I know there was no other witness that day in court. That's why you wanted anonymity. I knew it when they told me you would be giving evidence in a closed court.'

'Listen to you. So big, so macho like nobody would cross you, even when you killed someone. You can't handle the fact that one of your friends or gang or whoever *did* shop you to the police.'

'I need to tell you more and we're going to take a little boat ride, first.' He untied the rope, pushing the boat gently into the water. He held out his outstretched hand to her. She ignored it and backed away. 'Get in, Janey,' he insisted.

Free from his grasp, she stepped back, her hand falling to her pocket. 'Why do we need to go in the boat? Tell me here.' Her heart skipped a beat. Scared of what he had planned. Scared that yet again he was able to manipulate her so easily. Scared she wouldn't win this. But she needed to know what it was he wasn't telling her.

He sighed heavily. 'Do we really have to do this violently? Get in the fucking boat!' he roared, and she remembered Pauline saying, *nobody can hear you scream out there.*

'No, no, no, you tell me here. I'm not getting in that boat.' In one giant step he had her by the waist.

'Shut the fuck up and just get in. Stop lying to me, Janey. I'm not going to hurt you. I just want you to be honest with me.'

She believed that like she'd believed the lake wasn't wet. She pulled back; if she got in the boat that was it. She raked at his hand to release her. 'Get the fuck off me you mental fucker. Haven't you done enough to me?' She dug her nails deep into his flesh. He whipped round and slapped her. She lost her footing. Stars blurred her vision before he dragged her into the boat.

CHAPTER 38

She fell into the boat with a thud, scrabbling to the end as far away from him as possible. She tried not to think of the murky, dark water around her. Or the flimsiness of the boat should he try to throw her over. She felt inside her pockets. The comforting hardness of the Farb-Gel and her phone recording every word. Her hands gripped the sides. She had never been afraid of the water or her boat. *But I am now.* She twisted her body so she had maximum protection should he try to grab her. She wouldn't make it easy for him if he did. She was cold. A tremor of fear shook her body constantly.

'Not scared, are you?' he asked. She didn't reply. He pushed them away from the bank, climbed in, pulled the cord on the motor; the engine sound that had always soothed her terrified her now. Her fear making her breathless.

A wind picked up, rippling the water. She focused on Murk making himself comfortable, navigating the little boat out into the middle of the lake. They hit a current which made the boat bob furiously side to side. She gripped the sides, catching her breath; she'd not come across one herself but had heard occasionally if the wind was bad, you could encounter them. It was him, she gasped with realisation. *It was you! You killed Jasper!* 'My God, you killed Jasper, didn't you?'

He turned to face her. 'Such a sweet dog.'

Her blood boiled of all the things he'd done . . . this raged inside her boiling her blood. She hated him.

As soon as they were back on calm water, he turned off the motor. They bobbed gently. He took out a packet of cigarettes, pulled one out and lit it, casting his eyes into the openness across the lake. Then offered her one. She declined. He threw the spent match into the water.

Her hands had begun to cramp from gripping the edge of the boat so tightly. She relaxed a little to alleviate them, searching the shore for lights, but all was in darkness. Tendrils of smoke from his cigarette snaked up into the night sky; she watched them dissipate. He blew out smoke rings that floated towards her, growing in size on their journey until they too blew themselves out. She looked up to catch him watching her.

'What have you been thinking?' he asked. He turned the cigarette to face him, looking at the glowing end. For a moment she panicked, wondering if he was considering burning her with it. He smiled without looking at her as if he read her thoughts.

'Are you telling me that you're not a bad person? That all this was pinned on you?' Her voice sounded strange out in the darkness as if it wasn't hers at all.

He shook his head. 'No,' he said simply, not offended by her question. 'I am a bad person. Probably most of what you think about me is true.' He nodded his head out towards the blackness as if he could see something coming their way. She followed his line of vision. The moon still shone down covering a small area with its beam as if trying to illuminate something in the water, which of course, it wasn't.

'So, what are you saying? That the police framed you?'

A thought quickly passed through her mind of how he used to be when he was young — when they were both young. She thought of how he would hold her hand tightly in his when she was scared and had run into his bedroom, terrified of their father. How a smile would flicker across his face to let her know he would protect her. She thought of how much she trusted her brother to defend her. Then that day after Murk caught him in her bedroom, he lost control; he was bigger and taller by then, their father now afraid of him, but never thinking he would turn on him. Then there was blood under their father's head where he'd fallen. Murk was ashen, the iron, dripping blood, still in his hand. She remembered seeing the moment he decided to shift the blame; she was underage and with diminished responsibilities after the abuse she had gone through. She would be spared prison — whereas he was an adult and would go away for murder; at the very least manslaughter. Only fifteen at the time, she was sent to a sanatorium under the Mental Health Act. After the case was closed, the records were sealed because of her age. She hadn't seen him again until that day at the pub.

He laughed. 'They did. But I don't expect you to believe that. But you've been framed too. You might find that harder to believe, I suspect. Tell me, why did you buy this house on this lake?'

The question threw her. What did that have to do with it? 'I don't see the relevance of your question. We liked it. Simple.'

He nodded sagely and took a deep drag of his cigarette. 'I've got lung cancer. They've given me two years, max.' He looked at the cigarette again as if it held the answers. 'These are killing me. So, you see, I have nothing to lose right now. It's partly why I was given early parole. My brief was good. I wouldn't have got it if not for him. Cheaper for them to have me out rather than have to look after me in the slammer.'

She looked around her, squinting, trying to make out something that would give her answers. But there was nothing. Only the two of them bobbing in the middle of the lake. Alone.

'Do you know that the locals have their own name for this lake?'

'No.'

'Bermuda Lake. Do you know why?' She shook her head. Her brain struggled to make sense of where he was going with this. 'There's a body of water right in the middle of the lake that works a bit like a rip tide. Unusual in a lake, but it's something to do with the plates in the earth beneath the water. I'm surprised you haven't been told about it. They recommend you don't go near it, or you'll be sucked into it and disappear like with the Bermuda Triangle.'

She studied his solid features, catching the death stare with which he looked out onto the water, unsure whether to believe him or not. His cigarette burned down, close to his fingers; he didn't flinch.

'It's mentioned in the Domesday Book. Originally it was known as Devil's Lake. You can imagine why,' he said.

She gave a laugh. 'Is this supposed to scare me?'

'No,' he said casually. 'Just trivia I thought you might like to know. Someone should have mentioned it though. It could be dangerous.'

'If it were true, perhaps, but I really don't believe a word of it. The agents would have mentioned it when we bought the place.'

'You'd think. But then there are so many liars about, it's hard to believe anyone. Don't you think?'

She glanced in the direction he was looking and saw nothing untoward. Ignoring the question aimed at her, her heart hammered.

He pointed ahead of them where the boat was drifting towards the beam of moonlight. 'Can you see the ripples along the water? See how they ripple in opposite directions? Now look around at the rest of the lake. You'll see the water is still. Of course, folklore was greatly magnified by the moon beaming down right on the spot that took the lives of many unsuspecting souls over the years. This part of the lake is over fifty metres deep. That's deep, in case you're wondering.'

Was it true? Are there bodies down there? 'If what you say is true why haven't the bodies surfaced?'

301

He shrugged. 'I don't know. But people have seen them dragged in and drowned and never been seen again. Look it up and you see the countless eyewitnesses there have been over the years.' Murk stopped talking. Silence fell around them. He took the last drag of his cigarette and flicked it powerfully out onto the water. She watched as it sailed through the air, landing, the glowing end radiant in the darkness before going out.

'My son disappeared in there. It happened quickly.' He turned to her. 'I didn't know about it either.' His words came slow, dragged from a depth too harrowing to visit.

There was a deep ache in his voice and for the first time she felt sorrow for him not anger. Losing a child, no matter who you were, was tragic. 'I didn't know you had a child.' Her voice was quiet, torn that he was her brother and a killer, and the boy who'd died, her nephew.

'Why would you? He was eight when it happened. I couldn't help him.'

CHAPTER 39

Confused she turned to the side, looking out at the water; trying to see the ripples. There was certainly something happening on the surface. *Is he lying to me?* Would someone actually lie about something like that? Before she could open her mouth, he spoke again.

'I lived in your house with Pauline.' She gasped. 'Didn't you work it out? I love the look on your face right now.'

Now it made sense, Pauline helping him.

'After it happened, we broke up. Neither of us could cope. She owned the house and kept hold of it, then she got involved with Tony who moved into what is now their house but rented out your house. She didn't want to sell it or move away from her son. She didn't want to leave the lake and you can understand why, but she couldn't live in the house any longer.'

'How did it happen, the accident I mean?'

'The three of us were in the boat. We'd come out here to see the fireworks on New Year's Eve. You're asking yourself why I didn't go in after him? I did, but I slipped standing up and fell, banging my head and passed out.' He pulled out the packet of cigarettes, again, lit one and flicked the match into the water. 'They never found his body. I don't know how quick it was for him or whether he struggled to escape. Pauline said he went under almost immediately. She can't swim so couldn't do anything to help him. There was no evidence it had happened. We couldn't remember the exact spot. The police looked for some trace of him but found nothing. We didn't know about the lake at the time, otherwise we'd never have come this far out.'

She didn't know what or how to respond. This was not what she had expected. Her guard was down, she knew that. It left her vulnerable, but his story was too awful not to believe him. She kept her voice neutral. 'What happened with the police? Did they eventually believe you?'

'Eventually. They tried to say I'd killed him. Only because it was a way of getting me banged up, but they couldn't prove it. They had to take Pauline's testimony as the truth.' He turned to look at her. 'You see, all they could see was a violent man who had done bad things and that coloured their view of me. I loved my son and never laid a hand on him. I would have killed anyone who did. I won't lie about that. So, when you witnessed that day in the pub a few years later they were overjoyed.'

A wave of dizziness came over her. 'Wait. Did you say you lived in our house?' How could that be? And now it made sense. 'And that was why you wanted us to buy it.' He would know everything about the house. How to get in and out without being seen. 'You knew we were looking for a property around here and how much I wanted privacy, didn't you?'

'I did. Pauline helped persuade the couple who rented it to leave and sold it to you privately. You will have seen her name on the paperwork. It's innocuous enough to gloss over, but you didn't register it later when you met her. It was a gamble, but who takes in the names of the people who own the house you are buying?'

He would know where all the creaks and squeaks were. No wonder she never heard him moving about. 'You've been watching me all the time. You've known all the moves we've made.' She thought about what Pauline said about the lake being dangerous and how nobody could hear you if you got into trouble — like her and her son. She thought she'd been talking about the island, but she hadn't. 'Why didn't you tell me about the lake? Why didn't Pauline?' How cruel? 'Something could have happened to Lizzie?' She was his niece, for Chrissakes.

'Why would I?'

She was shocked by his reply. 'Because I'm your sister.'

'But you never wanted to see me or know about me. Why should I care?'

That wasn't altogether true. 'Well, not you then, but Pauline? Why didn't she tell me about the lake? She knew I was always on my boat.'

'I guess she just didn't feel like it, knowing what you'd done to me.'

'But, but that's just cruel. Lizzie might have got into trouble on the water. And I didn't do anything to you. I keep telling you.'

'Then I guess she was thinking an eye for an eye.' He shrugged at her denial and then surprised her by laughing aloud. 'Jane, people like me don't think like people like you.' He adjusted his seat. 'And Pauline had been my wife, she knew about you and what you did.'

'I, I don't understand how you became this person. You weren't like this growing up.'

'How innocent you were, even going through what you did. After Dad died, I lost it. I hated myself for putting you through what I did. I struggled with the guilt and my life spiralled out of control; I kept getting myself in trouble time and again.'

'Why are you telling me all this now. Why not just get on with whatever it is you want to do to me?' She didn't want to hear his remorse.

He took another deep drag of his cigarette.

'Jane, you just walked into the wrong place that day. I would never have contacted you otherwise. That boy was already half dead when he came in. Someone else beat him up. He was Pauline's nephew. I hadn't laid a hand on him. But he died in my arms.'

'But I saw you!' *Pauline's nephew! Can this be true?*

'No. You didn't. You saw what you wanted to believe. What your imagination made you believe.'

'But I didn't speak to the police, you have to believe that.'

'You gave your statement behind a screen. I heard your voice.'

'No, no you didn't. You heard another woman's voice, but not mine.' She shook her head. 'I didn't go to court. That wasn't me. You heard what you wanted to believe that day. You said yourself the police wouldn't tell you who the witness was. You imagined it was me, because of our history. But it wasn't me. Who else was there that day at the pub? Think about it. Who else could it have been?'

He pointed the cigarette at her. 'I told you to leave that day. That you had seen nothing. There was no other woman there.'

'You *threatened* me.'

He shook his head. 'No, I didn't. You thought I had because you were in shock at seeing me and that brought back all the past for you. You got confused.'

'I'm sorry about Pauline's nephew.' She spoke as the bits of lost information began to filter back to her of that day. He was right. The past had hit her like a truck. She'd not been able to get away from there quickly enough. 'Do you know who did beat him up?'

Murk shook his head. 'It was to get back at me. Some low life I knew.' He scowled. 'Motherfucker,' he growled. 'Twisted, motherfucker!'

'What? What have you thought of?'

An angry storm passed over him, warping his features. 'BITCH. THAT FUCKING BITCH!'

Fearing for her life, she pressed back into the boat, the frame digging into her back. 'What? WHAT? What is it?'

The boat rocked with his rage. He turned to her. She cowed away, pushing further into the frame of the boat to escape his wrath.

'It could only have been Pauline. She was the only other woman in the pub that day!' he roared.

Jane blanched in disbelief. 'What? Pauline? But—'

'We broke up because I didn't save our son. It wasn't my fault. I would have died for him. I was unconscious. I couldn't do anything. She never forgave me. The statement was her revenge. Keeping Ralph from seeing me while I was in jail was the same.'

'What?'

'Can't you fucking say anything else?' His voice boomed around the lake, echoing far into the distance.

'Ralph's your son?' It all made sense then.

CHAPTER 40

She moved her right hand from the side of the boat, pushing it into her pocket; the Farb-Gel was there if needed. She looked at the water. *Is he going to throw me in?* She edged away from the side, worried what he was going to do to her in his rage. If she'd really convinced him. Then he stopped, calmed a little and looked at her with understanding. A tension spread from him to her that choked her.

She watched him smoke, looking out into the darkness; smouldering after his initial explosion and lost in thought. He now looked at her intently; weighing her up. Weighing up what's she'd said. *Oh God, he's thinking it though. Working it out. Making the pieces fit. Shit. Shit. Shit.*

'What now?' she said, panicked. Needing to know what he was thinking.

He gave her a searing look. 'Yeah, about that little bit of information you just sowed, sister dearest.' His voice was jarringly quiet, with a fine sharp edge to it like a recently sharpened Sabatier knife.

'What? What are you going on about? What are you going to do about Pauline?'

He huffed, his temper calming but not extinguished. In its place was something worse; a bubbling rage under the

308

surface full of hate, anger — vengeance. He lit another cigarette, slowly, never taking his eyes off her. She pushed further
back as if the wood of the boat would give and give her more
distance. It wouldn't. She was trapped. 'I've thought about
what you implied about Pauline and it makes no sense.' His
voice was a slow rumble like a stampede coming towards her.
'And the thing is, Janey, that wasn't possible. It was you in the
witness stand. I did see you.'

'What? No, no, no, it was Pauline. Not me.'

'You tried to make me believe it was Pauline. I didn't
think you had it in you to be so smart. You very nearly did.
But she'd left the pub by then. She didn't see her nephew
come in. She couldn't have been the witness. You lying bitch.
You've not changed, have you? I knew you were the witness
who testified. D'you think I'd ever forget your voice? Revenge
is best served cold, dear sister — don't you agree?'

'What does that mean?' Panic made her voice tremble.

'I'm sure you can work it out. It means that here we are.
The two of us. Out on the water.'

He had always protected her; he had braved the wind and
rain to go conker hunting with her when she was determined
to win the competition at school.

'No, no, no that's not true. It was her, not me. I *didn't*
do it.'

Her grip tightened on the Farb-Gel.

She thought of the recording in her pocket and wondered
what she would do with it now. Nothing she guessed. 'Why
didn't you come back for me when I was in the sanatorium?'
she yelled at him, her fear driving her now.

'I was frightened if you saw me, it would be too much for
you. I cared about you, Janey.'

She shook her head. 'No. No, no, you didn't. You know
I kept begging them to contact you. You were my brother. I
was desperate to see you. You were all the family I had left.'

'I always kept an eye on you from a distance.' He was
quiet for a moment as if thinking something through. 'You
know they sent me photos of you and reports.'

309

'Nobody told me anything. I thought I was alone.' Tears burst free. 'When I was set free, I was terrified. I knew nobody. I thought I was alone in the world. Do you have any idea how scary that is?'

'You did all right with your illustrations.'

'I was lucky to catch a break with that. I'd started sketching in the hospital — it's what saved me.'

'And so, when you tumbled into the pub that day, you thought you'd get your own back, isn't that right? You ruined my life, you know. I spent ten fucking years locked up. I lost touch with Ralph until recently. When did you realise it was me haunting you?'

'When the Devon snow globe was moved and left on my desk. We only went to Devon because Patrick insisted. I never wanted to step on Devon soil again as long as I lived.'

She rose unsteadily to her feet, spreading her legs to distribute the weight to keep her balance. There was only one thing to do. She now had no choice.

She didn't see the blow coming until the pain in her face, powerful and shocking, brought her round. Her balance had failed her; she'd fallen backwards, hitting her head on the back of the boat. Slumped, trying to catch her breath and understand what had just happened to her, her eyes blinked to clear her fuzzy vision. She looked up in time to see his fist come down a second time. She felt the trickle of blood from her nose as she ducked intuitively out of the way of the next blow. She couldn't breathe out of her nose, and her lips felt swollen. Her breath was gasping, coming out raggedy as she saw him stand over her, boot raised as if to crush her.

Frenziedly she scrambled to the edge, desperately digging in her pocket for the Farb-Gel, tugging it free together with her phone that fell over the side. She pulled the lid off wildly and held it up in front of her. He froze. His look of surprise broke into merriment. 'Don't you dare come any further,' she screeched.

She pulled herself into a sitting position, wiping her nose along the edge of her shoulder; her shaking hand and aching face one ball of pain. She watched for his next move, knowing she was now fighting for her life. She recognised that look; she'd seen it plenty of times as a child but never aimed at her.

'This is not going to pan out the way you want it to, Curtis. You're not going to get rid of me,' she told him. Her swollen nose and lips made talking difficult. Her voice sounded weird, not at all like her. 'I am not going to fight you, spray you or push you overboard. Instead, we are going back to the house where I am going to call the police and you're going to tell them the truth about Dad.'

'What, that you killed him?'

'No!' she screamed at him. 'That's not true. You're trying to confuse me. You nearly had me believing it was me. But I remember what happened.'

'Do you? Are you sure, Janey?'

'You have to accept that you paid the price for what you did to that boy. I know what I saw.' She wiped her nose with the back of her hand. 'Besides, you can't honestly believe that nobody would look for me if I disappeared. Patrick would never stop looking for me. He knows about you.' Murk chuckled as if she'd said something hilarious.' She gave a grunt of dismissal. 'I can't believe I even for one second believed you.'

'Come on, Janey. What are you going to do with that spray?'

Her arm ached from holding it outstretched; she didn't know how much longer she could hold the position. 'You need help,' she said.

'What, the sort of help you had? I don't think so, Janey. I won't be locked up in a mad house. I'd rather be dead. Funny that because that's what's happening to me soon.'

She didn't laugh. There was only one way this could end now. Losing her phone was the final calamity. Again, she had no fucking proof. It was as if the gods were playing with her.

Suddenly, he stamped his foot so fiercely the boat rocked dangerously. She fell back, finding it more and more difficult to breathe through her nose. The brutal truth was that for her to be truly safe, he had to be out of her life.

She held on to the side with one hand, the Farb-Gel in the other, her finger at the ready on the nozzle. The pain in her face was a clear reminder of what he was capable of. And then it happened. His eyes locked on hers. His arm was there, his solid hand wrapping itself around hers like a serpent. She pulled back to release herself from his grasp and tried to regain her lost footing, but she was too slow and crashed to her knees.

The boot smashed into the side of her head, knocking her backwards and taking the breath from her lungs. Too swiftly for a man his size, he was upon her, his hands around her neck. Her windpipe burned. She gasped for breath. His fingers tightened. He was never going to fall into the water. She spluttered for breath. The can of Farb-Gel was long gone. With both hands she grabbed at his, trying to release him. She heard the can rolling back and forth on the floor. She kicked backwards with her heels, moving towards the engine. She let go with her right hand, reaching out for the can if only she could find it, for anything to use to help her. He slammed her back, knocking the breath from her again. Her head fizzed, her focus came in and out. Black spots appeared in front of her. He lifted her again, bending her backwards over the edge, pushing her head into the water. It lapped at her skull, splashing into her eyes, her nose and mouth. She gurgled and spat. The bulk of his weight was on top of her, crushing her. Her hand still flailed. Searching for purchase on something. Anything.

He's going to drown me. She felt a sharp slap of utter panic as she struggled to escape. Using both hands she clawed and pulled, raking her nails along his skin, trying to prise his hands from her neck. There was no chance of freeing herself that way. She brought her knees up, all the time gasping for breath that was impossible to catch. Then she recalled a film she'd seen; a woman was being attacked but she escaped. So she went limp. Stopped struggling. Stopped gasping until he loosened his hold. Played dead. Then, she went full-on attack mode. Her hands clawed at his face, his eyes, scratching, digging the nails in hard into his eyes. He yelled, pouncing back onto her. But this time, catching him off guard, she was able to bring her knees up and, with her feet against his belly, push him off with all her strength.

He stumbled, slipping backwards. She gasped in air, held on tight to the side of the rocking boat. The Farb-Gel was right next to her. She reached for it. She knew she only had seconds before he was back on his feet and coming for her again. This was the only moment she was going to have control. She ploughed into him, arms outstretched in front, palms flat for maximum impact. Using her entire body strength, she pushed him. The momentum of his huge bulk and gravity did the rest. A sharp crack ricocheted through the darkness as his head smashed the edge of the boat. He toppled, hands flailing, grasping at the air to find purchase on something, but there was nothing just the darkness and below, the inky water. Panting, she moved backwards out of reach. Terrified he'd grab her, taking her down with him if she got too close to the side. She did nothing to help him.

She sat, frozen, holding onto the boat as it swayed madly left to right. She watched him disappear under the water. Then, all was silent, only small ripples on the surface of the water. She leaned forward, looking everywhere, but there was no sign of him.

A body didn't disappear. It had to come up. There was nothing though. A fox screamed out in the distance; she shuddered. The only other sound was the blood rushing in her ears. She knelt down, wobbly, leaned forward over the edge of the boat a second time, this time more gingerly. Nothing. Just silence.

Then a rush of water. Two hands blindly clung to the side of the boat. Panicked. Disorientated, she fell backwards as the little boat was abruptly dragged down with the weight of him struggling to pull himself out. He was alive and coming for her. 'Tell me the truth, it was you, wasn't it?' he spluttered. 'I have to know.' She grabbed the can of Farb-Gel, holding it in her trembling hand; bracing herself with her feet against the side of the boat as he pulled it down. Water sloshed over her trainers. But he was tired and didn't have enough strength. If she did nothing, he'd take them both down.

The boat began rocking wildly, then a leg hooked itself over the side. She gasped, horrified. She moved to the edge where his face looked up at her. 'Yes. It was me.' And sprayed. 'And that's for Jasper.' She sprayed until it emptied. She threw the can down. He let go of the edge to wipe his face. Tiredness pulled him down. He sank back down into the dark water.

CHAPTER 41

Clearing up the mess was her next priority. Leaving him floating with his face sprayed with Farb-Gel would only indicate to the police he hadn't drowned.

The water was cold when she slipped in, taking her breath away instantly. Slowly, she swam towards the body and pulled him back by the foot. She tied some rope she kept near the engine around his ankle then wearily pulled herself back into the boat, only just managing it. She started the engine and navigated her way towards her island. There she climbed out gingerly. Every part of her ached and there was searing pain in her face when she moved, making her wince each time she turned her head. She tied up the boat to make sure it wouldn't get dragged out. She began searching for rocks and large stones, not easy in the dark. Taking the torch from her storage box she remembered where Ralph had dumped a lot of waste from clearing out her space. She began the laborious job of filling the bucket from her box with stones and heavy roots they'd pulled out, then lugging them back to the shoreline There she filled Murk's pockets. But it wasn't going to be enough. She dropped onto her arse, exhausted and out of ideas. She covered her face with her hands. *This is too much.* She didn't have the strength to carry on. Then she remembered the blanket in the box. If she wrapped it around his trunk, she could shove stones inside that, then tie the longer rope she had in her storage box, securing it all against his body.

It felt like an eternity by the time she was sure she'd done enough. Finally, losing the will to live, her body screaming for rest and pain relief, dog-tired and in more pain than she thought she could bare, she dragged herself back into the boat and took it out towards the larger part of the lake, as far away from her home as she dared, all the time, dragging him along. Then she removed the rope from his foot.

She watched him . . . float. *What if he doesn't sink?* Finally, with a slurp the lake took him. She looked around, terrified. Was this the part of the lake he'd spoken about with the rip tide? She shone the torch, looking for the ripples on the water, finding them further along. If she'd thought about it, she should have dropped him there. If it were true. Probably not.

It was only when she got back home, stripped off and was about to navigate herself into a warm bath that she saw just how bad her face was. The face that looking back hit her viscerally. My God. *Nobody can see me like this.* Her bruised and battered face and the throbbing skin around her neck looked angry and swollen. What excuse could she use? It wouldn't be long before his body was discovered. She was sure it wouldn't stay down long, but hopefully his face would be eaten by then, hiding what had really happened to him. Encrusted blood caked her nostrils and her neck where it had run. Her skin was beginning to change colour into different hues of purple and green. The collar of her jumper was beyond repair, soaked in blood. She didn't think her nose was broken. Just badly swollen. All this had to be dealt with instantly. And so, a plan formed in her mind. A mad plan, nonetheless. But it was the only one she could think of in her exhausted state. She had to do something to make her injuries look like something other than what they were. . . like a fall down the stairs, maybe. Not a fight with King Kong.

She wasn't about to throw herself down the stairs though; knowing her luck she'd break her neck. She knew enough to know she'd need conclusive injuries that marked her accident as real. Just in case he did pop up somewhere before decomposition.

The stairs looked steep. Steeper than she'd ever realised. The thought of falling down them was in no way appealing. But it was obvious something had happened to her tonight. It wasn't something she could hide. She couldn't think of any other way to explain it. Patrick would want an explanation, too. She had to have it on record she'd had an accident at home, just in case. It was always the *just in case* part of these things that ended up letting you down.

She sat on the top stair, figuring each way she could fall; none of which seemed safe. Finally, she moved away. It was too crazy.

Stiff, she staggered back to the bathroom, to the bath she'd run. She really looked a sight. Her nose didn't look so bad as she removed the blood. The bridge was swollen and there was a small split of the skin right at the top. Her lips looked terribly swollen as if she'd had a procedure that had gone badly wrong. Nothing seemed broken. The warmth of the bath water helped her aching body as she gently lowered herself in. She went under, gently wiping at her painful face, clearing the encrusted blood. Not letting Murk's face into her thoughts. She was only able to stay under a second or two before she had to breathe.

Changed into her pyjamas, she took her stained clothes and put them in the garden incinerator. Throwing a match in she waited, arms wrapped around herself, until all that was left were ashes.

As the adrenaline subsided, the shock hit her. *What have I done?*

She went back inside, glugged water like someone who'd been in a desert for days. Found the gin she kept for medicinal purposes at the back of the baking cupboard, and took a couple of shots of that too. She thought of Murk, face down in the lake.

She paced, unable to settle and looked at Pauline's house from the window. Did she know Murk had met up with her? Did Ralph? Christ. She couldn't think of that right now. It was muggy, the sun would be up in less than an hour.

She saw the lights go on at Penny and Gordon's. She went outside and hobbled to their house. Penny's shock was instant when she opened the door.

'Jane, oh my God, what happened to you?'

'I fell down the stairs a few hours ago. I was waiting for you to wake up.'

'Have you called an ambulance? Do you need me to take you to hospital? You look terrible.' She winced looking at her.

'I think it looks better than it feels. Because it hurts like hell. I'll be fine with some strong painkillers. I won't be going to Mumbles though,' she half-joked, and grimaced when she tried to smile.

'My God, Jane . . . it really looks bad. Don't joke like that. You could have killed yourself.'

Jane put up a hand to her face. 'No, no, I know. I know how bad it looks.'

'But you might have concussion?'

'I don't, really I don't. I've been lying in the bath, soothing myself. Feeling sorry for myself,' she said looking sad.

'Why didn't you call me or Pauline?'

'I didn't want to make a fuss. It's early hours, you know. I'm OK, and . . .' She laughed shyly. 'I can't find my bloody phone and we don't have a landline anymore. I saw your lights go on.'

'Come on, I'll come back with you. How did it happen?' She turned around to speak to Gordon as he came down the stairs and to tell him where she was going.

'Silly, really,' she said as they made their way to the house. 'I don't know how I did it to be honest. I was thirsty and half-asleep. I went to the kitchen for some water, but I misjudged the step, you know, and tumbled.'

'Jane, you could have killed yourself.'

'I know.'

Jane didn't really want Penny at the house but needed somebody to witness what had happened so that she had an alibi. 'I've run out of paracetamol,' she said, as they opened the front door. 'Do you have any? I'll get to the pharmacy later when they open. But I need something to kill the pain. I've had a couple of shots of gin to help with it, but I could do with some real pain relief.'

'You must go to the doctors when they open, get something stronger and get him to check you over. I'll come with you. Let me fetch the paracetamol and then you tell me when you make an appointment.'

'I'll be OK, I'll manage.'

'Don't be ridiculous! I won't take no for an answer.'

* * *

Jane was alone again, Penny having left. Now Jane prowled, unable to settle, everything seeming surreal. She touched objects, books, pens, pictures on the walls then began putting everything back that she'd strewn in the kitchen, searching for the hidden cameras. It seemed so long ago. But it wasn't, only hours ago.

She thought of the tale he'd told her of the Bermuda Triangle and his son dying in the water. She didn't want to think about her nephew dying that way. She had actually felt sorry for him. Somehow, with the grace of God, she'd come out of that situation alive. She didn't know how. She didn't know from where she'd found the strength but, shaking, terrified, thinking she would never see Lizzie or Patrick again, she had.

She pulled the fridge door open wide and looked inside. She was suddenly ravenous and craving food the way one did after a heavy night of drinking. Her demons slain. She could relax. And yet she couldn't. She was truly free. And yet she wasn't.

Bacon, eggs, baked beans and bread all come out. The hob went on, the microwave pinged, and the toaster popped the bread toasted to a perfect golden colour. She sat at the kitchen table and ate without thinking of anything until she'd consumed every morsel of food. Then finally, exhaustion claimed her. Staggering upstairs, collapsing onto her bed she fell into oblivion.

* * *

She woke to a ringing sound. At first, she thought it was ringing in her ears. Wrapped up in a sheet, she struggled to wake up. Sluggishly she opened her eyes, her senses trying to find her phone. She fished around the bed with her hand, then remembered it was at the bottom of the lake.

How long had she been asleep? She wasn't ready to get up. She untangled her body. Moving just a little sent a litany of painful tiny daggers into every single part of her body. She felt damaged as if she'd been beaten up with a sledgehammer, which was an interesting irony because Murk had been a sledgehammer.

There was no easy way of pulling herself out of bed. Moving slowly caused too much pain. She lurched quickly into a sitting position, grabbing her face as the pain made her cry. A tsunami of painful coughs followed and she had to catch her breath to stop herself screaming out in agony. *Oh my God. How can I hurt so much?* Memories crashed through her mind, tumbling one after another. She killed him. She actually killed him. Her hand instinctively went to her throat where it was still sore. Images of Murk with his hands wrapped around her throat, squeezing the life out of her. She repressed other images threatening to follow and reached for the glass of water by the bed.

Staggering she made her way downstairs, to the front door. 'Penny,' she said on opening it, 'stop ringing the bell, please.'

'I was worried when you didn't answer. Are you OK? I've called the doctors for you. Got you an appointment later today.'

'Oh, that's great, thanks. I've only just got up. I'm going to make some coffee.'

'OK, and the next thing is Patrick called me. He's been trying to get hold of you. I didn't tell him. I hope that was the right thing to do, but I said you'd lost your phone.'

Shit. I'm meant to be in Mumbles. Oh, fuck what a nightmare. *I told him I drove there!*

'Bless you Penny, thanks. Yeah, best not to tell him about my fall until he gets back.'

That was it. She never went but told him she had so he wouldn't worry. Perfect. Then she fell down the stairs and couldn't go anyway. Oh, sweet.

'Well, I said if he needed to get hold of you to call me and I'd fetch you to the phone. He sounded confused at that point but had to ring off or was cut off. I'm not sure he believed me.'

'I'm going to order another phone just as soon as I get some coffee.'

'Wait, let me go to town for you and sort it. I'll get you a new SIM card too with your old number. They can do that straight away.'

She was marvellous. She couldn't have planned that better. Penny the angel sweeping down and helping her. 'I didn't think of that. That would be brilliant, honestly, thanks, Penny. I'll settle up with you when you get back. Look here are all my details. Just say that you're me, otherwise they won't help you.' She went to where she kept all her paperwork and handed everything over. 'I owe you. Oh, and if Patrick calls again, please ignore it and I'll ring him the moment I have a phone.' She looked puzzled. 'He thinks I'm in Mumbles with you. I'll tell him I was too tired to drive that night and didn't relish telling him. I don't want him to wonder what the hell is going on if you talk to him.' *The lies just keep on rolling.* 'It's no biggie really. If you wouldn't mind, Penny.'

'Don't be daft. I won't answer. I don't like lying to him. I'll see you in a while.' She hugged her gently as Jane groaned when she squeezed a little too tightly. 'Sorry.'

Jane went back upstairs to begin the process of covering up as much as she could with make-up. She was pleased with the results, especially her neck. She tied a silk neckerchief around as extra coverage.

She made another coffee and drank it with some more of the paracetamols Penny had brought round.

As much as she tried to block out what happened last night, it wasn't working. Snapshots ran through her mind with HD definition. The boat, the Farb-Gel in her pocket. The lies he told. The fight. That made her wince just remembering it. The thinking she was going to die as he pushed her backwards into the water. The pummelling. The pain in her face as he punched her. The adrenaline rush that saved her life. Murk drowning. His reaching hand for her to save him and her recoil. Getting in the water after he was dead.

CHAPTER 42

Penny arrived two hours later, bustling into the kitchen. 'Here you go. I was so scared I was going to get caught out pretending to be you.' She laughed. 'It's the most excitement I've had in years. How sad am I? How are you feeling?' She put the new phone and SIM card in front of her. 'I wrote down how you transfer everything from your old phone onto this one.'

'Oh, Penny, you're wonderful. Thank you so much. Will you stop for a coffee? Oh, are you still OK to take me to the doctors?'

'Yes, I said I would. Gordon's around today so he can make the girls tea. I'll be over at five to collect you. I must dash now though. If I leave him too long with them it all goes to hell over there.' She leaned over, kissing her on the top of the head. 'I went over to Pauline's, but they must have gone away. The curtains are partly drawn, and her car isn't in the garage and Tony's isn't there either. Did she mention anything to you?'

Jane sighed. 'No. I've no idea where they've gone.'

It still played on her mind what to do about her situation. If they found the body. If it floated up somewhere. If the police connected the dots to her.

She picked up her new phone, signed into her Apple ID and set things up through the cloud. When all was done, she read a message from Patrick which he'd sent late last night. *Finished early and will be home today. Collecting some clothes and will drive to Mumbles to meet up with you.* She hadn't anticipated this. It was probably best to wait and see him rather than call him and tell him she was still at home. She would say she dropped her phone in the lake; it wasn't a lie.

Penny arrived to take her to the doctors.

When they returned, she let herself in, glad Penny had to get back to the girls. She put on some relaxing music, ran her finger around the inside of the turtleneck of her blouse. She remembered the recording she made last night and which had carried over to her new phone. She deleted it and everything else connecting her to Murk and Jon. She needed to calm down. Patrick would be home, and she wanted to show she was traumatised from the fall and nothing else.

Outside, she sat on a lounger listening to music on her new phone to help relax. Letting it seep inside her and work its magic. Dark clouds filled the sky, the predicted threat of rain imminent now. She worked on her breathing and emptying her mind. She dozed off, still exhausted, her body craving sleep to recover.

A while later a car pulling onto the drive startled her awake. Slowly, she went to the front door, looked out the side window and saw Patrick.

She ran through her story, making sure she had it straight. She woke in the night, thirsty, went downstairs half asleep for a glass of water, misjudged the top step and lost her footing. Exactly how she'd told it to Penny. He'd ask if she'd been drinking; she hated saying it, but it might be best if she made out she had had a little bit. No, she couldn't say that. There wasn't any wine in the house. Only the bottles in the walk-in pantry. Best not mention that. Nor the gin, the fact she had that hidden was best left out of the story. It would cause a different set of problems. She'd promised. No, no, it would be worse that way. Keep it simple. She watched him walk to the door. Her car was still in the garage. She breathed in slow and deep, slow and deep. She pinged her new rubber band a few times, slow and deep.

The key in the lock, then the door opened. She took a couple of steps back. His face went into shock when he saw her. Obviously, she wasn't meant to be here. She waited. Heart hammering. Sweat making her feel clammy.

'Oh my God, what happened?' His voice was full of concern as he took in her injuries.

'Don't panic, I'm OK. I just tripped down the stairs that's all. Stupid really.' She tried to make light of it.

'Are you sure? It looks really bad, Jane.' He approached slowly.

'It's not. I've been to the doctors. They were happy with me. Told me if anything changed to go to A&E. But it looks worse than it is. Penny came with me, so you can ask her if you don't believe me.'

'Why wouldn't I believe you? I can't believe they didn't insist on you having an X-ray.'

She chuckled to try and take the sting out of what he was seeing. 'I don't know why I said that. I'm just telling you that she drove me there. She's been terrific. They did suggest I ought to go. But I feel fine, really. If they'd not been happy with me, they would have insisted.'

Deep frown lines gathered on his forehead. 'Had you been drinking?'

'No.'

'But I thought— You texted me you were in Mumbles? You said the traffic wasn't too bad? Why did you lie?'

'Because when we were supposed to go, I was too tired. It's such a long drive, and if I told you I was staying here you'd have panicked, and I worried you'd come home, not wanting me to be here on my own. I'm sorry, I was protecting you. It was only a little white lie.'

'How did it happen?'

'So, so silly. I woke from a deep sleep. Thirsty, half-asleep, I staggered to the kitchen, misjudged the top stair, and fell. That's it. So daft, right? I can't believe how it happened.'

'My God. You could have been killed. Why didn't you text me or call me? Is that the truth?' He went quiet for a moment and said, hesitantly, as if the words were too awkward to speak, 'It wasn't that maniac, was it?'

'God no! No, no don't start thinking that way. We agreed there isn't anyone, remember?'

He held her at arm's length. 'You're not lying to me, are you? Because this looks really bad for a fall down the stairs.'

'What, are you now thinking I was telling the truth? Make your mind up, Patrick. Look, I fell and got myself bashed up. I haven't even thought about Murk. You were right, I catastrophised it all. Ask Penny, I went over to hers after it happened.'

'Still, you should have got in touch. I left you messages. Why didn't you get back to me?'

'Because I was fine, and I didn't want to disturb you. And I'd lost my phone. I dropped it in the lake accidentally. There's nothing you could have done anyway. And it would have affected your session, so that's why I didn't tell you.'

He wrapped her in his arms gently, afraid he might hurt her. It helped a lot and she melted into him. 'I feel awful leaving you now. I shouldn't have gone. I had a feeling something was off when I left.' She saw something whirring behind his eyes. Working things out about how they'd left everything when he went. Her fall, her lost phone.

She laughed, nervously. 'What, like a premonition or something?'

'Something like that, yeah.' He pulled back. 'Are you sure you're OK?'

'I'm fine, really.'

'Have you really not drunk anything while I was away?'

'No.'

Letting her go he walked to the kitchen, switched on the kettle and took a bottle of cold water from the fridge.

'OK.' He looked at the darkening sky. 'Did that storm ever get here?'

'Storm?' Oh, he meant the weather storm they predicted. 'No, it never arrived. Looks like it's not far away now though.' They both looked out at the gathering storm clouds and she had the distinct feeling they were thinking of wholly different storm clouds.

'Tea?' he asked finishing the water and throwing the bottle in the recycling. She nodded. 'Jane, we need to talk about getting you some help. I couldn't rest leaving you like I did. However bad this sounds, you really need professional help.'

'I know. I said we'd sort something when you got back.'

'I know what you said but you're good at brushing things under the carpet and I want to start the ball rolling today. You really scared me with that crazy story of yours, you know.'

'And I've spoken to the doctor today for a referral, so I have begun to get things moving.'

'Honestly?'

'Yes, we're going private, so he's getting a letter sent out this week to someone he recommends, and we should hear back at the latest next week.' It was a decision she'd made on the spot at the doctors.

'How d'you feel right now?' he asked concerned.

'Better that I've got it out in the open. Telling you what I was going through — I mean what I was *believing*, it made me suddenly realise how obsessed I'd become with my own thoughts.' She thought quickly, worrying that he wasn't going to believe her. 'Patrick, I'm scared too. I don't even know how it started. I must have terrified the both of you.'

He nodded, clearly thinking back over her behaviour. 'I think you really did. You need to apologise to Pauline and Ralph as well. And explain to them.'

'I will but I think they've gone away. Their cars aren't there, and the curtains are partially closed. Penny doesn't know where they've gone either.'

He looked puzzled. 'Well, when they get back then. Strange she didn't say she was going away. Maybe Lizzie will know.'

She looked down. 'Maybe.' But she doubted that. But that was a worry for another day.

* * *

He sipped his tea, scowling. She wished she could read his thoughts. He didn't ask her why she got that letter in the first place. The only saving grace there was that he never saw it. Should he remember it, she'd tell him she must have made it up like all the rest. There wasn't much he could say about it then. After all, she had sounded totally mad the other day.

'Let's go over to Penny's as you haven't seen Gordon for a while. I'd like to take her something. We've got a box of Lindt chocolates we haven't opened. I'll get her something better in the week,' she said suddenly wanting to be a million miles from there.

'OK.' He put the mugs in the sink. 'Good idea. You sure you're OK to go out? You look in pain.'

'I'm fine. I took some painkillers.' She really wasn't. She pulled the front door closed and turned to walk alongside him, taking his hand in hers. She felt the need to rub the back of her neck again. *Now I'm being silly.*

Her phone pinged with a message.

Unknown number:

Hello, Janey. ☺

THE END

ACKNOWLEDGEMENTS

Turning a manuscript into a book requires the efforts of lots of people, not just the author. So I want to acknowledge all the wonderful people at Joffe who have helped bring my manuscript to life and turn it into a book. The outstanding Senior Editor, Kate Ballard, amazing freelance editor, Sarah Tranter, fabulous Publishing Director, Kate Lyall Grant, superb Tia Davis, Marketing Assistant and all at Team Joffe.

A huge thank you to anyone I've missed! And a special thanks to the ARCers who read the books before anyone else.

And a huge, huge thank you to Team Joffe for all your support. It means more than you can imagine.

THE CHOC LIT STORY

Established in 2009, Choc Lit is an independent, award-winning publisher dedicated to creating a delicious selection of quality women's fiction.

We have won 18 awards, including Publisher of the Year and the Romantic Novel of the Year, and have been shortlisted for countless others. In 2023, we were shortlisted for Publisher of the Year by the Romantic Novelists' Association.

All our novels are selected by genuine readers. We are proud to publish talented first-time authors, as well as established writers whose books we love introducing to a new generation of readers.

In 2023, we became a Joffe Books company. Best known for publishing a wide range of commercial fiction, Joffe Books has its roots in women's fiction. Today it is one of the largest independent publishers in the UK.

We love to hear from you, so please email us about absolutely anything bookish at choc-lit@joffebooks.com.

If you want to receive free books every Friday and hear about all our new releases, join our mailing list here: www.joffebooks.com/freebooks.